YESTERDAY IS GONE

BEVERLY CLARK

Genesis Press, Inc.

Indigo Love Stories

An imprint of Genesis Press, Inc.
Publishing Company

Genesis Press, Inc.
P.O. Box 101
Columbus, MS 39703

ISBN-13: 978-1-58571-279-3
ISBN-10: 1-58571-279-5
Manufactured in the United States of America

First Edition 1997
Second Edition 2008

Visit us at www.genesis-press.com or call at 1-888-Indigo-1

To my husband Al, for so aptly inspiring the writing of such passionate love scenes.

To all my children: Catana, Alvin Jr., Dayna, Ericca, and Gloria. Without your understanding and help when the going got rough there would be no writing career, no *Yesterday Is Gone.*

To my mother Isabella Young, who instilled in me at an early age a love for reading and later an affinity for enjoying romance novels.

I'd like to thank HDRWA, my romance writers' group, for their support and help.

Special thanks to (Rag) Judy McQuarters, Doris Smith, Delores Williams, Kim, Margo, Denise, Polly, Adrienne, Rebecca, Lisa, and my other good friends.

PROLOGUE

"Congratulations, Doctor, on a job well done."

"Thank you, Dr. Murray," Augusta Humphrey answered proudly as she left the operating room. To have Dr. Thomas Murray, the leading heart surgeon in the country, observe her work and praise her skill was the best possible compliment she could receive.

With the thrill of accomplishment singing through her being, Augusta practically floated to the showers and then later out of the hospital, headed for home.

Ten minutes later, Augusta pulled her BMW up to an intersection only a few blocks from her house, and deftly guided the car into the left turning lane. She groaned in irritation because it was one of those busy intersections with four-way stop signs that the city officials had promised to replace with traffic lights but, of course, never did.

As she glanced to her right, she saw a bright yellow Porsche speeding up the cross street. To her left at almost the exact same moment she saw a little girl pedaling her bike into the crosswalk. Augusta's heart leaped into her throat. She shouted at the child to go back, but the girl must not have heard her because she froze in the center of the street and, like a rabbit held enthralled by the eyes of a snake, stared in shocked fascination as the swiftly moving vehicle speeded toward her.

Augusta's insides knotted in fear at the thought of what was about to happen. Without hesitation she shot her car into position in front of the terrified child.

Moments before the Porsche slammed into the side of her car, Augusta caught a flashing glimpse of the face of the other driver.

She wrestled in vain with the wheel, desperate to stay in control, but it was no use; the force of impact caused the safety glass of her window to crumble and sent her car careening crazily toward a nearby thrift store. The momentum violently propelled her car through the store's wide front window.

When the window shattered, fragments of glass blasted into her face. Excruciating agony tore through her brain.

The pain made Augusta scream again and again.

And then everything went black.

"She should be coming out of it any time now."

A deep male voice penetrated the dull fog enveloping Augusta's mind. The lingering lethargy from a deep, drugged sleep slowly fell away.

"Yeah, she's been under a long time," a different male voice answered.

As her confused senses cleared, she recognized the voices.

They belonged to two of her colleagues, Drs. Phil Curry and Mark Gregory.

Augusta felt a firm pressure around her head, and pain throbbed behind her eyes when she tried to open them. When she attempted to speak, the words would not come. Her body refused to respond to the command to move.

Distant hospital sounds and an antiseptic smell filled the air. What was she doing back at the hospital? She distinctly remembered leaving there. In fact it was the last thing she…

No, that wasn't right. Something was very wrong. Panic shot through her brain with the speed of a bullet.

"She's going to need all the courage she possesses," Mark said in a solemn tone.

"She was well on her way to being one of *the* best heart surgeons, black or white, this country has ever produced." Phil's voice sounded bleak.

Was silently screamed through Augusta's mind!

Was! That one word slashed through Augusta's brain again and again like the serrated edge of a knife destroying fragile brain matter.

"Dr. Hastings hopes that by the time the wrappings are removed, she will have healed sufficiently to allow her at least partial vision—but he isn't very optimistic about that happening."

"It's criminal that the medical profession has to lose her outstanding surgical skills so soon after celebrating their discovery."

"I agree with you there." A sad inflection tinged Mark's reply.

Augusta's heart sank, mired in abject misery. Not only was Dr. Ben Hastings an outstanding eye surgeon, he was also her friend. If that was what he thought, then it must mean that…

She began to tremble as shock set in. Tears Augusta couldn't hold back pooled in her eyes, and a pained sigh left her lips.

"It appears our patient is awake."

"Yes, I am, Phil," Augusta answered, her voice sounding brittle and harsh like the scrape of chalk across a blackboard.

Phil groaned. "Oh, Augusta."

"Augusta, I…" Mark began, forcing cheerfulness into his words, "We don't really know that you will be—"

"Permanently sightless? But it's the conclusion you've both drawn."

"It's much too soon after the surgery to be sure."

"Surgery!" She gasped as an uneasiness settled inside her. "They've operated?" It was one thing for Ben to say what he thought, but if he had operated, that had to mean that he was sure about his facts and set in his opinions.

Oh, God!

"When was the surgery done?" Augusta moved her shoulders away from the pillow in an agitated attempt to sit up. "How long ago, Mark?" Her voice broke.

"Calm down, Augusta," he said soothingly, while he gently but firmly pushed her back against the pillow.

"The accident happened a week ago," Phil answered. "Dr. Hastings made the decision to operate immediately, hoping that...But I'm afraid there was more corneal damage than he expected. It's too soon to tell how extensive."

Augusta started to remember something else. "What about the child? Was she hurt?"

"No. Don't worry, Doctor. She came through it just fine."

"Thank God!"

"Although she managed to escape without a scratch, she suffered a deep emotional shock as a result of having witnessed the accident," Phil explained, lifting Augusta's wrist to take her pulse.

"The Masons are in the visitors' room, eager to thank you for what you did for their daughter."

"What you did for that child..." Mark said, admiringly. "Not many people would have put their life on the line for a child not even theirs."

"I don't know about other people, but I couldn't let that reckless lunatic run her down. I suppose he drove away without staying to face the consequences of his actions."

"You're wrong, Augusta. He did stop. He wants to come in and talk with you."

"No way!" Instant hot anger swelled and then raged inside her like a violent storm. "I don't ever want that man in my vicinity. The thoughtless fool must have been going twenty miles over the posted speed limit for a school area. You say he is here in the hospital? I can't believe that. Why isn't he in jail?"

"You're getting yourself all worked up. The man assumed complete responsibility for causing the accident. He was let out on bail."

The man ruins my life and almost kills an innocent child, and the judge grants him bail!

Augusta sighed in disgust. "They'll probably give him a suspended sentence and he'll be back out on the street so he can do it again!"

"You're so hostile and angry," Mark said sadly.

"How would you feel, if you were in my place?" she shot back. When he didn't answer, the awkward silence intensified Augusta's discomfort.

Phil squeezed her hand. "We understand."

She couldn't stand the sound of pity in his voice. "Listen, I want you two to go."

"But, Augusta..." Mark began.

She cut him off. "Don't misunderstand me. I'm grateful to you guys for taking such good care of me."

"We only wish we could have done more."

Augusta heard regret in Phil's voice—or was it pity, the same as she'd heard in Mark's? "Please, just go."

"But..."

"I prefer that you do." She paused for a moment. "I want you to tell the Masons I'll see them in a few days when I've...I'll see..." The word *see* caused untold misery to slash through her insides. "Tell—tell them—"

"We'll handle it, Augusta," Mark affirmed.

A floating dizziness encroached. Augusta tried to hide the wave of pain that accompanied it, but an involuntary groan eluded her control. "Do you need something for the pain?" Mark asked.

"If it's bad," Phil rushed on, "we can..."

"It's not that bad." Augusta felt her composure begin to crumble. She had to get them out of there quickly. So she spoke more sharply to get her point across, "Now if you don't mind..."

Seconds later, the hush of the door signaled to Augusta that she was now alone.

The word *blind* screamed through her brain, reverberating like a piercing wail of horror over and over.

Augusta raised trembling hands to her temples, willing the pain to stop. Her fingers encountered the thick padding of cotton and bandages wound firmly around her head. This was all so unreal. She couldn't believe any of it—didn't want to believe any of it.

The lingering effects of the sedation she'd been under set in and seconds later Augusta closed her eyes, eager to escape this unbearable situation. She awoke to the gentle grasp of fingers on her wrist.

"How are you feeling this morning, Doctor?"

Augusta realized it must be morning, that the nurse was checking her pulse and blood pressure.

"When will I see—I mean, when will Dr. Hastings be in to see me?"

"I don't know, probably this afternoon. Is there something I can do for you?"

"No, I'm all right." That was a bald-faced lie. She would never be all right again unless she got her sight back. If she ever got it back. The possibility that she might not wasn't something she wanted to think about.

Augusta wanted the nurse to hurry up and leave so she could be alone. A feeling of bitterness and fury burned inside her.

It had taken her long years of hard work to become a heart surgeon. She had survived the poverty of the ghetto and an endless succession of foster homes following her mother's death from a heart ailment.

After finishing high school she had struggled, working every spare moment to put herself through college. She applied for a student loan so that she could attend med school, and then did a year's internship at Pennsylvania Memorial. It was hell, but she had managed to complete a seven-year residency with Dr. Thomas Murray, one of the country's leading heart surgeons.

She'd sacrificed, scrimped, and saved to pay back the loan, and had finally gotten to the point where she could buy a house and a car. And now at thirty-two, she was a surgeon who couldn't function as one, all because of some...she knew it wasn't Christian to harbor such hate, but at that moment, as God was her witness, she hated the man who had done this to her—hated him with a passion.

Her mind played back the seconds just before the crash. She remembered seeing the face of the other driver. His exotic mahogany skin and handsome Afro-American features were forever branded into her memory.

When the bandages were removed, she found that she was indeed blind. Totally—for all intents and purposes, her blindness would remain a permanent condition.

Tears of anger, frustration, and self-pity rolled down her cheeks. By evening, as she lay awake in her hospital room, an icy resolve had entered her soul. She'd cried her last tear over her loss.

Derek Morgan paced back and forth in the visitor's room, waiting for a chance to see Augusta Humphrey and talk to her and tell her…

Tell her what, Morgan?

What could he tell her? That he was sorry, that he wished the accident hadn't happened? What good would it do? She'd refused to see him time after time. After learning that the doctor was blind as a result of the accident, he was roasting alive in a hell of guilt and regret. Damn it, she had to see him!

As he waited, Derek saw the little girl from the accident. A cold sweat broke out on his forehead and his hands turned clammy. He'd come so close to killing that beautiful child!

The nurse came and told the girl and her parents they could go in and see Augusta Humphrey.

Derek approached the nurse. "When will I…"

"I'm sorry, Mr. Morgan. As I've told you before, Dr. Humphrey refuses to see you. There is nothing I can do." She smiled sympathetically at him and then returned to the nurses' station.

Derek slipped past the nurses' station to Augusta Humphrey's room and listened outside the door.

"How can we ever thank you, Dr. Humphrey?" Teresa Mason exclaimed.

"You've sacrificed so much for our little girl," Frank Mason added with a warm, yet sad, smile.

"Kelsey Ann was worth it."

"Thank her, Kelsey Ann," her mother prompted.

"Thank you, Dr. Humphrey. I was so scared, but you saved me. You were awesome."

Listening to her animated young voice, Augusta felt an ache inside her womb. If she had a daughter, she would want her to be just like Kelsey Ann Mason.

After the Masons had gone, a feeling of deep sadness washed over her. It wasn't like her to feel sorry for herself, but at the moment she was helpless to prevent its onslaught.

Derek stepped away from the door and watched the Masons as they headed for the elevators. A feeling of worthlessness flooded him. He couldn't stand this overpowering burden of guilt. What in the hell was he going to do? How was he going to live with himself? He had to think of some way to assuage his conscience, or else lose his mind.

CHAPTER I

Eighteen months later.

Augusta sat on her living room couch enjoying the mellow sounds of ballad singer Jeffrey Osborne drifting up from her stereo, when the peal of the doorbell intruded on her tranquility.

"I'll get it," her companion, Elaine Owens, who was seated across from her on the love seat, said before rising to her feet to answer the bell's summons.

Over the sound of her music, Augusta heard the low muffled cadence of a conversation taking place at her front door and called out.

"Who is it, Elaine?"

"A Mr. Todd Winters."

Augusta frowned; she didn't recall hearing that name before. She turned the volume down on her stereo. "What does he want?"

A deep, resonant male voice that sounded very much like that of the actor James Earl Jones answered. "To talk to you, Dr. Humphrey."

Augusta's eyes widened in surprise when she felt the couch cushion next to her sink down. Without invitation or permission, the arrogant man had the nerve to walk into her house and take a seat, beside her no less!

Surely he wasn't another salesman. She'd had her fill of that pack of pushy people targeting her door, primed and ready to execute every conceivable sales pitch under the sun.

"I don't know you, Mr. Winters," she replied in an annoyed voice. "You will in time, Dr. Humphrey," came his brimming with confidence reply.

Augusta heard Elaine move in her direction. "If you want me to, I can show, Mr. Winters to the..."

"No," Augusta interrupted, "It's all right, I'll handle this. Who are you, Mr. Winters? And what do you want? If you're some kind of salesman..."

"I assure you I'm not."

"Well, then..."

"I'm an instructor for the blind at the Braille Institute of Philadelphia."

She was puzzled. None of this made any sense. She hadn't..."I didn't contact there." Suspicion reared its head. "Who sent you here?"

"Dr. Ben Hastings asked me to stop by."

Augusta stiffened, comprehension dawning. "Ben!"

"Dr. Humphrey, I..."

She gritted her teeth. "Don't call me that."

"It is what you still are."

Augusta's insides tightened with hostility. "Look, if you came here to lecture to me, forget it."

"No, I didn't come here for that. Dr. Hastings thinks you've had more than enough time to adjust to your condition and should start your rehabilitation as soon as possible."

"He thinks? Of all the…I'm afraid he's wasted your time, Mr. Winters." Acid anger burned inside her. Just wait until she got her hands on Ben. Just because they were friends didn't give him license to think he could run her life. How dare he do something like this!

"It's my time, and I don't think I'm wasting it. From what Dr. Hastings tells me, it's been eighteen months since you lost your sight, and you've just recently exhausted the last possibility of a breakthrough any time in the near future. He also said you've put little or no effort into getting on with your life."

Augusta bit the inside of her cheek. Why, this judgmental…How would he know?

"I think you'd better leave right now, Mr. Winters. I resent you coming here like this! Now, if you don't mind…"

"Oh, but I do mind."

Augusta reached for the knob on her stereo and, finding it, turned the volume up.

She heard Todd get up. There was a click, and her music suddenly ceased.

The insufferable man had turned off her stereo!

Augusta reached for the knob to turn it on again and encountered the obstacle of long, male fingers. She jerked her hand back, zapped by the sheer male energy emanating from the contact.

Her voice a little breathless and shaky, she said, "What is your problem? I don't want you here. Can't you get that through your thick skull? Or are you hard of hearing as well as dense?"

Moments later, she felt the heated tension of his fingers on her shoulders. A strong whiff of his after-shave assailed her senses. Instant awareness blazed to life between them.

"Neither, Doctor," he countered, clearing his throat. "It's time you stopped wallowing in self-pity and learned to deal with your life." Wallowing in self pity!

Augusta jerked out of his hold, stung by his evaluation of her state of mind, and his analysis that she wasn't handling her life. "I want you out of here, mister. If you don't leave I'll..."

"You'll what? Have your companion call the police because you haven't learned how to do it yourself?"

"Of all the—"

Elaine, quiet during their heated exchange, now interrupted. "Mr. Winters, maybe you'd better leave."

"This is between the doc and me."

Augusta seethed. "Why you insufferable..." The sheer audacity of this man! To come into her house and...

"The name you're searching for is Todd, Doc."

"There are other names I'd like to call you."

"Such as?"

She could sense his amusement at her expense and it made her doubly angry. "Never mind, you really don't want to hear them." She drew away from him, yet at the same time she itched to get closer and...

"I've asked you not to call me 'Doc.'"

"Asked?" He laughed. "Is that what you called it? Could have fooled me."

"Whatever. A lot of good it did me. Don't you understand? I'm a surgeon who can't operate."

"With rehab you can...."

"What?" Augusta let out a poor facsimile of a laugh. "Learn to operate in Braille, cross my fingers, and hope every patient's heart, veins, and arteries are in the exact same place? Not to mention the nerves."

He replied, ignoring her sarcasm. "No, I'm not saying that."

"What are you saying?" She hurried on quickly. "Oh, then you're an evangelist who can restore my sight by the laying on of hands?"

"No. I'm certainly not that. I wish I could restore your sight." He hesitated briefly. "Unfortunately, I can do nothing to bring that about."

Augusta picked up on the odd catch in his voice. It sounded like more than just the polite regret you would offer a stranger. The confusing vibes radiating from this man deflated her anger.

Todd cleared his throat. "If you would just give me a chance to help you."

"Mr. Winters, surgery was my life."

"You have to find a workable substitute."

"Just like that."

"No, not just like that. You'll have to work at it, and even then it's going to take time and stubborn determination." He let out a wry chuckle. "Something, I don't need to guess, that you possess in abundance. And call me Todd, Augusta. You don't mind if I call you by your first name, do you?"

"Would it do any good if I said I did? If it makes you happy, go ahead, feel free, but I want you to know that I'm not ready for this."

"I believe you are, or you can be even sooner than you think. All you need is…"

Augusta rudely cut across him. "Right now, all I need and want is for you to get the hell out of my life!"

"What you want and what you need are two entirely different things, Augusta."

The way he said her name was—was soft, almost like a caress. She found herself strangely attracted to this man, and she didn't want to be.

The not-so-subtle hint of amusement was back in his voice, and she bristled. "Don't bother, Mr. Winters."

"Todd. And, Augusta, I will be back. You can count on it."

"You won't get in."

"Oh, I'll get in all right. I can't say it's been a pleasure, this time, but..." He let his voice purposely trail away. "You don't have to bother seeing me out, Elaine."

Todd Winters certainly didn't lack confidence, that was for sure, Augusta thought as she heard the front door close behind him. She was both glad and sorry at the same time that he had gone, and couldn't fathom the reason for the opposing emotions.

Unable to quell her inquisitive nature a minute longer, Augusta broke down and asked Elaine, "What does he look like?"

There was a slight hesitation before Elaine answered. "He's a very attractive black man—tall, lean, and vital. And he has the most incredible brown eyes you've ever seen."

It wasn't all Augusta wanted to know. "What do you think of him?"

"In what way?" Elaine probed. "Impersonally as a professional? Or personally as a man?"

At that moment Augusta wasn't sure which interested her more, so she said. "As a professional, I guess."

"He seems sincere, committed, and confident about himself and his work. What's your opinion of him?"

"I haven't formed one yet." Augusta knew that she lied. She did have an opinion about the arrogant, aggressive man. Never had she met anyone so determined to have his own way. For some reason, she wasn't satisfied with Elaine's impression. How she wished she could have seen him herself!

Augusta felt an overpowering urge to know more about Todd Winters the man. Despite her anger at his temerity in coming uninvited into her home, he aroused her curiosity.

One thing was for sure: she intended to have a talk with her good friend, Dr. Ben Hastings, about butting into her life like this.

Augusta had Elaine phone the man in question. As she heard her companion punch in the number, a shiver of frustration and irritation seeped into her because of the truth in what Todd Winters had said. That she hadn't attempted to learn how to use the phone on her own hit too close to home.

Damn him! How had he managed to make her feel this deep dissatisfaction with herself?

Elaine handed Augusta the receiver.

"Ben, this is Augusta."

"What can I do for you, love?"

"Don't you 'what can I do for you, love,' me. I called to tell you to stay the hell out of my personal life."

She heard his wry laughter. "You've met Todd Winters, I take it."

"This is *not* funny, Ben!"

"All humor aside, what did you think of him?"

She frowned in exasperation when he ignored her question and swiftly volleyed back one of his own. "Ben!"

"I did it for your own good, Augusta. I care about you."

Augusta sighed. How could she stay mad at a man who only had her best interests at heart? "I'm just not ready to..."

"What? Face a life that's not the way you want it to be?"

"I feel a lecture coming on. I see it was useless to call you. In the future don't do me any favors without asking my permission first. Goodbye, Ben."

"Augusta, don't hang up! Are you going to let him help you?"

"Goodbye, Ben."

The rest of the evening, all Augusta could think about was Todd Winters. She tried blocking him out of her thoughts by using her music, but it didn't work. Todd Winters had aroused a restlessness in her that nothing she did seemed to quiet. He brought home the reality of her blindness in a way no one around her dared do, except maybe Ben to a certain extent.

And if Todd Winters was a barometer of what her colleagues and people who knew her were thinking, she realized they must have all been walking on eggshells when around her. These past months, had they all been being more than just sympathetic—heaven forbid, pitying her? The thought of anyone doing that vexed her beyond reason.

But was she ready for this? If not now, when? Was Ben right when he questioned whether any time would ever be the right time? She certainly wasn't going to let him or Todd Winters rush or push her into anything.

No one had ever played on her fears or used her frustrations to get her attention as this Todd Winters had. Although not cruel, he had been firm. Augusta recalled the odd note of sympathy she'd heard in his voice. She frowned. Or was it pity? She shuddered to think it might be the latter. She'd had enough of that to last her a lifetime.

Augusta wished she could have seen Todd Winters' face for just a moment. She shook her head. It did no good to dwell on that because she would never know what he looked like. Even if she could see him, what difference would it make? The man meant nothing to her.

She had to admit that, although he'd only taken up less than fifteen minutes of her time, in that brief period it had been enough for him to arouse a need in her to question and reassess her life.

She felt curious to know what he would have to say the next time he came to her house. *What was she thinking?* Already her mind was planning ahead for that eventuality. There wouldn't be a next time, damn it! She didn't want him to come back. If he did, she just wouldn't let him in.

Despite her vehement denial, his confidently spoken words that he would return came back to taunt her.

One day passed, then two, and when Todd Winters hadn't made an appearance, Augusta assumed he wouldn't come back. She refused to admit that she had been anticipating his return.

A third day passed. Augusta found herself toying with the idea of exploring the perimeter of first her bedroom, then her living room, and eventually the rest of her house.

For so many weeks and months she'd spent the majority of her time in one clinic, hospital, or doctor's office or another all over the country. She'd rarely been in her house long enough to attempt to learn where everything was.

If she were to be completely honest with herself, she knew that wasn't quite true. She had used constantly being out of town as an excuse not to do what she dreaded: admit to the possibility that her blindness might be a permanent condition that she would have to force herself to deal with.

She thought about Elaine. She'd hired her as a helpmate.

Or are you using her as a crutch?

Augusta blanched at the thought that that might be the real reason. The concept was detestable to her.

She carefully eased her body to the edge of the love seat, then slowly rose to her feet. She managed to evoke a mental picture of how the love seat looked, and where it was positioned in the living room. Her heart began to pound. Until now she'd sidestepped any effort to commit any part of the house to memory, telling herself that once she got her sight back it would be of no use to her.

Augusta put her hand out in front of her, inching a step forward, then another, until her shin connected painfully with the corner of the coffee table.

"Ouch!" she swore under her breath. She realized that this was going to be a regular, everyday, common occurrence during the investigation and trying-out processes.

Augusta swallowed her apprehension, then took another tentative step. When she didn't blunder into another obstacle, she took another, and felt the soft-cushioned edge of the couch brush against her leg. Moving in front of the couch, she encountered her stereo. She ran her fingers over its smooth surface. The scent of lemon wax drifted up from it. How odd. She had never paid any attention to the scent before.

The sudden peal of the doorbell made her heart leap into her throat. Who could it be? Surely not...She thought about calling Elaine, who was on the service porch doing the laundry, but decided against it. Besides, the door wasn't that far away. Just as she took another step, she heard the bell again.

Indecision is the thief of time. Make up your mind, Augusta.

She stumbled forward, waving her hand from left to right in front of her. "I'm coming, I'm coming," she called out in irritation. The person at the door started knocking. Augusta was almost positive that Todd Winters was the idiot attempting to knock a hole in her door.

As the knocking persisted, Augusta found she was able to judge the direction from which it originated. By shuffling her feet forward along the carpet for what seemed like miles, but could only be a matter of several feet, she encountered the door. Then by sliding her hand across its surface, she found the knob. And with a feeling of triumph, she opened the door.

"Very good, Augusta."

"You!"

"Yes, me, Todd Winters, in the flesh. Don't sound so disappointed, Doc. The rejection might damage my fragile ego beyond repair."

"Fragile ego? I doubt if anything could ever do that," she answered dryly.

"Woman, you wound me to the quick. I'm glad to see you're finally curious enough about your surroundings to investigate. You really should ask who it is before you open your door, though. Is today the first time you've ventured out of the safe cocoon you've woven around yourself? It was, wasn't it? Are you alone here?"

"No, Elaine is on the service porch doing the laundry."

He took Augusta's hand and slid his other arm around her waist to guide her back into the living room.

At his touch, a quivering sensation jetted through her insides. Her mouth suddenly felt dry, and she found it hard to swallow. "What are you doing here, Mr. Wint...Todd? I thought I made it clear to you the last time you were here that..."

"You wouldn't let me in if I came back? But you have."

"I didn't know it was you on the other side of the door."

"Let's cut the bull. You've made an all-important first step, Augusta, and it's all that matters. It might be helpful if you acquired a cane or maybe a seeing eye dog, or both."

A cane or a dog or both! The image of a man she'd seen using a cane came to mind. At the time she remembered feeling pity for him because he had to use a cane to get around and to keep himself from tripping or blundering into someone or something. Now the thought that others might see her in the same light...It was more than she could handle right now, and she lashed out in angry frustration at the suggestion.

"You'd like to see me as an object of pity, helpless, wouldn't you?"

He pulled her up from the couch none too gently. She sensed that the iron control he expertly kept in check was threatening to slip. "No, Augusta, You're wrong. I wouldn't like it. As for you being helpless, you don't have to remain that way."

"But I'll still be blind." Now why did she feel that she had to challenge him at every turn?

"Yes, you will. But you can learn to live with it Augusta, and learn to adjust your life because of it. Others have. There is help out there, all you need..."

"Is you? Right? Mr. Ready, Willing and Able?"

She heard him sigh as though he were really trying the name on for size to see if it fit. Of all the arrogant...It was up to her to decide whether she needed his help or not, whether she would accept it or not. At the moment she wasn't sure about anything.

"All right, Augusta, I see you need more time to digest what I've said. I'll come back."

"You said that the last time you were here. If I need you, I'll call you."

"I don't think so. You know why? Because you won't know how."

Todd urged her a step forward and then another. When he guided her fingers to the phone receiver and moved them across the buttons, she felt the heat of his determination flow into her. He wasn't being condescending; he was lending her some of his confidence, and at the same time he was making her very much aware of him as a man.

"There are twelve buttons on the receiver. Three across and four down. Starting from the top it's one, two, three; next row four, five, and six, and so on. Then there is the star, the "0" for operator, and the pound sign."

He went on to move her fingers across each button, calling off its function. He did it again and again until she knew them by heart. Then he recited his phone number until she could say it back to him and show him she knew how to punch the numbers in by herself.

"You're a quick study. Now if you need me, you can contact me personally."

"Or call the police to throw you out."

He ignored the jab. "You might reconsider my suggestion about the cane. It might save you a few bruises."

Augusta allowed him to guide her back to the couch. Now that he was ready to leave, she was suddenly not as anxious for him to go.

"I can see myself out, Augusta."

Like the first time, Augusta felt strange, oddly disturbed after his visit. She rose to her feet, stepped over to the phone, picked up the receiver, and practiced fingering the buttons.

"I thought I heard the doorbell," Elaine said as she entered the living room.

Seconds later Elaine's voice seemed closer to Augusta.

"Who was it?" her companion inquired.

"Todd Winters."

"How did…you answered the door yourself?" Elaine sounded surprised, but pleased by the revelation.

Augusta smiled at the inflection in the other woman's voice and she answered proudly, "Yes, I did."

CHAPTER II

Derek Morgan turned on his answering machine and played back his messages, disappointed to find none from Augusta Humphrey. He knew he shouldn't get his hopes up, and yet he couldn't seem to help himself. He removed from his blue blazer the badge identifying him as Todd Winters. If he could only remove his deep sense of guilt at his deception as easily.

He knew he would have to find a way to tell Augusta the truth about himself, but it was just too soon for that. She hadn't reached the point where the news wouldn't cause a setback. When she made that all-important call agreeing to go to the Institute, then maybe, but that seemed a long way off.

Derek walked into his kitchen and reached for the coffee maker. Right now what he needed was coffee. As he waited for it to perk, he let his thoughts slip back to the day of the accident, the one day he would never forget as long as he lived. Guilt, like a slow-acting poison, seeped into every part of his psyche. How did one go about telling a woman like Augusta

Humphrey that he was the bastard responsible for ruining her life?

He walked over to the sink and looked out through the cafe-curtained window above it. Had it only been fifteen months since he'd gone to the Braille Institute and convinced them to train him to work with the blind? He couldn't remember doing any other work more satisfying than what he did at the Institute. He'd certainly never felt anything close to it about his company, Morgan Electronics.

When his coffee had finally finished perking, he reached for a coffee mug from the cabinet. After setting it down on the small, butcher-block kitchen table, he walked over to the refrigerator/freezer and delved into it to retrieve a TV dinner.

He was used to this kind of fare since he'd been living on his own. He didn't have to read the directions; he knew every one by heart. He popped the dinner into the microwave and set the timer for the required number of minutes.

He hadn't realized what a selfish, aimless, irresponsible existence he had lived before that fateful day months ago when he...He squeezed his eyes shut against the painful memory, seeking to banish the guilt. But it refused to be banished.

There was no escaping it. His father used to say you have to pay for everything you do. He, Derek, had never taken those words seriously and had lived a reckless and carefree lifestyle, damn the consequences. No matter how much he paid, would it ever be enough to compensate Augusta Humphrey for what he had taken from her?

The phone rang, jolting him out of his reverie. He picked up the kitchen extension.

"Hello."

"Derek?"

"Ben?"

"How's it going?"

"With Augusta Humphrey, you mean?"

"The very same. I got the impression from talking to her a few days ago that she wasn't altogether happy with your visit."

"But then you already knew what her reaction would be, didn't you? You're one crafty devil, Dr Hastings. Since that first visit, the situation has changed only slightly. Even though she's gotten over her initial anger at my intrusion into her life, she's still not exactly thrilled when I come around. But I'm hoping that she'll break down and call me once she comes to realize that going to the Institute can only help her."

"If she does, are you sure it's not you more than the Institute that's the real draw?"

"Has she said something to you?"

"No, not in so many words, but it's the impression I got."

"Would you mind telling me how you reached that conclusion with so little to go on?"

"I've known Augusta a long time."

"How long?"

"Eight years. We first met at Pennsylvania Memorial when I had just finished my residency in surgical ophthalmology and she was an intern on the chief of staffs service." He laughed. "You know, some of her colleagues used to call her Gusto, because she always put everything she had into everything she did. We became fast friends.

"You see, she has no family to speak of, unless you count an aunt and half a dozen cousins she hasn't seen in years. As a result of her background, she is more of a private person than most. My wife Myra and I sort of adopted her. She's like a younger sister, really."

Derek smiled. He didn't stop to wonder why he should feel so relieved by Ben's words.

"She's loyal to our people," Ben went on. "She isn't like some Afro-Americans who forget where they came from once they leave poverty behind. Instead of setting up her own offices in a plush part of town, Augusta chose to stay at Philadelphia General. And as you know, her house is situated near the heart of South Philly. The only luxury she's allowed herself is—was—her BMW."

Derek felt the point of guilt jab through him like a sharp needle. He was silent for a moment. "What you've just said has given me an idea how to reach her once she's made that all-important first step. If, as you say, she feels passionate about helping others, it may work in our favor."

"Our favor?" Ben laughed. "So it's gone as far as that, has it?"

"Ben!"

"All right." Ben quietly considered Derek's words, then said, "It sounds good in theory, but all of that was before the accident."

"What organizations were she involved with?"

"EC, Educate the Children, an organization geared toward keeping children and teens off the streets and out of gangs. And she was a staunch participant in a stay-in-school teen encounter group."

"It sounds like her interests lie with helping children. Any particular reason for it?"

"You'll have to ask her that."

"I can see our Dr. Humphrey was a mover and a shaker."

"You won't get an argument from me on that."

"If I can help, she will be again."

"Just make sure you don't hurt her in the process."

"I won't. Believe me, I've already done enough in that department."

"You've changed, Derek. Don't let your sense of guilt belittle what you've accomplished."

"I know you're right, but I intend to make it up to Augusta."

"Getting back to the point of this conversation, because of the accident I was sure she'd permanently isolate herself from the world, but, you, my friend, have apparently managed to find a loose thread in the seam of her cocoon. Whatever you do, don't stop pulling it."

"I haven't been pulling any strings, Ben."

"Yeah, and I'm Bill Clinton. When you came to me about her, I wasn't at all sure that what you had in mind would *work.*"

"And now?"

"So far, so good. Time will tell whether you'll be successful with the future phases of your plan."

"You make it all sound so cloak and dagger, and it really isn't."

"Whatever, Derek." He paused. "You shouldn't put off telling her who you really are."

"She's not ready to hear it, Ben. I need more time."

"Just don't wait too long, all right?"

"I'll keep in touch."

After hanging up the phone, Derek heard the beeps from the microwave indicating that his dinner was ready. As if by rote, he moved to take it out of the oven and then sat down at the kitchen table to eat the meal of Salisbury steak and potatoes and to drink his coffee.

When he finished, he tossed the half-eaten container into the garbage can. He had never realized until lately how monotonous all of this was.

He dismissed those depressing thoughts and headed for his study. He'd brought home pamphlets, reports, and books on retraining the blind for alternate jobs in the field they worked in before their blindness. He'd gone over the materials at length at the Institute with John Fuller, the vocational counselor, because he wanted to become familiar with the methods if and when Augusta declared herself ready to move in that direction.

It wouldn't be long now, because Augusta was—like it or not—becoming more cognizant of how her life could open up. The incident at the door and later with the phone indicated that he was right in thinking along those lines.

The call, when it came, would be the first important step toward a measure of independence for her. To see her well-adjusted and content was all he asked for. To see her happy would heal his conscience. But to do it all, he would have to return her sight to her. Unfortunately, that miracle lay beyond his power.

Augusta continued to explore her house, becoming more and more familiar with its rooms with each passing day. She couldn't fathom now why she had been so resistant to the idea.

Before, you didn't have Todd Winters around to drive in the stake.

Each new revelation about the furniture in the rooms gave her confidence to move on to other more personal items, such as identifying certain soaps or perfume by smell, size, and the shape of the bar, bottle, or jar.

The feel of the cool, slick-glassy surfaces of her jewelry, the tangy, menthol fragrance of mouthwash, and the minty taste of toothpaste—all of these normal, everyday things she'd once taken for granted now became exciting discoveries.

Augusta occasionally caught herself thinking about what Todd had said about using a cane or a dog, but she was unwilling to go that far, not yet. Something inside her rebelled at the idea that she might need one or both. Or Todd Winters. She still hadn't called him.

Why?

She knew it was pride.

Augusta was seated on the porch, where Elaine had left her while she did the housework. She heard footsteps advancing up her walkway and caught a whiff of a man's cologne. There was something so hauntingly familiar about it.

"Who's there?"

"It's me, Augusta, Todd Winters."

"What are you doing here?"

"Now, is that any way to greet a visitor? Besides, you knew it was me before I identified myself, didn't you?"

Augusta ignored his question. "I wouldn't exactly call you a welcome visitor, Mr. Winters."

"Maybe not. I thought we agreed it would be *Todd* and *Augusta.*"

"I don't remember agreeing to that."

"But you do recall saying whatever made me happy, feel free, don't you? And calling you Augusta does, so I will."

Augusta cleared her throat but didn't answer.

"You're very good at evasion, Doc. You still haven't answered my question. How did you know it was me before I spoke?"

"How could I have known whether it was you or not? I couldn't see you."

"In a way you did 'see' me, Augusta. You saw me with your other senses. Something about me projected an image in your mind, and you associated that something with me. What was it, Augusta? It couldn't be the way I walked because last time I was here I was in your living room and it's carpeted, muffling the sound. Was it my cologne? Do I have bad breath? What was it, Augusta? Tell me."

"Todd..."

"Answer me, Augusta."

She wanted to evade the intense probing firmness she heard in his voice. She could almost visualize the scrutinizing look he was no doubt beaming on her. "What will it take to get you to leave?"

"Don't sweat it, Doc. You don't have that kind of money, so save your breath. It's good to see you outside enjoying what nature has to offer. Describe to me what it feels like, the sound, the smell."

His abrupt subject change threw Augusta. She wondered what he was up to with the seemingly innocent shift in their discussion. She breathed in deeply. Before she knew it, she was answering him.

"My senses are drinking in the unique, perfumed scent of the marigolds planted on either side of the porch, the sweet fragrance of the roses growing along the trellis.

"I can feel the warmth of the sun and smell the fresh scent on the soothing, mid-morning breeze brushing against my face. I don't remember being conscious of either the smell or the feel of either in quite this way before. It's as though my other senses have suddenly banded together to compensate..."

"For your loss of sight? Not exactly, but they are becoming more keenly aware with each passing day.

You never realized what you and every other sighted person have taken for granted all your life and never taken the time to enjoy."

"I don't know what you mean."

"Oh, I think you do. And there's nothing wrong with that. When you begin your rehabilitation..."

"If I do," Augusta corrected him.

"*Once* you begin your rehab program," he re-corrected her, "it'll help you to be more perceptive about things and people."

"You seem so certain about that. You know, Todd, I have a thing about being steam-rollered into anything."

"Believe me, I'm not trying to pressure you, Augusta. It's enough for now that you're becoming interested on your own in the future possibilities at your disposal. Look, I have to be getting to the Institute."

Augusta heard the rustle of plastic against plastic.

"I brought several cassettes that'll give you some facts about the inner workings of the Institute, how it got started, and the progress that it's made over the years."

When he placed the cassettes in her hands, Augusta felt his warmth flow into her. She felt him looking at her and wished for a moment that she could literally see his eyes meet hers.

"I'll be checking on you, Augusta. Until then, later."

Did his voice sound husky? she wondered. Or was it her imagination? Augusta found herself listening for the rhythm of his footsteps as they receded seconds later, muffled in the carpet of soft grass beneath his feet. Next came the sound of his steps on the asphalt, then a car door opening and closing.

How had she failed to hear it when he had gotten out of the car earlier? Because as a former sighted person, she was used to taking things for granted, just as he'd said.

She realized now what he had been doing: playing mind games with her. It seemed that the man would do anything to drive his point home. As his car pulled away from the curb, she heard a slight ringing noise. Judging from the sound, it needed some kind of mechanical work. Now he had her listening for defects in his damned car!

She fingered the cassettes, then slipped them into her skirt pocket and rose from her seat on the couch swing. And as she shuffled toward the front door, she suddenly became aware of the creaky, in-need-of-oil sound the swing made when she moved her weight off it. She'd never paid any attention to the protesting sound before, but now, thanks to Mr. Todd Winters, she was conscious of it and a lot of other things she'd rather not be. She turned when she heard light, competent footsteps on the porch.

"Elaine?"

"Yes. Are you all right, Augusta?"

"I'm fine." She smiled.

"What happened to put you in such a good mood?"

Augusta couldn't keep the awed satisfaction out of her voice. "I heard your footsteps when you came outside and knew it was you. You probably think I've—never mind. Let's go back in the house."

Derek began to make driving by Augusta's house a habit on his way home from the Institute over the next days. He wanted to stop, but decided not to just yet. He wanted to give Augusta more time to consider going to the Institute.

One afternoon following one of his classes with the junior blind, he took his usual detour down Augusta's street. He saw the woman he hoped to see sitting on a bench under a tree with a cassette radio in the space beside her. He stopped and parked the car, having decided that he would have a talk with Augusta after all.

Just as he climbed out of the car, he saw a teenage girl walk over to the row of hedges that separated her yard from Augusta's and call out to her. Derek inched forward, being careful to remain hidden behind a tall dense shrub on the corner of the property.

"Augusta, it's me, Melody."

"Yes, Melody?"

"Can I come over and talk to you?"

"Of course you can."

Derek could see that an old pathway had been forged through the hedges. Evidently, over a period of time the girl had formed the habit of coming to visit her next-door neighbor. This pleased him. He was right in assuming that Augusta had a special affinity for kids and possessed a natural rapport with them. If only he could use that to help her help herself. For a few seconds he let his mind wander along that train of thought, then returned his attention to the pair under the tree.

Augusta sensed Melody's uneasiness when she came to stand behind the bench, so she smiled to reassure her, then asked. "What do you want to talk to me about, Melody?"

"I'm not sure how to begin. It's about me and Kevin. He's my boyfriend."

It was hard for Augusta to believe that Melody was almost a woman now. She and her family had moved next door seven years before, when Melody was ten years old. Augusta had watched her grow, transforming from an awkward, chubby child into a slender, attractive young lady. She'd regretted not having spoken to her more than a few times since the accident.

"Mama said I shouldn't bother you because you have enough problems to cope with, what with losing your sight and everything."

"You could never bother me, Melody. I may not be able to see you, but I can still listen. Come, sit down and tell me about you and Kevin."

"Melody! What are you doing over there? Didn't I tell you not to pester Dr. Humphrey?" a female voice loudly intruded.

"It's Mama, and she's coming over here," Melody said dully.

Augusta and Jean Cummings had never been overly fond of one another. Augusta believed that the woman was jealous of the rapport Augusta and her daughter shared. When she heard the other woman's steps halt, she said, "She's not pestering me, Jean."

"No? The last time Melody spoke to you was a few months ago, and you all but ignored her. You had my baby in tears."

Augusta remembered that incident. She'd just gotten the results from the last consultation and she had been depressed.

"I'm sorry. It was just a bad day for me, Jean. I would never deliberately set out to hurt Melody, and you know it."

"Well you did, and I'm not going to let you have the chance to do it again. Let's go home, baby."

"But, Mama, I want to talk to Augusta."

"She's not your mother, I am. You can tell me whatever it is."

"Jean, I..." Augusta began.

Jean interrupted. "Melody feels sorry for you just like everybody else, but you're not going to use my child as some kind sop for your ego because you can't see no more."

With that, the woman insisted that her daughter accompany her back through the separation in the hedges.

Augusta closed her eyes against the pain her neighbor's cruel words evoked.

It was all Derek could do not to go after Jean Cummings and shake the stuffing out of her for what she'd done, but he had to comfort Augusta. This would have to happen just when he'd made progress in drawing her out of her shell. He wondered if it would jeopardize his plan to lure her into the world outside her house.

"Are you all right, Augusta?"

"Todd!" Augusta swallowed down the pain and humiliation she'd just suffered. To know that Todd had overheard what Jean had said was almost more than she could stand. "I'm fine, Todd. What are you doing here?"

Derek could see that she was trying to be brave and it tore at his insides. If not for him, she wouldn't be going through this.

"I've made it a practice to drive down this street on my way home from the Institute. Today just happens to be one of the days I work with the junior blind. Their classes are of a shorter duration, so I leave the Institute early on those days."

"Junior blind? I didn't know you worked with kids."

Derek heard the spark of interest in her voice and he smiled. "Yes, I have for the last seven months, and I enjoy it."

Augusta shifted her attention. "I guess you heard what just happened?"

"I won't pretend that I didn't."

"I wouldn't want you to."

"So how do you feel about it?"

"How do you think I feel? What you really want to know is how I'm handling it, right? You once accused me of dropping out of life. Do you need another example of what my life is like?"

"All the more reason to change it, mold it into what you want it to be."

"It's easy for you say. You're not blind."

"No, I'm not blind, but don't tell me I don't understand what you're going through."

Augusta realized how self-pitying she sounded and grimaced in disgust at her behavior. She'd learned to face things head-on all her life and now to whimp out like this...

"I know it's not easy for you, Augusta. Getting to where you have took real guts. One way or another life isn't easy for any of us. We all have to learn to adjust when our life changes or fate slaps us down."

"What do you want from me, Todd?"

"It's not what I want that's important. It's what you want, what you expect from yourself. You can learn to deal with life on your own terms. All you need is help, and I'm offering it to you—the same way you were offering it to that girl a little while ago."

"You don't pull your punches do you, Todd Winters? I think you missed your calling. You should have been a politician, or maybe a preacher."

"Have you listened to the tapes I left with you?"

"You're pushing."

"I know So what have you decided?"

"I haven't."

"I guess you want me to leave you alone. I will for now because I do have to be going, but I'll be seeing you."

"Yes, you always will," she said bitterly.

"And so will you, one day, just in another way."

After Todd had gone, Augusta sat and thought about the last thing he had said. What had he meant by it? What other way was he talking about? He knew better than anyone else that in all likelihood she would never regain her sight. She just didn't understand the man.

Her mind replayed what had happened earlier with Jean. Knowing the woman as well as she did, she shouldn't have been hurt by her reaction to Melody visiting her. Jean had so much. She had a husband who loved her and a child—everything Augusta had hoped she would have one day, yet the woman wasn't generous enough to share Melody with her. Instead she felt threatened.

Augusta sought the play button on the cassette player and replayed one of the tapes Todd had given her. She had a lot to think about thanks to Mr. Todd Winters, damn him.

As the days went by he became a frequent visitor. Augusta often wondered what made him keep coming back, considering that she gave him little or no encouragement to do so.

His eagerness and devotion in wanting to help her bordered on the extreme, as if he had some deep hidden motive for doing what he did, apart from the obvious one.

She knew there had to be more to it and to him. And she intended to find the answers to both. Even if it meant going to the Institute, or at least promising to anyway.

CHAPTER III

Derek was concerned when he still hadn't heard from Augusta after several more days had passed. He'd thought for sure that he had reached hercat then reaching back. Following the incident with Jean Cummings and their talk afterward, and his subsequent follow-up visits, he was so sure that she would call. He had expected…

What had he expected? Whatever it was, it was more than he should hope for. If he were to be truly honest with himself, he knew he wanted more from their present relationship. There was a physical attraction growing between them, a chemistry he'd tried to deny from the first moment they'd met. But he knew it was there and sensed Augusta was aware of it, too, on some level.

He likened their relationship to a game of tug of war, where both sides pulled against the other. If either of them acknowledged these feelings and let go, there was no telling what could happen. Why was he worrying about that? Nothing would come of the attraction.

Though he fought against it, Derek's thoughts strayed back to the time when his fingers brushed hers that first day. Those smooth, slender fingers were silky-soft and damned arousing.

When he had looked into her dark, dark eyes and lower to her luscious full lips, he had wanted to taste them, delve his tongue between them into the sweet warmth beyond.

He was a fool. He had to stop thinking about Augusta like that and concentrate on helping her adjust to a life without sight. He dared not think past that.

Derek left his study and headed into his bedroom, shed his clothes, and stepped into the bathroom. As usual, there were no towels on the rack. He laughed, then walked to the linen closet to get some, showered, and then left the bathroom. Seconds later he slid naked between the cool sheets on his bed, letting his thoughts wander back to Augusta.

She seemed to be all he thought about these days. He had a lot to make up to her. His goal was to make her and others like her active, useful people again. *Who in the hell was he trying to kid?* This particular lady was special to him, and he knew it. And he knew that neither his guilt nor her blindness had anything to do with it.

His alter ego badge as Todd Winters in place, Derek got out of his car. Then, reaching back inside to retrieve a large, brown, leather-bound object, he headed up the walk to Augusta's house. He straightened his tie and knocked at her door. He heard the shuffle of shoes on the carpet and knew Augusta was on her way to answer the door. When he heard her call out, "Who is it?" he smiled. She'd remembered.

"It's me, Todd."

She opened the door and moved aside. "You're here bright and early. To what do I owe this visit?"

"I know you weren't expecting me; I just thought I'd drop by."

"Come on in, Todd."

Something was different—he could feel it, but couldn't quite put his finger on it. He'd have to be patient and wait until Augusta was ready to tell him what it was.

"I've brought you a present," he began soon after taking a seat on the couch next to her.

"What kind of present?" she asked warily.

"Don't worry, it isn't a snake."

"I hope not. I hate snakes."

"You and half the nation." He placed the book on her lap and waited.

Augusta touched the sleek, smooth surface and the rounded corners.

"Is it a book?"

"Of sorts. Go ahead. Open it."

"You know I can't see to read it," she said stiffly.

"My grandmother used to say there is no such word as *can't.* Look at it with these," he said, brushing his fingers across hers.

He could tell by the expression on her face that the contact had affected her. How were they ever going to get anywhere with that attraction working overtime to undermine them at every turn? He would just have to keep physical contact to a minimum. But how could he do that when seventy-five percent of instruction to the blind involved some form of touching?

"You remember the time you learned the parts of the phone receiver so you could call me? Which you haven't done."

"Todd!"

"All right. Getting back to that day."

"Yes?"

"We'll apply the same principle with this book." He moved her fingers to the edge and she unsnapped the catch, freeing the book for exploration. Derek found that her fingers were so warm and smooth and…These hands were surgeon's hands. And because of him they would probably never touch a scalpel again.

Derek cleared his throat. "Tell me, what do you feel, Augusta?"

She opened the book, guiding her fingers across the first page. She frowned. Something felt different about the page. And the surface was no ordinary surface. The texture was nubby. A strip of carpet? Or upholstery? What kind of book was this? she wondered.

"I see you've identified what's on the page. Go on to the next one, Augusta."

She turned the page. The faint fragrance of flowers wafted up her nostrils. It was not just any flower; this was a rose, a dry, pressed rose. She could tell by the scent.

"Todd, what kind of book is this?"

"One like the ones we use at the Institute to help our students learn to identify things by touch, feel, and smell." He took her fingers and turned the page.

She felt the roughness of tiny rocks glued to a coarse background.

Derek watched Augusta carefully. "Tell me, what do you feel?"

It was hard for her to concentrate when her sense of smell picked up his cologne and unique male musk. "These are rocks, very tiny rocks and each one feels different. This one is smooth. And this is—no it isn't rocks. It feels like sand. That's it, sand!" Her fingers stopped on a porous rock.

"Pumice?"

"Right again."

"And this one is uneven with many layers."

"Very good. It's a piece of petrified rock. Are you sure you haven't studied geology?"

Augusta smiled. "Of course. It was one of my majors in college."

"I knew that." Derek hesitated. "I noticed when you came to the door you seemed troubled. Is anything wrong?"

Augusta kneaded her bottom lip with her teeth. "I was going to call and tell you not to come by today."

"Why?"

"I wasn't up to—never mind. I was wrong. Your presence has lifted my spirits."

"Good. What do you think about going to the park?"

"I don't know."

He knew she'd probably feel self-conscious being around people because of what had happened with Jean Cummings, but it was something she would have to get used to.

"We can take the book and compare the things in the park to what you have in there."

"You make everything a learning experience. You're a born teacher, Todd Winters."

"I thought you compared me to a politician or a preacher." Derek was quiet for a moment. "I'm glad you have elevated me to the position of teacher.

Thank you for saying that. I like that title better. Where is your Elaine?"

"I gave her the afternoon off to do some shopping."

"Well, shall we go then?" Derek was pleased that Augusta was finding she didn't need her companion to do everything for her. Augusta was beginning to rely on Augusta.

She felt nervous about the outing, and her heart started to pound as Todd helped her out of the car. The birds seemed to be trilling a loud fortissimo in her honor. She heard voices, children's voices, and it sounded as if they were playing games. She could hear the slap and squeak of the rubbery bottoms of their tennis shoes as they contacted the concrete.

Derek took her elbow and guided her across the grass. "To your left, teenage boys are playing basketball. To your right small children are swinging and playing in the sandbox. Some others are hanging from the jungle gym like little monkeys." He felt her tremble. "Are you all right?"

"Yes. I was just thinking about the child I saved from that crazy driver who blinded me."

He felt a painful jolt deep in his soul. He'd done nothing but think about that little girl and how he'd almost killed her.

Derek remained quiet for so long, Augusta thought he might not know the circumstances of her blindness. "Ben did tell you how I lost my sight, didn't he?"

"Yes."

"Kelsey Ann is the name of the little girl involved in the accident." She smiled. "She's eight years old and very intelligent. Every time I think about how that reckless fool nearly…I'm sorry, I didn't meant to get into this."

"It's all right. Straight ahead there's a bench. Do you want to sit down?"

"Oh, no. I'd rather walk."

Several boys playing chase careened into them.

"Can't you guys watch where you're going?" Derek reprimanded them.

"Todd," Augusta said softly, "it's all right."

"No, it's not. I think they…"

"Man, the lady's blind!" said one of them.

"What does it feel like? Being blind, I mean," another asked Augusta interestedly.

She was too surprised to answer.

Still another said to his friends, "I don't think I could handle it, man."

"You're not the only one," the first boy answered. "We're sorry, lady?'

Not waiting for her reply, they ran off, resuming their game of chase.

Augusta felt a lump in her throat and couldn't speak.

Todd squeezed her hand. "If you want to, we can leave."

"I have to get used to people's reactions to my condition sometime. It may as well start today."

Augusta's attitude surprised Derek. He didn't know why it should. He knew she had spunk. She had to have it to become the kind of doctor she had been.

Derek and Augusta eventually ended up sitting on a bench. Together, page by page, they again went through the special book he'd given her.

During the ride back to her house, Augusta thought about the patience it took for Todd to help her—or any blind person, for that matter. And not for the first time she wondered why he did it. He obviously wasn't blind himself. Maybe someone in his personal life was blind. A mother, a sister. A wife?

Elaine said he looked to be about thirty-four or thirty-five and was very attractive.

Todd Winters was an enigma to her; he never talked about himself. To ferret information from him about his private life was like trying to extract a pearl from between the tightly closed shell of an oyster.

"A penny for your thoughts, Doc. Or is it a dollar these days due to inflation?"

"Why do you do it?"

"Work with the blind, you mean? It's a hard question to answer. There are many reasons, but I can tell you that helping the blind is more rewarding than anything I've ever done. To see a person, against great odds, make a life for himself or herself is a real turn on for me. I can't find the words to adequately convey that feeling to you. The Institute has become my life. I thoroughly enjoy my work there. What else can I say?"

"Nothing else," she replied softly. He had cleverly maneuvered the subject away from anything personal. She wondered why he didn't want to talk about himself. What reason could he have?

Derek glanced at Augusta and wondered if he had succeeded in making her forget about him personally. He hoped he had. His life wasn't a subject he wanted to discuss with her right now.

CHAPTER IV

Restless, Augusta swung back and forth in the porch swing, turning over in her mind whether she was ready to brave the Braille Institute. The thought of going there had at first intimidated her. But now she saw it as a challenge, one she felt more and more like taking up as each day went by.

According to Todd, the book he had given her was one among many he used in working with the blind. She knew why he'd given it to her: to wet her appetite for more. And it had worked. It had sparked just that response in her. She now hungered for more knowledge about how the blind learn to cope.

The cassettes he'd given her mentioned the number of counseling sessions prospective students were obliged to attend before being accepted into the Institute. She wondered what the sessions would be like and whether she could go through with them. They had to include probing into her feelings concerning the accident. Whatever the sessions included, her mind was made up.

Todd's persistent, caring, attitude, coupled with the episode with Jean and the incident in the park, had helped her to arrive at a decision. She reached for the cane by her side, which she had Elaine get for her. She no longer felt any shame, embarrassment, or self-consciousness connected with relying on the cane. She reasoned that it was made to help blind people, and she had to admit that that was her status.

There, she'd finally admitted to membership in that special group.

Augusta suddenly became aware that she wasn't alone. She immediately recognized her caller.

"Todd?"

"You and that swing are like a beacon drawing me here."

Augusta smiled. "Yeah, right."

"I'm serious. Every time I drive down your street, I'm automatically drawn to it like a moth to a flame."

"All right, all right, enough already. What have you got in store for me for today, Mr. Winters?"

"You make me sound so calculating and…"

"Well, aren't you?"

"I confess it's true. The lady is onto me," he said in mock despair. "You're a certifiable nutcase, Todd Winters."

Derek eyed Augusta closely. There was a light-heartedness about her today. Did he dare hope that she had, that it meant…

He didn't have long to wait for an answer.

"You've guessed right. I have decided to go to the Institute as a visitor. Your visitor."

"You won't be sorry, Augusta. You'll wonder why you haven't done it before now. I can arrange to get you in to see Diane Reichter, our resident psychologist, and John Fuller, who is our program advisor and vocational counselor, in..." he looked at his watch, "about forty minutes, if we hurry. I'll need to use your phone."

Augusta stood up. "Be my guest. I'll be ready to leave whenever you are."

Derek stepped over to her and hugged her. He realized his mistake almost immediately. The warmth of her softly curved body enclosed in his arms made his body respond.

Get a grip on yourself, Morgan. You can't afford to let these renegade feelings get the upper hand.

He released her quickly and stepped back, reaching for the front doorknob. The scent of her perfume seemed to follow him inside the house, taunting him unmercifully with what he had reluctantly chosen to cut short: namely, a chance to hold Augusta in his arms and...

He had to stop leave whenever you are.", but how in hell was he going to do it?

Augusta's heart thumped a heavy tattoo in her chest. She could still feel the tingle of sensation that being held in Todd's arms caused to course through her, even though the contact was brief and broken off quickly. She knew Todd's excitement wasn't personal and only meant that he was happy she had at last agreed to accompany him to the Institute. Anything else would be a fantasy on her part. She had to keep reminding herself of that.

A few minutes later Derek came back out on the porch, followed by Elaine with a tray of lemonade and three glasses.

"We have a while to wait before our meeting. John's in a conference. Elaine suggested lemonade, and on a day like today, I didn't have the will power to refuse." He knew they needed a chaperone. Chaperone! Where had that old-fashioned word come from? Thanks to Elaine, he and Augusta would be alone as little as possible. He had a job to do, and couldn't afford to let his attraction to her distract him from performing it.

"Sounds good to me," Augusta answered. Her chance to be alone with Todd was gone. She wished it were one of Elaine's days off.

When it was time to leave for the Institute, Derek breathed a sigh of relief. But it was short-lived when he realized that he and Augusta would be alone in the car. Since his awareness of her had suddenly intensified, any time alone with her spelled danger.

It was ironic. His aim was going to be to help Augusta become independent and not continue to use

Elaine as a crutch, while at the same time he himself was going to need her to act as a buffer between him and Augusta so they would not be completely alone together. Did this make any sense? What was the matter with him? He inwardly scolded himself. He was thirty-four years old, not eighteen. Surely he could exert more control over his libido than this.

When Augusta felt the car slow down, she tensed. Although she had decided to visit the Institute, she was still anxious about going there. She'd gone to the park, but it wasn't the same as traveling on the busy city streets.

Suddenly the everyday sounds of car horns blowing, engines revving, sirens blaring, and the voices of people talking loudly as they hurried by panicked her. Would there ever come a time when she got used to being hearing-oriented as opposed to sight-actuated?

She would have to reprogram her senses to accommodate her present situation. And she knew it wouldn't be easy.

Derek stopped the car. He sensed the fear Augusta was so courageously trying to play down.

"You'll like Diane and John. John's Australian and has an accent that makes him sound like Crocodile Dundee. And he even looks like him. Now, Diane has hair the pale color of cornsilk, and her accent is German." He laughed. "I told her once that she loolod like a modern-day version of Marlene Dietrich. If you could only have seen her blush."

Augusta smiled.

"That's better. Are you ready to go inside?"

"I guess." She unlocked her door and waited.

Derek gave her hand a reassuring squeeze, then got out of the car and walked around to the passenger side to open her door.

Her momentary panic began to dissipate when she felt Todd's sympathetic hand on hers. With his assistance, she climbed out of the car onto the sidewalk.

"There are fifty steps to the stairs, and from them twenty-five more leading to the front door of the Institute, Augusta."

Derek took her elbow Augusta silently counted every step. She didn't want to stumble at this stage of the game.

But on the last step she did falter.

"Don't worry about it, Augusta," Derek said gently.

"It's been known to happen to sighted persons; me, for one."

Although she knew he meant his words to calm and reassure her, they didn't banish her feelings of frustration and self-consciousness altogether. A whoosh of air greeted her when the door opened automatically, making her flinch, but she leveled her shoulders and let Todd escort her inside the building.

"We're approaching the elevators," Derek said.

When they reached them, he raised Augusta's hand to the wall on her left so she could feel the raised, Braille-dotted surface beneath her fingers.

"You'll learn what each tiny dot means."

Augusta's smile wobbled slightly as she nodded in agreement.

At last the elevator arrived. She hesitated. She had hated elevators when she could see. The feeling of losing her stomach always made her a little queasy.

Derek made a guess as to her thoughts. With a firm grip on her elbow, he ushered her inside the cubicle and turned her to face the closing elevator doors.

Just as Augusta closed her eyes, he spoke. "There are also Braille dots near the number designating each floor. You want to try it?"

"I think I'll pass this time."

"Diane's and John's offices are on the third floor."

The ding of the elevator bell when they reached the third floor was like music to her ears. She could hardly wait to step out on solid ground. Even though she had once used the elevator routinely to move from one floor to another to see patients or to get to an operating room, everything was different now and somehow intimidating.

Upon entering, Augusta found that both Diane's and John's voices sounded friendly and welcoming.

Though she felt herself relaxing, she held Todd's hand during the discussion.

She listened intently as John outlined the curriculum of the Institute.

"We expect our students to do their daily and weekly assignments faithfully, to the best of their ability."

Augusta was impressed. John made it sound like attending a university for credit toward a degree. When she thought about it, she realized it was a learning process with goals the same as with any degree in a specific field of endeavor.

Diane explained where she came in. "Our students have to feel emotionally as well as physically well to reach any modicum of success in learning to cope with their blindness, so they come to me and we discuss it," she further explained. "Denial, frustration, anger, bitterness, and depression are normal reactions to the loss of something as integral as sight. It's my job to help you get over the rough spots as painlessly as possible. So what do you think? Will you be joining us?"

Now that she had come to the decision-making part, Augusta hesitated, not sure if it was the right place for her.

"The one thing you'll have going for you is that you'll be working with Todd Winters, one of the handsomest instructors we have on staff, I'm told,"

Diane added, her voice teasing yet charmingly cheerful.

I'm told. Augusta digested this. It suddenly dawned on her what Diane had said.

"You're blind too, aren't you?"

"Yes," she answered candidly. "Does that bother you?"

"Well, no. It just never occurred to me that you might be. Why didn't you tell me, Todd?"

"I didn't think it would make any difference as long as Diane knew what she was doing and was good at it."

"Were you always blind?" Augusta asked Diane.

"No. The day I graduated from college, I fell down the steps as I was leaving the stage and hit my head. Over the years a tumor formed, pressing on not only the optic nerve, but other brain functions. To save my life I had to sacrifice my sight."

"It must have been devastating."

"It was, Augusta. I was at the pinnacle of my career as a portrait painter when I was forced to have the operation. You may have heard of me. I painted under the name Diana Mueller."

Augusta nodded. She did remember that name and had seen some of her paintings. She had gone to one of Diane's gallery showings a few years ago.

"I've been where you are right now, Augusta," Diane went on. "I, too, have had to find a substitute for something that was the center of my life. And believe me, it was the hardest thing I've ever had to do."

"I don't know what to say."

"Just say you'll give us a chance to help you. That's all we ask."

Augusta expected Todd to say something, but throughout the entire discussion, he had remained conspicuously quiet.

"I'd like to think about it."

"Take your time, but don't ponder it too long," John said. "Study long, you..."

" 'Study wrong.' I know."

"Remember, we're here to help."

Augusta heard John skirt his desk, and in the next moment he was shaking her hand. "It was nice meeting you, Doctor."

"You too. Both of you," she said, rising to her feet.

Derek was by her side when they exited the office and guided Augusta to the elevators.

"Are you up to a tour?" he asked.

"Not today."

Augusta heard shuffling footsteps and the tapping of many canes. If she became a student here, she would be just like the people whose canes she heard.

"If you're ready, I'll take you home."

There was a long silence during the first ten minutes of the drive back to Augusta's house.

"Are you angry with me, Todd?" Augusta asked.

"No. Should I be? It's a decision only you can make."

"But you are disappointed, though, aren't you? You'd like me to go, wouldn't you?"

"You have to want to go for yourself, Augusta. I want what's best for you. I hope you know that."

Yes, she did know that, and wished she were more to him than just another blind person he wanted to help. But wishing was definitely not going to make it so.

She had to think about her future and put any thoughts or fantasies about Todd Winters as anybody other than an instructor out of her head. Whatever she decided in the next few days would affect the rest of her life.

"You seem distracted this evening, Augusta."

"What did you say, Elaine?"

"You were miles away just now."

"I'm sorry. I've had a lot to think about the last few days."

"You mean whether you want to go to the Institute as a student?"

It was more than that, Augusta thought. She was so sure that Todd was angry with her about the Institute, but when she had time to think about it, she realized his mood had altered before they'd gone there. She wondered what had caused it. Had she said something? She didn't think she had.

"Augusta? Are you feeling all right?"

Augusta shook her head to clear it. "I'm fine. I think I'll go to my room now; I'm a little tired."

"I hope that's all it is, and you're not coming down with something."

Augusta smiled. "Believe me, it is. Good night, Elaine." She reached for the cane by the side of the love seat and made her way to her room.

She showered and prepared for bed, but found it impossible to fall asleep. The odd inflection in Todd's voice came back to haunt her. What had changed him? She knew of nothing she'd done to cause it.

Though faithful as ever about "checking on her." as he called it, Todd showed a quiet reserve that hadn't been there before they had gone to the Institute. And they were never alone any more.

She thought about the time he had invited her to go to the Independence Museum…

Friday evening she and Elaine were eating dinner when the phone rang.

"Hello."

"Augusta?"

"Todd."

"How would you like to go to the Independence Museum? I know you've probably been there a dozen times, but I thought you might like to go."

"You're wrong; I've never gone there."

"You mean you've lived in Philadelphia all your life and haven't gone to the city's museum? Shame on you! What would William Penn say?"

"Todd."

"All right, all right. Now here's your chance."

"Chance? Chance to do what?"

"Be patriotic, loyal to Mr. Penn's memory and all that. You understand."

"Oh, of course." She laughed. "You idiot."

"I know you aren't used to crowds just yet, but..."

"When do you want to go?"

"I thought you, Elaine, and I could go on Saturday."

"Elaine?" Augusta frowned, confused.

"You think she'll want to come?"

"I—well—I guess so."

"Then ask her, I'll hold on."

She covered the receiver with her hand, wondering why he wanted Elaine to go with them, and then asked Elaine if she would like to go.

"It's a go, Todd. What time will you be coming to pick us up?"

"The tour starts at eleven. I'll be by your house at ten-thirty."

"We'll be ready."

Augusta was preoccupied when the tour guide started to explain the significance of each piece on the different displays.

"This bed warmer, said to be made by Paul Revere, had to have hot coals placed inside. The long handle made it easy to move the warmer over the cold bed sheets..."

Derek laughed. "Wouldn't the colonists be shocked to know what the term "bed warmer" has come to mean since their time?"

Augusta frowned when she heard the teasing amusement in Elaine's voice as she said, "You're bad, Todd Winters."

Augusta didn't comment.

Derek's laughter faded, and he cleared his throat. "The tour is almost over. What do you say we eat lunch at the Colonial Restaurant?"

"I'm game. What about you, Augusta?" Elaine asked.

"It sounds fine," she answered coolly.

They ate in silence.

Augusta shook her head, banishing her reverie. Had she only just imagined that Todd had begun to include Elaine in everything they discussed or did? It was almost as though he were using Elaine to distance himself from her.

"You're getting paranoid, Augusta," she told herself. But was she?

And what about her decision to become a regular student at the Braille Institute? She was close to calling Diane to confirm it. Her thoughts returned to Todd. How would he feel working so closely with her now, if he really were trying to distance himself? Would he continue to be so cool and remote with her? Probably.

She knew instinctively the one thing that wouldn't change, and that was his caring attitude concerning her welfare. Was she just another project to him? If only she could get him to think of her in a different light.

Come on, Augusta, in your dreams. If what Diane had said and Elaine had seen could be believed, every female within a hundred-mile radius chased after Todd. Why would he want a blind woman when he could have any sighted one of his choice? But, according to Diane, he didn't seem to be aware of how attractive women found him.

What was it with Todd? What drove the man? For some reason, she couldn't shake the feeling that he had a very definite reason for being so devoted to teaching the blind. If she knew more about him, maybe she could understand why someone like him would do something so completely selfless.

He didn't have to spend so many hours with her. Why had he singled her out? After that first time, she felt sure it wasn't because Ben had asked him to.

What kind of private life could he possibly have? Was there a woman involved in it? And if there were, would she or any woman want to compete with his kind of schedule? The answer was yes, any woman would. Todd was special, warm, and genial, at least most of the time, and intense all of the time.

There was that strange sadness she picked up on at different intervals. She suspected that he was grieving about something. Had he lost someone close to him? Was he surviving a broken relationship? A divorce? What?

Augusta found herself wanting to solve the mystery of Todd Winters. She'd find a way to get him to talk about himself.

Early the next morning, Augusta picked up the phone and called Todd.

"Hello," came his sleep-husky voice.

"Did I wake you up?"

"It's all right. What's up, Doc?"

She laughed. "You're so original early in the morning."

"Aren't I just?"

"The reason I called is that I wanted you to be the first to know that I've decided to attend classes at the Institute."

"Very good. Do you want to go in with me today?"

"You don't waste any time, do you, Mr. Winters?"

"No, I don't. Can you be ready in, say, an hour?"

"Can you?"

"A question answered with a question. Maybe you and Diane have more in common than I thought."

"Do I hear a hint of chauvinism in there some place?"

"From *moi?* I'll be by your house in an hour, Doc."

Augusta smiled as she placed the receiver on its cradle. Todd sounded like his old self. She had Elaine choose an outfit for her, the most attractive yet casual one in her wardrobe.

When she came out of the shower, Elaine was waiting to talk to her.

"You've decided to go to the Institute, haven't you?"

"How did you guess?"

"I want you to know that I think you're doing the right thing. Although I'm wondering if it's for the obvious reason."

"Obvious reason?"

"Namely, to get close to one Todd Winters."

"That might have a little something to do with it," Augusta admitted.

"Only a little?"

"Todd will be here in a few minutes. I haven't got time for this."

"So I'll shut my mouth and help you get dressed."

Was she so transparent? Augusta asked herself. Would Todd suspect an ulterior motive? Would it make a difference if he did? She felt sure that he was attracted to her, but that was as far as it went. He couldn't possibly think of her in romantic terms. *But God, how I wish he did!*

Derek didn't know why he felt like a school boy on his first date. He was only taking Augusta to the Institute, for Christ's sake. Then why was he so on *edge?* he questioned, gazing at Augusta's house from his car, which was parked in front of it. Why was he still sitting out here instead of going to her house to get her?

Come on, Morgan, get out of the car. He finally left the vehicle and strode up the walk to the front porch. Before he could knock, the door opened. The sight of Augusta standing there in a cool peach sundress made his insides tighten with desire and momentarily struck him speechless.

"Well," Augusta said softly. "How do I look?"

"You look…"

"Yes?"

"Ah…nice. We'd better get started." He now noticed Elaine standing behind Augusta. "I'll have her back by four."

"You're acting as though I'm a teenager you have to return to the bosom of my family at a decent hour."

"Am I? I didn't realize." He sounded so serious.

"I'm only kidding, Todd, lighten up." She extended her hand. "Shall we go?"

Augusta's first session with Diane was scheduled for later in the week. Today she had an appointment to see John. They put together a personalized course of study for her.

"Until you know your way around, a guide will help you get from one class to another," John said. "We encourage our students to familiarize themselves with the Institute as soon as possible. You'll have awareness training and practicality adjustment with Joan Gordon, and Braille and mobility training with Todd Winters. In about six weeks, if you've progressed as well as we hope, you'll continue to more advanced Braille."

"With Todd?"

"Yes, with Todd. You two get along very well, don't you?"

Augusta smiled. "Yes, we do."

Augusta was mentally drained as well as physically exhausted by the end of the day. Todd had taken her around to the different rooms and then to the gardens and the cafeteria. He had explained the everyday routine to her as they went along.

"So what do you think?"

"I'm impressed. Maybe 'bowled over' better describes how I feel."

"You're bound to feel that way at first, but it'll get easier. You'll see." Augusta flinched.

"You will 'see,' Augusta. You'll just be doing it in a different way, using your other senses."

"You're slowly but surely becoming a balm for my vanity."

"Whatever you need me for, I'll be there for you, Augusta."

"Why do you put up with and spend so much time with me?"

"You need me, Doc."

"Yes, I certainly do." *In more ways than you know, Todd,* she silently added.

CHAPTER V

Derek gave Augusta's hand an encouraging squeeze as he guided her down the corridor to Diane Reichter's office.

"I know you're nervous about this session with Diane, Augusta, but after it's over you'll feel better, I promise. I'll be here to offer support or sympathy, if you need it."

"You'd think I could handle a simple rap session without having an anxiety attack, wouldn't you?"

"Listen, Augusta, where personal feelings are involved everyone is vulnerable, okay? Don't think I didn't have to go through something similar to this when I chose to learn how to work with the blind." For a moment Derek's mind drifted back to those days. He remembered coming here feeling unworthy and guilty as hell, but he had been determined to change, and after talking to Diane and John, his purpose was set. He couldn't say it had been easy, because it hadn't—but he *had* changed.

"What was it like for you, Todd?"

"It's a long story. I'll tell you about it sometime. We're here. You'd better go in. Diane's a busy woman, and we don't want to waste any of her time."

"No, we don't want to do that." Augusta was a little disappointed that she wouldn't get to hear more about Todd's life.

Derek looked at his watch. "I'll be back to get you in an hour. Your first session shouldn't last any longer than that." He caressed her cheek. "It'll be all right, Augusta," he said gently.

She offered him a wobbly smile. His heart dropped down to his feet. She was so beautiful.

Augusta listened as his steps receded, then taking a deep breath, she knocked on Diane's door.

"Come on in, Augusta," Diane said.

Augusta put her hand on the knob and turned it. She heard the smile in Diane's voice when she met her at the door and took her arm, guiding her to a seat in front of her desk.

"I know how you feel, Augusta. Please, relax. Do you want a cup of coffee or tea?"

"Coffee will be fine." Augusta heard Diane walk over to the coffeemaker and pour two cups of coffee. She wondered how long it had taken Diane to learn to be so at ease with her blindness. How much time would it take her before she could perform the same task?

Having guessed her thoughts, Diane answered the question for her.

"It won't be long, Augusta, I promise you. Joan Gordon will be your instructor and, believe me, she's the best around. The woman has the patience of Job. Now let's get down to the real reason you came here." When Augusta hesitated, Diane said, "Don't freeze up on me."

"Where do we begin?"

"How about with how you feel about your blindness?"

The bottom seemed to drop out of Augusta's stomach. She had been trying not to think about it because she got bitterly angry when she thought about the bastard who'd done this to her.

"Let the pain and anger out, Augusta. It's the only way you'll truly begin to heal."

"I'm not sure I know how, Diane. I've lived with it for almost two years." She began to tremble.

"Didn't you get counseling following the accident?"

"It was offered, but I couldn't bring myself to discuss it with anyone at the time. The pain was too raw, too deep, too much to bear."

"And now?"

"I still don't want to talk about it, but..."

"You feel that you have to because of Todd. You have to want it, too, Augusta. If we're to help you, you have to accept that you may never return to the profession you love."

Augusta laughed bitterly. "It's not as though I have a choice, is it?" she asked, taking a sip of her coffee.

"You have to mentally accept it. Deep inside you, the hope flickers like a candle that sometime in the future you will miraculously get your sight back. As long as there are people researching, there is always that possibility—but, Augusta, you have to live your life in the meantime. In case it doesn't happen for you, you have to consider a workable substitute."

"Is that what you did, Diane? Has it really worked? Can you tell me that you don't miss painting?"

"No, I can't tell you that. But we aren't discussing me." She gave a little laugh. "I used to be a master at evasion myself. It takes one to know one, and believe me, I know all the signs. You're a strong woman, Augusta. You've managed to cope with a situation that would have broken a lesser person."

"Right now you're still in denial. What that means is your subconscious has erected barriers against the harsh reality of what happened to you. Your mind has built up a protective mechanism to help you cope until a time when you can deal with the situation. Since you've agreed to come here, it means that you're finally ready to move out of that protective environment."

"And do what? What can a heart surgeon—scratch that—an ex-heart surgeon do with her life? Don't you understand what..."

"Oh, yes, I do, Augusta."

"I didn't mean to..."

"I know you didn't, but let's be candid with one another. You're hurting and you want to strike out at someone and relieve that pain. It's a normal reaction. Don't think I didn't do that myself because I did. Painting was my life, just as surgery was yours. I use the word *was* with emphasis, because for right now it's in the past. A satisfying future is what we want you to have, a worthwhile and rewarding future, one that will fulfill the need you have to help people. Yes, I know that about you, Augusta. That was the reason you became a doctor in the first place, isn't it?"

There was only one way Diane could have known this. "You wouldn't happen to know Dr. Ben Hastings, would you?"

"Ben happens to be a friend of mine as well as a colleague. We've worked closely on quite a few cases over the last five years. He does his best for his patients and when there's nothing else he can do, he steers them my way. We had a discussion about you right after he performed the surgery on your eyes. He knew what your reaction would be."

"I remember him approaching me on the subject of rehab, but I put it in the back of my mind. Then along came Todd Winters."

"Along came Todd Winters," Diane said with a fond chuckle. "And aren't you glad he did?"

"Sometimes I am."

"What substitution can we make that you think will work for you, Augusta? Have you thought about teaching?"

"No. I have an income from the insurance company of the man responsible for blinding me. I haven't thought about anything past learning to be independent. God, how I hate this." A sob escaped her control.

"I know you do. You have a right to your anger. Something precious and wonderful has been taken away from you. And you feel as if nothing is left." Augusta felt a warm hand close over hers.

"Augusta, there is a world out there waiting for you if you want it. Once you have accepted what your life can be like, you'll really be able to get on with living it."

"It sounds good in theory, but..."

"Just give yourself time, Augusta. You've managed to survive admirably so far. When I finally faced the fact that I would never paint again, I tried to commit suicide."

"You!"

"Don't sound so surprised. You can't tell me you've never considered it."

"I'd be lying if I said the thought hadn't crossed my mind, especially after my final visit to a specialist who told me he couldn't do anything for me, crushing my last hope of regaining my sight."

"What source of strength prevented you from going over the edge?"

"When you live some of your life in the ghetto, as I did, you learn two things. You have to develop the will to survive by taking life as it comes. Or you drop out of life, by turning to drugs, gangs, and a life of crime, eventually dying physically, spiritually, or both. I decided a long time ago to be a survivor and, by becoming a doctor, to help others do the same. After I'd made it through medical school, I worked hard to help children and teenagers see other alternatives to a life of drugs, gangs, and crime."

"Don't you want to get back to doing that?"

"Yes, but how?"

"That's where Todd, Joan, John, and I come in. Of course there will be times when you'll feel depressed, frustrated, and angry. But we know how to help you deal with that."

Augusta heard the rustle of papers.

"I'm checking my calendar to schedule your next session. We've developed a system to help me do it myself. Anything we can do ourselves, we do. You'll learn that once you get started with your classes. I know all of this seems overwhelming to you, but you'll get used to it. Just remember that help is always available if you need it."

"I'll remember."

"Is Friday next at, say, ten o'clock, all right with you?"

"That'll be fine."

They heard a knock at the door. It was Todd.

"How did it go?" Derek asked as they stepped into the elevator.

"I'd rather not talk about it."

"That bad, huh?"

"No, not really, I just need time to absorb it."

"I see Diane has worked another one of her miracles."

"What do you mean?"

"Once she's started to make you hunger for that something extra, it's just a matter of time before you find yourself caught up in a rush for life you thought you would never experience again."

"Is that how she made you feel, Todd?"

"She has that effect on everybody. Now you see why the Institute feels so lucky to have her."

Augusta was beginning to feel that she could really do this. Todd was right. It was hard not to get caught up in Diane's enthusiasm. Could she, Augusta, possibly find a special place for herself? Derek led her to his car, realizing that for the last ten minutes she'd grown quiet.

"Is anything wrong, Augusta?"

"No. I've been thinking."

"So when is your next session with our resident miracle worker?"

"Friday. You don't have to take me; I can get Elaine."

"What time is your next session scheduled?"

"Todd, I…ten o'clock."

"I'll pick you up at nine-thirty. No argument."

"No argument? You are one impossibly pushy man."

"Not pushy, just determined and very concerned about a certain lady. Relax and enjoy the attention, woman."

Augusta laughed. "You do have a way of putting things, Mr. Winters."

"And don't you forget it."

"I won't," she said softly.

CHAPTER VI

Augusta had several more sessions with Diane before being given the green light to begin classes. Today was her first day at the Institute as a student, and she *would* have to suffer from a severe case of nerves.

She had Elaine lay out several outfits. Augusta pictured how she looked in each one. None of them seemed to be quite right. Why was she getting so stressed out about how she looked? The other students were blind, just as she was.

But Todd isn't blind, a familiar voice inside her mind pointed out.

"How about the mint-green, linen pantsuit, Augusta?" Elaine sighed wearily.

"I'm sorry, Elaine. What did you say? I don't know what's wrong with me this morning."

"I do. You want to look good for Todd Winters."

"It's that obvious, huh?"

"I'm afraid so. But why you're worrying I don't know. The man is going to like you in any one of these outfits. But you wish he would do more than just like you in them."

"You're probably wondering why he should."

"No, I'm not, Augusta. Don't think I haven't picked up on the frustration you feel when he insists on including me in everything so that the two of you are never alone. If you think he's interested in me, put it out of your mind."

"How can you be so sure that he isn't?"

"Believe me, a girl knows whether that special something is there. It isn't, between Todd and me. Now, you'd better make up your mind which outfit you want to wear. Todd will be here any minute."

Elaine's words made her feel better. Why, she didn't know, because it didn't mean he was interested in her, Augusta Humphrey, as anything but a person in need.

Derek arrived, and they were soon on their way to the Institute.

"You're looking good, Augusta. That color of green complements your skin. Knowing you look good will help you breeze right through that all-important first day. You'll do fine, you'll see."

"I hope so."

Derek squeezed her hand reassuringly. "I know so."

Augusta found herself counting the steps as they entered the Institute. From the front door to the elevator she counted fifty steps. Her guide, a young woman named Dani Clare, who'd lost her sight in an accident similar to Augusta's, was waiting by the elevator to take her to Joan Gordon's class.

"I'll be waiting for you to come to my classroom," Derek said.

"Yeah, said the spider to the fly. Step into my parlor."

Derek laughed. Augusta thought it the most pleasing sound she'd ever heard.

"I've been called a slave driver and a few other names, but never a spider. I have to be getting to my class. Until later, Augusta."

Augusta swallowed past the lump in her throat and started counting the number of steps, as her guide had suggested. There were one hundred seventy-five from the elevator to Joan Gordon's room. With her guide offering encouragement, maybe the day would turn out all right.

Augusta found Joan Gordon to be everything Diane and Todd had told her she'd be. She didn't waste any time either. Before she knew it, Augusta found herself learning the practical aspects of a blind person running a house. By the time she'd left, she felt as though she could climb Mount Everest with no problem.

But two hours later, Augusta felt ready to chuck the whole idea of learning Braille. She had assumed it would be easy. She couldn't have been more wrong about that or Todd. She found Todd Winters, the instructor, a merciless taskmaster.

"The Braille system is based on a rectangular pattern of six raised dots," Derek patiently explained. "Using one to six dots, there are sixty-three possible combinations that can be formed with this pattern. Today we're going to start with the first ten out of the twenty-six used to translate the letters of the alphabet."

When he came over to her table to help her. Augusta found it next to impossible to focus on his words. His nearness was more of a distraction than a comforting salve for her fraying composure.

"You're not concentrating, Augusta." Derek guided her fingers across the flash card again and again.

He wasn't yelling at her, but he might as well have been. Tears pricked the back of her eyelids and she blinked furiously. She had several degrees, yet she couldn't learn to distinguish one set of dots from another. Humiliation burned like acid inside her.

She had learned to use the phone from Todd, and how to judge the perimeters of a new place from Joan Gordon. Surely learning Braille couldn't be that hard. Augusta sat up straighter and tried harder to recognize the patterns.

It became a matter of pride with her. She refused to be defeated. But at times over the next few days, the name Todd Winters was like waving a red flag in front of a bull. How she relished the idea of skewering him to the wall with her horns. At such times, she yearned with a passion to see his face.

And at other times, when she felt like giving up he wouldn't let her.

Damn him!

"Augusta, on the surface you want to learn, but deep down you may be experiencing a form of denial. Now wait a minute before you go off. Your subconscious is clinging to the hope that you'll see again, so it resists the rehabilitation. All your life you've used sight to learn things. You ask yourself, how is it possible to learn now when you can no longer see to read?

"Since the accident, at times you've vacillated between accepting help or sticking your head in the sand—in a way, running away from the problem. Am I right?"

Augusta nodded.

"It's no different with this. Augusta, you're not a weak woman. I sense an inner strength you haven't begun to tap. There will be times, very trying times, during your course of training when you may experience extreme anxiety. This, too, will pass."

Augusta smiled. "That day you came to my house I thought you were a pushy salesman. Was I too far from wrong?"

"All your flattery'll get you is a cup of coffee, Doc."

One day after a particularly grueling session in mobility training with Todd, Augusta had to stop to calm her temper.

"You're not ready to quit on me, are you, Doc?" Had he pushed her too hard too soon? He couldn't help wondering.

"Not on your ruthless life."

He relaxed and she heard the smile in his voice. "It's like that, hmm? You'd like to get you hands around a specific part of my anatomy and squeeze; namely, my throat."

"How did you ever guess?"

"You aren't the first to wish you could reserve that privilege all for yourself. There'll come a time when you're to the point that you can study my face with your fingers. Until you've passed this belligerent stage, there's no way I'm going to let you anywhere near my throat."

"I can hardly wait for that day." Her belligerent thoughts of a few seconds ago faded, changing into an acute awareness.

"I just bet you can't. You're doing fine, Augusta. I don't want you to think otherwise."

"But..." Now the thought of touching his face or any other part of him made her feel weak in the knees. She'd only felt this kind of reaction once before about a man. During her first year of surgical residency, she'd met Larry Giggins, who was also doing a residency in heart surgery. The relationship didn't last, because Larry couldn't get past his professional jealousy toward her.

But with Todd, that hunger was stronger, more enveloping, soul-devouring in its intensity.

"You don't have to say it. I know what you're thinking."

Augusta swallowed hard. "You do?"

"Augusta, it takes time to adjust to everything that's happened to you. The Statue of Liberty wasn't put together in a day. It took weeks, months even."

He didn't know, he hadn't guessed, thank God. She breathed a sigh of relief.

"Once your mind is relaxed and resigned to learning what it has to, to get in sync with your body, it'll come easy for you."

Augusta felt the heat of his dedication to her and all the blind people he would teach in the future. She felt his strength, heard it in his voice. She could imagine the feel of his strong arms protecting her, surrounding her with himself. If only some of that heated compassion found another outlet. *If only,* the two most frustrating, overused words in the universe.

Derek watched Augusta's face and let his eyes rove the lovely contours of her body with a yearning to caress her so strong, it threatened to drown him in sensation. It wasn't doing him any good to dwell on these intimate thoughts about her.

How could he tell her the real reasons behind his dedication? What excuse could he give for what he had done that terrible day? He found it hard enough living with the guilt. But to gain Augusta's love, then lose it…? Hell would be too mild a word to describe the soul-torturing experience.

Augusta sensed the shift in his mood, as though a chill had suddenly permeated the air.

"All I know about you is that you work here. How long have you done this, Todd?"

"A while. I think you've spent enough time here for today, Doc."

He'd done it again, closed the subject without giving her the answers to questions she wanted to know so badly. One day she'd get him to open up.

Derek spotted Augusta in the cafeteria eating lunch.

"How's the food today, Augusta?"

She felt the warmth of his hand on her shoulder and her heart began to race. "Todd!"

"Mind if I join you?"

"No, please do."

"Are you sure? The last time I saw you, you wanted to mutilate a certain part of my body."

"That was yesterday, and yesterday is gone."

"You mean you've mellowed toward me since then?" Derek took the seat across from her. "Should I believe her? Tell me, what brought this about?"

"When I tried to form a mental picture of a tyrant like my fourth grade school teacher with your voice, I burst out laughing and saw how ridiculous my attitude toward you was."

"This fourth grade teacher of yours must have been a real troll."

"And from what Elaine says, you're as far from that as the sun is from Pluto."

"I'll have to thank her for the compliment the next time I see her."

"Are you angling for an invitation?"

Derek took her hand in his. "Are you close to issuing me one?"

Augusta felt her heart perform like a Mexican jumping bean. "Maybe."

"Whenever you do, I accept."

She cleared her throat and eased her hand out of his.

Derek got to his feet. "That shepherd's pie you're eating looks good. I think I'll have the same."

The sound of Todd's voice and his male scent did strange things to her nervous system. She began to wonder whether she could accomplish anything around him, even something as simple as eating. Surely he must hear her heart pounding when he came close to her. And surely when his hand took hers, he felt it tremble like a novice tightrope walker teetering on the high wire.

Derek glanced back at the table where Augusta sat, glad she couldn't see him right now. There was no way he could hide his state of arousal. Luckily for him most of the people in the room were also blind. And those who weren't, weren't paying any attention to him.

How had he let himself become so emotionally involved with Augusta? It wasn't as if he needed a reminder about the true nature of their relationship. There could never be anything between them, ever, given his part in ruining her life. Yet in no way could he let himself off the hook by turning her over to another instructor. He owed her, and he intended to pay.

You were right, Dad, about payback being a real bitch.

Derek paid for his lunch and returned to their table.

After a few minutes, Augusta asked, "Good, huh?"

"Yes, very good."

There was a lengthy silence. Augusta wondered what had happened to Todd between the time he had gone to get his lunch and when he got back to eat it. She could almost touch the frost in his manner, and he had spoken only a few words.

"Is anything wrong, Todd?" she asked.

"No, nothing. I've got to be getting back. I have a meeting with John in a little while."

Augusta was sure it was more than that. For some reason, he wanted to get away from her.

Derek knew he hadn't convinced her with his lame excuse. He'd only succeeded in hurting her feelings. How was he going to handle this situation without causing her more hurt? *Or himself?*

After Todd had gone, Augusta sat thinking about the last few minutes of their conversation. Was Todd really trying to keep himself aloof for the reasons she thought? Students were always forming crushes on their instructors. Did he see her as one of those and didn't want to encourage her to think there could be any more to the relationship than that of student and instructor?

Augusta felt mortification rush through her. She was taking courses at the Institute to learn Braille, to give meaning to her life again, not to fall all over her instructor like some lovesick groupie. From now on she would concentrate her efforts on why she came there: to learn.

As the days went by, Augusta was polite, and she would immediately leave the room when class was over, never lingering to talk to Derek. He knew he should have felt relieved, but he didn't. He found himself craving the closeness they had begun to share before reality had painted him a true picture of how any relationship with her would turn out.

He remembered something Ben Hastings had said about Augusta being a private person and withdrawing into herself when hurt. Derek knew he had taken her from her safe cocoon by encouraging her to make that all-important metamorphosis vital to her well-being. He couldn't abandon her now. He had to maintain the friendly balance she needed to emerge a completely confident, independent person.

No matter what it might cost him personally, he owed Augusta every chance for as normal a life as it was in his power to help her obtain. He'd be her friend if it killed him. Considering his growing attraction to her, it could very well come to that.

CHAPTER VII

Since that day in the cafeteria, Augusta had formed the habit of packing a lunch and eating it on the Institute's garden-court terrace. She might not be able to avoid Todd in one of his classes, but she would otherwise, even though it might play havoc with her heart.

She might have become more adept at recognizing the different Braille patterns in her eagerness to master it, but Augusta found herself out of her depth personally where Todd Winters was concerned.

"Here you are."

"Todd!"

He settled himself on the bench next to her "We need to talk, Augusta."

"About what? I've improved my Braille."

"You learning Braille has nothing to do with us."

"Us? There is no us. We've barely been on speaking terms for quite some time."

Derek sighed. "I know, and it's my fault. Listen, Augusta, I don't want to be at odds with you. Can't we be friends?"

Augusta felt a stab of disappointment. His friendship was something precious to her. If that was all he could give her, she'd have to accept it. After all, friendships could evolve into something more, couldn't they? If she were patient, maybe…

"Yes, we can." She smiled.

Derek was relieved to see that his shifting moods wouldn't deprive him of her company. Damn it, why couldn't he control his feelings around her? His life would certainly be less complicated.

Three days had come and gone since Derek and Augusta had agreed to be friends. Seated in the study hall practicing the new Braille symbols she'd learned, Augusta thought about what the word *friend* meant. To her, it meant confiding in each other and caring about one another's welfare. Todd obviously believed in the latter, because he was very caring—but not the former, for he never confided anything personal to her.

She still knew precious little about Todd Winters, apart from his work at the Institute. She knew that he was a passionate and private man. He was so open and honest about everything else, it seemed almost as if he had something personal to hide. She had to stop thinking like this. She was beginning to get paranoid.

Though Todd seemed more relaxed since they had agreed to be friends, he still managed to keep her at a distance. It made her all the more determined to find a way to make him open up to her.

"Mind if I join you?"

"Diane." Augusta smiled. "How did you find me?"

"Todd said you were probably eating in here today, so I asked the cashier to tell me where you were seated. I counted the tables until I made it to yours."

"Please, sit down."

"Is everything going all right?"

"Yeah."

"You don't sound like you quite believe that. If you're having problems, Augusta, feel free to talk to me about them. I'll help you in any way I can."

"I'm afraid no one can help me with this."

"It's personal, I take it."

"Yeah, it is."

"Does Todd Winters figure into this?"

"How did you guess?"

"That first day in my office, I sensed a certain tension between you two."

"You're amazing, Diane."

"Not so amazing, just perceptive. It comes with the territory. I won't ask you how you feel about Todd; I can guess. Maybe if the two of you sat down and—"

"He doesn't feel the same way about me. I know he finds me attractive and he may even desire me, but he sees me as a responsibility, not a woman he wants to get involved with. I think he's afraid of hurting me."

"Are you sure that's it?"

"Pretty sure."

"Then there's not much I can tell you. Just hang in there and wait to see how things develop. Todd might surprise you."

"I doubt it, but thanks, Diane."

"Listen, I'm available any time you need me. We girls have to stick together."

"You've became proficient enough with your studies to go on to the next step in your rehabilitation program," John Fuller told Augusta in their meeting in Todd's classroom. "You're very special to us here."

Tears came to her eyes. "Thank you. You have no idea how happy this makes me."

"I think we do, don't we, Todd?"

"Yes." Derek studied Augusta's lovely face. To hear her describe herself as being happy meant everything to him. At last he'd made progress in paying back the debt he owed. But it wasn't over yet. The hardest part for Augusta was yet to come: the transition from student to teacher, utilizing her medical training. Knowing she would be helping others benefit from her knowledge would go a long way toward filling the empty spaces in her heart.

"I'm going to have to leave now, Augusta." John put his hands on her shoulders and gave her a friendly squeeze. "Again, congratulations."

"Thanks, John."

As soon as he had left the room, Derek cleared his throat "I think this calls for a celebration, Doc."

"Celebration?"

"You and Elaine can come to the Embers with me."

She and Elaine? Augusta was disappointed, more than disappointed really. She wanted to celebrate with him, *only* with him. Why did Todd think he needed a chaperone? Unless...She was curious to know why being alone with her was so difficult for him?

"If you're too tired, we can do it another time, Augusta."

"No, I'm not too tired. We'll have to check and see if Elaine is free to join us."

"You're right."

Derek breathed easier when Elaine agreed to go with them. As he looked at Augusta across the table in the restaurant, he decided that she was altogether too fetching in her aqua silk pantsuit, with its loose, sleeveless top draped enticingly across her full breasts. Her elegant upswept hairstyle with its wispy side curls framed her lovely oval face to perfection. And those dewy-soft, ripe lips and dark, fathomless brown eyes…

If not for Elaine's lust-restraining presence, he didn't see how he would be able to keep his hands off Augusta's warm, glowing brown skin.

He had never thought he'd feel anything close to this attraction when he first approached Ben Hastings about paying her a visit. He intended just to help her adjust to her handicap, and then get out of her life. Augusta wasn't supposed to make him step over the line past human caring and concern into…what?

He couldn't seem to stop himself from becoming more personally involved, no matter what he did or how hard he tried to fight the attraction.

"For someone who wanted to celebrate, you're very quiet, Todd," Augusta teased.

"Can you blame a man for silently admiring two of the loveliest ladies in town, whom he just happens to be sharing the evening with?"

"I love to hear you talk," Elaine bantered back.

Augusta smiled. "As I've said before, you're a balm to a girl's vanity."

An uncomfortable silence stole the moment. A waiter came to the table with a bottle of champagne. As Augusta sipped hers, she wondered if Todd admired Elaine as more than a simple dinner companion. *What if he did?*

She didn't know what Elaine looked like. Her voice and personality were warm and friendly. Could Elaine be wrong? Was Todd interested in her? That could be the reason he included her in things they did together.

"Now who's being unusually quiet?" Derek asked.

"It's the champagne. Maybe we should order now."

Derek was beginning to think the idea of a celebration was a mistake. The genial evening he had planned was turning into a tense episode. Controlling himself wasn't going to be as easy as he had hoped. But had anything in his life been easy since Augusta had entered it?

Her sessions in mobility training helped Augusta to feel more relaxed with her blindness, more confident in her ability to get around. She was certain that before long she wouldn't need Elaine. The scary part of her rehab would soon begin: the retraining that would start her on a different career.

Teaching at the medical school wasn't something she'd have ever considered if she...She'd never thought to have anything else to do with medicine during her recovery period in the hospital.

"If you're concerned about how you'll do as a teacher, don't be. I've seen you work with the children at the Institute. You have the patience of a saint. What do you say we stop for something to eat on the way to your house?"

"Todd, I...never mind. We can eat at my house. Elaine is making a pot of her famous Louisiana Creole gumbo tonight. You're in for a real treat."

For once the thought of sharing Augusta with anyone else didn't appeal to Derek. He was losing his struggle to stay just friends, and he knew it. He felt like a mountain climber who had lost his footing and was grabbing for a tree, hanging on for dear life, hoping against hope it would bear his weight.

What was he going to do now? He had many more weeks of close proximity to her. What had he gotten himself into? Why did he have to feel this way about her? Why couldn't their relationship have remained strictly professional?

Elaine excused herself soon after dinner. The tension between Derek and Augusta was stretched tighter than a rubber band strained to the limit. He knew he should go, but a voice inside his head kept urging him to stay.

Augusta sensed the struggle going on inside him. And the conflicting vibes were playing havoc with her mind. What did Todd really want to do? Was it…could it possibly be…

"Todd—"

"Augusta—"

Each blurted the other's name.

Derek reached for her hand. "I…"

"Yes," Augusta whispered, her heart pounding a mile a minute.

Derek pulled her into his arms. He groaned at the pleasure he derived from the warmth of her luscious body as it made contact with his. Her feminine scent excited him beyond bearing. His lips descended, drinking their fill. No wine was ever so potent, no kiss ever so sweet. His breathing grew labored as he deepened the kiss.

Augusta shivered with need. All of her fantasies were coining true. The taste of him on her tongue was the food of love. Yes, love. She had to confess to herself that that was exactly what she was feeling for this man.

His wandering fingers found her breasts and slid across her nipples. She threw her head back, reveling in the pleasure the intimacy of his touch evoked in her. He wasn't close enough; she wanted to absorb him into herself. She wanted him to make love to her.

Derek suddenly pulled his mouth away. The reality of what he'd almost let happen sobered him. A little more and they would have ended up in bed.

"Todd?" she whispered, her voice breathy, ragged with passion.

Derek adjusted her blouse. "I didn't mean for this to happen."

His words hit her like a glass of ice water thrown in her face. "What did you expect would happen when you started kissing me like that?"

"Look, I think I'd better go."

"Todd, what is it? Is it me? Is it my blindness that turns you off? You go so far and no further. It's all right to teach me, but not to make love to me?"

"No, it's not that. Augusta, I respect you, and I don't want to hurt you."

Augusta felt her insides wither and die.

Her stricken body shuddered within his arms. He despised himself for hurting her. He had never intended to do that. What was happening to him? Things never should have reached this point. He'd lost it for a moment and given in to the desire that racked his body night and day. He couldn't let himself slip again.

"Listen, Augusta. I didn't mean that the way it sounded."

"Oh, I think you did. You were right. It's time you left."

"I don't want to leave you like this."

"Don't worry about me, all right? I'll be ready to go to the Institute when you get here in the morning. Good night, Todd." She started for the door.

He stood there for a moment before following her. There was so much he wanted to say. Yet what could he say to her that would make a difference?

You could try telling her the truth.

Yeah, right. Oh, by the way, Augusta, I'm the one who blinded you.

She can't handle that right now.

You're the one who can't handle it. Coward.

Damn right! That was exactly what he was. He didn't want to see the derision on her face or hear the contempt in her voice.

"I'll be here at the usual time in the morning. Good night, Augusta."

That night as Augusta undressed for bed, her mind replayed what had happened between them. Could they be just friends now? The thought of his hands roaming feverishly over her body made her shiver with longing for a completion of what he had started. Was his reaction just a typical male reaction? Or was it more? What kind of mood would he be in in the morning? He could be so prickly at times, and then at others he could be so tender. Would she ever understand or know how to take him?

Derek paced back and forth, occasionally looking out his living room window at the quiet and empty street below, as quiet and empty as his life would be without Augusta a part of it. Tonight he'd lost it and almost made love to her. It was all he could do not to give in to the temptation to possess her.

What he felt for Augusta went beyond mere friendship. He'd seen how the passion in her came to life. To know she desired him that much was driving him out of his mind. How in God's name had he resisted her this long? He knew if the circumstances repeated themselves, he wouldn't be able to stop next time. What was he going to do? What? He was caught in a trap of his own making. How was he ever going to escape? The trouble was, he didn't really want to.

He headed for the shower. The tightness in his groin hadn't eased. It would have to be a cold shower, although he was sure it wouldn't help; he wanted Augusta, and he wanted her badly. A shower of ice couldn't quell the fire.

He had to face Augusta in the morning. What opinion would she have formed about him? The thought of seeing disgust written on her face chilled him to the bone and drained his ardor. At last the tightening in his loins eased.

It might have been eighty-five degrees outside, but inside Derek's car the next morning the temperature was ten below zero. He looked at the woman seated next to him and longed to smooth the frown from her face, to ease the quiet anger brewing inside her. He'd botched up last evening, big time, letting himself get carried away by desire. Augusta probably hated his guts. And he couldn't blame her. To her it no doubt seemed that he was leading her on, teasing her.

"Are you all right, Augusta?" he asked at last.

"I'm fine," she answered coolly.

"Amen to that."

"Todd, I..."

"Look, I'm sorry about last night."

She said in irritation, "You don't need to apologize again."

"I want you to understand where I was coming from."

"I understood, all right. I'm just another body."

"No, you're not just another body, Augusta. You mean more to me than that. I didn't want to take advantage of you."

"A kiss is not exactly taking advantage of me."

"Don't you see what it could have led to? You're an attractive woman!"

"An attractive *blind* woman."

"As I said last night, your being blind has nothing to do with it. You're damned sexy and desirable, blind or not."

"If that's the way you feel, then why...?"

Derek was silent.

"You don't have to answer." Her voice turned frigid. "I see."

"I doubt it," he said, stopping the car and killing the engine. They had arrived at the Institute.

How was he going to get through classes with Augusta now, he wondered, what with the added complication of sexual frustration chipping away at their relationship.

"If you want another instructor, feel free to change. I'll understand."

Augusta thought about it. She didn't think she could accomplish as much with a different instructor. Todd knew how to pull the best from her. Her adjustment to her condition had a lot to do with how Todd handled her. Did she want to start over with someone else at this stage?

"I don't want anyone else."

Derek breathed a sigh of relief. He didn't know what would happen between them if he continued to be around her every day, but God help him, he didn't think he could get through the days without seeing her. He was in a catch-22 situation, growing more fraught with tension by the day.

What in God's name was he to do? He was only human. And around Augusta, oh, how very human he was!

There had to be a middle ground; he'd better find it, and fast. Derek watched Augusta make her way down the hall to Joan Gordon's room. The sound of her cane tapping the floor caused fresh, renewed pain to well up inside him. There would be no need for her to ever go through this, if not for him. He'd been a reckless, thoughtless fool eighteen months ago, and Augusta had paid the price for it. If necessary, he would protect her against himself, he vowed.

Augusta found herself wanting to stay in Joan Gordon's class, but she knew she had to go to Room 312 sometime. If it killed her, she would learn to be around Todd and function in his class, in spite of what had happened between them. She was determined that from now on their relationship would be strictly professional and nothing more.

In the days that followed, Augusta found it an easier thing to say than to actually do.

Things came to a head just as she was about to leave Todd's classroom.

Derek caught hold of Augusta's elbow and turned her around to face him. "We can't go on like this. The 'cold war' has got to stop. The other students are picking up on the tension between you and me. Like you, they're keenly aware of what goes on around them."

"What do you suggest we do about it? Maybe I should transfer to another class or another institute altogether."

"I don't think that's a good idea. The other students look up to you as a role model. If you suddenly stop coming, well...you get the picture."

"Yes, I do."

"It could undermine their confidence in the program, and I don't want to be responsible for causing that."

"Neither do I. So what do we do?"

"We could try to go back to being just friends."

"Can we really do that? Not that we're exactly enemies."

"Augusta!"

"All right. Friends." She held out her hand.

Derek took it. "Friends." He had hopes this would work, but the feel of her hand in his almost caused him to blow their newly forged friendship.

CHAPTER VIII

Derek waited in Dr. Ben Hastings' reception room for him to get back from a consultation at another hospital. After a while, he got up from his chair and wandered over to the window, his hands thrust deep inside his pants pockets. For the second time, he and Augusta had agreed to be just friends. He wondered if he was being realistic to hope they could go back to the way things were.

From the beginning, their relationship had been more than just professional, making friendship a tenuous proposition. Augusta had jokingly said they weren't exactly enemies. It was ironic because if she knew the truth, they'd be just that. He'd never forget the look on her terrified face seconds before the accident. He shuddered now thinking about it. He still had nightmares about it.

And when she'd said she wanted to see his face, unaware that she had already done so, pain like he'd never known had ripped through his guts. His face was probably the last thing she'd seen before losing her sight. It would not be one she'd relish seeing ever again.

He'd gone beyond the boundary of friendship when he'd kissed her lips and caressed her soft, sexy body. Being friends with Augusta was going to be hell.

"Derek?"

"Ben."

"Have you been waiting long?"

"No. Listen, I need to talk to you about something."

Ben studied his friend for a moment. A frown of concern creased his forehead. "Come on into my office."

Derek followed him inside and shut the door behind them.

Ben loosened his tie. "Have a seat. How is Augusta doing at the Institute? I've been out of town a lot lately and haven't had a chance to talk with her about it."

"She's coming along," he said evasively, then his tone brightened. "At first, she had difficulty grasping Braille and the special instruction the blind need to deal with their daily lives. But she's gotten past those obstacles."

"Then the reason for your visit isn't a professional one?"

Derek sighed and then, looking away, said, "No."

"It concerns Augusta, though, right?"

"Indirectly."

"Want a cup of coffee? Something tells me we're both going to need it."

Derek laughed. "What I need is something stronger, but I guess I'll have to settle for coffee."

Ben walked over to a supply cabinet, brought out two Styrofoam cups, and then left the room, returning with a pot of coffee.

"How do you take yours?"

"Black."

Ben filled both cups then handed one to Derek. He dropped a cube of sugar into his. "All right, out with it."

Derek sipped his coffee. "I think I'm in love with Augusta."

"Think?" Ben smiled knowingly.

"All right, I know I'm in love with her. And I don't know what in the hell I'm going to do about it." Derek explained to Ben what had happened between him and Augusta so far.

"You do have a problem. It must be hell indeed trying to be just her friend."

"You'd better believe it. What do I do, Ben?"

"You could tell her how you feel about her. Better still, you could tell her the truth."

"I was afraid you were going to say that."

"Not much help, am I?"

"That day I came to you, I never envisioned that anything remotely like this could happen. I wanted to help her, and that's all. Period. But when I saw her sitting on her couch the first time, the woman took instant possession of my heart. I never had anything hit me so hard."

"You have my sympathy, man. Love isn't something any of us have any control over. When it ensnares us, we're helplessly caught in its embrace."

"But what do I do?"

"Other than what I've said before? I haven't got a clue. I'm sorry."

Derek sighed. "I guess I'd better be going." He put down his cup and rose to his feet.

"I still think you should tell Augusta the truth. She's a remarkable woman."

"I know she is, but it doesn't ensure that she'll forgive me."

"You're right, it doesn't. How is this, ah, 'friendship' of yours coming along?"

"I don't know. Sometimes I think it's working, and at other times… "

"Maybe you should let her really get to know you."

"You mean be a…"

"Real friend, a confidant? Why not? That's the way people really get to know each other, isn't it?"

"I'm not sure it's wise in this case."

"It could be the only way the two of you will be able to stand being in each other's company. Go to very public places and never allow yourself to be alone."

"I've tried that more than once."

"And did it work?"

"At first, but no matter where we are, just looking at her turns me on."

"Then I don't know what else I can tell you."

"You're her friend, I thought maybe...Never mind, I'll have to work this one out on my own."

"Good luck, Derek. You're going to need it, buddy."

Thanks to Joan Gordon's practicality adjustment class, Augusta was beginning to learn how to fix simple meals, although she still needed Elaine to help her do the shopping. Joan had taught her how to mark her frozen dinners. She reminded her to smell the meats for signs of early spoilage and to check fruits and vegetables for ripeness.

Joan explained that in identifying herbs and spices, all she had to do was remember the word for things and how they related to the scent of them—say, cinnamon and its spicy aroma, or the pungent smell of seasonings such as bay leaves or thyme.

One day in the not-too-distant future, she intended to fix Todd a home-cooked meal. When she could see, she'd never been much of a cook. Generally speaking, she had been on the run and had eaten out a lot. She still had an awful lot to learn, but learn it she would. She was determined to change the boundaries of their friendship.

Augusta cursed, rubbing her forehead when it made contact with the open door of one of her kitchen cabinets. Learning to cook in her kitchen was proving to be an obstacle course, fraught with pain and dangers. It had been days since she'd started to become more familiar with her kitchen.

A blind person had to remember many things when entering or leaving a kitchen. The first rule of thumb was to find one's way around. Augusta learned that if she forgot any of the rules, she ran the risk of being cold-cocked by an open cabinet door, done in by a dust pan, battered by a broom, or struck in the stomach by silverware drawers that had been left open.

It would take time, a determination to succeed, and a lot of pride to overcome the obstacles and master the culinary skills needed to produce adequate meals. Augusta wanted to offer Todd more than just an acceptable meal. She wanted to be proud of what she cooked for him.

She heard Elaine enter the room.

"How's it going?"

"Good, if you don't count a concussion, scorched fingers, and injured arms, legs, and other bruised parts of my anatomy."

Elaine laughed. "That bad, huh?"

"And that's the good part. I never thought it would be a picnic, but..."

"Hang in there, you'll do it."

"I certainly hope so. Did you pick up the things I asked you to get?"

"Yes. Are you sure you're ready for this?"

"As ready as I'll ever be."

Augusta knew it was ambitious to try stuffed green peppers, but try it she did. After finishing, she sat down and waited to find out what Elaine thought.

"Well?"

"It's...I mean, ah..."

"Did you like it?"

Elaine cleared her throat. "It, ah, is different."

"Different how?"

"I was afraid you'd ask me that."

"Do you think Todd would like it?"

"Oh, yes."

Augusta tasted one and nearly choked. Tears came to her eyes. "It's a little spicy, isn't it?"

"In a word, yes."

"Then it's back to the drawing board for me." Augusta laughed and soon had Elaine joining her.

After that disaster, Augusta experimented daily for the next week.

A few days later Todd called.

"Augusta, it's Todd. I'd like to spend Saturday afternoon with you."

"Alone?"

"Yes, just the two of us. We need to talk about some things."

"What time will you come for me?"

"Is eleven too early?"

"No, it's perfect. How should I dress?"

"Jeans will be fine."

"I'll see you then."

"Goodbye."

Augusta could hardly believe what she'd just heard. Todd had actually invited her to spend the day with him, and he hadn't included Elaine. What did he want to talk about? Was he ready to really be friends, tell her about himself, confide in her? She could only hope.

Would she finally get to know the real Todd Winters? Could this friendship lead to—no, she wouldn't let herself hope for something more this soon. She'd be patient, take it slow, and see how things went. A true test of his friendship would come when he tried her cooking.

Augusta went to her closet. She'd replaced all of her metal hangers with wooden ones. She had marked in Braille what each item of clothing was and its color. Thanks to a swatch book Joan used in the classroom, Augusta had learned how to recognize materials by feel. Some like silks or denim were easy, but others that blended different textures and materials were harder.

Often, the smell of them when they were new gave her a hint.

She was also learning to mark her garments by sewing French knots into the labels, using the Braille system. The feeling of becoming more independent with each new thing she learned lifted her confidence level.

Augusta put on jeans and a simple cotton, short-sleeved white shirt. Where was he taking her? she wondered. Just as she finished tying her Nikes, the doorbell rang.

Todd was here!

In her eagerness to get to the door, she bumped her shins on obstacles no longer supposed to be obstacles since she had become familiar with her house. She had to laugh because she had quite a few battle bruises and bumps acquired in the process of learning every nook and corner of her home.

"Are you ready to go?"

Augusta smiled. "And just where are we going, Todd?"

"I'll let you figure it out once we get there."

"Sounds suspicious to me."

"Come on out of there, woman." Todd took her hand and led her out the door.

After they had driven for a while, Augusta grew restless with anticipation.

"Aren't you going to even give me a hint?"

"You're like a child eager to know what's in the packages underneath the Christmas tree. No, I'm not going to give you a hint, so stop trying to wheedle the information out of me."

"You're a mean man, Todd Winters."

"So I've been told. We'll be there soon, Augusta." When she heard the amusement in his voice, she wanted to strangle him.

Augusta smelled river water. Was it the Schuylkill or the Delaware? He really had her curious. The scent of flowers filled the air. It must be the Schuylkill River. But where on the river? Fairmount Park? Was that where he was taking her? It had a lot of flowers and greenery, but so did Bartram's Home and Garden. Where was he taking her?

Derek parked the car and then walked around and opened the door for her.

"Todd."

"All right, Augusta," he said in mock irritation. "Have you guessed where we are?"

"We're near a river."

"Yes. Which one?"

"I'd say the Schuylkill. Bartram's Home and Garden."

"The smell of flowers gave it away. I was afraid of that. Let's walk, Miss Marple." He took her arm and wrapped it around his own. "When I was a kid I used to come here. My buddies and I would slip through the fence onto the grass and pick the flowers."

"As I recall they have 'keep off the grass' and 'don't pick the flowers' signs all over the place."

"They did then too, but it didn't stop us. We made bets on who could pick what flower and get away with it."

"It sounds like you were a regular little demon."

"Oh, I was that all right." Derek grimaced. If he'd only learned how to curb that tendency a lot sooner.

They toured the garden and then headed down to the river. Augusta hadn't been here since she was a little girl growing up in South Philly. They crossed the bridge and walked along the beach.

The sound of children busy at play surrounded them. Augusta visualized them tossing frisbees and running in and out of the water after them. As they continued up the beach, the voices grew faint and eventually faded, to be replaced by the caw of gulls as they wheeled overhead.

Derek brought Augusta to a crop of huge rocks and seated her on one.

"You said yesterday that you wanted to talk, Todd."

"And I do," he said, sitting down next to her. "I know you've been curious about me and what I do outside of the Institute. It's a subject I don't really like to talk about."

"If it's hard for you, Todd, you don't have to talk about it now."

"I want to, Augusta. Before I became an instructor for the blind, I lived a self-indulgent existence. My parents were well-to-do and spoiled me rotten, I guess because I was their only child. You see, I was a late-in-life child. They'd given up on ever having any children.

"My father headed a large company, one he'd started from nothing. And of course, as his only son, he wanted me to follow in his footsteps."

"You weren't high on the idea, I take it?"

"When I was growing up, it seemed far in the future and I was interested in the here and now, and having fun like most kids. I'd never had to work at anything. I breezed right through school. Even college presented no problems at all. After I graduated, I went to work in the family business to please my father."

"What kind of business is it?"

"Electronics. We specialize in electronic watch parts. Anyway, I saw it as just another job. Then about three years ago, my father died of a heart attack. A few months later my mother was gone too. They were so close. Without my father, she was lost. I knew it was only a matter of time before she joined him."

"You must have been devastated. I know I was when my mother died from a heart ailment when I was eight years old. That day I made up my mind to be a heart surgeon."

"It couldn't have been easy. What about your father?"

"He and my mother were only married a few months when he was drafted into the army. I was two years old when he was killed in Vietnam. My mother never got over it, and never remarried. After she died, I was placed in an orphanage."

"Didn't you have any relatives who were willing to keep you?"

"I have an aunt, but she had six kids of her own and couldn't take me. My father didn't have any people, as far as I know."

"What was it like?"

"It was hell sometimes, but not always. There were a few foster homes that weren't so bad."

"But no one wanted to adopt you?"

"No."

"You must have been very lonely without a family."

"I can see you find it hard to fathom growing up without one."

"I have to admit I do."

"How did you come to be an instructor at the Institute, Todd?"

Derek hesitated. He had the perfect opening to tell her the truth. "Something happened to change my whole outlook on life. After my parents' deaths, I went a little crazy.

"I didn't need to work, so I hired a manager to oversee the business and lived life in the fast lane—gambling, drinking, chasing women, and racing cars—the whole bit. It took a tragedy to open my eyes. I realized what an empty life I was leading and decided it was time to change. You see, I met and fell in love with someone..."

"Who was blind? And you became an instructor at the Institute so you could help her."

To hear Augusta talk about him as though he were some kind of hero, humbled Derek. He answered, "Yes, and I..."

"Lost her."

Derek hoped not. *Tell her the truth, man.* He could hear Ben Hastings' words. "Augusta is a remarkable woman, she'll understand." But would she forgive him? He couldn't risk it. Not now. Not yet.

"After losing your parents and then the woman you loved, it must have been hard. Was she blinded in an accident?"

"Yes." Derek couldn't completely keep the anguish out of his voice.

"Todd." Augusta's heart went out to him. His pain was still too recent, too raw. No wonder he didn't want to talk about it. She could almost feel his misery.

"Did I bring back the pain? If I did, I'm sorry. That first time I met you I was so awful to you."

"I understood, Augusta. Helping you was like..."

"Helping her. I've always sensed that there was a more deep-seated reason why someone like you would dedicate his life to helping the blind."

"Someone like me! What do you mean?"

"There is something different, I don't know, something special about you, Todd Winters. And I'm proud to be your friend. Now can I see your face? I can assure you that I'm over my belligerent stage and won't strangle you." She laughed.

"Yeah, tell me anything."

"Come on, Todd, I am, really." She raised her hands to his face and started exploring his forehead with her fingertips. It was wide and intelligent, his skin warm and smooth.

"What color are your eyes?"

"An ordinary brown."

"I'll bet there is nothing ordinary about you, Todd Winters." She began to concentrate. He had a mixture of strong, classic Afro-American features of full lips and a broad, slightly flattened nose with a touch of Native American ancestry in his high, chiseled cheekbones. His chin was determined, his neck muscular, all in all a strong face. And for some reason it seemed strangely familiar. Had she actually *seen* him somewhere before?

"Do you like what you see?"

She smiled. "Yes, I do."

"Are you done?"

"For the present."

"Are you hungry? If you are, there's a place not far from here called Mama's on the River."

"I know of it. In fact, I used to eat there almost all the time when I was a starving intern at Pennsylvania Memorial. As I remember, they serve the best crab leg stew this side of the Mississippi, in the world probably."

"It's one of my favorite dishes."

"You don't seem like a crab leg man to me."

Derek laughed wickedly. "But I'm definitely a leg man, Augusta."

She smiled. "On second thought, I'll just bet you are."

"Well, do you want to eat at Mama's?"

Augusta stood up and brushed away the sand from the seat of her jeans. "Yes, I'm starved." She held out her hand, he took it, and they were on their way. In rare times like these that she shared with Todd, she wished with all her heart she had her sight back.

"I really enjoyed today, Todd."

"We'll have to do it again. I'll see you Monday morning, Augusta."

She heard him turn to leave.

"Todd."

He stopped "Yes."

"'Would you like to come in for coffee? I can now make a decent pot all by myself."

"Joan has you doing that now? All right, I'll be your guinea pig."

"Well, I like that. I'm going to make you eat...no, drink those words."

"We'll see."

Derek followed her into the kitchen and watched while she measured the coffee and put it in the pot. When it was ready he noticed how she determined the amount to pour by feeling the level of heat rise as the coffee filled the cup. Joan had taught her well. He could see what a receptive pupil Augusta had been. He couldn't help wondering if she would be as receptive to his lovemaking.

"Do you take your coffee black, or would you like some cream or sugar with it?"

"Black will be fine. You're becoming a pro at this. I'm proud of you."

"Thank you, kind sir."

"Kind? That wasn't what you said about me a few weeks ago. I distinctly remember you calling me ruthless, among other things."

"That was yesterday."

"And yesterday is gone, I know." He laughed. "And I'm damned glad it is too."

"You are?"

Derek took her hand in his. “Yes, very,” he murmured softly in her ear.

Augusta sighed just before a yawn escaped her lips.

Derek caressed her hand. “I think it’s time you went to bed before you fall asleep on me.”

“It was all that fresh air and good food.”

“‘We’ll have to do it again sometime.”

“You said that already.”

“I know.”

Augusta walked him to the front door.

“Good night, Todd. I’ll see you Monday morning.”

After he’d gone, Augusta leaned back against the door. He had almost kissed her. Considering what she had learned about him, it was unrealistic to hope for more, right now. Competing with a dead woman wouldn’t be easy, but if she were patient she could make him choose her. She could never take the other woman’s place, but she could at least carve a place of her own in his heart.

CHAPTER IX

In the time that elapsed after Todd had taken her on the outing by the river, Augusta felt good about the direction their relationship seemed to be headed. Todd's manner was more open now since they'd both shared a part of themselves with the other. She felt that it had helped them to really come to know one another better.

"You've gone as far as you can with us at the Institute, Augusta," Derek said during the ride to her house after leaving the Institute. "It shouldn't be too long before you get your teaching credentials."

"You aren't thinking of abandoning me now, are you, Todd?"

"I'd never do that. As long as you need me, I'll be there to help you, in any way I can." He cleared his throat. "I mentioned to John that you once enjoyed working with children and teenagers. He wanted to know if you would consider helping us two days a week with the junior blind once you know what your schedule will be."

"I suppose it was Ben who told you about my work with EC." She went on, not waiting for him to answer.

"I don't know, Todd. I'll have to think about it." She had to admit that she missed working with the kids at EC. But things were different now, she couldn't see how to…Her thoughts trailed off. The kids would be blind like herself. Could she handle their special kind of problems? Was she strong enough to stand hearing the anguish in their young voices at having a condition thrust upon them that they could do nothing to change?

She could understand why Todd and John thought she'd be the perfect person for the job because of what had happened to her. But she *wasn't* so sure that was true.

"There will always be someone there to offer you support if something happens that you feel you can't handle, Augusta."

Todd had correctly hit on her own self-doubts. "You into mind reading now, Mr. Winters?"

"No, but I know where you're coming from. When I first started, I felt some of the same anxieties you're experiencing. I had John, Joan, and Diane to help me through it, the same as you will. And you know I'll help too."

"I'll think about it and get back to you."

"You really would be perfect, Augusta. I've seen you with your next-door neighbor's daughter. You have a rare, natural rapport with kids."

"Haven't I always said you reminded me of a pushy salesman?"

He laughed. "And quite a few other people, too, as I recall."

She loved hearing Todd's laughter.

"By the way, this is Elaine's last week with me. Now that I've completed my classes and don't need a full-time companion, she's decided to move back to Louisiana with her parents and finish her degree at Tulane."

"Have you lined up anyone to come in and clean and do the heavy-work?"

"Yes, that's all been taken care of. What I need is someone to help me in the mornings once I start teaching, if I'm accepted at the medical school."

"You will be. Those people aren't stupid. They know when they have a good thing. They're damned lucky you want to do it."

"There's nothing like having your own one-man cheering section."

Derek pulled into her driveway. "I meant what I said about helping you, Augusta. I won't be working mornings at the Institute. My classes for the junior blind will be switched to afternoons starting in September. We have a new instructor that John will be working with. So for the next eight months they'll be taking over my early morning mobility class."

Augusta realized that Todd was willing not only to relinquish part of his time to help her, but also share his work with the junior blind with her. What a loving, giving person he was.

"Now, no more arguments. You'll be needing someone to photocopy your lectures, help grade papers, exams and other things like that. Who better than *moi.* Give me a call when you're ready."

"I can always hire an assistant."

"I know, but why? I'll be all the assistant you need, Doc. We're a team, remember?"

"I won't forget, Mr. Winters."

To Derek her voice sounded husky and passionate. Then he gazed into her face and beheld a raw, hot desire simmering there. If he didn't get out of there fast, he'd break his resolve to remain just friends. And once he'd done that, there would be no turning back.

He got out of the car and helped Augusta carry her books and papers into the house.

She put a restraining hand on his arm when she heard him move to leave.

"Todd, I'm going to miss riding with you to the Institute every morning."

"So will I. Don't worry, you'll get tired of my presence once I become your assistant."

She could never get tired of his presence. "We won't have to think about that for a while, since I haven't gotten my credentials yet. In the meantime, do you promise not to make yourself a stranger?"

"I promise. I've really got to be going."

After parking his car, Derek didn't go up to his apartment right away. He remained inside the car, mentally sweating. He knew Augusta had wanted him to stay. And God, how he had wanted to! It had taken every ounce of will power he possessed, and then some, to leave her.

He was only too human. Resisting Augusta was like tearing out a piece of his heart.

Yet you've done it for weeks now.

Now that I've volunteered to be her assistant it will continue for many more weeks to come.

There won't be an Elaine to play chaperone the next time around.

You think I don't know that?

Well then, are you crazy, or do you have a masochistic streak, Morgan?

I love her. I promised myself I'd protect her.

Even from yourself? How much longer do you think you can keep that promise?

Derek couldn't answer that question.

As Derek passed by the door to the Institute library the following morning, he saw Augusta busily at work researching, probably a subject for the classes she hoped to teach in the fall.

His heart constricted in agony, knowing she had to settle for teaching rather than doing what she loved: operating. All because of him. There was nothing wrong with being a teacher, but when he thought about the specialized surgical training and God-given talent Augusta possessed and couldn't use...

If only he hadn't been driving so fast. If only the tree limb hanging across the stop sign hadn't obstructed his view. If only that little girl hadn't wheeled her bike into the street. If only, if only, if only. He had to stop this. It did no good to dwell on the past and let it become a ghost haunting him in the present.

"Are you coming in, or are you just going to stand there blocking the doorway?" Augusta asked.

"I didn't expect to see you here. Elaine drop you off?"

"Yes, she did."

"You knew I was standing there all along and didn't let on. You're good, Doc."

"That's the kind of flattery I like to hear. Pull up a chair."

"Sorry, I can't. I have a meeting with Diane in a few minutes."

"Before you go, I want to invite you to dinner at my house." Before he could answer, she said, "And I won't accept any excuses, Mr. Winters."

"I wasn't going to offer any. When do you want me?"

Right here, right now, forever, Todd darling. "How about Thursday?"

"Crab leg stew?"

"What else?"

"I'll definitely be there."

Augusta cut fresh flowers from her yard and set candles on the table. She knew in her heart of hearts this was going to be a special night for her and Todd.

She'd never considered herself a seductress, but a woman in love could be anything she wanted to when it came to getting her man. She took a long, leisurely bath in her favorite bath salts. Augusta chose to wear a cream silk, thin-strapped evening dress that molded her full breasts and hugged her slender hips, making her feel as though she were being cherished in the passionate hold of a lover. If her plans to seduce Todd worked, later that night her bare body would know the full benefits of a far more intimate embrace.

She worried about her hair since she couldn't see how it looked. Finally she decided on a single French braid, and fashioned her shoulder-length hair into one. She added a splash of Chanel No. 5 behind her ears and on her wrists for extra confidence. What was she thinking? Confidence wasn't what she needed to induce Todd to make her his. A little luck wouldn't hurt.

Derek prowled the confines of his living room, pacing back and forth like a panther in a cage. He'd showered and dressed more than an hour ago. It was almost six o'clock, but he couldn't make himself walk out that door. His insides were in turmoil. He'd been putting this night off for as long as he yearned for it to come about.

God, he wanted to make love to Augusta until neither of them could move. He'd fantasized how her husky voice would sound as she uttered sweet little moans of pleasure when he made her body burst into flames of ecstasy.

The tightening in his groin was almost unbearable. Just the brush of his pants against that volatile area was making him crazy.

He'd finally found the one woman in the world for him, yet his fear that she would never forgive him once she knew the truth stood like an invisible barrier between him and happiness.

Tell her, Morgan.

I want to, but...

You're afraid she'll despise you.

I know she will, and I can't blame her. If our situations were reversed, would I be able to forgive so easily?

You can't put off telling her forever. Eventually the truth will come out.

Maybe it won't, maybe…

And maybe you're fooling yourself, Morgan.

Derek stopped pacing and straightened his shoulders. He would tell Augusta the truth tonight.

Just as he was about to walk out the door; the phone rang.

"Hello."

"Derek?"

He tensed when he heard the voice of his plant manager, Ronald Williams. "Yeah, what's up? I was about to go out."

"I'm afraid we have a problem. We need you to come down here as soon as you can."

Derek sighed. "I'll be right there."

He would have to call Augusta and cancel their dinner plans. Derek knew he should count himself fortunate that he'd escaped the temptation she presented and he did, but at the same time he felt profoundly disappointed that he wouldn't be seeing her.

Derek picked up the receiver and punched in Augusta's number.

"Augusta, I'm afraid you'll have to give me a rain check on tonight's dinner."

"Why? What's wrong? Are you all right?"

"I'm fine; it's my company. There's a problem and I have to take care of it personally. I hate to cancel out on you at the last minute."

"Don't worry about it. We can do it another time. You do what you have to do. Good night."

"Good night."

Augusta felt the frustration deep in her soul. She had wanted to be with Todd so much she could almost taste it. She got out of her clothes, put on a caftan, went back into the kitchen, and turned off the stew.

Am I wrong to want him so very badly?

He does seem to be resisting your overtures.

He said my blindness isn't the reason.

But can you really believe he's telling you the truth? Of course I can. He hasn't lied to me so far.

So far as you know.

I have to know one way or the other.

She cleaned the kitchen and reached for the light switch. Then she remembered she had already turned the light off after Todd called. God, would she ever get used to the darkness? No matter how many times she turned on a light switch, she was not going to see.

Feeling a little sorry for yourself, Augusta?

No, I'm not. I refuse to give in to that weakness. I'll adjust.

But what to do about Todd?

Derek finally tracked down the breach in security around midnight. It seemed that a nest of mice had eaten into some of the wiring of the security system, setting off the alarm. He'd literally been saved by the bell. But the problem could have been handled without his help. Sometimes he wondered about his plant manager.

Stop fooling yourself, you jumped at a chance for a temporary reprieve. That's all it is, you know.

Derek showered and went to bed, but he didn't fall asleep right away. He fantasized about Augusta and how she would look wearing next to nothing. Or better still, in nothing at all.

You've got to stop thinking about her like this.

You have any suggestions?

You're avoiding the inevitable and you know it. She won't give up on you. Why fight it? Let it happen.

You know why I can't do that.

Then tell her the truth and get it over with.

During the next days after Todd cancelled out on dinner, Augusta set about learning anatomy by touch, not sight. When she touched certain parts of the cold rubber and plastic man, she wished that it was Todd's warm, hard, male body she was caressing and bringing to rapture.

Whoa, girlfriend.

Damn it, she wanted to see Todd, hear his voice, or the familiar rhythm of his footsteps on the walk. She picked up the phone and called him.

"I'm glad I caught you before you left for the Institute."

"Something wrong, Augusta?"

"No, nothing like that."

Derek felt his insides tighten in anticipation.

"I just happen to be having crab leg stew on the menu for dinner, and I was wondering if you could make it tonight."

Augusta. He groaned inwardly. Derek knew he should say no. So far, by sheer force of will, he'd managed to keep himself in check, especially after the last time when they had almost…

Didn't she know what she was doing to him?

Augusta waited for him to think of an excuse to get out of it.

"Do you want me to bring anything'?" he said finally.

She smiled triumphantly at the resigned sound in his voice. "No, just yourself. I'll expect you at six o'clock."

I know what I'm doing, Todd. If I have anything to do with it, our friendship will blossom into a loving, honest-to-God relationship.

After he'd hung up, Derek scolded himself. Why hadn't he told Augusta he couldn't make it?

You didn't want to, that's why.

Nothing can happen between us.

You want to bet?

Why can't life be simple?

Augusta heard Todd's car pull into the drive and then his footsteps on the walk. Did his steps sound hesitant, as though he wanted to stop, turn around, and go back to his car? No, her imagination was working overtime. She waited for him to depress the doorbell.

"Todd?"

"Yes, it's me, Augusta."

She rubbed her hands together to dry her palms and opened the door.

"You look—you look beautiful, Augusta." And sexy and…

She smiled. "Thank you. Please, come on in."

"What's that wonderful smell?"

"You know very well what it is. I sure hope you're hungry, because I have enough crab leg stew to feed a small army. Would you like to listen to some music?"

"Yes."

"Go ahead and choose something while I see about dinner."

Derek searched through her CDs and came across Anita Baker's "Rapture." He knew he was cruising for a bruising, but put the CD in the player anyway. The first song, "Sweet Love," began to play. Anita Baker put her heart into the lyrics, singing for all lovers who longed to embrace and protect.

Listening to the words that so accurately described his emotional state, Derek moaned in sweet agony.

"Are you all right, Todd?"

He hadn't heard her coining. "I'm fine."

"Just now you sounded as though you were in pain. Does the music remind you of…"

"No, it's just that when the words…" He cleared his throat. "You need any help with anything in the kitchen?"

"I have everything under control. Would you like a glass of wine?"

"Will you have one with me?"

"Yes."

He watched her walk into the kitchen to get the wine. The sweet, even, throaty tones of the singer penetrated his concentration, weakening his resolve. His mind conjured up an image of Augusta lying naked on a bed holding out her arms to him, beckoning him into them. But when Anita Baker got to the part about trust…

Did he dare trust that Augusta would forgive him? This was hell on his libido, but it was sheer torture on his vulnerable heart.

She returned with a chilled bottle of wine on a tray with two glasses and set it down on the coffee table.

"Let me fill these, Augusta," Todd volunteered, his voice husky.

Augusta smiled knowingly.

With none-to-steady hands, Derek poured two glasses of wine and handed one to her.

They sipped at their glasses, listening appreciatively to the next song, each thinking that the description of the joy of love perfectly suited what could be.

Derek placed his glass on the table. "Dance with me, Augusta?"

She nodded and put down her glass. Derek stood. Pulling her to her feet and taking her into his arms, he held her close as they swayed to the beat of the music.

They embraced in the dance, fitting perfectly, moving wonderfully together. Augusta felt herself tingling at every place their bodies touched, helpless to censor the wild and intimate scenes flashing through her mind, dream sequences programmed by the dance and by the lyrics promising a wondrous love and joy. Dizzy, she heard someone breathing raggedly and for the life of her couldn't tell whether it was she or Todd.

The music finished at that moment, giving Derek a chance to control the overpowering urge to do more than just dance with Augusta. Once that urge took over, he knew he would be lost.

She'd almost done it; she'd been so close. Augusta swallowed hard, and her voice came out shakily. "Are you ready to eat?"

"I think we'd better, don't you?"

"Ah, yeah, ah." She inched away until she felt the edge of the coffee table against the back of her leg.

"Is there anything you'd like me to do, Augusta?"

"You could light the candles."

When Derek entered the dining room, his breath caught in his throat. The ambiance reached out to embrace him, even more than the music. Moments later he realized that the candles were flickering. Had he lit them? He must have, but he couldn't remember doing so. What was happening to him?

Augusta carried the tureen of stew to the table.

"Are you ready to eat?"

As soon as she put the stew down, Derek eased her away from the table and, circling her waist with his arms, led her back into the living mom.

"Todd, I..."

He stopped, pulled her into his arms, and showered hungry kisses on her lips. She trembled when he released her mouth.

"Augusta, my Augusta, what are you doing to our friendship?"

"I invited you here to dinner, that's all," she said innocently.

"Uh-uh, your goal was to seduce me."

"And will I accomplish my mission?"

He didn't answer.

"I want more than friendship, Todd. You've become very special to me."

"You're special to me too, girlfriend."

Derek kissed her eyes and buried his fingers in her hair.

"So soft, so sweet," he murmured in her ear.

Derek dropped kisses over her throat and moved upward to taste her lips. The flavor of wine, mingled with her own unique honey, caused his insides to riot and he was suddenly intoxicated, high on passion, drowning in her passion.

Augusta felt her senses reel. Her lips parted, and Derek delved his tongue deep inside her mouth, searching for the perfect mating. Finding it, he tasted and drank seemingly endlessly, until they both quivered with need.

"Oh, Todd," she moaned. "I've wanted you to kiss me like this since that first time weeks ago. But you pushed me away, and I thought…"

He stopped the flow of her words with his kisses. "I didn't mean to hurt you, Augusta, I swear I didn't."

She said when she could catch her breath, "You told me you wanted us to be just friends."

"The hell with being friends. I've wanted to do this for so damned long."

He lowered the straps on her dress, easing the bodice down her body, baring her to the waist. "Have mercy, you're so fine," he groaned, lashing a breast with his tongue, circling the tip repeatedly until it peaked like chocolate frosting on a cake. By the time he had tasted the other, he could have sworn it *was* the flavor of chocolate.

What was he doing? The song "Caught Up in the Rapture" filled the room. That was exactly what he was. Caught up in the rapture that was Augusta. He'd fought it as long as he could, but he could fight it no more. He was lost in love.

"I know you spent a lot of time cooking my favorite dinner, but all I want to do right now is make love with you."

"I want that too," she said huskily.

"Are you sure, Augusta? I don't want to take advantage of you. I care too much about you to *ever* hurt you like that. Once I make you mine, there is no turning back. I want you to understand that before we go any further."

"I do, Todd. And, my darling, I *am* sure." She moved out of his embrace.

"Why are you leaving me?"

Holding up the bodice of her dress over her bare breasts, she said,

"There's something I want to do first."

He watched her make her way down the hall and disappear into a room. She was the sexiest woman he'd ever known. Looking at her set his body on fire. He'd been burning in hell for weeks, and tonight she would give him relief.

When he thought he couldn't wait another minute longer, the song "Mystery" began to play and Augusta entered the room. Derek nearly swallowed his tongue at the sight of her in a filmy black negligee. He had no idea she'd planned his seduction quite so well.

Augusta reached his side. "How do I look?"

"Like the fantasies dreams are made of."

"I'm no dream. I'm a real flesh-and-blood woman." She wound her arms around his neck.

Derek's breathing quickened when her skin made contact with his. "You definitely won't get an argument from me about that." He slipped his arms around her waist.

"Arguing is the last thing I want when I have something far more pleasant in mind."

Derek felt her warm breath on his cheek. When she kissed his ear, he shuddered.

"What you do to me, Augusta." His voice was rough with passion.

"What do I do to you, Todd?" She flicked her tongue in his ear, and the shuddering turned into a violent tremor.

"You know very well what." He breathed raggedly, his heart pounding wildly in his chest.

"The first thing we do is make you more comfortable."

He allowed her to unbutton his shirt. When she slid her fingers inside and caressed his nipples, he jerked in reaction.

"Don't you like it?"

"I like it too much." He removed his shirt at warp speed, carelessly tossing it to the floor. He sat down on the couch, bending to untie his shoes. Augusta went down on her knees and pushed his fingers away to unlace his shoes, slipping them off his feet, along with his socks.

Next to come off were his pants and briefs. Augusta let her imagination take over, visualizing how his body must look.

Derek opened her negligee, easing it off her shoulders, letting it drift to the floor where his clothing lay strewn.

"God, Augusta..." His breath sucked in.

She placed a finger across his lips. "Don't talk with these."

"With what then? These?" He moved his fingers across her nipples and then bent his head and kissed one, then the other.

Her breasts seemed to ache and swell. She whimpered, "Oh, Todd."

He didn't say a word, just raised his head higher, branding hot kisses along her neck until he reached her full ripe lips. He splayed his fingers over her shoulders, sliding them down her back along her spine, kneading her buttocks.

When Derek felt her shiver; he moved her body closer until her femininity cradled his hard, hot flesh.

He moved his hips in a reflexive action against the arousing motion of hers. Desire, like the exotic beating of a drum, throbbed through them both, urging them into the prelude of an ancient ritual dance.

He lifted her onto his lap and wrapped her legs around his waist, allowing his hard hot maleness to impale her wet supple femininity.

Augusta cried out.

He lay back on the couch, her legs still straddling him. She moved her body in strong, circular motions against him. As his breathing grew more labored, Derek moved upward, crying out his pleasure. "Yes, yes, oh God, yes!"

Augusta joined his litany. Her body and his tensed like coiled springs, pulling tighter and tighter, the friction driving them both insane with pleasure.

The spring let go at the moment of climax, sending them both reverberating into space in a profusion of ecstasy that inundated every part of their souls.

Lovemaking had never been like this for him, Derek thought in wonder. Being in love made all the difference.

Augusta moved her fingers over his damp face. "You were wonderful, Todd."

"And you're beautiful, baby."

"I'm not, but you make me feel that way."

"To me you *are* beautiful, and always will be."

They lay for long moments, still intimately joined, reveling in the magic of love, although neither spoke the words. There was no need.

Augusta dozed off, but Derek lay awake, thinking about later when he had to tell her the truth. He hoped that what they felt for each other would transcend everything else.

God, he loved this woman more than life. She *was* his life. He felt himself harden within her at the thought.

Augusta gasped. Without opening her eyes, she began to move against him.

Again they were climbing that wild, magical stairway only lovers climb, striving to reach that special room of rapture at the top.

CHAPTER X

Augusta woke to the strong, steady beating of her lover's heart against her ear. She lay tucked in the safety of Todd's arms. His relaxed and regular breathing indicated that he was sleeping soundly.

She breathed in his masculine scent, becoming immediately aroused. Augusta moved her fingers down his flat stomach to the apex of his thighs and the thick forest of hair surrounding his manhood. His velvety length began to firm at her touch, and a groan escaped his lips.

"Play with fire, woman, and you will get burned."

She continued to caress him. "Is this the match?"

He rolled her under him, parted her thighs, and stroked the pulsing, striking pad of her desire with himself. Sparks ignited, bursting into flames that soon raged out of control and utterly consumed them both.

"Baby, you can wake me up like this any time," Derek said much later.

"You like it then?" She moved her hips against his.

"You're an insatiable woman, do you know that, Doc?"

"Only for you, Todd. You know, we never got around to eating that crab leg stew."

"You mean you're hungry for something other than yours truly?"

She playfully punched him in the ribs. "Get up, and let's go do justice to that stew."

"She hurts me first, then offers to feed me. What's a man to do with a woman like this?" He fondled her breast.

"Oh no you don't, mister. I'm starved."

"So am I."

He kissed her, and she kissed him back. The thought of food was temporarily suspended again.

Later they dressed, went out on the front porch, and sat in the swing. With Derek's arm around her, Augusta rested her head on his shoulder. "You're awfully quiet, Mr. Winters. No regrets?"

"Not a one, pretty woman." But a pang of guilt at his continued deception did painfully prick him.

"You sure?"

He tilted her chin and kissed her thoroughly. "Is that convincing enough?"

"I like your method of proving your case." Even though he spoke the right words, Augusta felt that he was holding back something. What was bothering Todd? she wondered.

He sensed that he hadn't completely convinced her. "If I'm quiet, it's because your stew filled me to the gills."

"Humans don't have gills."

"Very funny. You know what I mean. I won't be able to eat for at least two days."

"I'm glad you enjoyed it. We'll have to do it again sometime."

"Which part? The eating or the loving?"

"Now who's insatiable?"

"I wasn't suggesting..."

"Oh, yes, you were, and you know it."

"I really should be going."

"You don't have to be at the Institute until one."

He looked at his watch. "It's twelve-fifteen now. I need to go home and change."

"Will you be coming over tonight?"

"Do you want me to?"

"If I had my way, you wouldn't be leaving me now."

His voice turned husky. "Really?"

She kissed him "Really."

After Todd had gone, Augusta stayed out on the porch thinking about her life. Was she being fair to Todd, saddling him with a blind woman? They hadn't talked about commitment, but knowing him as she did, it wouldn't be far off.

She loved him so much. She'd never thought to find love, considering everything that had happened. Deep down she'd nurtured a fantasy of having it all: a career, the man she loved, and a child. She had lost the career she'd prepared for, but found another way to be a part of medicine, if only by helping others to become skilled, caring surgeons.

Did she dare hope for the other part of her fantasy? Todd cared about her, desired her, but he'd never mentioned marriage. Would he offer commitment out of love, or a misplaced sense of pity or obligation? She had to know which before they went any further.

A knock on his classroom door brought Derek out of his reverie.

Ben Hastings walked in. "Where were you just now?"

"Lost in a daydream. What are you doing here? Sit down. Can I get you some coffee?"

"No, thanks. How's it going, man?" He relaxed in the proffered chair and waited for an answer.

"With Augusta?" He arched a brow. "In what way?"

"Any way you want to talk about."

Derek sighed. "We're closer than—let me put it this way. We are as close as two people can be."

"How did she take the..."He paused, checking out his friend's expression. "You haven't told her, have you?"

"I know what you're going to say, but I just couldn't. I love her so much, Ben. I don't want to lose her."

"You're not sure you will. Knowing Augusta, she wouldn't have become involved with you if she didn't care deeply."

"What you're saying is true, but…"

"Trust in her feelings for you."

"Being a surgeon was her life, Ben. I've taken the most important part of it from her. Can any woman, even one as special as Augusta, forgive that?"

"There's only one way to find out."

Derek rose from his seat behind his desk and walked over to the window, digging his hands deep into his pockets. "I know you're right. I'll see her tonight and tell her."

As Ben watched Derek, his respect for the man went up another notch. He certainly didn't envy him what was to come. He'd told him that he felt sure Augusta would forgive him. But was it wishful thinking on his part?

"I'm in your corner. If there is anything I can do…"

"There isn't, except wish me luck."

"It goes without saying."

"I've heard from the board at the medical school, Todd," Augusta spouted excitedly the moment she opened her front door to Derek.

"You'll be gainfully employed in September, I take it?"

She hugged him tight and then, arm in arm, they walked into the living room. He smiled at the delighted satisfaction animating her lovely features.

"I didn't think I'd be this deliriously happy, but I am."

He sat down on the couch and pulled her onto his lap. She laid her head on his shoulder. "Have you thought about your other offer?"

"Other offer? You mean working with the junior blind? Todd, I don't know if I'm qualified."

"There is no one more qualified than you, Augusta. You have something most teachers wish they had with their students."

"You really think I'm right for the job?"

"Absolutely."

"You have the confidence of a politician."

"Not that again." He kissed her neck.

"It must be true what they say."

"What they say?" He stopped kissing her.

"About politicians being better lovers."

"Why you—I'll get you for that."

"You promise?"

"It's a promise I definitely intend to keep."

Augusta snuggled closer.

"I need to talk to you about something."

"Having to do with the junior blind?"

"No, it's along a more personal vein. Have you thought about getting a seeing eye dog?"

"You think I need one?"

"It would be more than just company for you, Augusta. Since you live alone, the dog would double as a bodyguard."

"I hadn't thought about that."

"I have. I don't like the idea of you being here alone."

"You could always move in with me."

"Don't tempt me, woman. Seriously, you need time to adjust to your new life. I'll be over here as much as if I lived here, but for now I think we should wait and see where our relationship is headed before we get into something that may not be right for us."

Augusta felt a jolt in the region of her heart. What did he mean? How deeply did Todd's feelings for her run? He had confided some personal things to her, but not the things she wanted and needed to know about him. Could she be rushing their relationship? Or was he backing off?

Derek could almost see the wheels turning in her mind.

Tell her, Morgan.

Augusta kissed Derek, catching him off guard. Whatever he was about to say flew out the window.

"Augusta."

"I want you, Todd. I've missed you."

"It's only been..."

"I don't care." She stroked the front of his pants. "Make love to me."

He felt himself harden beneath her inquisitive fingers.

"Oh, God, Augusta. Woman, I..."

He rose from the couch with Augusta in his arms and headed for her bedroom. He lowered her to her feet and slowly undressed her, enjoying every moment. Then he shed his own clothes.

Looking at her made his heart soar with love.

Her voice turned husky. "This will be a double celebration."

"A double celebration?"

"I have another piece of my life in place, thanks to you."

"And the other?"

"My celebration as a woman. Before you came into my life, I hadn't thought of myself that way in a long time. So you see, I have two reasons to celebrate."

"Augusta, I have to tell you..."

She put a finger across his lips. "No more words, Todd." Augusta kissed him, then led him over to the bed.

Derek decided to tell her some other day. Being with her like this was addictive, and right now he needed a fix.

You'll always need a fix. Tell her the truth, now.

Derek closed his mind to that persistent voice of reason.

On Saturday morning, Augusta could feel the warmth of the sun shining through her window on her skin. She smiled, thinking about last night. She'd had a heat of another kind warming her body.

Todd was everything a woman could want in a lover. He could be as gently sweet as he could be savagely exciting when he made love to her. She'd tried to talk him into—or, she should say, tenderly persuade him to stay the night. She knew he wanted to, because she'd heard the struggle in his voice, but in the end he had dressed and gone home.

It was almost as though he were afraid to stay, but that was crazy.

Your brain is working in overdrive again, Augusta.

She sensed a kind of—she didn't know, she couldn't pin it down—but there was something.

Don't borrow trouble.

She needed to talk to someone about her doubts, his feelings for her as well as hers for him, and her other fears and insecurities as well. She'd call her friend Myra Hastings. Both Myra and Ben had been her very best friends for years—more like family, really.

But there were some things a woman could only discuss with another woman. Myra was warm, loving, and a good listener. Augusta had almost forgotten that in the nearly two years since her accident.

Augusta shook her head to clear it. She'd have to push this to the back of her mind for now and get showered and dressed before Todd arrived. He was going to take her to the Seeing Eye Dog Center today. This was another sign that he cared deeply for her. She'd give their relationship space, more time to grow.

Maybe he needed the time as much as she did. He also had to adjust his life. Just because he worked with the blind didn't mean he didn't need time to adjust too. She wondered if he'd gotten used to loving the other woman before she was taken from him. Was he afraid to commit so soon because of what happened with her?

"How do you like her?"

Augusta eased her fingers across the soft, furry head of Bella, a seven-year-old, female German shepherd. "She seems to like me."

"Who could help it?"

"Thank you, although I think you're a little biased."

"You'll have to go through a training program with her."

"I always seem to be in training for something."

Augusta's innocent remark made Derek recoil internally. "It only takes four to six weeks; then you two will be inseparable."

"Like you and me."

He squeezed her hand. "Yeah, like us."

Augusta and Bella sailed through the trial period, and before long they were working together like parts of a well-oiled machine. Bella seemed to sense what Augusta needed before she knew herself. Though never before fond of animals, Augusta soon developed a loving relationship with Bella. She hadn't known the closeness of a family for a long time. She hoped that one day she and Todd, and possibly a baby, might share that kind of togetherness.

She had to stop projecting things into the future. Todd hadn't asked her to share his life. Should she let nature take its course? Or should she help it along?

"Myra, it's Augusta."

"Augusta? Long time no see…I mean…"

Augusta laughed. "It's all right, Myra, I know what you mean."

"I know I should have called you," they both said at the same time.

"I guess we're both equally guilty," Augusta admitted.

"I think you're right," Myra agreed. "So let's do something to fix it, girlfriend. When do you want to get together for a rap session?"

"For the wife of a prominent doctor, you are down to earth, Myra Hastings."

"I can't help but be down to earth. I haven't forgotten where I came from. I wasn't raised in the prim and proper suburbs of Newark, New Jersey."

Augusta *had* almost forgotten that. "How about having lunch together on Thursday? Next week I'll be knee deep in preparation for my classes at the medical school."

"That's right. Ben told me you'd be teaching. I have to admit that it surprised me."

"Me too. I would never have considered it if not for Todd Winters. In fact he's the one I need to talk about."

"Ah, woman's age-old dilemma: how to deal with her man."

"And you would know about that? Come on, Myra, you and Ben have one of the most stable, loving marriages I know"

"You would think so, wouldn't you? But there are times when..."

"Out with it, Myra. Is there something wrong between you and Ben?"

"Not really, I'll talk to you about it when I see you on Thursday. We can have lunch at my house."

"You don't have to go to all that trouble. We can eat out."

"It's no trouble. You know how domesticated Ben has made me. Look, I really have to go. I have an appointment in half an hour and I don't want to be late, so I'm going to have to cut this short, I'm afraid."

"I understand. All right then, I'll see you on Thursday."

Augusta wondered about that odd conversation. Myra really had her curious now. What could possibly be wrong between her two best friends? Surely it wasn't as serious as Myra had made it sound. Whatever it was, she intended to find out and help if she could.

Every time she and Bella got on the bus, it was an adventure. Today was no exception. Ben and Myra lived across town. To get there, she and Bella had to change buses. Most people were very considerate when they realized she was blind.

The bus driver told her precisely how to get to the address she gave him. When they got off the bus, she and Bella had only to walk down Maple to the intersection, cross at the light, and walk halfway down the block. According to the driver, the house should be the third one on the left.

Before Augusta reached the house, Myra came out to meet her, offering apologies.

"I should have come to your house and picked you up. I just wasn't thinking straight."

"Don't get so upset about it. Bella and I needed an adventure. We've only been on the bus twice since we became a dynamic duo. We needed the practice." Augusta remained silent as the three of them made their way up the driveway of the Hastings' house. As they reached the porch, Augusta began to speak. "You're always Ms. Calm, Cool, and Collected, Myra. But today I sense a barely contained tension in you, girlfriend. It's not like you to overreact like this. What's wrong?"

Myra opened the front door and waited for Augusta and Bella to follow her inside.

"I thought you came here to discuss your problems, not mine."

"Now you're being defensive."

"I'm sorry."

Augusta frowned, mentally picturing her petite friend with her pixie face and hairstyle, large sherry-colored eyes, and caramel skin. Whatever was bothering her, she knew it had to be serious to have this strong woman in a state very near to tears.

Myra glanced at Augusta, wondering how she was going to get through lunch without breaking down.

Her visit to the doctor had been a real downer. She'd been to so many doctors in the last five years.

"I've set up lunch in the breakfast room. Your dog must be thirsty. I'll put a bowl of water down in the kitchen for her."

"Thank you, she'll appreciate it." Augusta patted Bella's head and let Myra lead her out to the kitchen where she instructed the dog to remain.

Taking Augusta's hand, Myra guided her into the breakfast room to a chair at the table.

Augusta recognized the smell of oil and vinegar dressing, tomatoes, lettuce, turkey, ham, and eggs. "Chef's salad. My favorite."

"I remembered. But how did you know that was what we were having?"

"Since losing my sight I seem to have developed a keener awareness of things, using my other senses. One of the first things we learn at the Institute is to rely on our senses, particularly the sense of smell."

Augusta and Myra were well into their meal when Augusta put down her fork.

"What has you so strung out, Myra?"

"I thought we were going to talk about your problem," she said evasively.

"It can wait. You're on edge and I want to know why, especially after that cryptic remark you made the other day about the state of your marriage."

"There's nothing wrong with my marriage."

"Myra, this is me, Augusta, you're talking to. I know I've neglected our friendship and I'm sorry, but it doesn't mean that I don't care about you and Ben. You know that. If there is any way I can help, please let me. Even if it's just to listen."

Myra thought it over before deciding that she, too, needed to confide in a friend.

"All right, but when I'm done I want to hear about your problems, okay?"

"Okay," Augusta agreed.

Augusta heard a resigned sigh and imagined the expression on her friend's face. She waited for her to begin.

"You know that Ben and I have been trying to have a baby for a long time."

"Yes."

"We've been going to a fertility clinic for the last five years. Every test there is, we've had it done. Every procedure, we've followed it faithfully. So far we haven't had any luck. The doctors say there seems to be no physical reason why we can't have a baby. But, Augusta, I'm not getting any younger. In a few more years it won't be possible."

"Have you considered adoption? The process isn't nearly as complicated as it used to be."

"I know you were an orphan and—but, Augusta, I want my own baby from the love Ben and I share. It may sound selfish and unfeeling not to want to adopt when there are so many children who need homes. If after we've exhausted every possibility and nothing happens, then I'll consider adoption. But the way I feel now, it wouldn't be fair to bring a child into our home under those circumstances."

"I never knew you were this desperate for a baby, Myra. How does Ben feel?"

"Oh, he's being philosophical about the whole thing, saying if we never have a child I'm all he'll ever want and need, but I know how much he wants a baby. I feel like such a failure." She broke down.

Augusta skirted the table to reach her friend's side and took her hands in hers.

"Myra, don't cry. It's usually no one person's fault. Sometimes it's just not the right time. There must be a doctor somewhere who can help you. Have you considered artificial insemination or *in vitro* fertilization?"

"With artificial insemination periods need to be regular, and mine are so irregular it's hard to determine when my fertile periods begin and end. Every time we've tried *in vitro* fertilization it hasn't taken. I refuse to use anybody else's sperm but Ben's.

"As I've said, I've gone through every test and procedure there is, and I still haven't had any luck in getting pregnant. You have no idea what it's like." Myra laughed. "I have to say that Ben certainly enjoyed making love at the odd times of the day he was required to do so when I was keeping a record of my temperature, when we were following the ovulation method."

Attempting to lighten the mood, Augusta added. "Yeah, I'll just bet he did, knowing Ben. I'm sure he didn't need that kind of incentive to make love to you, though. The man is crazy about you, Myra."

"I know," she said softly. "I'm just as crazy about him."

"During my residency at Pennsylvania Memorial, several friends of mine decided to go into gynecology and obstetrics. I could contact them and see if there are any new procedures they know of that might help you."

"'Would you? I'd be so grateful."

"Of course, it's going to cost you."

"What?"

"I'll expect a special dinner when this ends in a miracle baby. And of course I'll have to insist on being made the baby's godmother."

"It's a deal. Oh, Augusta, I'm so glad I decided to open up to you."

"So am I. There's no guarantee it'll work. Nothing may come of this, you know."

"I know, but I've almost given up hope. Will you come with me to the doctor?"

"Do you need to ask?"

"Now it's your turn."

"You've met Todd Winters," she began. "So what do you think of him?"

"He's gorgeous."

"Myra!"

She laughed. "Ben would probably kill me if he heard me saying that about another man."

"Elaine, the companion I had, said pretty much the same thing about his looks. But what I want to know is, what you think of him as a person?"

"He seems like a strong, responsible man. Ben has told me about his job at the Braille Institute and his work with the junior blind and his other projects along those lines."

"Todd has told me a few things about his life. I know he has a business. Do you know anything about it?"

"No. From what I've gathered, he has a manager handling things. Working with the blind seems to be…well…an obsession with him. Of course that's only my personal opinion. I could be all wrong about that."

"I trust your instincts, Myra. I get the same impression. At any rate, he won't talk about it in any depth. For some reason, I think he's not being completely candid with me."

"But whether he is or not, you're attracted to him." Noting the expression on Augusta's face, she asked,

"It's gone beyond mere attraction though, hasn't it? You two have become lovers, haven't you?"

"You always manage to get right to the heart of a situation. Yes, we are. I love him very much, Myra."

"But do you trust him with that love?"

"Not completely, but I want to. I'm trying very hard to be patient and wait until he decides to confide the more personal aspects of his life to me; like whether he loves me. It isn't easy—the waiting, I mean."

"It's never easy to trust another person with your heart. No one ever said loving someone was easy. It can be hell sometimes," she said reflectively. "Believe me, I know."

"What can I do to encourage him to open up more with me?"

"What women have been doing since the beginning of time: Wait to see what happens and continue loving your man no matter what."

"Did you and Ben ever go through anything like this?"

"Oh, yes. I made Ben think that he was doing the chasing, until I caught him." Augusta found herself unable to resist joining in her infectious laughter.

"You're crazy, Myra Hastings. I'm glad I called you, girlfriend. You make me feel better."

"That's what friends are for, to lighten the load. You've definitely lightened mine. When do you think you'll know anything?"

"I don't know. You'd better give me a couple of weeks to set something up." Augusta moved her fingers over the face of her watch. "Better collect my dog. I really have to be going. I'm expected to attend a meeting at the medical school. I've thoroughly enjoyed my lunch and the time we've had to talk."

"Me, too. We'll have to do it again real soon."

"Yes, we will. Now if I can take your advice. Patience has never been one of my strong suits."

CHAPTER XI

Her preparations for the semester kept Augusta very busy over the next two weeks, but she did manage to contact several doctors about Myra's problem, finally getting an appointment for her with Alicia Crawford, a fertility specialist.

"I'm nervous, Augusta."

"I know you are, Myra, but please try to relax. If memory serves me right, Alicia is a very warm, caring doctor."

No sooner had they sat down in the waiting room and filled out some papers than Myra's name was called.

"Augusta!"

"Don't panic, I'll be with you. You really should have had Ben come with us."

"No, I don't want to raise his hopes until I'm sure Dr. Crawford can help me."

"I can understand that, but—all right let's go in."

Augusta and Myra were ushered into a large pastel office, done in mauves, blues, and beiges. A smiling, dark-skinned woman greeted them.

"Augusta, it's been a long time."

Augusta felt a moment's anxiety because she hadn't been around Alicia since her blindness, but made herself ignore it. "Yes, it has. You're famous now."

Alicia laughed. "Hardly." She shifted her gaze to Myra. "Mrs. Hastings? You wouldn't happen to be Ben Hastings' wife, would you?"

"I'm afraid so," she said seriously, but spoiled it with a giggle.

"Knowing him as I do, I would have thought he'd be here with bells on."

"He would have if he'd known I was coming here."

"You don't want to raise his hopes when nothing may come of this, do you?"

"I see you understand. I wasn't sure I'd like you, but I do."

"I'm glad to hear it. You brought a copy of your medical file. That'll help considerably as well as saving me the trouble of sending for it. Give me a few minutes to look it over. While I'm doing that, I'll have my nurse show you to an examining room."

Augusta squeezed Myra's hand. "Go on, I want to talk to Alicia."

"All right."

Alicia switched on the intercom and instructed her nurse to come in.

After Myra had left with her, Augusta cleared her throat.

"Having a baby is more than a little important to Myra, Alicia. If after you've examined her and run all your tests, you find you can't help, please contact me."

"But..."

"As one doctor to another, of course."

"All right, Augusta. I was sorry to hear about the accident. Is there any hope you'll regain your sight?"

"Not in the immediate future. But I didn't come to discuss me; I came with Myra to lend moral support. She's the important one here."

An hour later, Augusta and Myra again seated themselves in Alicia Crawford's private office.

"Well, Doctor, what's the verdict?" Myra asked.

"I've done a thorough physical and can find no reason why you shouldn't be able to conceive. Of course, I'll need a profile on your husband. Can you get one for me?"

"I can give you the name of the doctor."

"Wonderful. I'll have to wait on the lab work to come back to give you a conclusive assessment of your case, Myra. I'll call you as soon as I know anything, all right?"

"All right."

Once inside the cab Myra pumped Augusta for information.

"You spoke to Dr. Crawford in private. Did she tell you anything more than she told me? I have to know, Augusta."

"If she did I would have told you. It's too early to predict anything yet. Be patient. Listen to me, the queen of impatience."

"Where were you this afternoon?" Derek asked Augusta after he arrived at her house that evening. "I tried to call you and got the answering machine. At first I thought you'd gone to the college, so I went over there. When I found you weren't there, I got worried."

"I'm sorry for worrying you. I was helping a friend."

"What friend is that?"

"It's..."

"If it's confidential, I won't pry." He laughed. "Male or female?"

"Todd!"

"All right. I have more important things on my mind."

"Like what?"

"You want me to give you an example?"

"I think I would like that, yes."

"You're a brazen hussy, Augusta Humphrey."

"You made me that way, Mr. Winters."

"Well, since I've created this vision of loveliness, it's only fair that I enjoy my creation." He undid the buttons on her blouse and easing his fingers inside her bra, caressed her nipple.

Augusta felt her stomach do somersaults and her heart pound erratically in her chest. All this man had to do was touch her and she went up in flames.

"Todd."

"Yes?"

"I guess you're determined to do this."

"Yes, I am, so don't give me any trouble, woman."

"I wouldn't dream of resisting when surrender is so sweet."

"Oh, Augusta, I...care about you so much."

As he finished undressing her, Augusta thought about what he almost said, but didn't. He had changed his mind for some reason. She was sure he was going to say he loved her. Why hadn't he said it? she wondered.

"I do more than care about you, Todd."

"I'm glad, Doc. We are good together, aren't we?"

"Very good," she said, helping him out of his clothes.

Minutes later they lost themselves in the rapture of their lovemaking.

Before she knew it, September arrived. In two weeks time she would begin her work with the junior blind. She didn't know which one of her teaching assignments she was looking forward to most.

Don't you, Augusta? The junior blind is close to Todd's heart, and that's where you want to stay. Admit it.

As the first order of business, she acquainted herself with both of her classrooms. The one at the college had to be carefully set up for her convenience and safety. Derek helped her with the seating arrangements, the assignments in and out baskets, and the anatomy displays. Her students were instructed not to move things such as seats, other furniture, or displays around without first consulting either Augusta or Todd. Some of the students were surprised their instructor was blind, but no one objected.

Bella inspected and sniffed each student, becoming familiar with their scent. If anyone she did not know came anywhere near her mistress, Bella greeted the strangers with a warning growl. In a matter of days Augusta was as familiar with her classroom at the college as with her own home.

Next came her classroom at the Institute.

Derek guided her through the Institute garden to the solarium where the class for the junior blind met.

As they walked, Augusta could feel the cool afternoon breeze whispering around her while she enjoyed the refreshing scent of flowers and other greenery.

"There are…"

"I've been counting the steps from the main building to the solarium, teacher."

"Well, excuse me." Derek drew out the words.

"Todd, I have to do this myself, my way, okay?"

"Okay, Doc. Proceed."

Augusta smiled, knowing he had been teasing her more than instructing her. She didn't have Bella with her today; she was on her own. While they walked, she continued to count the steps and, using her cane, she found the glass double doors to her classroom.

"Todd!"

"I'm here, Augusta."

Relieved despite the brave front she had put on for his benefit, Augusta opened the door to the classroom and walked inside. She sensed that the room was different from any of the others at the Institute.

"We try to make it less like a classroom and more like a place where the kids can just hang out. It's the aim of the Institute, by forming this chapter of the junior blind, to make learning a fun process as well as an educational one."

"That's a wonderful concept. I like it."

Augusta walked around the room, fixing in her mind the semicircular arrangement of chairs and the sliding glass door leading out to the garden.

Breathing in the smell of outdoors that filled the room, she could picture what the room would look like when the sun shone brightly through the glassed-in porch in summer and the sparkling-white beauty of fresh fallen snow in winter on the grounds just the other side of the glass. She could imagine the orange and red-gold color of the leaves in autumn and the many shades of glistening greenery and colorful profusion of flowers in the spring months.

Yes, this was a very relaxing atmosphere.

But the real test was the kids. Todd had told her how hostile, resentful, and bitter some were. He was concerned about one in particular. Augusta was eager to meet the girl.

In the conference with Todd, Diane, and John, she had learned that Tammy Gibson—seventeen, bitter, and rebellious—trusted no one. And after hearing about her background, and adding to that the girl's recent blindness, she could well understand why she acted that way. Hadn't she too felt that same way not so long ago? It had to be more devastating for someone of Tammy's age.

The girl didn't attend the class because she wanted to; a judge had decreed that she must. As a ward of the court, she had no choice but to obey his decree. John had said she had a bright mind and if channeled in the right direction she could make something of her life, if she wanted to.

Diane had mentioned that a lot of emotional debris stood in the path of Tammy's rehabilitation. But if she could be reached before it was too late, there was real hope for the girl.

The problem lay in how to reach her. So far no one had managed to do so with the exception of Todd, and he only to a limited degree. Would she, Augusta, have any better luck?

Derek watched as Augusta's slender fingers repeatedly moved across Tammy Gibson's name in her roll book, making it obvious what she was thinking about or he would have asked who. He shifted his gaze to her face and saw the play of emotions as they swelled and ebbed like waves washing over the rocks at the beach. Considering what had been said at the meeting, she was probably more than a little anxious to meet Tammy Gibson.

When he thought about Tammy Gibson, his heart went out to her. She'd suffered so much in her young life. Something about her reminded him of Augusta. Both were orphans and had lived a life totally alien to his. If they hit it off, he believed they could help each other.

"So what do you think, Augusta?"

"As soon as I know my way around this room and more about the kids I'm going to be working with, I'll be ready to start earning the trust and confidence you and John and Diane have in me."

Trust, Derek thought. Oh Augusta, how am I going to keep yours once you know what I've done? How am I going to ever tell you the truth? How are you ever going to understand and forgive me?

Augusta sensed a change in Todd. "Todd, are you all right?"

"Yeah, why?"

"You wandered away from me. You're so quiet, and I feel that you…"

"I'm fine, Doc." He went on quickly, "Do you want to stay and explore a while longer, or are you ready to go home?"

Augusta wanted to say more, but refrained from doing so. Maybe Todd was just deep in thought about his pupils. If she could, she would help this girl for Todd. He'd helped her, Augusta, and spent a lot of time with her when he really didn't have to. Yes, she'd do this for him, the man she loved.

"Whenever you are." Augusta smiled. "You are going to stay a while and 'spend some time' with me this evening, aren't you?"

At her brazenly suggestive question, Derek returned the smile. She knew he wanted to do that more than anything. "Maybe I'll consider it."

"Todd Winters, don't you play games with me."

"I thought the whole point of 'spending some time' together was to do a little playing."

"As I've said before, you're wicked."

"Admit it, woman. You love it."

I love it and I love you, Todd.

CHAPTER XII

Her first day as an instructor at the Institute, Derek walked Augusta to the solarium. They stopped just outside the door.

"Augusta, after I've introduced you to the kids, if you want me to, I can stick around until you've..."

"I don't think I'll need you to do that. If I'm to build any kind of rapport with the kids, I'll have to be the one to cement the first brick. If I need your help, you better believe I'll give a yell."

"Augusta, they can be something else when they want to be."

She kissed away his concerned warning. "So can I, don't forget."

Derek smiled. "It's not very likely that I will."

"Are you trying to say I used to be a dragon-tongued, obnoxious twit?"

"You said it, I didn't." She could tell he had covered his mouth to muffle his laughter.

She socked him on the arm. "You're going to pay for that, Todd Winters."

"I have no doubts that I will. I'm anxious to know just how you intend to exact punishment."

"You think I'm going to tell you that? Hey, I've got time and the element of surprise on my side. Believe me, I'll think of something creative."

"You ready to go in, Doc?"

She knew what he had been doing, and it had worked. "Ready as I'll ever be."

As Derek and Augusta entered the room, the loud raucous voices that had emanated from within quickly quieted, then ceased altogether.

"Kids, I'd like you to meet our new associate teacher, Miss Augusta Humphrey. I've told you about her and now here she is, in the flesh."

She didn't know what to expect, but above the vocal buzz of curious reactions, Augusta heard one voice rise in volume above the others.

"You gonna leave us with somebody we don't even know?" Augusta recognized the voice as being female and instinctively knew it belonged to Tammy Gibson.

"I'm not abandoning you, Tammy. I'll be around if I'm needed. Miss Humphrey won't be a stranger for long; she's here to help me help you?"

"Yeah, right," Tammy answered sarcastically.

Augusta felt the girl's hostility like a whiplash across the face. She wondered if she'd ever sounded like that. If she had, how had Todd put up with it and still kept coming back to visit her? She now wondered if she had what it would take to deal with this girl.

"I know you're all going to show Miss Humphrey the respect she deserves."

"You ain't leavin' already?" Tammy asked.

"For two days out of the week, I'll be turning the class over to Augusta—I mean Miss Humphrey, starting today."

Augusta swallowed hard as she gathered her composure. "We'll be all right, Todd. You can go now."

"All right, but—I'll be back in two hours."

A grimace etched a path onto Augusta's face. Two hours! It could seem like ten if she didn't carry on as she had planned.

Derek walked over to the door and then looked back at Augusta and the class. He wasn't so sure he should leave her alone with them just yet.

"I'll be ready when you get here, Todd."

The note of dismissal he heard in Augusta's voice told him that she wanted him to leave. He opened the door and walked out.

The sound of the door closing made Augusta's nerves jangle; she was all alone with the kids.

"First thing I'd like to do is get to know every one of you and relate the name to the person. Who wants to go first?"

Silence met her words. Then a boy spoke out.

"My name is E.J. Baker and I'm thirteen."

"Kelly Farmer," said another. "I'm fifteen."

Augusta judged the voice to be female, although it did have a husky timbre. There were twelve students in the class, and nine more identified themselves. Tammy Gibson's voice wasn't one of them.

Augusta instructed the kids to sit down in the seating arrangement she and Todd had worked out. All sat in their respective chairs, she assumed. Then she heard one sigh of boredom near the sliding glass door. It didn't take two guesses to know who it was.

"Tammy, I'd like you to sit over here."

"What if I don't wanna sit over there?"

So it was beginning; the challenge was on.

"If you don't want to sit there, where do you want to sit?"

"If Mr. Winters ain't gonna be here, I don't wanna be in here at all,"

"Suit yourself. Now, E.J., tell me what your initials stand for," Augusta said, completely ignoring Tammy's hostile rejoinder.

"Eric Baker, Junior," he began. "My mother didn't want people to confuse me with my daddy so she started calling me Eric Junior. When I was little I couldn't say my whole name, so she shortened it to E.J."

Augusta moved on to the next student after E.J. had finished.

"Tell me something about yourself, Kelly," Augusta encouraged.

"What can she tell you that you don't already know? She's just as blind as the rest of us," Tammy blurted.

An awkward silence enveloped the room. Then Augusta heard Tammy noisily shuffle her feet on the floor. Ignoring her as if she hadn't been so rudely interrupted, Augusta continued with her get-acquainted program.

"There are assignment sheets on your desks. I want each of you to study yours, and I'll ask you some questions if we have time. If not, then the next time we meet." Augusta rose from her seat and walked over to where Tammy stood.

"Won't you come and join us, Tammy?"

"What for?" she answered rebelliously.

"We could all get to know each other better. According to Todd, your grasp of Braille is exceptional, considering the short time you've had to learn it."

Her voice softened. "He—Todd—I mean Mr. Winters, told you that?"

Augusta realized that Tammy had a crush on Todd and that half of the reason for her antagonism toward her was simple jealousy. She'd have to be very careful how she handled things with this girl. She remembered how those intense feelings connected with loving someone could affect a girl growing into womanhood. In Tammy's case, the wrong move could be disastrous.

"Yes, he did."

"I can hardly wait until he comes back to teach us."

Augusta quirked her lips at Tammy's words. She wasn't the only one who could feel a twinge of jealousy. Augusta, too, wanted to spend every spare moment with Todd.

"That's another day; for now you're stuck with me and have to make the best of it. Since having me here is what Todd wants, we wouldn't want to disappoint him, now would we?"

Augusta assumed the girl was thinking it over when she didn't answer.

"If he left you here with us, he must think you're all right. Not that I agree with him."

Augusta touched the face on her Braille watch. "Since we have another hour to go, maybe you'd better get started on your assignment, Tammy. I'll expect you to hand it in before you leave."

A resentful sigh of defeat left Tammy's lips. Augusta had her at a distinct disadvantage because if she wanted to stay in Todd's good graces, she knew she would have to do as her new instructor said.

Augusta smiled, realizing at the same moment Tammy did that she had no choice but to do as she said. Though the girl didn't like it, she was learning what it was like to be an adult, that everything wasn't going to always go her way.

The students left the solarium, all except one. Augusta wondered why this one in particular was lagging behind.

Tammy brought her paper up to Augusta's desk. "I can't answer these questions."

"Why not? They weren't hard."

"You wouldn't understand."

"Maybe I would."

"I doubt if anyone who smells like expensive perfume and probably wears designer clothes can."

"Even if I do, what does that have to do with you completing the assignment?"

"I told you, you wouldn't understand."

"I only asked what your goals are."

"That's a joke. What kind of goals could a blind girl from the ghetto have?"

Augusta realized where this girl was coming from and knew it wasn't going to be easy to make her see that she could make a life for herself without sight. After all, it hadn't been easy for Augusta herself to come to that same realization. It took Todd's caring attitude.

"If you're gonna lay this trip on me about how my life could be so good, forget it!"

Only a few months ago she'd said almost the same thing to Todd, different words of course, but the meaning was the same. Augusta realized now why he wanted her to help him with this girl and why she was eager to do it. And it wasn't all because of Todd, either.

"Your life isn't over just because you can't see, Tammy."

"I don't need this or you preaching to me. I gotta go."

"Tammy, I..." She heard the girl unfold her cane and head for the door.

Augusta sighed. Well, there was always the next session. She didn't know how long she had sat there when she heard Todd speak.

"How'd it go?"

"Todd. I'm not sure. I thought for a while I was making progress with Tammy."

"She lay it on you pretty heavy?"

"You could say that."

"We'll talk about it later. You've had a full day. How about having dinner somewhere quiet? Say Corkie's on Roosevelt?"

"It sounds like heaven to me right now."

"You know, Tammy Gibson has a thing for you." Augusta took a sip of her coffee and waited for an answer.

"Oh, yes. She lets me know it in every conceivable way known to womankind. I want you to understand that I'm not encouraging her."

"I didn't say I thought you were. You've probably become a lifeline to the girl. She's made you her goal instead of venturing out and finding a true one of her own. Is that where I come in?"

"I knew I couldn't fool you. I didn't know what else to do about her. I thought if you two could hit it off…"

"Well, we haven't. I'm afraid I represent a threat to her. It's going to be touch and go until she can put her feelings for you into proper prospective. If she can."

"I was afraid you were going to say something like that."

"Doesn't she have—I mean, isn't she interested in anything else?"

"Singing," Derek said thoughtfully, almost to himself. "Tammy has a beautiful singing voice."

"Maybe…"

"I know what you're going to say. Diane tried to encourage her to pursue a singing career."

"Tammy said she wasn't going to have anyone pitying the poor blind girl. Her self-esteem had suffered even before she lost her sight, if what we learned from her file is any indication. If we can somehow make her believe in herself…She was raised very much the way you were in some ways, shuffled from one foster home to another.

"Her father left the home when Tammy was eight years old. You were more fortunate than Tammy; you had a loving mother, but hers died from a drug overdose when Tammy was twelve. The only thing that woman cared about was when she'd get her next hit on the cocaine pipe. She spent every spare dime on her addiction."

"Tammy's two brothers and her sister were adopted by a San Francisco couple. As you may have guessed, the adoptive family didn't want Tammy. After that rejection, she became even more rebellious and wild. The foster parents she had at the time couldn't exert any control over her, handle her behavior, or cope with her attitude."

"How did she lose her sight, Todd?"

"The sister of her foster mother had a seventeen-year-old son who was into motorcycle gangs. I guess he spotted a kindred spirit in Tammy. They soon became more than friends, and her foster parents were ready to send her back to the Mary McLeod Bethune Residential Home for Girls."

"Tammy and the boy decided to take one last joy ride on his motorcycle. They crashed through the plate-glass window of a department store. As a result, Tammy lost her sight. Once the boy knew it, he refused to come see her in the hospital or have anything more to do with her. You can imagine what it did to her. To Tammy it was just another person who had either abandoned or rejected her."

"I can see how her deep sense of hurt might block any efforts at rehabilitation. It looks as if whatever feelings she had for that boy, she's transferred to you."

"Exactly. So you can see the danger if her feelings for me deepen."

"Oh, yes, I do. A woman can be every bit as territorial as any man. I'd say maybe more so, depending on the woman."

"Are you trying to tell me something, Doc?" She heard the desire in his voice.

"Definitely. I think we should continue this discussion at home."

After making love, Augusta lay awake, her head resting on Derek's chest. His deep, even breathing said that the man she loved was asleep. Her thoughts shifted to Tammy Gibson. If the girl knew just how close she was to Todd, she'd freak out and any hope of helping her would be impossible. So what did she do next?

"Where did you go just now, Doc?" Derek asked sleepily.

"Nowhere, I'm right here with you."

"Uh-uh, you're not getting out of it that easy. Come on, give."

"I was thinking about Tammy and how to handle her."

"She's really gotten to you, hasn't she?"

"As you intended that she should. But it's not that so much as that I identify so strongly with her. She's at a rebellious stage in the growing-up process that could adversely affect her adjusting to her situation. If she doesn't have something to offset these feelings of possessiveness about you and her rage at fate and fear of rejection, there isn't much that any of us can do to help her."

"Okay, Dr. Freud, what are you going to do?"

"I don't know yet," she sighed, "but I'll come up with something."

"Knowing you as I do, it's just a matter of time."

By Augusta's third week at the Institute, she hadn't made any progress with Tammy, and it bothered her. She'd always had a way with kids, especially teenagers. Knowing what Tammy had gone through, she had thought that she would be the perfect person to break down her barriers, but instead the girl resisted every effort Augusta made to be friendly.

Augusta had thought that not having Todd walk her to class or pick her up afterward would help, but it hadn't. There had to be a way of reaching Tammy; she just hadn't discovered it yet. She wasn't giving up, though.

When class ended and the last student had left, Augusta got on the elevator. She realized that she had left her homework bag in the classroom. And just as she stepped off the elevator to go back and get it, she heard the piano. Her heart gladdened at the sound. It had to be Tammy. Augusta was glad she'd had Todd get the piano. She wondered what had made the girl come back and play.

As quietly as she could, Augusta eased the door to her classroom open and stepped inside. If she'd made a lot of noise, Tammy wouldn't have heard her. She was so into her music a bomb could have exploded and she wouldn't have been aware of it.

Augusta had been that way about surgery. When she was operating, nothing and no one else existed outside that room. She eased into the nearest chair and sat listening. Suddenly, Tammy broke into song. Augusta was held spellbound by the rich, hauntingly beautiful sound of the girl's voice as she sang "Killing Me Softly."

The song reminded Augusta of her mother; it had been one of her favorites. Tears rose to her eyes and she sniffed. Tammy suddenly stopped singing and let her senses take over.

"Miss Humphrey?"

Still overcome by the song, Augusta couldn't immediately respond.

"I know it's you." Tammy made her way to Augusta's side and then reached out her hand to touch her moist cheek. "You're crying!"

"It was because of the song and your voice." Her throat tightened with emotion. "It was—I can't describe it—it was so beautiful. No, more than beautiful. Please, finish the song."

"You really want me to?"

"Yes," she sniffed again.

"But if it makes you so sad…"

"I'm not sad. It just brings back memories that are so precious to me."

Tammy hesitated for a moment, then returned to the piano. Moments later she was totally absorbed in her playing and her singing. Augusta sat listening and enjoying Tammy's performance. The girl had real talent; her voice was a cross between Roberta Flack and Toni Braxton, yet uniquely her own.

Tammy finished and returned to Augusta's side.

"Listen, are you all right?"

Augusta stood up. "I will be in a minute."

"I've never had anyone react to my singing like this," Tammy said in an awed voice.

"You reached something in me, something I've kept buried since my mother's death."

"My mother's dead, too. But I'll bet your mama wasn't like mine."

"Everyone's mother is different, special to them in ways only they understand. Whether a mother's good or bad, she'll always be your mother and you'll always love her, no matter what."

"My mama was a crack addict, but there were times when she…"

Augusta sensed the onset of tears in Tammy and reached out to draw her into her arms. Oddly enough, she didn't pull away. But the moment of comforting ended almost as soon as it began.

"I understand what you're feeling, Tammy. I miss my mother, too."

She stiffened in Augusta's arms, then backed away. "I gotta be going."

"See you in class on Thursday."

"Yeah." Tammy gathered her backpack, unfolded her walking cane, and headed for the door.

A change took place in the classroom atmosphere after that. Augusta seized the opportunity to tell Todd about it one evening as they relaxed in front of the fireplace. The weather had turned chilly, and he had insisted on starting a fire.

"The change in Tammy—it's like a miracle, Todd."

Derek liked hearing the happiness and awe in her voice. "I knew that if anyone could reach Tammy it Would be you, Doc."

"Now I know how you feel every time you've helped someone."

She had no idea why he'd…*Oh, Augusta, how I need to tell you the truth.* His love for this woman knew no bounds.

The more he thought about telling her the truth, the more convinced he was that in time what he had done wouldn't make her hate him. Maybe Ben was right and Augusta could forgive him. He just needed more time. Just a little more time. He reached for her and held her tight.

"Todd?"

"I was thinking about how much you mean to me."

"You mean just as much to me, my darling."

Bella padded up to her and nuzzled her hand. Augusta patted her head. "You mean a lot to me too, girl."

Derek felt almost jealous of Augusta's affection for the dog. He couldn't help wondering if after he had told her the truth her feelings for him would be less than what she felt for Bella.

Augusta kissed Derek and snuggled closer into his embrace. "Todd, I want us to be this happy for the rest of our lives."

"Me too."

CHAPTER XIII

"How about you coming to my place tonight, Doc?" Derek said as he opened the classroom door.

"That'll be a first. You've never invited me to your inner sanctum. I wouldn't know how to act, and besides, I wouldn't know my way around."

Derek kissed Augusta's neck. "It would give me the utmost pleasure to instruct you on the finer aspects of a man's abode; namely, his bedroom."

"Of course you would pick that particular aspect. But this isn't exactly the place to discuss it."

He cleared his throat. "Unfortunately, you're right. It isn't. The kids should start filing in any minute. I was hoping to secure a few moments alone with their teacher. Oh, well." He moved a step further into the room, ushering Augusta inside.

Augusta heard Derek's stunned gasp.

"Todd, is anything wrong?" Augusta called out in alarm.

"No, nothing is wrong, Miss Humphrey," Tammy answered.

"Tammy!"

"I wanted you to hear a song I—never mind."

"Tammy," Derek started toward her, but the girl backed away from him.

Augusta touched his arm. "You'd better be going, Todd. You'll be late for your meeting with John."

"But…"

Augusta smiled reassuringly. "I can handle it."

"You sure?"

"Yes, I'm sure."

He glanced from Augusta to Tammy, then reluctantly moved to leave the classroom.

"You don't have to leave right now, T…Mr. Winters."

Derek turned.

Tammy switched her attack to Augusta. "You couldn't wait until you got him home to get it on, could you, Miss Humphrey?" Tammy spat. "Mr. Winters, Todd, must be something else between the sheets."

Augusta was momentarily stunned past answering.

"Wait just a minute, Tammy," Derek began sharply. "I'm not going to let you talk to Augusta like that."

"What you gonna do?"

"Todd." Augusta nudged his arm. "Your meeting. Remember."

"You ain't gotta leave, I'm outta here," Tammy said acidly.

Then Augusta heard her unfold her cane and rush to leave the room, stumbling, nearly falling in her haste to be gone.

"Tammy!" Derek called after her.

She continued on out the door.

"Let her go, Todd."

Derek walked over to Augusta. "Maybe I should go after her."

"This is something Tammy and I have to resolve."

"But she's pretty upset."

"How do you feel about Tammy, Todd?"

Augusta heard him sigh and then answer, "Like a brother or a father. She's almost young enough to be my daughter, for Christ's sake."

"What we have to do is convince Tammy that deep down, that's the kind of love she feels for you."

"A major big-time miracle is what we need here, I'd say."

Augusta kissed his cheek. "You worked one for me, don't forget."

"How can I? But, Augusta, this is different."

"I know it is."

After Derek had gone to his meeting, the kids filed into the classroom. As much as she wanted to go after Tammy, she had a class to conduct. Augusta hoped that Tammy would return, but she doubted it, considering what had happened.

Finally it was lunchtime. Augusta headed for the solarium garden.

She had an idea that she would find her pupil there.

"Tammy," Augusta called out.

"Yeah," Tammy answered coldly.

"I thought I'd find you here."

Augusta heard Tammy move to leave.

"Stay so we can talk."

"I ain't got nothing to say to you."

"On the contrary, I think we have a lot to say to one another."

Augusta sat down. "I know how you feel."

"Yeah, right."

"I do. You see, Todd used to be my teacher, too."

"For real! He didn't tell us that."

"Come on, sit down?"

Without uttering another word, Tammy sat back down on the bench.

"I'm not going to tell you that what you heard wasn't exactly what it seemed because it was. I happen to love Todd very much."

"Does he love you back?"

"He hasn't said so."

"But you think so?"

"Yes." She paused. "Don't hate us, please. We care about you, Tammy."

"I've heard those words before, and they ain't never been true."

"I'm sure you have. I used to hear the same thing from the foster parents I had just before they sent me back to the home."

"You lived in a foster home?" Tammy whispered in disbelief.

"Yes, from the time I was eight-years-old until I turned eighteen."

"But I thought that you were…"

"Were what? Rich? And just doing this out of boredom to pass the time? Hardly. I was born in South Philly, Tammy."

"I bet you don't ever go back to the 'hood."

"I haven't forgotten where I came from, if that's what you mean. My house is near the heart of the old neighborhood—'hood." Augusta changed the subject. "In college I had a professor I was crazy about."

"You gonna try and tell me what I feel for Todd is like that?"

"No, I'm not going to tell you that. Only you know how you feel about Todd. What you need to do is examine your feelings closely, Tammy."

After a week passed following her talk with Tammy, Augusta began to worry. Tammy had missed one week of classes. Then it was Tuesday of the following week. Would Tammy come to her class today? she wondered. Todd said that Tammy hadn't attended any of his classes either.

When it came time for class to begin, Augusta gave up on Tammy and started the day's lesson. Then she heard the door. She knew it had to be Tammy and gave the girl time to reach her chair before continuing.

When class was over and all the other students had gone, Tammy Gibson stayed behind. Augusta knew she wanted to talk. Was that a good or a bad sign? She couldn't help wondering what she would have to say.

"Miss Humphrey, I've been doing a lot of thinking about what you said. You know, about my feelings for T...Mr. Winters."

"And have you come to any conclusions?"

"Yeah, I think I have. I thought...wanted to believe..." Her voice faltered and then she continued. "He never said anything to make me think he was interested in me in any way, other than as an instructor in a student. I wanted there to be more to it. You understand what I'm saying?"

"Yes, I think I do. But he's not the only one who cares about you, Tammy."

"He thinks I can really sing. What do you think? You think I gotta chance to make it?"

"Do you believe you have?"

"I don't know?'

"*If* you think you have, it's up to you to do something about it. Stevie Wonder is a perfect example to follow. He didn't let his blindness stop him from attaining his goals, and neither should you. You'll have to work at it. It won't be easy. Don't get me wrong—it's going to take guts."

"Augusta," came a familiar male voice.

"Todd," Augusta answered anxiously, wondering what his sudden appearance at this fragile moment might do to Tammy's resolve.

"If I'm intruding, I can come back later."

"You're not. Is he, Tammy?"

"No, he ain't. Look, T…Mr. Winters—I'm sorry about what I said."

"I understand what you were feeling."

"You do?" She sounded skeptical.

Derek walked over to where Augusta and Tammy were sitting. "I had a serious crush on my eleventh grade English teacher, let me tell you."

"Miss Humphrey said the same thing happened to her in college."

"I guess it happens to everyone at some point in their life. They get over it and sometimes don't even remember feeling that way."

"After what I said, I wouldn't blame you if you never wanted to talk to me again."

"It wasn't that serious." Derek didn't dwell on it and quickly moved on to another subject. "I've missed not having you in my class this past week."

"I been doing some heavy thinking." Tammy reached for her backpack and eased the strap over her shoulder. "I've gotta be going."

Derek watched her leave and was silent for a few seconds afterward.

"Is she going to be all right?" he asked Augusta.

"I think so. Of course, we'll have to give her some encouragement. But yes, I think she's going to be all right."

By the end of the day Augusta felt exhausted, but it was a nice kind of exhaustion because she and Tammy had reached an understanding. She snuggled closer to the man she loved. They were at his apartment, sitting on the carpet before his fireplace and listening to music, enjoying each other's company.

The weeks of summer had flown by and autumn had arrived, Derek realized, and he had yet to tell Augusta the truth. Gently grazing the top of her head with his chin, he thought about confessing, but it was a distant thought that grew more distant with the dawning of each day and every satisfying night of loving. His life was so good right now that he didn't want to rock the boat. Telling her the truth would do more than that. It could cause his life to capsize.

You've got to stop this, Morgan.

"What do you have planned for tomorrow, Doc?"

"Nothing that I know of. Why? Have you got something in mind?"

"Maybe."

"Come on, tell me."

Derek laughed. "I think I'll let it be a surprise. Wear something warm and casual."

"Is that all you're going to tell me?"

"Uh-huh. I know, I'm a mean man, and you love it."

"You would think that."

Derek arrived at Augusta's house just before noon on Saturday.

"All right. Where are we going?" Augusta demanded.

"You wouldn't want to spoil my surprise, now would you?"

"You are impossible, Todd Winters."

"Come on, you know you love me." He kissed her deeply.

Yes, she sure did. "If you keep that up, we're never going to get out of here."

"You're right, so put your ass in gear, woman."

"I didn't know you could be so crude, Todd Winters." She said in mock indignation.

"It's the least of the things you are going to find out about me."

Derek surprised her with tickets to the Philadelphia 76ers exhibition basketball game.

"The game was exciting, wasn't it, Todd?" Augusta managed to relay to Todd over the boisterous din created by enthusiastic Sixers fans as the sports arena slowly emptied.

While the game had been going on, Derek had done a play-by-play commentary on the game. He loved watching her expression and could tell that she was imagining the different moves and how each player looked while making them.

"Yes, it was. When I got the tickets, I had no idea you were a basketball fan."

"Oh, I've been hooked since I was thirteen. One foster family that I lived with loved basketball and the Sixers. They took me to all their games. My favorite player was Dr. J."

"Do you have another one now that he's retired?"

"Not really. I haven't gone to a game since before the accident."

"I'm sorry, I didn't mean to make you think about that day."

"It's all right, Todd. A few months ago it would have bothered me, but not now" She smiled. "You've made all the difference."

You certainly have, Morgan. Tell her the truth, man.

"...What do you think?"

"I'm sorry, I didn't catch the first part of what you said."

Augusta frowned. "Are you all right, Todd?"

"Yeah, I'm fine. See how you've got me acting? My mind just wanders."

Augusta smiled. "Really? And just where had it wandered to just now?"

"To a certain woman and how she looks buck naked."

"You're wicked, Todd Winters."

"I know. You wouldn't like me any other way. Are you hungry?"

"Not really."

"You want to go for a walk in the park and work up an appetite?"

"Yeah, I think I'd like that."

They left the sports arena and headed for Roosevelt Park.

Derek hooked an arm around Augusta's shoulder as they walked. He could see that she was taking in the atmosphere of her first autumn without sight since her new awareness.

"The air smells so dry and crisp. The sound of leaves crunching under our feet as we walk seems strange. I'm trying to visualize the different shapes of the leaves, the shades of gold, brown, and red in them, the squirrels and the sparrows flitting about the trees."

"I never noticed the woodsy smells before. I've always enjoyed fall, but never really paid attention to all that was going on around me."

"I think it's true of most people. Only when you can't see do you become more keenly aware of what you've been missing."

"You're probably right."

"I know I'm right."

"Thank you, Mr. Know-It-All."

"You hungry now?"

"Starved. All this walking has given me an appetite."

"How about the Spaghetti Factory?"

"Sounds good to me."

When Derek and Augusta walked into the Spaghetti Factory, the aroma of Italian cooking assailed their nostrils.

"What kind of pizza do you want?"

"Let me think." Suddenly she could visualize a giant pizza with pepperoni, mushrooms, olives, and sausage, covered with lots and lots of mozzarella cheese and tangy Italian sauce on a thick crust. She mentally licked her lips.

"Well, Doc?" Derek said with mock impatience.

"Don't rush me. I smell the one I want." She described it down to the tomatoes.

Derek smiled, because a waiter had just brought that exact pizza to the table next to theirs.

"That's fantastic! How'd she do it?" their waiter wanted to know. When he realized Augusta was blind, he offered an apology. "Listen, I'm sorry, Miss. I didn't..."

"It's all right; I'm not offended."

Derek heard the relief in the waiter's voice. He sympathized with the man. He had to be feeling uncomfortable after tossing out those careless words.

"We'll have the special." Derek indicated the table next to them.

"That is what they're having, isn't it?"

"You're right it is. Spaghetti and your choice of salad come with our special. Would you like wine with it?"

"Augusta?"

"Yes, I would."

After the waiter had gone to fill their order, Augusta said, "I didn't mean to embarrass the man."

"You just got carried away with the ambiance of the place. He can't fault you for your enthusiasm."

"You're a..."

"Don't say it. I'm a balm for your vanity, right?"

She could hear the smile in his voice, and she loved hearing it. She loved him. Period.

Derek studied the woman he'd come to love as she tucked into her pizza with gusto. He smiled, recalling Ben saying that her colleagues had nicknamed her "Gusto."

She personified everything a man could want in a woman. She was warm, loving, full of spirit, strong and compassionate. Augusta had put her life on the line to save a child who wasn't even her own. She had helped troubled teenagers in her community. What Augusta Humphrey had in abundance was character. Could she understand his lack of it eighteen months ago, when it had cost her so much? If he revealed the truth now, would she believe that something more than his sense of guilt had moved him to turn his life around? That he had grown to love her, really love her for herself? That it wasn't out of some misplaced feeling of pity and compassion?

If you were in her place, would you believe that, Morgan?

I've tried to make it up to her.

The bottom line is, will she think you have done enough?

She's got to.

Does she really?

"There's one piece of pizza left, Todd. It's your last chance."

Derek laughed. "Be my guest, Doc. You smelled that one piece of pizza. You sure you're not part bloodhound?"

"That's not nice. Bella wouldn't like you referring to her mistress as another category of dog."

"You're crazy, you know that, don't you, Augusta Humphrey?" And God, how I love you, he silently added.

Derek and Augusta stood outside the Spaghetti Factory, ready to get into his car.

"Augusta, are you sure you can squeeze in after all you ate?'

She playfully punched Derek's arm. "What are you trying to say?"

"Oh, nothing. We had a good time, didn't we?"

"But then we always do. You've added a new dimension to my life, Todd. Before you came along, I didn't have very much to look forward to, or so I thought then. For the first time in a long while, I'm truly happy."

"You give me too much credit."

"I don't think I give you enough. You deserve every bit of it, and more."

Derek drew her into his arms and bent to kiss her.

"You know the one part about being blind that I have to say I love, is being the recipient of your spontaneous kisses, not knowing when you're about to lay one on me."

He kissed her. "You mean like now?"

"Yeah, like now." She pulled his head down and kissed him back. "You're not bad at that yourself, Doc."

"What I'd like to do is go home and practice some more. Are you game, Mr. Winters?"

"Definitely, Doc. Practice makes perfect, don't you know."

"Then let's go and practice so we can become experts."

"Your wish is my command."

"You know, it seems as though we were made for each other," Augusta said, sitting in her living room listening as Todd built a fire in the fireplace.

"I feel that way, too. I never enjoyed doing the simple things so much. I used to crave excitement above all else."

"I can't imagine you ever being like that, Todd."

"Believe me, I was. After my parents died, I was at loose ends. I had no direction in life and didn't want one. All I wanted was to have a good time. Then something happened to change my outlook on life."

"I'm glad you're not like that anymore. I like you just the way you are."

Oh, my sweet Augusta, you wouldn't have eighteen months ago. You would have loathed the irresponsible bastard I was. Derek walked over to the couch, pulled her to her feet, and hugged her tight.

"What was that for?"

"For being you."

Augusta slipped her arms around his waist and laid her head against his chest, breathing in the fresh masculine smell of him, feeling the strength emanating from his body At that moment she felt cherished and loved. She knew it would only be a matter of time before he told her what she longed to hear.

They undressed before the fire and made love. It was close to midnight when Derek went back to his apartment.

CHAPTER XIV

"Everything checks out fine, Augusta," Ben Hastings said after concluding his examination.

"Everything except that my sight shows no sign of returning. Not one glimmer or even any gray shadows." Disappointment edged her voice.

"I detect a more complex reason for your despondency.""

"I had hoped there was a change that—I never wanted to see more than I do now. If you must know, there is a special man in my life."

"Todd Winters."

"Is there anything you don't know, Ben Hastings?"

"He and I are friends, too, remember? I don't see anything wrong with my two friends getting together."

"Has he said anything to you about his feelings for me?"

"That's something you'll have to discuss with him."

Her lips formed a pout. "I was your friend first."

"And you think that gives you a prior claim on my loyalty?"

"Well, yes."

"Women."

"Men."

"All right, I'll tell you this much; he cares very deeply for you."

"How deeply?"

"You'll have to judge that for yourself. How about having lunch with me?"

Augusta knew she wouldn't get any more from her cagey colleague.

"You're on."

Derek went to Augusta's house after finishing at the Institute.

"How'd your check-up with Ben go?"

"He found no change."

The disappointment in her voice seared his heart. Surely there was a doctor somewhere who could help her. "Whether you get your sight back or not, it doesn't matter to me. I…"

"Yes?"

"My feelings for you won't change."

"And just how do you feel about me, Todd?"

"You know I care for you, Augusta."

It wasn't what she wanted to hear. But she knew one day he would put into words how he felt about her.

"I've got a stack of exams for you to grade." She handed him her grading bag.

"Are you happy teaching, Augusta?" He took the exams and spread them out in sections on the coffee table. "I know I kind of pushed you into the job at the Institute."

"I don't regret a minute of the time I spend there. You know how I feel about working with the kids. The answer to your question is that I'm happy most of the time. But there are times when I..."

"When you miss being a surgeon."

"I know it's useless to dwell on it. That part of my life is over, and I know I have to accept it."

"There's always the chance that you'll get your sight back one day."

"A miracle *could* happen. But I can't count on it happening anytime soon, if it ever does. The miracle of you is my only reality right now."

"Are you sure I'll be enough for you, Augusta?"

"What do you mean?"

"Oh, nothing. Don't mind me." He reached for the answer book. "I'd better get on with grading these exams."

Augusta wondered in silence what he could be alluding to.

Ben sat behind his desk studying a medical journal when his nurse buzzed him.

"Derek Morgan is here."

"Send him in, Rebba."

Seconds later Derek walked in.

"I knew I'd get a visit from you."

"I don't mean to make a nuisance of myself, Ben, but Augusta is important to me. She seemed a little down after her check-up."

"Have a seat, Derek." Ben closed the journal.

"Any breakthroughs at all?"

"A Dr. John Eekong in Nigeria is doing some amazing work with corneal restoration using laser surgery."

"Is it worth considering?"

"Maybe. I want to conduct my own investigation before I give the thumbs up on telling Augusta about it. I don't want to get her hopes up, only to let her down."

"I understand. If only..."

"You've got it bad, haven't you, my friend? As bad as I have it for Myra."

Derek nodded. "I want to do so much for her." He let out a frustrated sigh. "I feel so helpless knowing there is nothing."

"I know how you feel, but when you've done all you can..."

"Are we just talking about my situation now?" When Ben didn't answer right away, Derek said, "Friendship cuts both ways. If there is anything I can do to help, you only have to ask."

"Yes, I know." A frown furrowed his forehead. I'm worried about Myra. She's been on edge so much lately. You see, she's been trying to get pregnant for a long time now. I'm afraid of what might happen to her if it turns out we can't start a family."

"You guys are still young, Ben. You'll probably end up having a whole houseful."

"Right now I'd settle for just one. Getting back to you and Augusta, you've done everything you can for her, Derek."

"It's not enough, damn it!"

"Guilt can be a destructive emotion if you let it eat away at you. Believe me, I know. I've let it torture me where Myra is concerned. I can't help thinking that in some way it may be my fault that Myra hasn't conceived."

"You don't know that for sure. And there is always adoption."

"Myra is adamant about having our own child. I've tried to reassure her that I wouldn't mind adopting, but she doesn't want to hear it."

"I don't know what to tell you, man. We're certainly a pair. We can't solve each other's problems; we can only commiserate and share the guilt."

"Guilt sure can obstruct your view of all the good, can't it? As far as Augusta is concerned, you have to stop blaming yourself. What's done is done, and no matter how much you would like to go back and change it, you can't."

"I know you're right, Ben, but it's damned hard when you know that you're responsible."

"I can only imagine what you are feeling. If I were to find out it was my fault that we couldn't..." Ben shook his head to dispel his momentary reverie. "I'm sorry about going on and on about it like that."

"You love Myra and want to see her happy. Maybe you should sit down with her and talk about your fears and apprehension."

"You're probably right. In fact, I know you are." He laughed. "Can you picture the great Ben Hastings at the mercy of a pint-size woman?"

"Oh, I can. Getting back to Augusta."

"I've told you that the woman loves you."

Derek arched his brows in hope-filled curiosity. "Did she tell you that?"

"Not in so many words. She asked if you'd said anything to me about your feelings for her."

"And what did you say to her?"

"That she would have to discuss it with you."

Derek's eyes lit up and a smile spread across his face. "You have no idea how happy it makes me to hear that piece of news."

"I have some idea," Ben said dryly.

Derek rose from his seat and walked over to the window and looked out. "I've wanted to let her know how I feel, but I've hesitated because—well, you know the reason why."

"Now that you're sure she loves you, there's no problem, no reason why you can't tell her the truth, is there?"

Derek didn't answer.

"I'm not going to say another word on the subject; you'll do what you want to anyway. You know my feelings."

"Yes, I do. And I appreciate your advice." Derek looked at his watch. "I've got just about enough time to take care of some unfinished personal business before I visit my lady."

"What kind of business?"

Derek grinned. "You know everything else; I'll let you figure it out."

"You don't have to be a genius to read that look in your eyes. Congratulations."

"Maybe you should go into mind reading as a sideline."

"I wish I could make everything all right for you and Augusta, Derek."

"And I wish I could do the same for you and Myra. Where Augusta is concerned, it looks like the next move is mine. I just hope I make the right one."

Augusta had a feeling that tonight would be the turning point in their relationship because Todd's voice had had a different sound to it. He had called to tell her that he had made reservations for dinner somewhere special, but he wouldn't tell her where, much to her irritation.

When he called back an hour later to say he was running a little late and to be ready to go the minute he got there, she knew something was going on. Did she dare hope the day she'd dreamed about had finally come?

She took special pains with her appearance, choosing to wear a royal purple velvet dress with a high neckline. The back was cut out in the center in the shape of a heart, the point plunging to her belted waist.

She and Bella went down to the beauty shop. Augusta had her hairdresser, Andre, style her hair. She had to laugh at the way he described her, commenting that she looked like a cross between Nefertiti and Salome. Whatever that meant.

At the sound of the doorbell, Augusta's heart fluttered wildly in her chest. "Oh, God, let this evening go the way I want it to."

Bella padded to the door ahead of her. Augusta could hear her sniffing it. She assumed that the dog was satisfied that whoever was on the other side posed no threat to her mistress because when Augusta reached the door, Bella moved away, allowing her to open it.

Derek didn't say a word, just kissed her boneless.

"If you're a salesman, I'll buy whatever you're selling," she said breathlessly.

"If your response is any indication, I think I'm going to like working this territory."

"You think!"

He kissed her again. "I know I will."

"That sounds better."

"Are you ready to be wined and dined, Doc?"

"Wined and dined, huh? Is this some special occasion I've forgotten about?"

"You'll have to wait and find out."

"Todd…"

"Augusta…"

Uninterested in their by-play after having witnessed it many times, Bella loped back into the living room, eased down on the floor before the fireplace, and closed her eyes.

Derek pulled Augusta out onto the porch and closed the door behind them before sweeping her up in his arms and walking out to the car.

"Todd, put me down."

He continued to carry her, ignoring her half-hearted protest. Only when he reached the car did he lower her feet to the ground.

"You're one stubborn man, Todd Winters."

"Man being the key word."

"I won't argue with you on that point. You are most definitely all male."

"And you are most definitely all female," he said huskily, pulling her into his arms, reveling in her beauty, which was no surface illusion. Her rare kind of beauty reached to the soul. He knew himself to be a most fortunate man. More fortunate than he deserved, but if fate was kind, he would spend the rest of his life loving this very special woman.

Both remained quiet for a moment, each delving deep into the emotions that consumed them.

"I think we'd better be going," Derek said, opening the car door and turning to take Augusta's hand to help her.

Once inside and on their way, Augusta tried to engage Derek in a conversation geared to extract information about the evening he had planned.

Derek cleverly maneuvered the conversation around to talking about the Institute and her work.

"How is it going with Tammy?"

"She's making great progress, as you well know. Todd, stop changing the subject. You know what I want to talk about."

Ignoring the annoyance in her voice, he continued as though she hadn't uttered a word.

"We've concentrated mainly on your work at the Institute, but what about your work with the medical school students?"

"Todd!"

He laughed. "We'll be there soon, Doc."

"You're impossible."

He muffled his laugher when he heard the sigh of frustration enter her voice. *Just a little while longer, my love.*

Derek glanced at Augusta every now and then, glorying in the fact that she loved him. He intended to make sure she never had any reason to regret it. The life he envisioned with her would be rich and full. They would have children. He knew how much having a child meant to Augusta. Every time she heard children playing in the park or a baby crying, her face lit up and a tender expression infused her features.

She had her sense of purpose back in her life. It wasn't surgery, but he could tell that what she did was important to her. What would telling her the truth now accomplish? It wouldn't bring her sight back. She'd be hurt, angry, and bitter.

He hoped once she realized how deeply committed he was to making her happy, that when the time came to tell her it wouldn't matter so much, and then surely she would forgive him. He knew he was risking their future happiness on that uncertain premise.

Derek pulled his car into the valet parking area, then walked around to the passenger side to help Augusta out.

She heard Todd hand the keys to the parking attendant, who politely greeted her before getting into the car and driving away.

"I always like the royal treatment we get when we go where there's valet parking."

"You deserve it, Doc."

"Todd, are we at the Staircase?"

"Augusta."

"Aren't you going to tell me where we are now?"

"You are one persistent lady, aren't you, Miss Humphrey? But no, ma'am, I'm not going to even give you a hint. You'll find out what I have planned in due time."

"Yeah, whenever that is," she pouted.

Derek laughed. "Don't be so impatient. You'll be glad you waited once you know the reason for the wait."

"You're a silver-tongued devil, Todd Winters."

"And you're my sacrificial victim."

"Very funny."

The door was opened by a doorman and Derek escorted Augusta inside. Immediately the scent of roses greeted them. The sound of a crackling fire and the warmth drifting toward them in welcome added further to the intimacy of the restaurant.

When they had first come to the Rose Room weeks ago, Augusta remembered Todd describing each dining room. There was the yellow rose room reserved for family dining. The winter-white rose and pink rooms were for surprise birthday and bachelor or bachelorette parties.

The red one was reserved for romantic purposes such as parties for newlyweds, anniversaries, and engagements. When the maitre d' directed them there, her whole being rioted with joy.

After they were seated, the waiter arrived with champagne nestled in a bucket of ice.

Derek smiled at the smug look on Augusta's face. "I can tell by your expression you think you know why I brought you here, Miss Smarty Pants."

"You may be right, but I'm not going to spoil your special moment, Mr. Winters."

Derek signaled the waiter to open the champagne.

Excitement that Augusta could barely contain bubbled up in her throat.

Derek enclosed her hand in his. "Augusta Humphrey, will you marry me?"

"Oh, yes, my darling." Tears came to her eyes.

Derek kissed each one away. "These *are* tears of happiness, I assume?"

"You know they are, you idiot. I love you with all my heart."

"I love you, my beautiful Augusta."

She heard a tiny creaking sound as he opened the ring box, and moments later she felt him slip a ring on the third finger of her left hand.

Augusta ran her fingers over it. A large, heart-shaped stone dominated the center with smaller stones surrounding it.

"The heart is a ruby, and there are fourteen diamonds encircling it."

"Oh, Todd!" She cupped his face with her fingers. "You won't be sorry. I intend to make you a happy man. I'm so lucky to have you."

"I'm the lucky one, Augusta."

She heard Todd pour champagne into their glasses and then he handed her one.

"To us," Derek said and clinked his glass against hers.

Augusta took a sip. The popping bubbles tickled her nostrils.

"This is the most beautiful day of my life." She kissed him thoroughly before releasing his mouth.

"You keep that up and we won't make it through dinner."

"Would that be so bad?"

"Augusta..."

She kissed him softly on the lips. "The only thing I'm hungry for right now is a taste of you, Todd."

"Don't you want to set a wedding date?"

"We have plenty of time to do that. Do you mind if we leave now?"

"Say no more. Waiter!"

Derek unlocked Augusta's front door and pushed it opened. He heard Bella growl. She stood at attention just inside the door, her eyes alert, her ears pointed, ready for action.

"Easy girl, easy, Bella," Augusta said to the dog in a calm, reassuring voice. "You know Todd, he won't hurt me." The dog quieted immediately.

Derek turned Augusta's face to his and kissed her.

They stayed in that position for a while, enjoying the kiss.

Reluctantly, they drew apart, came all the way inside the house, and shut the door.

Derek laughed when he saw the dog lope over to her usual resting place in front of the fire, lower her body to the floor, then close her eyes.

"Bella's enthusiasm is overwhelming."

"Oh, leave her alone. She's seen us do this plenty of times and is probably bored by it."

"Surely you're not bored with me, Augusta."

"I could never be that where you're concerned." Augusta laced her arms around his neck. "Now let's get back to the reason we left the restaurant so early."

"A lady with a one-track mind. I love it."

"And I love you."

He kissed her again. "How did I get so lucky?"

"Build a fire, Mr. Lucky; it's getting cold in here."

"I definitely want to keep you warm. In fact, I'd like to make you hot."

"You do have a way with words, Mr. Winters."

He parted the lapel of her coat and cupped her breasts. "I think I'm better with body language, don't you?"

"Oh, definitely, but I think you'd better see about the fire first."

"You're one cruel woman, Augusta Humphrey," Derek grumbled in protest, then reluctantly left her side to rekindle the fire. He soon had the room warm and inviting.

"Now to get back to where we left off." Derek eased her coat off and caressed her bare back with his lips.

Augusta felt shivers of delight move up and down her spine, and a moan escaped her lips.

Derek tossed her coat onto the back of the couch and moved his fingers inside the heart-shaped opening at the back of her dress, lovingly fondling her satin-smooth flesh. Eager for more, he undid the clasp at the neckline and opened the dress, peeling it down to her waist. He snaked his hands around her body and cupped her breasts, teasing the nipples in circular movements against the palms of his hands.

Augusta cried out, arching her back and pushing her breasts deeper into his warm hands.

Derek pulled the dress, half slip, and purple silk panties down past her hips and let them drift to the floor. His breath caught in his throat at the sight of her lush, full breasts, small waist, rounded hips, and soft, yet firmly padded, buttocks.

To him, her skin seemed to glow as though from a vibrant inner light. He couldn't resist caressing her body.

"Baby, your skin is like silk." He lowered his face to her throat, breathing in her scent. "And your body has the exotic fragrance of a field of wildflowers."

Augusta moaned again. She wanted to say something, but at that moment she was lost in the heady sensation of his fingers moving erotically over her body. Wanting to give him the same pleasure he was giving her, she turned and began to undress him.

"You smell wonderful yourself, Mr. Winters." The scent of Pierre Cardin momentarily mesmerized her. A few seconds later she moved her fingers over his skin, exploring his hard, muscular male body, all the while envisioning how devastatingly magnificent it must look.

Noticing her intense concentration, Derek asked, "What are you thinking?"

"How you look fully aroused and ready."

"Here, feel what you do to me," he said, placing her hand on his hard, velvet-sheathed male organ.

When he bent his head to suckle her nipple, a sensation of sheer pleasure trickled down her belly and poured into her center of creativity. Her breath caught somewhere between her lungs and throat when he treated the other nipple to the same rapture. Her entire body now reduced to a mass of throbbing, passionate need, Augusta cried out.

"Oh, Augusta, I want you so much, baby," he murmured in her ear. "I want to celebrate our happiness in your bed, but if we don't go now we might shock Bella."

Her voice low, vibrant, and breathy, she answered, "We wouldn't want to do that."

Derek lifted her in his arms and strode into the bedroom. Then he eased her down on the bed and slid his lean male nakedness over her.

He moaned at the contact. "I can't wait," he murmured in her ear.

"Neither can I," Augusta rasped, her voice barely above a whisper.

He thrust his smooth, hard flesh deep within her to the hilt. Her body shuddered violently, suffused with pleasure so acute her breathing altered, growing more labored as she writhed against him. They started the climb up the mountain, higher and higher. They reached the summit and slowly tumbled down the side as though in slow motion into a seemingly bottomless chasm of euphoria.

All through the night they tasted rapture, then finally fell asleep in exhaustion just before dawn.

Derek studied Augusta as she slept. They'd made love before, but this time was special, more binding. Becoming engaged put a seal on their love. They were truly and deeply committed to each other. He kissed her lightly on the lips. God, how he loved her.

Augusta moaned softly, shifting onto her back. Derek trailed passion-trembling fingers across her hip to the core of her desire and stroked and teased the bud between the dewy folds of her femininity until her breathing changed, growing more erratic with each stroke. When she parted her legs, he slid between them, seeming to bury himself to her very heart.

"Yes," she cried out at the peak of bliss.

Derek followed her into the cloud path to heaven.

"What a way to wake up," she said, her voice lazy with contentment and supreme satisfaction.

"I take it you approve of my technique."

"Most definitely."

"Let's shower together."

Of course, they couldn't resist making love.

"You know what I like about your bathroom?" Derek asked.

"No, what?"

"You have plenty of towels. I always seem to forget to put some in mine."

"After we're married I'll take care of that."

He kissed her. "And I'll take care of you."

Later they went to Derek's apartment so that he could change. They had lunch at Romano's and then returned to her house, tiptoeing past a sleeping Bella to Augusta's bedroom.

As they lay entwined after making love, Derek's conscience pricked him.

You should have told her the truth before you became engaged to Augusta. Now it's going to be that much harder when the time comes. And it will come.

I know.

"Are you all right?" Augusta asked.

He kissed the top of her head. "I'm here with you, aren't I?"

Augusta smiled. "Yes, where you belong."

"You're a possessive lady, aren't you?"

"You'd better believe it."

"I do, my beautiful Augusta. Do you want to go dancing tonight?"

"Dancing!" Augusta swallowed hard.

"I know what you're thinking. But, Augusta, darling, I'll be with you. There's no need to feel self-conscious."

"You know me so well."

"Yes, I do. I'm going to teach you how to relax and enjoy life. So put on your red dress, sour dancing shoes, and some of that sweet perfume, and let's go party."

A coat-check girl took their coats. As they waited at the top of the stairs to be escorted down to the restaurant in the Chateau, an exclusive supper club with live music and a dance floor, Augusta felt her anticipation build.

"The staircase is like those leading into the ballroom that Cinderella went to. It's made of a pale lavender marble and leads down to the restaurant, where there are about fifty tables surrounding a dance floor and a stand for the entertainers."

"The decor is dream-like, with crystal chandeliers and copies of famous paintings done by the masters."

"I'm beginning to feel like a princess. And you're my Prince Charming."

"Flattery will get you the best table in the house."

"You mean you arranged all this?"

"Yes."

She could hear the amusement in his voice. "How did you manage it on such short notice?"

"That's my little secret."

"Your table, sir," the waiter said, indicating the one near the front of the stage.

Augusta could hear the excited murmur of people's voices as they talked and laughed, and the clinking of glasses as they passed their tables. The scent of jasmine filled the air, and "Unchained Melody" played in the background. She visualized how the people must look swaying to the music in such a romantic atmosphere.

"I have a surprise for you." Derek stood up. "I have to leave you for a moment, Doc, but don't panic, I'll be right back. There is someone I have to see."

"Todd!"

"Be right back."

She heard him walk away and wondered what he was up to. By bringing her here she knew he wanted to make the evening special for her. The music to one of her favorite songs began to play.

"Augusta?"

"Todd?" She realized after she'd said it that it wasn't. She knew that voice anywhere.

"You must be his special lady," came the deep rich voice of Jeffrey Osborne.

"Yes, she is." Derek took her hand in his and raised it to his lips. "I dedicate this song to you."

The singer crooned the words to "On the Wings of Love." Immediately the voices in the audience quieted.

When Jeffrey Osborne finished singing and moved away, Augusta's eyes shone with joy. "He's one of my favorite singers. You knew that, and you arranged this just for me."

"I remembered that on the day I first came to your house, one of his songs was playing."

"I wasn't exactly the soul of graciousness that day."

"Your temper is something else, Doc. And I can't say I want it aimed my way anytime soon," he commented wryly.

"I wasn't that bad."

"It depends on your interpretation of bad."

"Todd."

"Don't worry none, my spirited little filly," he said in his best Texas accent. "I love you a whole bunch."

"You're crazy, you know that?"

His voice gentled. "Crazy about you."

As if on cue Jeffrey Osborne started singing that song.

"Did you plan that, too?"

"No, but I have to say his timing is perfect. Care to dance, my love?"

"I don't know..." Dancing in her living room was a far cry from doing it in public. A shiver of panic streaked through her.

"Come on, Doc." Derek pulled her up from her chair into his arms and led her onto the dance floor.

Awkward at first because she felt self-conscious about being the center of attention, Augusta soon let herself go with the flow of the music, following Derek's smooth lead. He was a wonderful dancer. She truly felt like Cinderella tonight, floating through a fantasy of love and the promise of forever after.

"I was thinking that Tammy could use some help in starting her singing career. Do you think Jeffrey would..."

"She's blind," Augusta heard a feminine voice utter in a low astonished voice.

"What I wouldn't give to have that hunk she's dancing with pay attention to me. Whatever she has going for her, it's working for her big time," said another.

Augusta stiffened at first, but then relaxed. These women were actually jealous of her. They couldn't understand why a man like Todd was with her, but she knew and it pleased her no end. She moved closer to her man.

"That's my girl. I knew you could handle anything."

"For those women to react like that, you must be Denzel Washington, Mario Van Peebles, and Billy Dee Williams all rolled into one."

"Not hardly."

"Modesty in a man, I love it."

"You're some kind of woman, Augusta Humphrey."

When the music ended, they left the dance floor and returned to their table.

As Derek seated her, Augusta said, "About Tammy..."

"All right, Doc, I'll talk to Jeffrey about her."

"Thank you, Todd."

"You don't have to thank me. If I didn't have my mind so wrapped up in loving a certain lady, night and day, I'd have thought of it myself."

A waiter appeared with the menus and discreetly handed them both to Derek.

"What would you like to eat, Doc?" Derek asked.

It felt strange to Augusta, not being able to read a menu and having someone order for her when she had been so used to doing it for herself.

"What do you suggest?" Derek asked the waiter.

"The *coq au vin* is very good, sir."

"Chicken in wine sauce. All right, we'll have that then."

The waiter smiled. "How about a Chardonnay?"

"Sounds wonderful," Augusta answered.

"You're easy to please."

"Not always."

"Does that hold a special meaning?"

"I'll explain later," she said, her voice sensual, hinting at joys to be experienced in the not-too-distant future.

Later, after they had finished their dinner, Derek danced with Augusta again.

"You see, I told you you'd do all right."

Augusta smiled. "So you did."

"You *are* enjoying yourself, aren't you?"

"You know I am."

"Just checking."

Augusta leaned her head against his shoulder and delighted in the warmth of his body. She loved this man with all her heart. And she, Augusta Humphrey, was going to be his wife. Christmas was only six weeks away. They could have a Christmas Eve or New Year's Eve wedding. She smiled. Maybe Valentine's Day; that would be so romantic.

"I'll be Mrs. Todd Winters. Such a nice ring to it, don't you think?"

Derek winced. What would she think if he were to tell her the truth: that it would be Mrs. Derek Morgan? Augusta despised that name and the person that went with it.

You know what she would think and say.

How do I tell her now?

Augusta knew the moment his mind wandered because she felt his body tense.

"Todd, darling what is it?"

He'd better be careful because Augusta was a very perceptive person. *Considering how deceptive you are, Morgan, tell her the truth now.* The music stopped, saving Derek from his thoughts. He guided Augusta back to their table.

What could be bothering him? she wondered. There had been many moments lately when he'd become preoccupied. She hoped that he wasn't having second thoughts about marrying her.

"Todd, if you have any reservations about marrying me, please say so now."

"Augusta, darling, I don't. It's not that, I swear it isn't. Problems at my company have me distracted is all. I'm sorry, I didn't mean to bring them with me tonight."

Augusta wasn't sure she believed his explanation. If it wasn't really troubles at his company, and if marrying her wasn't the problem either, then what else could it be?

Derek sensed that he hadn't convinced her.

"The chocolate soufflé is delicious."

"None for me. I don't think I can find a place to put it, maybe next time."

"I want the evening to be perfect for you."

"And it is, Todd. But I think it's time we left."

"But the night is still young."

"Oh, I have plans for the rest of it," she said, in her most sexy, mysterious voice.

"You going to give me a hint about these plans?"

Teasingly she murmured, "You don't need one."

"Oh, I'm going to like them, then?"

She could visualize his brows arching in mock surprise. "Todd."

He laughed. "By all means let's go, Doc." He stood up, then helped her to her feet and escorted her up the stairs.

When they reached the top, Augusta said, "*This* Cinderella isn't going to turn into a pumpkin."

Derek whispered in her ear. "No, she's going to turn into a woman hussy before the night is over."

Augusta laughed. "You taught me everything I know."

The mood had lightened, much to Derek's relief. He suddenly wanted her all to himself. He refused to allow any further negative thoughts to spoil the rest of the evening.

CHAPTER XV

Augusta couldn't remember ever being this happy, not even when she could see. She felt so lucky to have Todd. Everything seemed so perfect that she feared something might happen to spoil it. But that was crazy.

She'd come to really enjoy teaching, more than she ever thought possible. Surprisingly, teaching others to do things she could no longer do herself didn't bother her. In fact, to know that one day the talented hands belonging to one of her students might be those of a surgeon because she had helped him or her provided a real high.

Augusta smiled as she went about the kitchen preparing Thanksgiving dinner for Todd. It was quite an experience, cooking a turkey and not being able to see if it was brown enough. In Joan Gordon's class she had learned to rely on her sense of smell and taste in knowing when food was done or brown.

She heard Bella sniffing around the stove.

"You're hungry, huh, girl?"

The timer went off on the stove, alerting her that the turkey had cooked the prescribed number of hours. She opened the stove door and took out the bird, sniffing for doneness. She wasn't satisfied that it had cooked long enough.

"It'll be a while longer, I'm afraid, Bella." She popped it back into the oven and set the timer for another half hour. That should give her time to get changed before Todd arrived.

Just as she came out of her bedroom, Augusta heard the doorbell and patted her upswept hair style, smiled, and then smoothed her hands down the hips of the forest-green, velvet dress she'd bought for the occasion. The salesgirl had assured her it looked as if made for her alone. The form-fitting sheath boasted three-quarter length, filmy-green tulle sleeves.

Augusta opened the door. "I smell flowers. Let me guess. Chrysanthemums."

"Right on the money. You're something else, Doc." He kissed her softly on the lips and walked in. "It smells good in here."

"The turkey!"

"Don't stress yourself; I'll take it out for you."

"No, I want to do it myself."

"Is it all right if I follow? By the way, you're looking good tonight. But then you look good any time I see you, and in anything you wear—or don't wear," he added wickedly.

"Todd, you ought to be ashamed of yourself."

"I'm not, though. He slipped his arms around her waist and kissed the nape of her neck. "I meant every word."

She eased out of his embrace. "Oh no, you don't," she said and walked over to the stove, opening the oven door to take the turkey out. "I spent too much time cooking this dinner."

"Come on, baby, a short delay won't hurt it." He came up behind her and cupped her breasts.

Her breath sucked in. "You behave now, Todd Winters."

He reluctantly let his hands drop to his sides. "All right, but I want to be compensated for my long-suffering."

"Long-suffering, is it?" she asked, her voice husky and full of promise. "I'll put you out of your misery soon."

Derek wiped his mouth. "I haven't had a home-cooked turkey dinner like this since my mother died. Delicious! I thought you said you weren't much of a cook."

"With Joan's help and my determination to be a good wife to you, I've learned through trial and error. I'm glad you enjoyed it. How about a slice of sweet potato pie?"

"You'll spoil me."

"I can hardly wait to do that."

"I hope that eagerness to please extends beyond the dining room."

She shook her head. "You're incorrigible, Todd Winters. But I love you in spite of it."

"Thanks a lot," he said in mock hurt.

After dessert, Derek helped Augusta take the plates and remaining food into the kitchen.

"Now for my other dessert." He kissed her lips and let his hands wander over her breasts.

"Todd!"

"I want you, baby."

Augusta kissed him back. "And I want you. I know where we're going to spend most of our early married life."

He nuzzled her ear. "Not just the early part."

"Oh, you'll get tired and take me for granted, as most contented husbands do their wives."

"Never."

"Is that a promise?"

"Cross my heart."

The next morning Augusta fixed breakfast for them.

"Do you have anything special planned for today?" Derek asked.

"Not really, since I have no papers that need grading and neither you nor I will be going in to the Institute today. What did you have in mind?"

Derek laughed. "Well…"

"Oh, you, not after last night?"

"You can't blame a guy for trying. Seriously, I thought we might drive to Palmyra this afternoon to hear the Junior Blind Choir sing Handel's *Messiah*. Tammy has a solo."

"That's wonderful! She did tell me she was trying out. I am so glad she got a part. This is a perfect opportunity for her, Todd. Oh, yes, I definitely want to go. But then, you knew I would. Is this a program that's done every year?"

"Yes, it is. It took some convincing to get Tammy to try out, but I finally got her to agree."

"Have you told her about our engagement?"

"Ah, no, not yet."

"You're the worst procrastinator, Todd Winters."

"I know." Derek looked intently at Augusta. She just didn't know how much of a procrastinator he really was. "It might snow, so you'd better wear something warm. If you need any help dressing, I can offer my services, for a fee of course."

"I can do it myself, thank you."

"You can't…"

"I know, you can't blame a guy for trying. You're really something else."

"No, I'm not, I'm all male."

"How well I know that."

Augusta centered her attention on Tammy Gibson when it came her turn to solo. She had the voice of an angel. And when she had finished her part and joined the rest of the choir, Augusta sat in awe listening to the young voices.

Augusta had been thinking about Tammy a lot over the past few weeks. She reminded her so much of herself at that age. She'd felt just as alone and had erected just as many barriers. How she would have loved to have someone who really cared about her!

She wanted so much to help this girl with whom she felt a deep kinship. Though no longer as resistant to her overtures of help, Tammy still kept a tight rein on her thoughts and feelings, as if she dared not open herself to anyone. Augusta couldn't help believing that having someone take a more personal interest in Tammy might make all the difference in the woman she would become.

Once more, she found herself wondering whether she herself ought to be that "someone." Would Tammy consider letting her become her foster mother? Or maybe even adopt her? Would she want to after she found out about her engagement to Todd? Once they were married, Tammy could be a big sister to the children she and Todd planned to have. It wouldn't make up for the loss of her brothers and sister, but maybe it would help.

Augusta squeezed Todd's hand.

"What is it, Doc?"

"What do you think about my becoming Tammy's foster mother? We'd probably be more like sisters, though."

"Wow, that's quite a question, Doc. How long have you been thinking about that?"

"A while. What do you think?"

"I think you're exactly the kind of person Tammy needs. But are you sure you want to take on that responsibility? Tammy can be moody and damned difficult, as you've already found out."

"I know that, but I want her, moods and all. That girl needs somebody to love and care about her, Todd. I want to be that someone."

Augusta's announcement didn't take Derek totally by surprise. Though he had said nothing, he had observed her growing attachment to Tammy. And Tammy was at a precarious point in her young life. She could just as easily go in the wrong direction as otherwise, unless someone who really cared provided support and encouragement. "I think it's a great idea," he answered. "But you'll have to go before the judge. The court may or may not agree."

"You mean because of my blindness? That's discrimination. I'd make as good a mother as any sighted person. Just let me speak to that judge."

Derek smiled. His Augusta could be a formidable adversary when riled. He pitied anybody who opposed her when she was in a mood like this. She was magnificent. "I'm sure with the Institute behind you, you won't have too much of a problem. Diane and Joan can attest to your abilities. Not to mention yours truly."

"You realize that that'll mean, if I can convince a judge to let me have her, Tammy will be living with us after we're married. Or maybe even living with me before that. Are you sure you won't mind?"

"Maybe just a little."

"Todd!"

"That's only because I've become accustomed to making love to you anytime I want to."

"Are you sure that's your only objection? You'll have just as many other things to adjust to as Tammy and I will." Then Augusta flashed him her sexiest smile. "She won't be around all the time, darling. She's seventeen. We probably won't have her with us long before she becomes absorbed in her singing career. Wouldn't it be wonderful if she went to Julliard or some other music school?"

"You're kind of getting ahead of yourself, aren't you? We don't know if you'll be able to get her yet. She may not even want to live with us."

"You mean because of her feelings for you? I've thought of that. I agree that it might be a problem."

"To test the waters, I think we'd better tell her about our engagement first. Don't you?"

Augusta caressed his cheek. "Oh, and while we're on the subject, after we're married I want us to have three kids of our own."

"Oh, you do, do you? All at once, or one at a time?"

Augusta playfully punched him in the ribs. "One at a time, of course."

"The lady has a heart as big as all outdoors."

She ignored his teasing. "I hope they'll all be like Kelsey. She's such a sweet child. You remember her from the accident."

"Yes, I remember." How could he ever forget?

On the way back to Augusta's house, Derek was quiet.

Augusta touched his arm. "Are you thinking what I'm thinking?"

He glanced at her. "I don't know. What are you thinking?"

Augusta teased him again in a deliberately husky voice. "About how wonderful it's going to be after we're married."

"Yes, I was thinking that exact same thing. It proves that great minds think alike. That reminds me. We haven't set a date for the wedding. How about next week?"

"I was thinking more along the lines of New Year's Eve or Valentine's Day."

"Valentine's Day! That's a little...corny."

"Romantic," Augusta responded and pinched him.

"Ouch—that isn't funny." He rubbed the abused area on his arm and groaned as though he were in extreme pain.

"Oh, you!" She kissed it better. "What do you really think?"

"Whenever you want to get married will be fine with me, Doc."

"Don't just agree with me, I want feedback, any suggestions you may have—within reason, of course."

Derek took her in his arms. "I say the sooner the better. It's already impossible to keep my hands off you as it is. Three more months of waiting will kill me."

"No, it won't. You do think I'm worth the wait, don't you?"

"Honey, yes." He kissed the space behind her ear and traced a path of kisses down her neck.

"It's still early. You want to go for a walk? I think Bella needs some exercise. Since you've been hanging around all the time, she and I haven't gone out much."

"Hanging around?"

She could picture the expression on his face. "You know what I mean."

"Yes, I do. I wouldn't want to deprive Bella in any way, since it was my idea that you get her in the first place."

"Had you only known that you would be personally keeping me from being alone."

"Are you intimating that I've become your lap dog?"

"Oh, no, I would never insinuate such a thing about you," she said in a serious tone, but spoiled it by letting a giggle escape.

"Why you—I'll get you for that," he grabbed her fleeing figure and wrestled her to the carpet.

Augusta said breathlessly, "You promise?"

Derek caressed her cheek, then kissed her mouth. "If we're going to go for that walk, we'd better go now or we might not make it at all."

Derek built up the fire after they returned from their walk. Joining Augusta on the love seat, he put his arm around her shoulders and pulled her close to him.

"I'm going to be out of town this weekend."

Augusta took his hand in hers. "Oh, why?"

"I've been chosen to represent the Institute at Help the Blind Children Read Foundation in Charlotte, North Carolina."

"That's quite an honor, isn't it?"

"I wish I could go with you."

"Me, too. Not that I need moral support, you understand."

"Oh, no, you just want a warm body to keep you from getting cold at night."

"You got it." He laughed.

"Seriously, Todd, I would like to hear you speak."

"It's going to be shown on…"

"You were going to say television, weren't you? Todd, darling, things like that don't bother me anymore. I can hear it even if I can't see it." It warmed her heart that he was so sensitive to her needs. Todd was a very special man, one in a million, and all hers. She thanked her lucky stars for him.

"It's going to be broadcast at six o'clock, Monday night on Station WCEB, the educational station."

"I'm so proud of you."

Derek hugged her tight. He wanted to say, "You are responsible, my darling. You've changed my life. You are my life." But he didn't. He just held her close, enjoying the feel of her soft, warm body against his.

Before long Augusta fell asleep in his arms. He brushed a stray wisp of hair away from her face and kissed her cheek. "You're so precious to me, my love.

You're the kind of woman a man searches a lifetime for and rarely, if ever, finds," he whispered. The thought of losing her sent chills racing down his back and fear stampeding into his heart. He had to tell her the truth, but...

But what?

Her love for me is strong.

But is it strong enough?

That was the two million dollar question. Would anyone's be that strong, considering all she'd gone through as a result of the accident. The pain, the sense of loss, the depression. All the time in the hospital, the surgeries to remove the scarring caused by the shards of glass that cut her face. She'd survived it all.

But can she survive your deception once she knows the truth?

He eased Augusta out of his lap and stood up.

"Todd?" Augusta called out in a sleep-husky voice.

"I'm right here, baby."

"You're not leaving yet, are you?"

"I really should be going. I have a lot of things to take care of before I leave for North Carolina on Friday."

"I know I'm being selfish, but I want you to stay a while longer."

"All right, but just for a little while." Derek laughed softly.

Augusta smiled and held out her hands to him. He pulled her to her feet, then lifted her in his arms and carried her to the bedroom.

Shortly before dawn, he finally went home.

Derek came to the solarium to pick Augusta up after her class ended. He purposely arrived earlier than usual because they had decided to tell Tammy about their engagement and broach the subject of Augusta becoming her foster mother. The last of the students were shuffling out of the classroom as he approached.

Before Tammy could leave, Augusta asked her to wait because she had something she wanted to talk to her about.

"What is it, Miss Humphrey?" Tammy asked. "I've done all my assignments."

"Yes, you have, and I'm proud of you. I wanted to congratulate you on your fantastic performance in the Christmas concert. After hearing you perform in public, I think you have a good chance of making it in the music industry. But that isn't all I wanted to talk to you about, though." Relief flooded through Augusta when she heard Todd's reassuring footsteps.

"*We* have something to tell you," Derek added.

"'Tell me what?"

"Augusta and I are engaged to be married."

A pregnant silence enveloped the room for what seemed liked hours but could only have been a matter of seconds.

Augusta broke the silence. "There's something else." She swallowed hard then said. "What would you say to my becoming your foster mother?"

Tammy remained silent.

"Talk to us, Tammy," Augusta said anxiously.

"I don't know what to say. I mean..."

"I know we've hit you with a lot in one shot," Derek began. "But..."

Tammy interrupted and addressed the engagement issue first. "When did you get engaged?"

"A few days ago. How do you feel about it?" Augusta asked.

"Well, I'm not surprised. I know that you two love each other. I've accepted it...and I'm happy for you."

Derek watched the expression on Tammy's face, wondering whether to believe her.

As though sensing his doubt, Tammy said, "I'm telling it like it is, Mr. Winters. I really am happy for you both. I'm over my feelings about you."

Augusta was relieved to hear Tammy say those words. "About the other—how do you feel about me becoming your foster mother?"

"Why do you want to? Do you feel sorry for me?"

"Feel sorry for you? No, Tammy, I care about you, you know that. I want to make a home for you."

"Why? 'Specially after the mean things I did and said."

"I knew you were only saying them and acting like that because you were hurting. I understood, believe me."

"What about you, Mr. Winters? What do you think? You sure you gonna want me hanging around all the time after you're married?"

"Listen, Tammy, I care about you just as much as Augusta does. Having you in our home would make us both very happy."

"You really mean that?"

Augusta put her arm around Tammy's shoulders. "We really mean it."

"If you really want to be my mother…" She couldn't finish her sentence; emotion clogged her throat.

"I want you to be my daughter, Tammy." Tears slid down Augusta's face.

Derek felt his own eyes misting at the poignancy of the moment.

"Will the judge let you be my mother?" Tammy asked uncertainly.

"He'd better," Augusta answered softly, but with purpose.

Derek made up his mind to use every ounce of influence the Institute had to ensure that the judge would rule in their favor. He knew that Diane and

John would back him up. It might take some time, but Augusta would have Tammy in her home.

Augusta waited anxiously on the couch with Bella at her side for the program to come on. When she heard Todd's voice, her imagination started working overtime, visualizing how he looked. Then the interviewer asked.

"How long have you worked with the blind, Todd?"

She heard the hesitation in his voice before he answered, "Fifteen months."

Fifteen months? But she thought that it had been a lot longer. He must have started right after her accident. She hadn't realized the death of the woman he loved had occurred that recently. No wonder he seemed so distant and so sad at times. Did he still love the other woman? Of course he did. Was it stronger than his love for her? She couldn't help wondering.

The interviewer continued to ask questions. "What did you do before you started working at the Institute?"

"I have an electronics business I inherited from my father."

"Are you very involved with it now?"

"Only in a limited capacity. I have a business manager who handles the actual day-to-day work."

"How did you get started working with the blind?"

Derek's voice faltered slightly as he formed his answer "S—someone I love dearly was my inspiration."

Was he referring to the other woman or to her, Augusta couldn't help questioning. Surely he didn't consider her simply a substitute for his lost love. Of course he didn't. Why was she letting her insecurities jerk her around like this? Todd loved her for herself.

Try as hard as she might, Augusta couldn't completely erase from her thoughts the possibility that he might feel that way. She heard the interviewer ask Todd questions about the Institute and what he did there, the latest techniques and equipment they used.

Augusta only half-listened to the rest of the program. She missed Todd so much. It had been the longest two days of her life. She needed him here with her now. She was convinced that he was truly her soul mate.

As though sensing her mistress's anxiety, Bella rubbed her cold nose against Augusta's hand.

She patted the dog's head. "I'll live, Bella," she laughed softly. "It just seems like I won't. I know he loves me."

Augusta had just showered and changed into her gown and robe when the phone rang. She hurried to answer it.

"Is that you, Todd?"

"Yes, it's me, baby."

"When will you be home?"

"In two hours. I'm calling from the airport. I can hardly wait to get home to you."

"Those are the most precious words in the world to me right now."

"Are you crying?"

"Tears of gladness, my darling."

"I hear the last boarding call. Got to go. See you in the morning. Good night, Doc."

"Good night, Todd."

Augusta drifted to sleep with joy in her heart.

CHAPTER XVI

It had been a week since she'd gone before the judge. Augusta felt sure she had made a good impression. She recalled what he'd said.

"Dr. Humphrey, are you quite sure you're prepared for the responsibility of a teenager, a blind teenager with a troubled past?"

"Yes, I am, Your Honor. I, better than anyone else, know what it's like to be shuffled from one foster home to another, one residential home to another. I also know what it's like to be blind."

"I don't doubt your sincerity, Doctor. I just question if you're really ready for this after so recently losing your own sight and having to redirect your personal as well as professional life."

She ignored the latter part of what he said. "It's because I so recently lost my sight that I'm the best person to deal with Tammy since she, too, so recently lost hers."

"You're certainly determined to help this young woman, aren't you?"

"Yes, I am."

"Why?"

"She needs me, Your Honor, as much as I need her."

"You'll be the fifth foster family I've placed her with in the last year. Are you aware of the attitude problems she's exhibited in the past?"

"Oh, I'm aware all right. She's done that in my class at the Institute."

"And how have you handled it?"

"With understanding and a willingness to listen."

"Has that always worked?"

"For the most part. Look, I know what you're trying to do, and believe me, I'm aware that there may be problems. But I'm willing to take them on."

"I'll give careful consideration to everything you've said." Augusta fervently hoped he would decide to rule in her favor. When would she know?

Surely he'd grant her request to become Tammy's foster mother. He just had to.

She put the dishes in the dishwasher and went into the living room to sit in front of the fireplace and practice her crocheting. Myra, so oldfashioned in so many ways, had insisted on teaching her the craft. She said it would come in handy once the babies started coming. Her friend seemed so up since going to Alicia Crawford. Augusta hoped that everything would work out for Myra and Ben, that they would produce the family they both wanted so desperately.

She had just finished a row when the doorbell chimed. Bella rose from her place by her mistress and padded to the door ahead of her.

"Augusta, it's me, Todd," he called out.

The dog recognized Todd's voice and moved aside, but remained alert. Augusta opened the door.

"I brought you a surprise."

"A surprise?"

"It's me, Miss Humphrey."

"Tammy!"

"I'm all yours. If you still want me."

Augusta hugged her. "If I want you? Oh, I want you all right! I'm so happy. Call us by our first names, please!" Then she turned and asked, "Why didn't you call me, Todd?"

"It wouldn't have been a surprise if I'd done that, now would it?"

"Come on in."

"I have to go back out to the car and get Tammy's things."

Augusta introduced Tammy to Bella and listened as the dog sniffed her hand and then loudly lapped it.

"I think she likes you."

"I've always liked dogs, but I've never been allowed to have a pet."

"Bella is more than a pet; she's my eyes as well as being a guard dog.

Augusta led Tammy into the bedroom Elaine had occupied. It had its own bathroom and a small sitting room.

"I hope you like it."

"Oh, I do!"

Derek brought Tammy's bags into the room.

"While you're familiarizing yourself with everything, Todd and I are going into the living room to talk."

"Okay. Can Bella kick it with me?"

"Sure she can. Stay, Bella," Augusta commanded the dog. Then she and Derek returned to the living room.

"I could kiss you for bringing her here."

"Nothing's stopping you, Doc."

They sat down on the love seat.

Derek said. "I think you and Tammy are going to work out fine."

"Me, too. She and Melody should hit it off. They're the same age."

"How's your relationship with Melody's mother?"

"That's another story. I don't think Jean Cummings and I will ever be close friends."

"As long as you and I remain close friends, that's all I care about."

"Oh, I think we always will. We are more than just close friends, Todd, we love and trust one another completely."

Tell her, Morgan.

"Augusta, I…"

"You guys done talking?" Tammy asked upon entering the room.

"Yes, we are. You and Bella getting along all right?"

"Oh, yes. She's great."

Derek rose to his feet. "I'd better be going, Doc."

"Oh, do you have to go so soon?"

"I have a heavy schedule tomorrow. The new man John hired is out with the flu and I have to take over his classes."

Outside in his car minutes later, Derek scolded himself for being a coward.

He should have stayed to tell Augusta the truth. *You'd better find the right time, Morgan.*

I know, but there never seems to be one.

Derek helped Augusta finish grading the last of the semester exams from the college. Tammy was next door visiting with Melody.

"You're a compassionate instructor, Augusta, to give the exam before the Christmas holidays. I remember an instructor I had in college who enjoyed watching his students sweat it out."

Augusta laughed. "I can tell he was one of your favorites."

"Don't mock me, woman."

"Would I do you like that?"

"In a word, yes."

"You don't trust me?"

The hint of amusement suddenly left his voice. "I do, baby."

"You sound so serious."

"I am about you. I trust you with my life."

Augusta frowned in concern at his vehemence.

"Darling, I was only kidding, I know you do, just as I trust you."

You're cracking up, Morgan, tell her the truth, man.

Derek opened his mouth to tell her.

"Todd, I have some last-minute Christmas shopping I want to do this afternoon. Can you drop Bella and me off downtown?"

Tell her.

"Augusta, I—"

"If you're too busy to take us, we can always go on the bus."

"It's not that. The icy sidewalks can be treacherous."

"Then you'll take us?"

"Yes, I'll take you."

Coward.

"I have something I have to do at the Institute. Call me when you're finished and I'll come and get you."

"You don't have to. We can…"

He kissed the tip of her nose. "Call me!"

"Yes, sir."

"I love you."

Augusta smiled. "I know."

Derek dropped Augusta and Bella off in front of Gold's Department store. At the information desk, the clerk told her what floor the music department was on and directed her to the elevators. As she and Bella stepped off the elevator seconds later, a saleswoman approached her.

"May I help you?"

"Yes, I want something special for my daughter. She's interested in a singing career. She wants to make a tape, but we don't have a piano. What would you suggest?"

"We have music keyboards with special features."

"That sounds perfect."

"If you would follow me."

Augusta prompted Bella forward.

Later, after she'd chosen her gift, Augusta and Bella left the store. With the help of a policeman, they found the other place she wanted to go to: Vandiver's Jewelers. The sound of Christmas carols and the animated voices of shoppers assaulted their ears as they entered the store.

"Ma'am, animals aren't allowed—oh, I'm sorry," came a young male voice to their left.

Bella pulled against her harness, alert and ready to act if necessary. "Easy, girl, the man doesn't mean me any harm."

Augusta heard him gulp nervously. "N-no, I..."

"Bella won't hurt you. Maybe you can help me."

"My name is Edward, and I'd be only too happy to, ma'am," he said in a relieved voice that relayed his eagerness to make amends for his blunder.

"First, I'd like to see your best collection of gold watches."

"Ah, yes, right away. Would you step this way, please." He guided her and Bella to a display counter across the large showroom floor.

Bella lay down beside Augusta's chair. Augusta heard the clerk slide a glass door aside. He guided her hand to a tray of watches. She examined several before coming to a watch with a large face and a heavy gold chain wristband.

"This is the one I want."

The clerk said in a surprised voice, "You've made an excellent choice considering..."

"Considering that I can't see it?" Augusta smiled. "The soul of tact you aren't, but you'll learn. I want it engraved with these words: 'To the man I will love forever, from Augusta.' How soon can you have it ready?"

"Friday. Would you like it gift wrapped?"

"That would be wonderful."

"Where would you like it delivered?"

Augusta gave him the medical school building's address. "It has to be delivered after one o'clock, not before."

"I'll personally see that it is."

Days before Christmas Eve, Augusta called on Ben Hastings.

"You're not due for a check-up for another three weeks, Augusta."

"I know, but I came to see you for a different reason."

"Let me guess: Todd Winters."

"You think you know everything."

"Most of the time where you're concerned, I do. Now what do you want to know?"

Augusta laughed. "You're priceless, Ben."

"He loves you, Augusta."

"I know that, but…"

"But what?"

"He's been so moody lately. There's something bothering him, and he won't tell me what it is. I thought maybe…"

"I might know what it is? I do, but he has to be the one to tell you about it, Augusta."

"Can't you even give me a hint?"

"No, I can't, I'm sorry."

She could tell by the way he said it she wouldn't get anything else out of him. He could be as closed-mouthed as a clam. Damn him!

"I know you're calling me all kinds of names in that fertile mind of yours, but I can't betray his confidence."

She said in a frustrated tone of voice, "I expected as much and I understand, but I don't like it."

"Be patient; he'll tell you when he's ready."

"I hope you're right. I don't like it when he suffers in silence. Doesn't he know that he can confide anything in me?"

"I'm sure it's not that, Augusta. I won't say any more; just be patient, all right?"

"All right." She sighed. "Now on to the other reason I came to see you. I'd like to invite you and Myra to join Todd and me and Tammy for Christmas dinner at my house."

"You doing the cooking?"

"Ben!"

He laughed. "We'd be happy to come. Myra's been complaining about not seeing enough of you lately."

"I've been so busy adjusting to teaching and recently getting the semester exams together, and, most importantly, adjusting to having a daughter."

"How are things going with Tammy?"

"I wish I could say it's always been smooth sailing."

"She giving you much trouble?"

"Not really. We've had our problems adjusting to each other's ways. For example, she's not used to anyone being concerned about what she wears. She told me that it didn't matter what colors she wore since she couldn't see whether they clashed or not. I had a hard time getting her to understand it mattered to people who see her." Augusta laughed ruefully and then added, "We've been working on her wardrobe."

"What about this attitude problem Todd mentioned?"

"She definitely has one, but I think it's a defense barrier against being hurt. We've talked about it. And it's getting better, a little bit at a time."

"You're really enjoying being a mother to this girl, aren't you?"

"Yes, I am, Ben. It's going to work out, you'll see." Augusta changed the subject. "I'm going to spend more time with Myra." As they talked, she realized that Myra hadn't told him anything about going to Alicia.

"Augusta, you're too much."

"At times so are you, Ben." She laughed.

"Everybody wants to be a comedian," he grumbled.

"Derek."

He looked up from some papers he was sorting through. "Ben! What are you doing here at the Institute?"

"Is that any way to greet a friend?"

"Sorry." He laughed.

"As a matter of fact, I had a meeting with Diane and thought I'd kill two birds with one stone, as the saying goes, and come see you."

Derek grinned. "Come on in and take a load off."

"That's better. By the way, I had a visit from Augusta yesterday. She's invited Myra and me to Christmas dinner."

"Yeah, I know. What did you say to her?"

"Don't worry, I didn't give anything away. Man, when are you going to tell her yourself? I thought you were all set to do that the last time I talked to you."

"Have you become the voice of my conscience or what? I was going to tell her, but every time I started to, it just didn't seem like the right time. I'll tell her soon."

"You've been saying that for months. Mark my words, you're going to regret putting it off so long."

"I intend to tell her after the holidays. I can't go on like this. The guilt is eating me alive." He rose from his chair, stretching his arms and swiveling his neck. "She's going to be hurt, Ben. And that's the last thing I want to do."

"It may not be as bad as you think."

"Get real, Ben. You know Augusta better than anyone."

"Haven't you heard that love heals all wounds, forgives all things?"

"Sure it does."

"Don't sound so skeptical. She'll forgive you. It just may take time for her to forget, that's all."

"How much time?"

"I can't answer that."

"Exactly." Derek sighed. "I know she has to be told sooner or later. I just wish it could be much, much later, like never."

"Life can be a real bitch, can't it?"

"You got that right."

Augusta put the last ornament on the tree, all except the top one.

"I guess you're waiting for me to do the honors," Derek said wryly.

"It took you long enough to get the tree. You've got to be the biggest procrastinator of all time, Todd Winters. Besides, you're taller than me."

"Me, too." Tammy added her two cents worth.

"What a cop out! Women!" You're so right about the former, Augusta. Procrastinator or not, he was going to tell her the truth. It was one New Year's resolution he would keep. He placed the angel on top. "There, I've done it. Satisfied now, Doc?"

"I hope you've got it on straight." Augusta placed the presents under the tree. "Don't you think I deserve a reward for orchestrating this whole thing?"

"What kind of reward did you have in mind?"

"I'll tell you later," she whispered in his ear. "Ben and Myra will be here any minute. I'm going to check on dinner."

The doorbell pealed.

"Would you get that, Todd?" Augusta said over her shoulder as she headed for the kitchen.

"The dinner was delicious, Augusta," Ben remarked appreciatively.

"Jammin'," Tammy eagerly seconded.

"Where did you learn to cook like that?" Myra asked.

"Joan Gordon's Cooking School."

"Joan Gordon? I've never heard of her."

"She teaches at the Braille Institute."

"Maybe I should go over there and take a few lessons."

"Amen to that."

"Oh, shut up, Ben," Myra shot back.

"You guys aren't going to start *Family Feud* in my living room, are you?" Augusta laughed.

"No, I'll bop him on the head when I get him home."

Ben looked to Derek. "Maybe I should go home with you tonight, buddy."

Derek shook his head and smiled. Ben and Myra reminded him of the way his parents had gotten along, always teasing one another in fun. He hoped that he and Augusta would have the chance to be together long enough to enjoy that kind of rapport.

After clearing the table and washing the dishes, the couples and Tammy sat relaxing before the fireplace, drinking hot apple cider and talking.

"By the way, have you two set a wedding date?" Myra asked.

Derek looked anxiously at Augusta. "Augusta thinks Valentine's Day would be the perfect time."

Myra sighed. "It sounds so romantic."

"You women, honestly." Ben teased.

In an aside loud enough to be heard by the two men, Myra confided, "Between you and me, he's about as romantic as a soda cracker."

"I resent that. I distinctly remember buying you quite a few dozen roses and boxes of candy over the years, Mrs. Hastings."

"Maybe we should renew our vows when Todd and Augusta take theirs."

"I had to open my big mouth."

Myra punched him in the arm.

"Hey, watch that, woman!"

Derek, Augusta, and Tammy laughed at their antics.

"We wouldn't mind if you joined us and made it a double wedding," Augusta said. "Tammy's going to be my maid of honor. She could be yours too, Myra."

"What kind of dresses are you two going to wear?" Myra asked.

"We've all got to be coordinated."

"Here we go with the woman's page," Ben commented.

Myra stood in front of her husband, hands on hips. "Ben Hastings, you're cruising for a bruising."

"Listen to the mouse that roared, would you," Ben put in.

They all laughed because Myra barely made five feet two inches in her stocking feet, tipping the scales at a hundred pounds, soaking wet.

"It's time to exchange presents." Derek rose from his place in front of the fireplace, pulled Augusta to her feet and then took Tammy's hand.

"I'm all for that," Ben said, tugging at Myra.

They walked over to the tree. Derek handed the gifts he and Augusta and Tammy had gotten for the Hastings to Ben and Myra. Ben reached for the ones he and his wife had gotten for Augusta, Derek, and Tammy.

"Who wants to go first?" Augusta cleared her throat.

Ben spoke up. "Me."

Myra snickered. "You would."

"Now, Myra, my love, you know I am but a child at heart." He unwrapped Augusta's gift to him. It was an engraved, nickel-plated optical light, the kind that clipped onto a shirt pocket. "Augusta, it—it's..."

"The great Ben Hastings is, for once, at a loss for words," Myra teased. "I love it!"

Ben kissed Augusta's cheek, then opened the gift from Derek. "A matching pen-and-pencil set with a crystal paperweight."

"If you kiss me, so help me I'll deck you," Derek said.

"In that case, I guess a simple thank you will suffice."

"I don't know you very well, but I like you both," Tammy said to Ben and Myra and handed them her gift.

"Thank you, Tammy," Myra said softly.

"Add my thanks to Myra's, Tammy," Ben added. "If I had any doubts about your coming to live with Augusta, I don't any more. I'm glad she has you."

Ben took the wrapping off the present. It was a cassette tape. He walked over to the stereo and put it in the cassette deck. They all sat mesmerized by the beauty of the voice on the tape.

"Is this you?" Ben asked Tammy.

"Yes."

"You have a beautiful voice, Tammy!" Myra exclaimed.

"Thank you. Do you really like the tape?"

"Yes, we do," Ben and Myra said in unison.

Ben turned to Augusta and Derek. "Hey, you've got a kid with real talent."

"We know," Derek answered. "Now for my present to you, Tammy."

Derek handed her an envelope.

"What is it?"

"Open it up and find out."

Tammy broke the seal on the envelope and pulled out the paper written in Braille. Derek watched while she read it.

"I can't believe it. It says that I have been accepted at Julliard School of Music. It's what I..."

"And Jeffrey Osborne has agreed to work with you on a demo tape when you're ready."

"Jeffrey Osborne! I love his music. Are you serious?"

"Yes, I am."

"Oh, thank you, Todd." She hugged him tight.

"Now for my gift to you, Tammy," Augusta said, guiding her hand to a large present.

"It's big, what's in it?" She tore the wrapping off, opened the box and ran her fingers across the surface of her present. "It's a keyboard! Oh, thank you, Augusta. I love you so much." They embraced fiercely.

"It's our turn," Ben inserted. He handed the present to Tammy.

"From the Hastings to you, Tammy."

She unwrapped a small box and lifted out an oval object. "It's a music box!" She examined it with her fingers, found the winder on the side near the base, and turned it. "Hero," one of Mariah Carey's songs, floated up. "I love it. Thank you both."

"It was our pleasure, Tammy," Myra said gently.

"Now it's your turn, Myra," Augusta chirped excitedly.

"Before I open it, I have an announcement to make. Ben, after seven years of marriage I'm finally going to give you what you really want."

"You don't mean..."

"Yes, a baby," Myra laughed softly. "He's speechless twice in the same night. Don't you just love it?"

"Congratulations, you two," Derek said in a pleased voice.

Augusta picked up on the excitement in his voice. Having children was definitely important to him. She remembered him saying how lonely he was as an only child. Once they were married, she would give him a family to love and care for.

Ben spoke gently to Myra when he finally found his voice. "When will the new addition to our family arrive, my love?"

"July. Any preferences?"

"No. Just that it be healthy and beautiful like its lovely mother."

"Now if that isn't romantic, I don't know what is," Augusta commented. "Now, open my gift."

"The box is heavy." Myra lifted it up and down. "What have you got in here? Lead?"

"You have to open it and find out."

She tore the wrapping paper off and opened the box. "Three boxes?" Myra opened the first one. "A cup with 'Mother' written on it." She opened the next one. "A cup with 'Father.'" Myra handed it to Ben, then opened the last one. "A training cup that says 'Baby.' Oh, Augusta." She sniffed. Myra hugged her friend. "Thank you, we'll treasure them always."

Ben put his arm around Myra's shoulders and kissed her cheek. He placed a hand on Augusta's shoulder and simply offered his thanks.

Derek could tell by Ben's expression he wished he could do more for Augusta. Damn it, there had to be a doctor who could help her. He would never stop searching for him or her.

"All right, my friends, open your gifts from us," Ben said.

Derek guided Augusta's hand to the box and let her tear the wrapping paper off. She felt something soft. Was it yarn? Sweaters? No. She frowned, confused.

"They are twin afghans, Augusta. I crocheted them myself," volunteered Myra proudly. "The pink one is yours and the blue is Todd's. It's for those cold nights after you're married."

Ben let out an amused sigh. "I told her body heat would..."

"Ben Hastings!" Myra sputtered. "Be quiet, there's a minor in our midst."

Augusta and Derek laughed. Tammy grinned.

Later, after Ben and Myra had left and Tammy had gone to her room, Derek and Augusta picked up their presents to each other.

"Open yours first, Todd."

He carefully removed the paper and opened the watch case. "It's fantastic, Augusta." He brushed his lips across hers.

Augusta smiled. "Read the inscription."

"'To the man I will love forever.'" Derek's eyes misted with emotion. "I'll treasure it always." He took his old watch off and slipped the new one on in its place.

Augusta reached for her present. She could tell it was a jewelry case after she removed the wrapping paper. She opened the lid, moved her fingers over a large heart-shaped pendant, and lifted it out of its velvet bed.

"Turn it over, there's an inscription."

Augusta read the Braille engraving with her fingers. "'I cherish you.' Oh, Todd, I love you so much!"

"I love you more, Augusta. Please, don't ever doubt it, no matter what. Now, before the doorbell interrupted us, what were you saying about a reward?"

Augusta hugged him tight. But his words "no matter what" struck her as strange. Something about them made her frown in concern. Of course she'd love him no matter what.

CHAPTER XVII

On Christmas morning, Derek, Augusta, and Tammy ventured out in the front yard and made a snowman.

After they finished the man of snow, Tammy placed a hat on his head. "What do you think, Todd?"

"Looks—great."

"How does the nose I stuck in look, Todd?" Augusta asked.

"Great."

"I'll have to take your word for it that I put it in the right place."

"Don't you trust me?" Derek kissed her cold cheek. "Now, would I lie to you?" He winced at his accidental choice of words.

Glancing at Tammy, he thought about how far she had come in accepting him as a part of Augusta's life. He remembered an incident that had happened soon after she moved in. He'd come to see Augusta…

"You promised to help me finish my project after dinner," Tammy said to Augusta with pointed emphasis.

"I will a little later, Tammy. Todd hasn't been over in..."

Tammy sighed exasperatedly.

"Maybe you'd better..."

"No, Todd. Tammy has to learn to be patient and considerate of other people's feelings. As we all must. Now Tammy, you apologize to Todd."

For a moment he had thought Tammy would stomp away in a huff, but she surprised him by telling him she was sorry. He could see that it wasn't easy for her to bow to another person's will. Augusta chastened her in such a loving way that Tammy found it hard not to do what she said.

Sensing that Derek and Augusta wanted to be alone, Tammy quickly interjected, "I've been invited to spend the day with Melody. Mrs. Cummings wants me to eat dinner and stay the night. Is it okay?"

"Yes," Augusta answered with a smile. Tammy had come a long way from that rebellious girl she had been. If it had been a few weeks ago, she would not have asked permission; she would have simply announced what she was going to do. There had been times when Todd came over and Tammy seemed almost jealous and reacted predictably. Yes, all three of them had experienced growing pains, and no doubt would continue to do so. Getting used to each other definitely was not a piece of cake.

"I'll go and get my things."

Derek waited until Tammy was on the Cummings' porch, then said, "What do you want to do with the rest of the afternoon, Doc?"

"Well…"

"I thought so."

Augusta pressed her lips on his. "The best way I know to get warm is to share body heat."

"I'm not arguing the point." Derek lifted her in his arms and carried her into the house.

Later, wrapped in only the Christmas presents Ben and Myra had given them, Derek and Augusta sat before the fire.

"This is the best Christmas I've had in a long time. I guess because it's my first Christmas with you and Tammy."

"I feel the same way, Augusta. You're everything I've ever desired. And having Tammy around is like having the little sister I always wanted." He slipped the afghan off her shoulders. "Enough talking., woman." Derek kissed Augusta's throat and her collarbone, then moved lower to her breasts. He cherished a nipple with his tongue. Augusta quivered, and a moan of pleasure left her lips.

"Oh, Todd, what are you doing to me?"

He worried the other nipple until it was taut.

She gasped. "I can't stand it."

He bared the rest of her. "Yes, you can," he whispered against the soft, yet firm flesh of her stomach. He found her bud of desire and teased it with his tongue.

Augusta cried out when an instant wash of ecstasy rushed over her. "This is for you, my love." His voice thickened. "I want to pleasure you out of your mind."

Augusta moaned. "What mind? I don't have one left."

He shook his afghan off and eased his body over hers, settling himself between her thighs. In one swift movement he was inside her, working his magic, driving her to the brink and beyond.

Augusta wrapped her legs around his hips and moved beneath him in love's unique ritual. Derek meshed their bodies together, the friction of their joining building, building toward that infinite, human implosion of love.

When he felt her passion erupt, only then did he join in the celebration. Their cries of rapture as they soared to the heavens blended in a jagged harmony.

"My love, you were magnificent," Derek gasped, his voice ragged. "It just gets better and better between us."

"I know. Each time I tell myself it can't, but..."

"I want you to come to my place for a private New Year's Eve party. I'll provide the food."

"But you don't cook."

"Mama's has agreed to deliver their New Year's Eve special. Black-eyed peas, ham, and cornbread. And a side order of crab leg stew for me. I'll make the eggnog from my father's recipe."

"You're lucky that Tammy's spending that night with the Cummings."

"I'm a lucky guy, all right. Tammy and Melody have certainly become close friends, haven't they?"

"I'm glad. Tammy needs a friend her own age. And so does Melody."

"You're a born mother; you worry about everybody." Derek kissed Augusta again. "Now, about my invitation?"

"I take it Bella isn't invited either?"

"Not this time. I want you all to myself when we ring in the new year. You know, whatever you're doing when the new year begins, you'll be doing it the same time next year. And, Augusta, be warned, I want to be making love to you on the stroke of midnight every New Year's Eve."

"I like the sound of that. I'll be there with bells on."

"I thought we agreed that you would leave Bella at home. Gotcha."

"You know what? You are a complete nut!" She kissed him quiet.

"The ball at Times Square has almost reached the top, Augusta, hurry up out of the shower."

"I'm not finished yet."

Derek rushed into the bathroom and joined her. He lifted Augusta and wrapped her legs around his waist, lovingly impaling her just as the clock struck midnight."

"Determined to get your own way, weren't you?"

"Any objections?"

"Not a—ooh, Todd." She gasped as he moved her against the wall and loved her.

It was the longest shower they'd ever had.

Afterward, they shared a bottle of champagne and fell asleep intimately entwined.

Derek and Augusta spent most of the next day making love and lounging in bed. At three o'clock she got up and showered. When she came out of the bathroom, Derek was waiting for her by the door.

He wrapped his arms around her. "Do you really have to go now?"

"Yes. I have to get home before Tammy does. And I have to take care of Bella."

"I need taking care of, too."

Augusta laughed. "Poor baby."

"I'm serious." He teased a nipple.

She gasped and eased out of his reach. "I'm sure you are, but I have to go."

"Let's go out later."

"All right. Where do you want to go? I'm getting to be an expert at going out, thanks to you."

"I've never taken you to the Cameo Room."

"I like the name."

"It's an intimate night club and restaurant. The food is excellent, and they have a dance floor. I'll pick you up around seven-thirty."

"I'll be ready. Now, if you would please move out of my way so I can put my clothes on."

"I like you better without any." He reached for her.

She evaded him. "I know you do. How well I know it."

After Derek dropped Augusta off at her house, he drove aimlessly for a while, thinking.

Tonight's the night.

Finally. It's about time you 'fessed up.

Oh, God, give me strength.

You? Praying?

I haven't done so well on my own. Maybe I could use some divine intervention.

It couldn't hurt.

He imagined every conceivable outcome with Augusta, each scenario worse than the one before it.

After a while he went home to dress for his evening out with the woman he loved. It might very well be the last time, but he hoped not. He did more than hope; he prayed.

Augusta stroked her fingers over the hangers in her closet until she came to the one she sought. On it a soft, black wool dress hung. She'd splurged and bought it a couple of months before the accident. It fit her body like a second skin. The neckline was draped with an antique-white lace collar, fashioned into a cape that covered her shoulders and tied like a scarf in front.

"Are you and Todd going to discuss your wedding plans tonight, Augusta?" Tammy asked.

"I think so. I got the impression that he wanted to talk about something important. It could only mean one thing. I'm so happy, Tammy. I love him so much."

"I know you do."

"You don't mind staying here by yourself this evening?"

"I'm not a baby, Augusta; I'm almost grown. I can spend an evening alone. You aren't staying out all night, but if you and Todd decide that you want to, I wouldn't mind. I have Bella for company and protection, and Mrs. Cummings won't mind if Melody comes over. You can stop worrying, all right?"

"Oh, all right. It's just that I've never had a daughter to worry about before. Bear with me?"

"I wish you had been my real mother, Augusta."

"What a wonderful compliment! And you know what? I love you as much as I would my own flesh-and-blood daughter."

After Tammy left the room, Augusta concentrated on setting a closer wedding date. No more waiting. She'd decided that although Valentine's Day was romantic, it was too long to wait. Tonight she would tell Todd that she wanted to be Mrs. Todd Winters as soon as they could arrange it.

Augusta took a long leisurely bath, then dressed for her evening out. She fashioned her hair into a French braid and attached a pearl-studded clip on the end. Her make-up was simple. Kelly, Joan Gordon's assistant, had shown her a few tricks. It took a while, but she'd mastered the technique of applying make-up.

Augusta's heart pounded in a heavy rhythm when she heard Todd's car turn into the drive. Tammy had insisted on going to her room early, to give the two of them time alone.

Augusta smiled as she went to the door and thrust it open.

Derek took her into his arms. "I've missed you."

She kissed him. "And I've missed you."

"You could have stayed longer, you know."

"I know, but there are Tammy and Bella."

"Tammy is almost grown up."

"I've heard the same lecture from the person in question. Have you two compared notes or something?"

"No, we just understand each other, that's all. Now will you come on, please."

"Impatient?" she kidded. "All right, I'll get my coat."

Derek looked at the dog. "I'll bring your mistress back safe and sound."

Augusta returned to the room. "Did Bella tell you she'd admonish you if you didn't?" she quipped.

"Very funny."

"I thought so."

Derek checked their coats at the cloak room of the Cameo Room. They waited in the reception area for a hostess to come and show them to their table.

"The ambiance here is incredible," Derek remarked. "All the hostesses dress in embroidered, white organdy, Victorian costumes, with their hair up in a bun. And around their necks they wear a black velvet ribbon choker with a cameo brooch in the center."

As they followed the hostess' lead, Augusta tripped.

The hostess quickly asked, "Are you all right?"

"Yes. Todd forgot to warn me about the steps. You see, he's my eyes whenever we go out."

"I see…I mean…"

Augusta smiled. "I'm not offended, I know what you meant. Now, Todd, how does the place look?"

"The dining area is placed back against a circular wall with the tables set in tiny alcoves that edge an expansive dance floor painted to resemble the ivory silhouette of a woman's face."

"Like a cameo brooch. Sounds like a club that caters to women. And I called you a closet chauvinist once, didn't I?"

"Uh-huh. Now you know I'm not. By the way, they serve the best burgundy beef in town."

"If I didn't know better, I'd think you were setting me up for something."

He was, he thought guiltily. Maybe I should...

Get on with it, Morgan. Tell her.

Right. He cleared his throat.

"What would you like?" a waitress came to the table and asked.

Augusta smiled. "I hear the burgundy beef is delicious."

"Yes, it is. Would you like to order that?"

"Yes, we would," Derek answered. "We'd also like a light Chianti with it."

"A very good choice. Enjoy your dinner."

"We will, I'm sure. Thank you," Augusta graciously replied.

When they were alone, Derek braced himself to tell her the truth.

"There's something I..."

"Derek Morgan, you son-of-a-gun! It's been a long time. Felicia thought she recognized you, so we decided to come over and make sure. Listen, I hear you're the head honcho at Morgan Electronics now. have any openings? If you do, I thought I might hit you up for a job."

Derek nearly choked. "Perry!" Of all the times to run into him and his wife. He hadn't seen them for several years.

"I'm Felicia, the one who puts up with this big bear. Is this your wife, Derek?"

Augusta gasped in shock, feeling as though she'd been run over by a Mack truck. "Todd! Derek! I don't understand."

"Augusta, I…"

"Perry, I think we'd better be getting back to our table. I think we've…ah…interrupted something," Felicia said.

Perry cleared his throat. "Ah…yeah…See you around, Derek."

Augusta tried to speak, but the words clogged her throat.

"Baby, let me explain."

"Don't you 'baby' me. Are you the bastard who…Of course you are! You're the man who blinded me, aren't you?"

Derek put his hand over hers. She jerked it away.

"Don't touch me! You—I can't believe it!"

"I was going to tell you tonight, Augusta. I swear I was, but…"

"But what? You've had months to tell me. If you ever intended to, Todd—no. It's Derek Morgan, isn't it?"

He reached for her hand. "Augusta, please, you've got to let me…"

"I said don't touch me, damn you!"

"All right, I won't, but you've got to listen…let me…"

"No, I don't want to hear it. You've deceived me all this time. I just can't believe it."

Derek started to speak, but misery bankrupted his tongue.

Augusta thought about the television broadcast. When Todd...Derek was interviewed, he'd admitted to being with the Institute for only fifteen months. That should have clued her in. But no, she was too much in love, too blind to...

What about the other woman who...

"It was all a lie, wasn't it? There never was any other blind woman you loved before you met me, was there? What a fool I've been. Do you get off on making fools of blind women? Or more to the point, just one blind woman in particular?"

"You can't think that I don't love you?"

"Was it guilt that made you change, Todd, or should I say Derek?"

Augusta shot abruptly to her feet.

Derek followed suit, quickly skirting the table to take her hand in his. "Derek, I don't want you touching me." Tears slid down her cheeks.

He brushed them away with his fingers. "Baby, don't cry, I never meant to hurt you, I swear I didn't."

"That's a good one. You've hurt me more than anyone else ever could."

"You don't understand."

"I understand, all right. Well, you understand this: I don't want to have anything else to do with you!"

"You can't erase what we've been to each other. Augusta, darling, I love you!"

She pulled out of his hold and cried, "You love me! That's got to be the joke of the century. You just feel guilty, that's all. Oh, and you probably pity the poor blind woman who fell so easily under your spell."

"Don't talk like that, Augusta."

"Why not? It's the truth."

"No, my darling, it isn't." He stepped closer. "You're just upset."

She backed away. "You're damn right, I'm upset, and with good reason!"

"Augusta..."

"How was I? Did I measure up in bed to a sighted woman?"

Derek grabbed her shoulders and shook her. "Don't ever say that!"

She struggled. "Stop it, Augusta! I never saw you as some kind of conquest or as a notch on my bedpost."

"Yeah, right."

He looked around them and saw the hostess and the waitress looking their way. "This isn't the place to discuss it."

"No place will ever be the right place as far as you're concerned."

She wrenched out of his grasp and stumbled as she tried to pass him.

Derek moved to steady her. "Augusta, I…"

"Save it, I don't want to hear it!"

CHAPTER XVIII

Augusta wanted to storm out of there, but she didn't know her way around the place.

"Is something wrong?"

Augusta recognized the voice as belonging to the hostess who'd met them at the door when they came in. She'd no doubt come over to see what the commotion was all about.

Derek touched Augusta's arm. "We have to talk."

She ignored his words and asked the hostess, "Could you show me to the ladies' room?"

"Why, yes, of course." The woman took her arm. "This way, please." The hostess guided Augusta away from Derek, in the direction of the ladies' room.

He waited outside for her to come out. His soul was in hell, and he was suffering the torment of the damned.

After what seemed like hours, Augusta hesitantly exited the room. The misery he read in her face broke his heart. He wanted to gather her into his arms and soothe away the hurt and disillusionment he'd caused.

"I seem to be at your mercy once again, Mr. Morgan," Augusta said coldly.

He answered, his voice pained. "Augusta, don't."

"Tell me, *Derek,* what would you have me say? Oh, I don't mind that you've only wrecked my life, destroyed my career, and broken my heart."

He knew it was useless to try to talk to her now, but maybe later...

You hope.

Yes, I hope. That's all I have.

Finding the wall, Augusta followed it. Derek had described the place as circular. Eventually, she would reach the door where they came in.

Derek started after her. "What are you doing?"

"That's a stupid question. I'm trying to get the hell away from you, that's what."

"But you can't..."

"According to you, there's no such word."

"You can't leave things like this between us."

"Just watch me." She came to some steps and tripped.

He steadied her. "Baby, you love me."

Tears coursed down her cheeks. "That's why what you did hurts so much. I never thought you, of all people, could deceive me like this."

"I didn't mean to. You have to believe me."

"Do I?"

Derek closed his eyes in an attempt to will the pain out of his voice.

"What about our love?"

"Our love! That's a laugh. It never existed, except in my imagination. Guilt and pity prompted you."

"At first it did, I'll admit that. But then I got to know you and fell hopelessly in love."

"You mean you could tell the difference? Move out of my way, Derek! Hostess!"

Within seconds the woman appeared.

"Yes?"

"Would you call me a cab?"

Before the woman could answer, Derek interrupted. "There's no need. I'm taking the lady home."

"Derek, I don't want you to," she said through gritted teeth.

"I'm taking you home, Augusta. And it's not negotiable."

Derek eyed the hostess, daring her to disagree with him.

"You don't have to go with this guy. Is it what you want to do?" she asked Augusta.

Wanting to hurry up and get the hell out of there, she answered. "Yes, it is." Damn him. Augusta swore, wanting to scream at Derek and tear out his heart as he'd done hers. She wanted to hate him. Because of him, her heart had sustained a shock greater than losing her sight—one she didn't know if she would ever recover from.

Todd Winters had been her lifeline. She had loved him with all her heart, and nothing could change that—but at the same time, she couldn't deal with the fact that he was also the Derek Morgan who had not only cost her her sight, but had deceived her all these months.

And you still love him.

Oh God, how am I ever going to cope with this?

She said to the hostess, "I seem to have left my purse in the ladies' room. Would you mind seeing if it's still there?"

"No problem. I'll get it for you."

"Augusta."

She stiffened. "Yes, Derek."

"You say my name as though you hate me."

The hostess returned with Augusta's purse. "Here you are. Luckily there was no one else in there. Or if there was, they didn't take it. You want to check to see if everything's still in it?"

"That won't be necessary. I heard my keys jingle when you handed me the purse, and they were the only things I had in it."

"If that'll be all, I..."

"Yes."

"You're sure?"

"I am, thank you." Augusta listened as the hostess walked away. "You said you were going to take me home, Derek. I'm more than ready to leave right now."

He took her elbow and guided her to the cloak room. As he helped Augusta into her coat, Perry and Felicia came to retrieve theirs.

Perry walked over to him. "Listen, Derek, man, if I caused any trouble between you and your lady I'm sorry."

Derek felt Augusta tremble beneath his hand. "It's not your fault." He wanted to blame someone, but the only one he could honestly condemn was himself.

Minutes later, he helped her into the car. She remained quiet during the ride home. He shot quick glances her way every once in a while. She looked so elegant sitting there with her hands folded in her lap. Only her sad expression gave away the pain she was suffering. All because of him.

It was over. The conversation he'd dreaded all these months had finally come to pass. He was numbed by the experience. What could he say to make her forgive him?

He should have followed Ben's advice, and his own conscience, and told her the truth a long time ago. But then hindsight was 20/20, wasn't it? He'd brought this heartache on himself. He'd procrastinated too long and he'd lost it all, maybe forever.

Don't fool yourself, Morgan, you wanted to be let off the hook. All along you were hoping you would never have to tell her the truth. Admit it.

No, it's not true.

Isn't it?

Derek pulled into the drive and cut the engine, then turned to face Augusta. "Can't you find it in your heart to forgive me, Augusta?"

"I don't know, Derek. Listen, I don't want to talk about this right now."

Despair seared his insides. She was so cold now, so distant. And she had been so warm, so loving.

And ignorant of your deception. Stop torturing yourself, Morgan. Give her time.

"Augusta, will you ever be ready to talk about it? I'm sorry. I should have told you the truth. I made a mistake. I'm only human. If I could change things and restore your sight and your faith in me, you've got to know I would do it in a heartbeat."

She didn't answer him. Instead she sat, recalling all that had been said tonight, the feelings of betrayal and disillusionment that had swamped her when she heard the words that had brought her world crashing down around her. Pain and a sense of loss crushed her heart—pain and loss worse than what she'd suffered after waking up from the accident and discovering her sight was gone.

She'd promised herself then that she wouldn't let anything hurt her again. But the fickle hands of fate had dealt her a stunning blow, guaranteed to make any other pain she'd ever felt pale in comparison.

Augusta shuddered, thinking about what could have happened to little Kelsey Mason if she hadn't intervened. It was hard to fathom that the man she thought she knew, and had come to love, had been so reckless and irresponsible.

Derek's words came bobbing to the surface of her mind. What they had shared was special—*was* being the operative word. He was the one who had taught her body to sing. Just his nearness could make her melt.

But that was all over. They could never go back to the way things were. Yesterday was gone forever.

She heard him unfasten his seat belt. "Don't bother to get out. I can make it to my door without your help, thank you."

Ignoring her words, Derek got out and walked around to her side to help her out.

"I said…"

"I heard what you said, Augusta. Give me your keys."

"Derek!"

"Augusta."

She sighed angrily, then opened her purse and took out her keys, angrily thrusting them into his palm. "All right, fine, do what you want to do."

"You won't give an inch, will you? No matter how you try to deny it, you still love me, you still want me.

One day when the hurt subsides and you can forgive..."

"Don't bank on it. It's over between us, Derek."

"I can't accept that, I won't believe it."

"You mean you don't want to accept it, you don't want to believe it. Believe it! It's over!"

Derek walked her to her door and unlocked it. He waited for Augusta to enter, then followed her into the hall. Bella greeted them, and, as though sensing the tension between Derek and Augusta, eyed Derek warily.

Augusta patted Bella on the head. "Not to worry, girl, Derek is leaving."

Derek scowled, looking down at the dog. She seemed to be waiting for him to make a wrong move. He knew from experience how sensitive and protective seeing eye dogs were of their masters.

"Before you go, Derek, I want to know one thing."

"What is that?"

"Why did you deceive me?"

"You wouldn't have had anything to do with me otherwise."

"You have that right. I wouldn't. You had to have known that I'd find out the truth sooner or later."

"As I said before, I was going to tell you."

"Poor Derek, ever the eternal procrastinator. Right? I've always thought it was strange that a man like you would be so dedicated to helping the blind. Now I know the real reason why."

"I doubt it." He knew it wouldn't do any good to tell her she was wrong about him and his motives. She wouldn't believe it, for one thing—and for another, everything having to do with him was now suspect.

"Don't bother coming back, all right? I'll get someone else to help me at the college from now on."

He tried one more time. "Won't you even..."

Augusta twisted off her engagement ring and threw it at him.

"I hate you for what you've done to me."

"Those are just words. I know you love me as much as I love you." He bent down and picked up the ring. His voice filled with pain, he said, "One day you'll realize we belong together. When that happens, I'll be waiting to put this back on your finger."

"Don't hold your breath waiting for that day. Now if you would please just get out."

"All right, I'll get out, Augusta. I'm not going to beg. Goodbye."

After Derek left, Augusta thought she would feel vindicated, but her rejection of him only saddened and hurt her more.

Would the pain of his betrayal ever cease? She didn't think so. Platitudes, like time heals all wounds, were just that: platitudes. She felt sure that no amount of time would make the pain stop. It was there to stay.

"Augusta, did I hear you and Todd arguing?"

"Tammy, I—you're still up."

Tammy touched her watch. "It's early. Did you and Todd have a fight or something?"

Augusta sighed heavily and took a deep breath before she answered.

"I'm afraid there isn't going to be a wedding."

"What? Augusta, what happened? Is it because of me? You didn't have to take me into your home."

"Tammy, it has nothing to do with you. It's because of something he did."

"What could Todd have possibly done that would make you…Is it another woman?"

"Oh, Tammy," Augusta broke down.

Tammy made her way to Augusta's side, and they embraced.

"I can't believe he would do something like that."

"It's not another woman. Todd isn't who he says he is. His real name is Derek Morgan."

Tammy gasped. "But isn't that the name of the man who—oh, Augusta," she cried and squeezed her foster mother tight. She couldn't believe what she was hearing, didn't want to believe it. Not Todd—Derek.

Augusta told Tammy what had happened at the restaurant. "What a way to start off the new year," Augusta said bitterly.

"There has to be a mistake. That man loves you, I know he does. You can feel it whenever you two are together."

"I thought so too, but evidently not. I gave him his ring back."

"Maybe the two of you will make up and..."

"Don't count on that happening, Tammy. There is no way I can trust him now."

"You're just saying that now. Later you'll feel different."

"I don't think so. It's over. If you can't trust the man you love, then who can you trust?"

Tammy started to cry.

"Don't cry, Tammy." She hadn't meant to do that. Augusta realized this would profoundly affect the girl because she practically worshiped the ground Todd—Derek walked on. She hoped it wouldn't ruin Tammy's relationship with him or destroy the progress she had made.

Bella padded over to them and rubbed her head against Augusta's leg, making sympathetic little noises, then brushed her nose against Tammy's hand.

"We girls have to stick together," Augusta said, running her fingers over the dog's smooth, furry head. "Right, girl?"

"Augusta, I can't believe this. It's just so unreal."

"I know, I..." The tears came and Augusta couldn't stop them. No matter what he'd done, she still loved him, but there was no way they could go back to the way things had been. Augusta moved away from the fireplace, took off her coat, and laid it across the back of the couch. Suddenly she felt numb and disoriented, as she had right after surgery when she learned of the damage to her eyes. This time she was hurt beyond repair.

"What are you going to do, Augusta? Will you forgive him?"

"I want to, Tammy, but I don't see how I can—after what he's done."

"I felt the same way when my—David, the boy I was in love with, deserted me after the accident. I don't think I'll ever be able to forgive or forget what he did."

"I'm sorry you had to go through that."

"He didn't love me like I did him, but, Augusta, I know that Todd—Derek, whatever he calls himself, loves you. Maybe he…"

"I don't want to talk about it any more; I'm too wiped out."

"I understand. But what are you going to do, Augusta?"

"I don't know, Tammy. The pain is just too deep, too raw. I don't want to think or feel anything right now. I'm going to bed."

Augusta knew she wouldn't get any sleep. God, she hurt. Would the agony ever go away?

CHAPTER XIX

The gloomy, gray Saturday suited Derek's mood. He stood above the Delaware River and watched its icy waters lap in slushy, irregular waves over the shore. Oblivious to the freezing-cold weather, he walked along the bank. Had it only been two days since his world had fallen apart?

He felt so alone. And from now on his life would be empty, without Augusta and Tammy. He had no illusions about how Tammy would react. She was loyal to those she loved, and she loved Augusta almost as much as he did.

No matter what happened between him and Augusta, one thing he would never give up on finding: a technique that could restore Augusta's sight, whether she appreciated his efforts or not.

He believed, like Ben Hastings, that one day Augusta would forgive him. She was too compassionate to do otherwise. He was also sure she wouldn't take him back. His deceit stood in the way of that.

In such a short time, she'd come to mean everything to him. He'd never meant to hurt her. But in procrastinating so long, he'd done just that. He had intended to tell her that night. He really had.

Yeah, and hell is hot.

I should know I'm scorching in the depths of it right now.

What are you going to do, man?

Do? Damned if I know—wait, I guess in the meantime, I'll devote more time to my company and put in more hours at the Institute. Maybe if I fill my life with work…

It won't lessen the pain. It won't make it go away. And it damn sure won't bring the woman you love back to you.

No, it won't, but what other choice do I have?

Finally the frigid weather penetrated his sheepskin jacket, chilling his bones and urgently persuading him to go back to his car.

Augusta sat before the fire in her living room listening to the wood as it crackled, imagining how the orange-yellow flames looked. Bella lay down by her side, seeming to absorb Augusta's mood.

"I thought I knew him so well, Bella. All the time he was deceiving me. How could he have done that to me?"

Bella rubbed her soft, furry muzzle against Augusta's foot in commiseration.

Augusta smiled. "I know you don't have the answers, girl." She patted the dog's head. "At least I still have you. And I have Tammy."

Augusta was worried about Tammy. The girl had been so withdrawn the last few days. She hadn't said much of anything since that night her world shattered.

Forgive him, Augusta, her inner conscience strongly suggested.

Oh, she would in time, but it didn't change anything. She could no longer trust Derek. Derek. He had been Todd Winters to her for so many months. And he'd lied to her from day one.

Day one?

Ben?

He'd known who Todd Winters was from the very beginning and had gone along with the charade. And she'd thought he was her friend. Was there no one she could trust? She wondered if Myra—no, she was sure she hadn't known. Honest to a fault, Myra would never go along with such a deception.

Augusta thought unforgivingly about her friend Ben. Evidently men stuck together to protect each other. And she had an appointment with Ben for a check-up next week. She wasn't sure she was ready to face him.

She still couldn't believe that it had only been a matter of days since she'd found out the truth. It seemed more like decades ago. She missed T—Derek. Would she ever get used to thinking of him as Derek Morgan instead of Todd Winters? He'd gone to such lengths to deceive her. But then, guilt was a heavy burden to carry.

Tears slid down her cheeks, and she wiped them away. Crying wouldn't do any good. It wouldn't lessen the emptiness she felt.

Exhausted, Augusta rose to her feet and made her way to her room. As she undressed, she accidently brushed her breast. She instantly remembered the last time she and Derek had made love. The nipple tightened. She shook her head to clear it. She had to stop thinking about him like this. It was over.

Hours later she lay awake, willing her body to cease its craving for Derek's touch. To never feel his strong arms, warm and reassuring, around her body or the tingle from his kiss was going to wreak havoc on her sanity.

"Merciful heavens," she cried, "why did it have to be this way? Why?"

Derek paced back and forth in his kitchen. He had finished off his second pot of coffee and knew if he drank any more, the cleaning lady would have to peel him off the ceiling. He just couldn't sleep, damn it! He felt as if he never would again.

Augusta had completely cut herself off from him. He had just begun to serve his sentence, and had only an inkling of what the rest of his life would be like without the woman he loved.

After walking into the living room, he turned on the stereo. As fate would have it, "I'm Only Human" by Jeffrey Osborne started to play. He wondered if Augusta might be listening to it.

When the song ended, Derek turned off the stereo. He took her ring out of his pocket. He didn't know why he'd been carrying it around with him.

Maybe because its a reminder of all you have lost. Face the facts, Morgan—you blew it.

He hurt so bad. Anguish burned deep inside him. He carried the ring into his bedroom, put it on the night stand, then sat down on his bed and stared at it.

"This belongs to you, Augusta. I had it made especially for that special woman in my life: you."

He climbed into bed and lay thinking. If he had told her the truth when he first met her, she would have hated him. Now that she knew, she hated him, or thought she did. No matter when she found out, he would have been in a catch-22 situation: damned if he did and damned if he didn't.

Keep trying to convince yourself of that, Morgan. You know the situation between you and Augusta was never that cut and dry. He closed his eyes and tried to close his mind as well, but it was no good. There was no way he could get any sleep tonight.

As much as she longed to take time off, Augusta knew she wouldn't. Work was her salvation. And she didn't know what she would have done without Tammy and Bella.

Tammy was spending a lot of time with Melody. Augusta was glad she had a close friend. Their time at the Institute was strained, wondering when they would run into Derek.

Augusta had encountered Derek in the elevator. The air was cold, thick, and as impenetrable as a block of ice—at first.

"Are you all right, Augusta?" Derek had asked.

"I'm perfectly fine." She willed the elevator to hurry to the ground floor. But as luck would have it, it stopped on the next floor and let on more people.

"Augusta, we can't..."

The elevator stopped, and the door opened. Derek put a restraining hand on her arm, allowing the other passengers to get off the elevator. When the last one had stepped out, he closed the door and pushed stop.

"Derek!"

He didn't say another word, just drew her into his arms and kissed her. Augusta struggled at first, but gave in to the betraying clamor of her body for his touch, only for a moment. Then she pushed him away.

"Derek, open the door, please," she said shakily.

He raised his hand to touch her cheek. "Augusta, we love each other. Can't you forgive me?"

Seeing the stubborn jut of her chin, he let his hand drop in frustration. "All right, have it your way," he said with a defeated sigh. Then he studied her for a long moment. "You still want me as much as I want you. I proved that a few seconds ago. You might tell yourself you hate me, but we both know it isn't true."

She could feel his eyes on her back as she left the elevator. More than anything, she wanted to turn and rush back into his arms. In the end, she couldn't do it. She couldn't allow him to chip away her barriers and hurt her all over again.

Augusta interviewed several students for the job of classroom assistant. She didn't think getting help would be that difficult, but soon found out differently. None of the applicants seemed right for the job. Finally she settled on a female graduate student who had recently transferred from another medical school in upstate New York.

Somehow she didn't want to work with another male. Every time she thought about Derek, her heart ached. It had been a week since that disastrous night.

And the pain hadn't eased one iota. If anything, it had worsened.

Augusta's check-up with Ben, only two days away, was staring her in the face. She had thought about cancelling it, but knowing Ben he'd come looking for her. She had to face him some time, so it might as well be now. Augusta wanted to call Myra, but she just couldn't build up the nerve to do it. She would have it out with Ben first, she thought grimly.

"I'm surprised you kept your appointment," Ben said when Augusta entered his office.

"You know about what happened between *Derek* and me." It wasn't a question.

"I suppose you're never going to forgive me for helping him deceive you. Damn it, Augusta, the man loves you."

"I don't want to talk about him with you, Ben. Let's just get on with my check-up, all right?"

"Augusta..."

"I mean it, Ben."

Always one to bite the bullet, he plundered on. "Augusta, Derek is a changed man from the one who caused your blindness. No one is more sorry than he is for what happened."

Augusta gritted her teeth and allowed him to have his say.

"All the bills you thought his insurance had paid? Derek's own private funds paid for them once that ran out. If you'd thought about it, you would have questioned it. You know that hospital staff insurance covers just so much of your expenses. And so does accident insurance."

"The many specialists you've seen over the last fifteen months—do I need to say more? Derek paid for what the insurance didn't cover. And he did it because he cared. He loves you."

"You say he loves me, cares about me. I call it guilt and pity. And you—Ben Hastings, my good friend—helped him deceive me all this time. I can't forgive either one of you for what you've done."

"Maybe we were wrong and maybe not. The point is, we cared about you."

"You were my friend, and yet you went along with this."

"Were? Am I not still your friend, Augusta? All right, when Derek first came to me I wouldn't consider what he had in mind. But once I saw how sincere he was, I relented. I told him what a forgiving woman you are."

"I forgive him, but I can't forget how he deceived me."

"My dear Augusta, the only way you can truly forgive is to forget."

"Don't tell me I'll get over it, because I won't—I promise you. If all you're going to do is talk about Derek, maybe I'd better go. *Maybe* I should make an appointment with another doctor."

Ben frowned. With Augusta in this kind of mood, he knew it was useless to continue talking to her.

"That won't be necessary, Augusta. Step into the examining room."

After he concluded the usual battery of eye exams, Ben guided Augusta back into his office.

"Listen, Ben, if you're going to..."

"No, I'm not going to talk about that subject, at least not directly anyway."

"Ben!"

"Sit down, Augusta."

The sound in his voice convinced her to do as he said. Something was on Ben's mind and she might as well listen and get it over with. Suddenly a renegade thought raced through her mind.

"I'm not getting worse, am I?"

"It's nothing like that. I haven't found any evidence of regression in your condition."

"Then?"

"A Dr. John Eekong has developed a new technique for corneal restoration surgery using a drug he developed and the laser."

"I didn't know there was such a thing. I thought that once the tissues were severely damaged, nothing could regenerate them and a corneal transplant was the only option."

"That's true for the most part. I've talked to the doctor, and he explained that in rare cases the fragmented cornea can regenerate. He's had amazing success with his new method of treatment."

"Are you saying…?"

"There is every hope he can help you—yes, that's exactly what I'm saying. Derek has arranged everything if you decide to…"

"I should have smelled a trap. Ben, I…"

"No one is trying to trap you, Augusta. We all want what is best for you. Is that so hard to believe?"

"Oh, I believe you all right."

"Well, then, what do you say?"

She didn't answer for long moments.

"Indecision is the thief of time, Augusta. Please don't waste this chance to see again—to possibly operate again."

Relentless in his determination to convince her, Ben offered a powerful argument. The possibility of having her career back was one she couldn't ignore under any circumstances.

Even though she didn't want to be beholden to Derek for anything else, she had to give this some thought—very serious thought.

Ben smiled. He knew when he had her. She would consider the proposal.

"Where is this hospital?"

"The Eekong Clinic/Hospital is on the outskirts of Lagos, Nigeria. According to Dr. Eekong, the patient undergoes the treatments there and is well enough to leave in a matter of weeks."

"Sounds almost too good to be true."

"There is the possibility it won't work, but in your case the odds for success could go as high as sixty percent. Isn't it worth a try to be able to operate again?"

"All right, spell out the terms."

Ben had known that he couldn't completely get away with his plan.

"Derek wants to see you and accompany you to Africa."

"I won't see him or go with him."

"Be reasonable, Augusta."

She rose from her seat and headed for the reception room door.

"Augusta, wait."

She turned. "You tell Derek that I'll go if he agrees to stay here and keep out of my way."

"Augusta..."

"Tell him to take it or leave it." She walked out of the office. Bella, who had been patiently waiting for her mistress to come out, hurried to her side. "Let's go home, girl."

Ben opened the door and stood watching as Augusta left his office suite. He shook his head. What a stubborn woman, he thought. He went back to his desk and punched in Derek's phone number.

"Hello."

"Derek?"

"Ben, what did she say?"

He hesitated.

"I want the truth."

"She doesn't want to see you or…"

"Let me go to Africa with her, right?"

"I'm afraid so. But Derek, I think all she needs is time and she'll come around."

"You can't be sure of that."

"The possibility of getting her sight back is a powerful inducement."

"I won't push her like that. Tell her I withdraw the conditions."

"But Derek, I really think you should insist."

"Never mind, I'll tell her myself. Don't worry, I intend to try to convince her, but if I see it isn't working, I'll withdraw the conditions."

"You two are more stubborn than a team of mules."

"Thanks for the compliment, Ben."

"I guess there's nothing else I can say, is there?"

"Goodbye and good luck, Derek."

"Goodbye, Ben."

Several days later Derek stood outside the medical school, waiting for Augusta to leave the building. When he saw her, his heart skipped a beat. God, how he loved the woman.

"Augusta."

She froze in her tracks at the sound of his voice.

"We have to talk."

"Did you think meeting me face to face would change my mind? If you did, you're in for a rude awakening." She signaled Bella forward.

Derek put a restraining hand on Augusta's arm. Bella growled.

"Easy, girl. All right, since you insist, Derek, we can talk at Maxine's."

He agreed. They had frequently gone to the coffee shop after Augusta started teaching at the medical school. He considered it one of their favorite places. God, it was hell being alienated from Augusta. Was this what he had to look forward to for the rest of his life? He didn't think he could stand it.

"What'll it be today, Doc?" Maxine, the owner, chief cook, bottle washer and waitress, said when they walked through the door. "Haven't seen you in a while, Todd."

Derek cleared his throat. "Well, I've been…ah, kind of…"

Augusta cut across him. “Just two coffees, Maxine.”

Derek wanted to say more when he saw Maxine frown and shake her head in confusion, but he didn’t. He noticed that Augusta had made her way to a different table from the one they usually occupied at coffee break times.

“All right, Derek, talk.”

He flinched inwardly at the cold, impersonal quality in her voice.

He’d done this to her.

“Augusta, I’ve tried to call you. I’ve left numerous messages on your answering machine.”

“I know, I was there when most of them came through.”

“You just chose not to answer.”

“You got it. But you’ve managed to get your way.”

“We have to talk, damn it!”

“*You* have to talk, not me.”

Derek sighed in annoyed frustration. “Listen, Augusta, I want you to go to Africa.”

“But only if you accompany me.”

“You mean you’d consider going if I modified the conditions?”

“Maybe.”

He hesitated for a moment. “All right, Augusta, you win. You go alone.”

“How nice of you to give me permission.”

"Augusta."

"I said maybe."

"Since you believe I'm motivated by guilt and pity, why don't you pacify my conscience by going? After all, I owe you for what I did." He sat thoughtfully quiet for a moment. "You don't want to be obligated to me for anything, do you?"

She didn't answer.

"I thought that was the case. You go to Nigeria. You undergo the treatments, and then we'll no longer be obligated to each other. Does that sound fair enough?"

Maxine brought the coffee.

After the woman had left them alone, Augusta pondered Derek's words.

As he waited, Derek voraciously drank in the loveliness of the woman he loved, committing to memory every aspect of both her outer physical appearance and the inner beauty she tried to keep hidden, but that managed to seep out in spite of her. He knew deep in his heart that in all likelihood the memories would have to sustain him in the long days and weeks to come until she forgave him—if she ever did.

"All right, Derek, I'll go."

"Do you want me to call Ben so he can set things up?"

"That won't be necessary; I can do it."

"Anything you say, Augusta." He took her hand in his. He felt her try to pull away from him. "I love you, Augusta."

"Derek, please, I…"

Reluctantly, he let her hand go. "All right." He wanted to say so much more, but knew it wouldn't do any good. He rose from his seat. "Baby, this is so long, not goodbye. I'll never say that."

Augusta heard him leave and tamped down the urge to call him back.

It was over. It was best this way.

Augusta gained Maxine's attention.

"You want a sweet roll or a donut to go with your coffee, Doc?"

"No, thanks. Would you bring me a phone?"

"Sure thing."

Maxine returned with the phone and then left her alone.

Augusta punched in a number.

"Dr. Hastings' office, Rebba speaking."

"Rebba, this is Augusta Humphrey. Is Ben in?"

"Yes, hold on. He's with a patient."

She hadn't expected Derek to give in so easily, as though almost guessing what she would say. Maybe he had. A sharp needle of guilt at the way she had treated him pricked her.

"Augusta."

"Yes, Ben. I've talked to Derek. He withdrew his conditions. You can make the arrangements with Dr Eekong. I've decided to go to his clinic."

"I'm glad to hear it, but I still think you should reconsider and let Derek go with you. You really shouldn't be alone."

"We're not going to get into that again. Besides, I have Tammy. Even if I didn't, my decision is final."

"Augusta, I think you're making a mistake."

"I know you do."

"Is there nothing I can say to change your mind?" Her silence gave Ben his answer. He knew it was useless to say anything more on the subject. In a resigned voice he said, "I'll get back to you in a few days about the details."

"I'll be waiting. Goodbye, Ben."

"Augusta...goodbye."

CHAPTER XX

"Hello."

"Augusta, it's Ben. Dr. Eekong can see you in two weeks. You really should…"

"Ben, we've been through all this. I don't want Derek to come with me."

"If I could, I'd come with you myself."

"I know you would. Stop being such a mother hen. I'll be fine."

"Myra would do it if I would let her, but at this stage in her pregnancy it isn't a good idea."

"Ben."

"I can't help worrying about you, Augusta. I guess it's become a habit I can't seem to break. I wish you all the luck in the world."

"If you don't get off this phone you'll have me crying."

"Will a guilt trip make you change your mind?"

"I thought not. You can't blame a doctor for doing all he can for his patient. Or a friend for wanting the best for his friend, can you?"

"I suppose not. Enough of the guilt already."

"Okay. Myra will be over to help you and Tammy pack. You did say that Tammy is going with you, didn't you?"

"Yes."

"All right then."

"Goodbye, Ben."

"Goodbye."

After she hung up, Augusta thought about Tammy's reaction to going with her to Africa without Derek.

"Can't Todd—mean Derek—come with us?" she'd asked.

"Tammy, I thought you understood that it's over between Derek and me."

"Well, I do understand, but you need him, Augusta."

Augusta didn't say anything to that, just thought about what Tammy hadn't said. The girl was in essence saying that she too needed Derek. After all, they were going to be a family before…

Damn him for doing this to me! Damn him for making me love him!

Damn you, Derek Morgan!

"You love him, Augusta, you know you do. I hate seeing you hurting so much," Tammy said.

"I'll be all right in time. You're still going to come with me, aren't you?"

"Of course I am. You'll be all alone. You'll need me. I've never felt needed like this before."

Augusta smiled. "I definitely need you, Tammy. You are my daughter in every way that matters. And I love you very much."

"And I love you, Augusta. I hope this doctor can help you."

"Me too."

Augusta felt lethargic when she woke up a few mornings later. She put it down to anxiety over her breakup with Derek. She filled her days with work and more work. But at night she suffered from loneliness and a sense of something missing. She knew what that something was, but it couldn't be helped.

She hadn't gotten much sleep lately. When she closed her eyes at night, dreams of Derek invaded her sleep. In the dreams she could see him. They would be making love, and suddenly he would drift away. She'd call out his name, but he seemed not to hear her. Then he would disappear altogether and she would wake up crying.

Her mind might have been set against Derek, but her body craved his with a passion she found impossible to ignore. Her mind might have understood, but her heart certainly didn't. After what Derek had done to her; how could she feel like this about him? Was love always so illogical?

Was it logical to hate Derek one minute and love him beyond reason the next? To forgive him and yet not forget? God, how she wanted to forget. But she just couldn't.

When Augusta got home from the college one afternoon, she found Tammy waiting in the living room, sitting before the fire.

"I'm surprised you're not over at the Cummings' house." She unfastened Bella's harness and put it away before removing her own coat. "You and Melody have become good friends, haven't you?"

"Yes, we have."

Augusta smiled at the strong note of loyalty to her friend she heard in Tammy's voice. "Are you ready to go to Africa?"

"Yes," she said hesitantly.

"Aren't you excited about going?"

"Oh, yes. Who wouldn't be?"

Augusta picked up on her reluctance and assumed that Tammy was still upset about Derek not coming with them. "I know you wanted Derek to come with us, but it just isn't possible."

"It's not that—I just..."

"What is it, Tammy?"

"I hate to leave Melody right now."

"Why? Is she in some kind of trouble?"

"Well, sort of, kind of—I mean..."

Augusta became instantly concerned. What was Tammy trying to keep from her?

"I thought we were close. Can't you tell me what it is?"

"I promised that I wouldn't say anything to anyone."

"Say anything about what?"

"I can't tell you. Melody will have to be the one to do that. I could call her and have her come over and—but you know how Mrs. Cummings feels about you and Melody."

"Yes, I do, but if Melody is in some kind of trouble maybe I can help. Go ahead and call her. If there's any problem with Jean, we'll just have to deal with it."

Tammy made the call, and minutes later Melody arrived. Augusta could sense the girl's fear and her unease. It saddened her. They had been so close. A frown furrowed Augusta's forehead, as she wondered what could be bothering Melody. It must be something really serious.

"Tammy, what do you want to do this afternoon?" Melody asked a little too cheerfully.

"Melody, I called you over so you could talk to Augusta. You need advice that I can't give you."

"Tammy, you promised that you wouldn't..."

"I didn't tell her anything."

"Listen, Melody," Augusta began. "We've always been friends. Don't you remember when you first came over to see me? You were a little bitty girl and so cute and eager to make friends."

"Yes, I..." She broke down.

Augusta reached for the distraught girl and pulled her into her arms.

"Come on and tell me what's wrong."

Melody allowed Augusta to lead her over to the couch.

"I just can't talk to Mama. She doesn't like Kevin and thinks he's not good enough for me, but I love him, Augusta."

"I don't understand."

"Once she finds out, she'll hate him and me."

"Your mother could never hate you. You're her only child; she loves you very much. We may not see eye to eye on a lot of things, but I know how much she cares about you."

"You just don't know. I'm pregnant, Augusta."

"Pregnant!"

"Almost three months. I thought about getting an abortion, but I just couldn't do it. This baby is a part of me and Kevin. If my mother finds out, I know she'll insist on me having one."

"You can't keep this from her much longer, Melody."

"I know. Kevin wants me to marry him."

"You're only seventeen, Melody. How old is Kevin?"

"He's nineteen."

"It's kind of young to be considering marriage. Is this what you really want to do?"

She hesitated. "It's the only way I can be with Kevin."

"It's a mistake to use an innocent baby to get what you want."

"I won't have an abortion!"

"I'm not suggesting that you do that. It's up to you and Kevin—and your mother. You have to tell her, Melody. Don't you see that? She's your mother; she loves you."

"Then what? She'll kick me out."

"I don't think she will. Why don't you let me call her?"

Tammy gave Melody's arm an encouraging squeeze.

Augusta picked up the phone and dialed the Cummings' number. "Jean, this is Augusta. Can you come over here? No, Melody isn't sick. But it's important. I'll explain when you get here. If it weren't I wouldn't be calling. Yes. All right. Bye." Augusta placed the receiver on its cradle.

"How did she sound?"

"Don't worry, Melody."

A few minutes later Jean Cummings knocked on Augusta's door.

Tammy went to answer it. Jean brushed past her into the living room.

"Where is my baby? If you've done anything to hurt my child, Augusta Humphrey, blind or not, so help me, God, you're going to have to answer to me. I mean that."

"Please, come in and sit down, Jean," Augusta said patiently. What she had to say to the other woman wasn't going to be easy for her to take. She had to be very careful how she broached the subject. Melody's whole future hinged on it.

"What is all this about? Melody?" Jean said sharply, then turned to Augusta.

"Melody has something to tell you. Let her tell you in her own words."

"Melody, baby, what is it?"

"Mama, I..." She started to cry.

"Baby, what's wrong?"

"I'm pregnant, Mama."

"Oh my God. It's that Kevin Thomas, isn't it? I told you to stay away from that boy."

"Mama, I love him."

"You don't have any concept of what love is all about. It's not jumping into bed with some boy."

"Mama..."

"Oh, be quiet. You're coming home with me. Why did you have to tell the whole world?"

"Augusta is not the whole world, Mama. She's my friend."

"I'm your mother. Why didn't you come to me?"

"Because you hate Kevin. I knew you wouldn't understand."

"So you came to Augusta instead of me!"

"Augusta listens and doesn't judge."

Jean turned on Augusta. "I guess you're happy now, Ms. Helpful."

"Jean, listen to yourself. Do you really think it makes me happy to see Melody in trouble and so miserable? Do you?"

Jean ignored Augusta's words and directed her attention back to her daughter. "Why, Melody? Didn't I teach you better than this?"

"You never liked Kevin and I wanted to be with him, but you wouldn't give me permission to see him, let alone go out with him."

"Now it's all my fault you got yourself in trouble."

"No, Mama, I'm not saying that."

"What *are* you saying?"

"Augusta made me see that I wasn't being fair to my baby using it like that."

"Your mistake can be corrected."

"If you mean get an abortion, I'm not going to do it."

"Of course you will. I'm not going to stand by while you ruin your life. How far along are you?"

"Mama, you're not listening to me. I'm not going to have it done. I want this baby."

"You don't know what you're saying. What about all our plans for you going to college?"

"I never wanted to go. That was your idea, not mine. I wanted to go to art school, but you wouldn't even consider it."

"If you insist on having this baby, you won't be able to go to art school or any other school."

"I can manage if you'll help me."

"You're not old enough, or mature enough, to be making this kind of decision alone."

"I'm not a baby, Mama. And besides, I have Kevin."

"You think you do. Just wait. He'll show his true colors soon enough."

"Then you can say I told you so."

"Don't you talk to me like that, young lady."

"Jean, this isn't getting either of you anywhere," Augusta intervened.

"You need to sit down and…"

"This is not your business, Augusta Humphrey. This is between me and my daughter."

"No, it's not. Melody made me a part of it by confiding in me."

"We can remedy that. Come on, Melody, we're going home to discuss this."

Jean moved to take her daughter's hand. Augusta stood in front of Melody.

"Do you want to alienate your daughter, Jean? Just keep on treating her the way you are, and I guarantee that's what will happen. Melody needs all the help we can give her."

"You say *we,* but what you mean is you—you want to take my place. You always have. I won't stand for it. Do you hear me?"

"Mama, Augusta isn't trying to do that."

"I don't want to hear it. You're coming home with me right now."

"No, Mama, I'm not—not if you're going to act like this. You think if I go home with you I'll do what you want."

"You're my daughter, and you *will* do what I say."

"Jean, this is not the way to…"

"You think because you have Tammy, that makes you an expert on raising a daughter all of a sudden?"

"No, I don't. But I've worked with troubled teens enough to know that you have to listen to them. You have to work together to solve problems, and listening to one another plays a major role in accomplishing it."

"I'm not trying to take your place with your daughter. I'm only offering her advice. It's up to both of you whether you choose to take it or not."

"Mama, please listen to her."

Silent until then, Tammy spoke out. "Mrs. Cummings, Augusta knows and understands. She helped me get it together at a time when I didn't see how I ever would. She not only took me into her home, she took me into her heart."

"Tammy, why don't you and Melody go to your room while Jean and I talk."

"All right. Come on, Melody."

"Mama, promise me you won't..."

"I'll listen, but I'm not promising you anything more than that." After a moment of tense silence, the girls left the adults alone. "Melody is thinking about marrying Kevin Thomas, Jean."

"Marrying! Is she out of her mind? She's too young to be considering such a drastic step."

"That might very well be true, but she's contemplating doing it just the same. Since she won't consider having an abortion, you have to give her your support, whatever her decision might be. Let her know that you care about her feelings and what she wants."

"Suppose what she wants isn't what's best for her? What then?"

"You have to let her make her own mistakes. What you both decide will affect the rest of her life. Help her, Jean. Help her make the right decision. And once she has, support her. If you don't, you'll lose your daughter."

"For the record, I've never tried to take her away from you. All I ever tried to do was be her friend and yours too, but you wouldn't allow it."

"Oh, God, have I really been that kind of a petty bitch?"

"No, you were just being overprotective of your child. I understood that, but she's no longer a child, Jean. She's almost grown. I realized that when she came over that day a few months ago to talk about Kevin and you came and got her. I think it was a turning point in her relationship with him."

"Are you trying to say I drove her into his arms?"

"No, I'm not, Jean. What I'm trying to say is that you saw me as a threat when I really wasn't. You might have done the same thing where Kevin was concerned, unconsciously making him seem more attractive to Melody."

"If only I'd listened to her that day, I might have prevented this."

"Maybe, and maybe not. Who can really say? What we have to do now is help Melody. She's the important one in all this. You need to get together with Kevin and his parents and discuss what to do."

"You're right. And, Augusta, I'm sorry about the way I've treated you."

"I believe you mean that."

"I do. I'm not one for apologizing, but I'm doing it now. Considering how I've acted, you'd be within your rights not to accept it."

"I accept your apology, Jean. All I want is what's best for you both. I never intended to come between you and Melody."

"I know that now."

Augusta called the girls back into the living room.

"Mama."

"Don't worry, baby, we'll work it out. Thanks, Augusta."

"I hope I've helped."

"Believe me, you have. Come on, Melody, we're going home and discuss this with your father."

"What about Kevin, Mama?"

"Augusta has convinced me that he should be in on this discussion, since it's his baby too."

"I need to say something to Augusta, Mama. I'll be home in a few minutes."

"All right." Jean walked to the door.

As soon as her mother had gone, Melody hugged Augusta. "Whatever you said, thank you."

"Take care, Melody. Your mother really does have your best interest at heart, you know."

"I guess so, but sometimes..."

Augusta gave Melody's shoulder an affectionate hug. "You have to understand how hard it is for your mother to realize you aren't a child any more. She's used to making all the decisions for you."

"I hadn't thought about it like that. Well, I'd better be going." She kissed Augusta's cheek. "I hope you have a safe trip to Africa. But most of all I hope you get your sight back."

"So do I. Tammy will walk with you to the door."

A few seconds later Tammy returned, joined Augusta on the couch, and took her hand into both of hers.

"You're really something, Augusta. I'm so proud to have you for my mother."

Augusta put her arm around Tammy's shoulder and held her close.

"I'm the lucky one. I don't know what I'd do without you."

"We're a team, remember. I'll be there for you, Augusta, whenever you need me. But I can't help wishing that Derek was—I promised I wouldn't mention him, didn't I?"

"It's all right. There is no way that we can 'X' him out of our lives completely. And I really don't want you to. You love Derek almost as much as..." She couldn't finish the sentence because of the pain constricting her heart.

"I wish there was some way you two could make up."

"There isn't, so let's not talk about it, okay?"

Derek sat at his desk at the Institute, sorting through the exercises he had planned for his class that day. Although he was as dedicated as ever to his work with the blind, he'd lost that extra incentive Augusta always inspired in him.

He wanted to go to Africa with her. Knowing there was a chance that she might see again lifted his spirits, but being there if it happened would bring him the ultimate satisfaction.

Derek put down the papers and rose from his chair. He had to get out of this room. He left his classroom and headed down to the Institute garden. Immediately he saw the bench Augusta had used the many times she'd tried to avoid him, when their situation was escalating beyond mere friendship into love. He could not escape the memories. No matter where he went, they haunted him. The snow-covered garden seemed lonely and empty.

An idea came to him. He could go to Nigeria anyway, and just not let Augusta know he was there. Ben had said that Augusta would be heavily bandaged for a while. He wouldn't interfere in her treatment; he just had to be there, be near her.

That evening before he went to Morgan Electronics to talk to his manager and inform him he'd be out of the country indefinitely, Derek made reservations on a flight to Nigeria scheduled for a week earlier than Augusta's. He had to talk to Dr. Eekong and assure himself that Augusta would be in good hands.

Yeah, right, Morgan. Don't kid yourself, you know Ben has already done that.

I have to know personally.

Any port in the storm, Morgan. Admit it. You just want to be close to her.

I want that more than anything. Even if she doesn't know I'm there.

CHAPTER XXI

"Is that everything you want to take, Augusta?" Myra asked.

"Yes, I think so."

"I'm glad to see you chose the most colorful pieces in your wardrobe. When the bandages come off and you can see, you..."

"Whoa, Myra, it's not a certainty that I'll get my sight back."

"You will, mark my words. When it's all over and you and Todd—I mean Derek...It's hard for me to get used to calling him Derek. When it's all over you and he can..."

"I'm afraid not. We won't be getting back together."

"But, Augusta, you love the man."

"He deceived me."

"But with the best of intentions. He loves you."

"Pity is more like it. And guilt, let's not forget the guilt."

"It's not like you to be so..."

"What? Hard? Unforgiving? Oh, I've forgiven him as far as the accident itself is concerned. And

I can understand that he didn't mean to intentionally hurt me. But, Myra, he pretended to be someone else all these months, letting me fall deeper and deeper in love with him when all the time he was...I'm sorry, but I can't forgive him for that."

"You two belong together."

"I'm afraid this story isn't going to have a fairy tale ending. We're all finished. Ben should be here any minute to take us to the airport. Would you be a sweetheart and see if Tammy needs any help?"

"No problem. I really like that girl."

"Me, too. I think I'll keep her."

When Ben arrived a few minutes later, he took the bags out to the car. Myra followed him. Augusta had had Bella picked up and taken to the seeing eye kennel. If she got her sight back, Bella would no longer be with her, and she would sorely miss her constant companion. She'd come to love the dog very much.

Augusta had Ben check the house to make sure it was secured before they left. She thought about calling Derek. She longed to hear his voice and have both his moral support and physical presence. On impulse, she walked over to the phone, punched in the number, and waited. When his answering machine came on, she hung up.

During the long flight to Paris and the even longer one to Nigeria, Augusta tried to channel her thoughts onto the procedure that could restore her sight, but it took a back seat to her love for Derek Morgan. Why couldn't she erase him from her thoughts and dreams, even for a little while? Was there no respite from this pain?

No, because he will always be a part of you, that's why.

Augusta and Tammy were captivated by the sounds around them, the squeal of wheels from baggage carts and the voices over the loud speakers announcing incoming and outgoing flights. They had fun trying to distinguish the differences in the languages of the people as they walked by.

"Madam Humphrey and her daughter?"

"Yes. Are you the driver the Eekong Clinic sent to pick us up?" She waited, mentally crossing her fingers and hoping the man's command of the English language was good enough to communicate.

"I am. Oswan at your service. I will get the luggage for you."

Something about his voice sounded oddly familiar to Augusta, but she couldn't put her finger on it. He spoke surprisingly good English and she told him so.

Derek smiled affectionately at Tammy, but hungrily drank in the sight of Augusta. He read the frown and the thoughtful expression on her face, guessing that she had picked up some nuance in his voice. Knowing how perceptive she and Tammy were, he had changed his cologne and now realized that he'd better not speak much. If he were around either one of them for any length of time, one or both of them weld be sure to guess his identity. He'd bribed the driver to let him drive Augusta and Tammy to the clinic.

He'd had a college friend from Africa and had practiced imitating Haakeem's accent until he had it down pat. Then he and his friend had worn ceremonial dress and pretended to be brothers on more than one occasion, fooling many strangers.

Derek smiled to himself during the ride to the clinic. Had he really been so carefree and crazy? It seemed him a lifetime ago. He glanced at Augusta. How you've changed my life, my love.

"Are we almost there?" Augusta asked the driver.

"Just be a few more minutes, madam."

"Have you worked for the Eekong Clinic long?"

"No, not long."

Augusta realized that Oswan didn't want to talk and didn't try to draw him out again. When the car came to a stop, Augusta grasped Tammy's hand.

"We are here, madam, mademoiselle," said the driver.

Just as Augusta made to climb out of the car, she suffered a dizzy spell and sat back on the seat waiting for it to pass.

"Are you all right, madam?"

"I'm fine. I guess it was the blast of heat hitting me all at once. I'll be all right in a minute."

It took all the control Derek had not to pull Augusta into his arms and hold her. It probably was the heat. At least he hoped that was it. God, how he worried about her.

Derek extended an arm to both Augusta and Tammy, then escorted them into the lobby of the clinic. He returned for their luggage and brought it inside, taking one last look at Augusta before going back out the way he came.

"Dr. Humphrey?" a female attendant asked.

"Yes, I'm Augusta Humphrey, and this is my daughter."

"Would you please come with me? We have a bed waiting for you. We have prepared a room next door to your room for your daughter. Tomorrow we will be pleased to start your testing program. Once you are settled in, Dr. Eekong will be in to see you. This arrangement is satisfactory to you, yes?"

"Yes, it is." Right away Augusta felt welcomed. It was quite an experience listening to the precise language spoken by the English-speaking people. It would take some getting used to.

She and Tammy talked for a few minutes in Augusta's room. When Tammy went to her own room, Augusta sat down in a chair to take in the fragrance of flowers drifting into the room. No sooner had she relaxed than she heard a knock at the door.

"Dr. Humphrey? I am John Eekong. May I come in?"

"Yes, of course, Doctor."

"I am familiar with your work. You performed open heart surgery on a friend of my family. Perhaps, three years ago?"

"What was his name?"

"Kinte Mali."

"I remember him well. He was a kindly, older gentleman."

"I am now in a position to repay you. Believe me, I will do everything in my power to restore your sight so that your skilled hands may help others. We are also testing your daughter to see if we can help her."

"If it is at all possible, I'm sure that you will help us both, Dr. Eekong."

"Please, call me John. May I call you Augusta?"

She smiled. "By all means, please do."

He patted her hand. "Tomorrow you are going to have a busy day. You get some rest tonight, yes?"

"I will, John."

Getting up from her chair, Augusta made her way to the closet and took out a gown and robe. The nurse's aide had unpacked her things and hung them up. She searched through her shoes for her slippers, then went into the bathroom.

Showered and relaxed, Augusta slipped into bed. God, she was tired. She wearily closed her eyes, seeking sleep. But her tired mind drifted to thoughts of Derek, making sleep an elusive thing. What was he doing at this moment? She'd never forget the sadness in his voice when he'd said goodbye.

She had to stop thinking about him, but how? Tears welled in her eyes and spilled down her cheeks. She wiped them away. What was wrong with her? Why did she feel like crying most of the time lately? It just wasn't like her.

After a long while, Augusta finally fell asleep.

"It is time to get up, Dr. Humphrey," a nurse with a heavy African accent said, waking Augusta with a gentle nudge.

Augusta yawned and stretched. "Already?"

"Our early morning routine is the same as in your American hospital, yes?"

Augusta smiled. "Yes, it is." She realized the woman referred to her as Dr. Humphrey. Evidently John Eekong had been busy singing her praises.

"First, we take the blood tests, the physical examination with Dr. Umani. Tomorrow the special eye exams with Dr. Eekong."

"Sounds like a full day."

"By the end of the day you will fall asleep the minute your head touches the pillow."

"I don't doubt it for a minute."

After completion of the blood tests, a nurse brought breakfast around. Tammy joined her. Augusta took one whiff of the exotic fare and became nauseous. She drank the tea and just nibbled a piece of dry toast without butter.

Dr. Umani was very thorough, Augusta thought later, after his nurse helped her out of the stirrups and down from the examining table.

Exhausted by the time they finished with her, all Augusta wanted to do was sleep when she received a phone call from Philadelphia. She tensed.

Could it be Derek? Reluctantly she took the receiver from the nurse.

"Hello."

"Augusta?"

She breathed a sigh of relief when she heard Ben's voice, yet experienced a letdown feeling because it wasn't Derek. Again those damned tears threatened.

"Ben, I'm glad to hear your voice."

"You're all right, then?"

"Couldn't be better."

"You sound funny."

"They're very nice here. Everyone is cheerful and warm."

"All right, Augusta, you can cut the snow job."

"Is it still snowing there?" She laughed.

"You can't put me off that easily, Augusta. You ought to know that by now. The truth: Are you really all right?"

"I'll survive. How is Myra?"

"She's fine and wants to talk to you."

"Augusta, I'm worried about you. I wish I could have gone with you and Tammy. But you know Ben the worrywart."

"Yes, indeed I do. As I told him, and now I'm telling you, I'm all right."

"Have you seen Dr. Eekong yet?"

"I met him yesterday. Tomorrow I'll him professionally and he'll start his eye exams. I have to admit that I can't help being a little anxious."

"It's only natural with so much at stake. You know you have our love and support, don't you?"

"Yes, I do."

"Here's Ben again."

"Augusta, have you heard from Derek?"

"No, I haven't, and I don't expect to."

"I won't mince words. I was hoping that you would change your mind and call him."

"Ben, you know my feelings."

"Yes, I know how stubborn you can be, but I was hoping you'd put it aside and—never mind. I won't keep you from your rest. Our prayers go with you, my friend."

"Thank you, Ben. And thank Myra for me, too. Good night."

"Good night, Augusta."

Augusta showered and got into bed. As the nurse had predicted, the minute her head touched the pillow, she fell asleep.

"I am sorry to tell you, but there is nothing we can do for your daughter. The optic nerve was too severely damaged."

Augusta felt her spirits plummet. She had hoped against hope for a miracle for Tammy.

"I was hoping..."

"I know you were. Let us get on with your examination." When he had finished his exam, John had Augusta wait in his private office.

"So what do you think, John?"

"There are large fragments of the corneas still intact."

"Is that good?"

"The doctor who did the surgery did a superb job."

"That would be Dr. Ben Hastings," Augusta said proudly.

"You have had the best of care. When I talked with him on the phone, I was very impressed with him. A lot of doctors would have removed the fragments. The corneas are fragile tissues and not easily, or quickly, healed. I can see that under Dr. Hastings' care they were left to regenerate naturally, but unfortunately they have not."

Augusta picked up on the slight hesitation in his voice. "Is that bad, John?"

"Not necessarily. We will do more testing. There is...."

"What is it you found? Is something wrong?"

"Not wrong precisely."

"What exactly? Please, tell me."

"Dr. Umani found something in his examination."

Her heart rate speeded up. "What did he find? Not cancer or..."

"Do not get so upset. It is nothing like that. When did you last have your monthly cycle?"

"What?"

"You are approximately four to five weeks pregnant, Augusta."

"Pregnant!" Augusta gasped in shock. Of all the things he could have said, it was one possibility she'd never ever considered. She remembered the last time she and Derek had made love, in the shower—New Year's Eve—at his place. Their lovemaking had been so frenzied—the protection he was using had slipped off. Caught up in the thrill of the moment, they couldn't stop.

It occurred to her that her pregnancy might complicate her treatment.

As though he had read her mind, John said, "Do not worry, Augusta, this will not change anything.

"The application in our procedure is topical. There will be no danger to your child, I can assure you."

A baby! Augusta couldn't believe it.

She was carrying Derek's baby!

She didn't know how to feel about this latest development. She'd always wanted a child. Next to her career...her career. Would she get it back too? She had everything but the man she loved in this human equation.

"I can see that you were not prepared to hear this. You look somewhat distressed by the news. Do you intend to *keep* the child?"

"Oh, yes. Although this pregnancy wasn't planned, I love this baby already, John."

"I am glad to hear this. Dr. Umani says you are a bit run down. We are going to take a couple of weeks to build you up before we begin the procedure. We intend to see that you get plenty of rest and exercise. We want a healthy mother and infant. Hopefully, and with the grace of God, you will be able to see this child. Since you just found out yourself, I assume the father does not know. Are you going to inform him?"

"Yes—no--I don't know right now. I need time to get used to the idea myself."

"It is understandable."

Did John sound distracted for some reason? she asked herself later after she returned to her room? She shrugged the idea away. It must be her imagination working overtime.

There was a knock at the door, then it opened.

"Augusta, how did our tests come out?" Tammy asked.

Augusta heard both anxiety and hope in her daughter's voice. She hated to have to extinguish that hope with cold, hard facts. "Come over here and sit on the couch beside me."

"It's not good, is it?" Tammy guessed. She found her way to the sofa and sat down.

"Dr. Eekong said the damage to your optic nerve was too severe." Augusta waited anxiously for Tammy's reaction to this discouraging news.

After a moment, in a voice devoid of emotion, Tammy said, "I understand. It's all right. Dr. Hastings explained to me before we came that the odds were against me."

"Knowing Ben, he probably set up the test just because I pushed him to. I'm sorry we got your hopes up." A sob escaped her throat. "Oh, Tammy." She pulled her into her arms. "I wish…"

"I'll live," Tammy sniffed. "Now, what about you?"

Augusta was not fooled by the bravado she heard in her voice. After years of emotional deprivation, Tammy had conditioned herself to expect nothing. And if she did allow herself to hope, she tried to pretend she hadn't. "We're going to have to deal with your disappointment. You have every right to feel angry about not getting your sight back."

"I'm not angry."

"If you're not, I'm angry for you. I wanted you to see again as badly as I want it for myself."

"Augusta, I—"

"Let out your pain, sweetheart. Don't lock it up inside you."

"I hoped..."

"I know you did, baby. Let it all out," she coaxed gently. Augusta felt the drops of healing tears soak through her dress as she held her daughter close. "I'll always be there for you, Tammy."

"I'm so lucky to have you, Augusta."

"You'll always have me. I love you." She continued to rub Tammy's back. "You know, you can still have your singing career, Tammy. You have a rare and beautiful gift of song and music. You don't have to see to brighten the world with it."

After a moment Tammy straightened up. "I'm okay," she said, blowing her nose on a Kleenex. "Now what did the doctors say about you?"

"Two things. First, there're no guarantees, but they want to do the procedure on my eyes." Augusta paused, wondering if her next news would help or "Second, they told me something that might make you feel better."

"What?"

"They told me that I'm a little bit pregnant."

"You're going to have a baby?"

Tammy didn't say anything for a moment. August waited, hoping that her "good news" wouldn't have the opposite effect.

"Oh, Augusta, this baby will be like having a brother or sister again. I can't wait for it to be born. This makes me so happy!"

Augusta let out a sigh of relief. Tammy's disappointment over her own diagnosis seemed, for the moment, forgotten in her happiness over the baby.

"Are you going to tell Derek?"

"I don't know, Tammy."

"You have to. He has a right to know, Augusta. I'm sure he would marry you and…"

"Slow down, Tammy. Do you remember what I told Melody? A baby is not the right reason to get married."

"A baby deserves to know his father. You and I know what it's like not to have one. Mine ran out on us and you never got to know yours. Don't do that to this baby! Please!"

"Tammy, I don't know exactly what I'm going to do. But you're right; a baby does deserve to know its father, and Derek…"

The phone rang. Augusta answered it.

"Hello."

"Augusta?"

"Derek!" she answered in a strangled voice.

His tone gentle, he asked, "How are you, baby?"

"I—I'm all right." She swallowed with difficulty.

"You don't sound like it." Concern laced his words. "Are you sure everything is..."

"Yes, I am." She tried to sound reassuring.

"I just called to give you moral support."

"I'm glad you did."

"Augusta, I could—never mind. I wish you all the best, you know that."

"Thank you, Derek." She bit her lip to keep from crying. They were so stilted with each other. It was truly over.

Not quite. There is the baby we both created.

"Augusta?"

"I'm still here, but I have to hang up now."

"I—I understand. I love you, Augusta. Please, remember that, will you?"

"Goodbye, Derek." She put the receiver on its cradle. "Oh, Derek," she cried, "I love you, too."

Tammy hugged her foster mother and wept with her.

As she lay back on a padded lounge chair in the garden outside her room the next afternoon, Augusta wondered what Derek would say if he knew about the baby.

Would knowing about her pregnancy increase his sense of guilt and responsibility?

Of course it would.

I couldn't stand it if he pitied me and just married me because of the baby.

That's your pride talking, Augusta. Tammy is right, you know. You have to tell him.

Derek watched Augusta from his bench seat across the courtyard. She was so deep in thought he wondered what was going on inside her mind. Dr Eekong had assured him everything was fine. Maybe she just felt anxious about the treatments. The doctor had said he found her slightly anemic and a little run down, but he expected her condition to improve very rapidly because he was prescribing a daily regimen of vitamins and exercise. Only when satisfied with her progress would he proceed with the treatments.

Following his phone conversation with Augusta, Derek longed to go to her, take her in his arms, and kiss her until he made her shiver with wanting. Both day and night, he was haunted by the memory of the little sounds she made when they made love and the wild abandon that took her when they were on the brink of oblivion. He got hard even thinking about the ecstasy they had experienced together. Love made what they had shared all the more special.

If only there were some way to get through to her. Augusta loved him, he was sure of it. And he loved her beyond reason. Surely if she loved him that much she might give him another chance.

Wishful thinking, Morgan?

You're probably right.

Over the next week Derek watched over Augusta like a guardian angel. With each day that went by, he seemed to see an improvement.

For some reason, Augusta felt as though she were being observed. It wasn't a negative feeling; in fact, just the opposite. A sense of protection and caring seemed to envelope her, follow her through the days and nights.

Tammy and Augusta spent every spare moment together, growing closer with each passing day. Today they sat on the garden terrace enjoying the wonderful smell of the flowers.

"How do you feel?" Tammy asked.

"I'm feeling fine; don't worry about me." Augusta touched her watch.

"It's almost time for me to take my vitamins." She reached for her cane.

Tammy moved to follow.

"Don't get up. You just got here. Stay and enjoy the coolness of the garden. I heard you talking to two of the young patients this morning. I'm glad you've managed to make some new friends so you won't have to spend all your time with me."

"Augusta, I like being with you."

"I know, but you need to be in the company of people your own age sometimes, too. Look, I'll see you at dinner."

"All right."

After a while Tammy got up and started back to her room to change her clothes. When she suddenly tripped, hands reached out to keep her from falling.

"Are you all right?"

"Derek! What are you doing here?"

Derek swore inwardly. In his concern for Tammy he had forgotten to disguise his voice. "You've got to promise not to tell Augusta I'm here."

"Why? You guys love each other. Why can't you make up and get back together?"

"It's not as simple as that, Tammy. God, how I wish that it were."

"Have you been here all along?"

Her eyes widened in realization. "You were the driver who drove us here from the airport, weren't you?"

"Yes, but how do you know that?"

"Augusta and I both agreed that something seemed so familiar about that driver."

"Now that you know, I want you to keep me posted on Augusta's progress."

"If you're here, that means you're in touch with her doctor."

"Well, I am, but he will only tell me about her general health. I want to know what Augusta is feeling, Tammy. Only you can help me there."

Tammy considered telling him about the baby, but decided it was up to Augusta to do that. She didn't agree with her, but it wasn't her place to interfere.

"All right, Derek."

Augusta had just finished her lunch when Dr. Eekong came to see her.

"How is our favorite patient today? Or should I say *patients?*"

Augusta blushed. "We are both doing fine."

"According to Dr. Umani, he is satisfied that you are in excellent health."

"Does that mean you are ready to proceed with the treatments?"

"Yes, it does. We want to begin in a few days, with the special drops I have developed from a plant that grows here in Africa. I have found its properties to be quite remarkable."

"After several weeks we remove the bandages to check the healing process. If the corneas are sufficiently regenerated, we use the laser to seal together any fragments that may not have sealed properly on their own. Then we apply more of the drops and wait a few more weeks."

"How long does it take before you'll know if the procedure is successful?"

"It varies from patient to patient. Your condition may be more conducive to the healing process. Mother Nature generously lends extras to mothers-to-be. I know you will think this an old wives' tale, but we in Africa believe this to be so."

"Far be it from me to question Mother Nature." Augusta laughed.

"Your laughter has a delightful sound, Augusta. You must do it more often."

"What? You mean you like to hear me laugh?"

"Yes, it lights up not only your face, but your entire being. It is a most attractive attribute. I must go now I have other patients to see this afternoon. I will see you in the morning."

"All right, John."

After he had gone, Augusta sighed. The big day was almost here. The procedure would work. She had to believe that. She would see again. She would see the face of her child. And, God willing, she would operate again.

What about Derek?

What about him?

Are you going to let him know you are carrying his child? Your child deserves to know its father. Derek deserves to know he has a child.

He'll want me to marry him out of some misplaced sense of responsibility.

You don't know that to be true, Augusta. He wanted to marry you before there was a child.

I can't decide what to do now.

You mean you don't want to decide, don't you?

CHAPTER XXII

After they'd had dinner together and Tammy had gone to her room, Augusta decided to go to the garden. She entered and found a seat. "Augusta?"

"Yes, John?"

"What are you doing out here all alone?"

"I like the peace of the garden after everyone has gone in for the night."

"Would you care to join me in a walk around the grounds?"

"That would be very nice. If you're sure you don't mind."

"Dear lady, nothing would give me more pleasure."

"Won't your wife mind your being late?"

"I am not married."

"Why not?"

"I have been so busy with my career, I have not had the time. I am a research scientist as well as a physician. With my schedule there are not many women who are willing to put up with me."

"I know what you mean. It's the same reason I haven't married and raised a family."

"What about the father of your child?"

"Our relationship just didn't work out. I'll be raising my baby alone."

"Maybe you will meet someone else and..."

"I doubt that."

"I do not; you are a very lovely woman, Augusta. Any man would be proud to make you his own. You and I, for example, have a lot in common, do we not?"

Augusta realized that John's concern went beyond that of a doctor towards his patient.

"I've suddenly gotten very sleepy. I think I'd better go back to my room."

"I will accompany you there. We do not want to tire you out."

When she heard the door to her room close behind John, Augusta let out a sigh of relief. The last thing she wanted to do was become involved with another man. Maybe she was reading more into it than there actually was, but in any case, she wasn't taking any chances. From here on in she would go out of her way to keep her relationship with John Eekong strictly professional.

Derek watched Dr. Eekong escort Augusta through the garden gate, and jealousy raged to life inside him. Augusta belonged to him. Surely she wasn't romantically drawn to the doctor! He had enough to worry about without that added complication. He intended to question Tammy about it and keep an eye on the situation.

"The drops may cause a slight discomfort. I want you to be prepared for that eventuality before we start, Augusta," John stated.

"I understand completely."

"Are you ready to begin?"

"Whenever you are."

Augusta did feel a slight stinging sensation when the drops splashed into her eyes.

"How do you feel?" John asked.

"A little uncomfortable, but it isn't bad."

"If it becomes unbearable, I want you to let me know, all right?"

"All right. What will it mean if…"

"We have to consider the possibility that you may be experiencing an allergic reaction to the drops, and we would have to stop the procedure."

During the next few hours Augusta prayed that she wouldn't have an allergic reaction. To her relief, the discomfort ceased.

The next morning the doctor increased the dosage of the drops and placed padded bandages over her eyes to keep out the harsh sunlight. They continued that dosage for three days.

At the end of the week, Dr. Eekong increased the drops to two applications a day.

Augusta began to get impatient. One afternoon she questioned Dr. Eekong.

"John, isn't there some way you can find out whether the drops are working?"

"We have found that we get much better results if we do not try to test the eyes before we use the laser."

"I'm sorry. I don't mean to tell you what to do."

He patted her hand. "I quite understand, Augusta. Try to be patient a while longer. Will you do this for me?"

"I'll try."

"I cannot ask any more than that from you."

It was the end of the second week following the laser surgery.

"We will remove the bandages tomorrow, Augusta. I know how anxious you have been. Since your system did not reject the drops, we can take it as a positive sign."

With all her heart, she wanted to believe this was true.

Derek was under just as much stress, and just as anxious as Augusta—and said so to Tammy when he met her in the garden one afternoon after Augusta had the drops applied and was resting in her room.

"I don't know how long I'm going to be able to stand this not knowing, Tammy."

"I know what you mean. It's getting to me too. I can't even imagine what Augusta is going through."

"If it wasn't for me, she wouldn't be going through this in the first place."

"Derek, you have to stop beating yourself up about that, okay? You didn't mean to do it. Augusta has forgiven you for the accident. Why can't you forgive yourself?"

"How did you get so wise?"

Tammy smiled. "It must be the company I keep."

"I'm glad Augusta has you."

"Derek…"

"Yes?"

"Oh, nothing. It's just that I hate it that you and Augusta haven't made up. You belong together."

"No one regrets that any more than I do. I blew it, Tammy. I should have told her the truth a long time ago. Maybe then she would have—but that's only guesswork on my part."

"There was nothing they could do about my sight, but Augusta *is* going to get hers back, I just know she will and then maybe you two will get back together."

"I can only hope that'll happen." Derek hugged her. "I'm sorry that they couldn't help you."

"Me too, but I didn't get my hopes up too high. Dr. Hastings said there was only a thirty-five percent chance. I'd better be going."

Derek studied Tammy's face, thinking how well she seemed to be adjusting to her disappointment. He thought he detected Augusta's fine hand in the matter. "Tammy," he said.

She turned. "Yeah, Derek."

"You know, I care about you. If I can help you, you know I'll do it, don't you?"

Tammy smiled. "I know."

"Before you go, what do you think of Dr. Eekong?"

"He seems to know what he's doing. Why?"

"I just wondered. He spends a lot of time with Augusta, doesn't he?"

"Are you jealous?"

"Of course not."

"Augusta loves you, Derek. I'm sure she only sees him as a doctor."

"I wonder. She does call him by his first name. That could mean that they are closer than just doctor and patient."

"Maybe, but I doubt it."

"Why?"

"I have my reasons."

"And you're not going to clue me in, are you?"

"It's just a feeling I have, Derek."

"I think it's more than that."

Tammy didn't offer any further explanation.

Derek watched her leave, then sat back down to continue thinking about the woman he loved.

The outcome of this procedure held the hope for the restoration of a dream. Her career was so important to her, probably more important than her feelings for him right now. At that moment he couldn't help being jealous of John Eekong and resenting her career just a little.

You've wanted this for her from the first moment you found out you'd ruined her life, haven't you, Morgan? As for John Eekong, you'll have to see.

But am I strong enough to accept the possibility that with the return of her sight I stand to lose her forever? Or that another man may take my place?

I won't think about it. Any of it.

Tomorrow would tell the story. Dr. Eekong had agreed to have the removal of the bandages done in a room with a two-way mirror so he could watch.

Augusta awoke the next morning earlier than usual. She'd had trouble falling asleep. It was only natural given the circumstances. She was more than a little anxious about what would happen today. The procedure just had to work. Her eyes and the area around them felt numb this morning. She didn't know what to make of it. What could it mean?

Augusta heard the door to her room open and footsteps as two people entered. They had come for her. She straightened her shoulders and took a deep breath.

"Are you ready, Doctor?" the orderly asked.

"Yes, I'm as ready as I'll ever be."

"Do not be nervous." The nurse gave her shoulder an encouraging pat.

The orderly helped her into a wheelchair and they were on their way.

By the time their small entourage reached the examination room, her nerves were stretched to the breaking point. She'd decided not to have Tammy in the room with her in case things didn't go well. She wasn't sure how Tammy would take bad news after her own disappointment.

"We have been waiting for you, Augusta," John said. "Shall we proceed?"

He helped her into the examining chair, and she heard the nurse close the blinds.

Slowly Dr. Eekong unwrapped the layers of gauze and then removed the cotton padding.

"Miss Tinkanga, I want you to open the blinds in degrees when I give the signal."

"Yes, Doctor."

"Now, Augusta, I want you to open your eyes slowly, gradually giving your eyes a chance to adjust to the light."

Augusta felt frozen to the spot.

"You will be fine, Augusta. Take it slow and easy."

She took a deep cleansing breath and then opened her eyes. Her eyelids felt heavy at first; then she blinked several times and waited.

She saw only darkness.

The procedure had failed!

"I can't see anything." Her voice came out sounding tight, strained, and shocked.

"Do not upset yourself, Augusta," Dr. Eekong said calmly, soothingly. "Close your eyes and wait for a few moments. Then when you open them again, I want you to tell me if you can you see anything—anything at all."

Augusta did as he said and then opened her eyes again. This time the darkness was a dull dark gray, then eased into gray, shadowy horizontal lines converging on the periphery of her vision. She heard the nurse manipulate the blinds.

Gradually the light filtered in.

She could see! Not a lot, but she could see!

The nurse opened the blinds a fraction more until eventually they were open all the way. The first thing she saw was a red sun setting over the city of Lagos. To her a sunset had never looked more beautiful.

"I can see! Thank God, I can see again!" she cried, a trail of tears streaming down her face.

Her prayers had been answered. She took in the things in the room. Everything had a vignette quality about it. John Eekong looked just as she had imagined he would, dark and handsome in a distinguished way with wings of gray at his temples. She took him to be in his early forties.

He smiled at her. "Things may appear hazy to you for a while."

"But my vision will continue to improve?"

"We hope so. But you have to face the possibility that it may not improve enough for you to operate again, Augusta."

"I know you're right. Just to be able to see anything at all is so miraculous. But to be able to perform surgery again would be the ultimate in miracles."

The look on Augusta's face thrilled Derek to the core as he watched her from his place behind the two-way mirror. For a moment his heart had stopped when she couldn't see. But now to know that she could see…

Where did that leave him? He sobered at the thought. He guessed that he would have to wait and hope. He had done all he could to make amends. But was it enough? Would seeing his face bring back all the anger and pain she had suffered because of him?

Derek backed away from the glass and turned to leave. He had come to make sure Augusta was all right. He'd done that. And now that he had, he could only go back home and wait for her to make the first move.

If she ever does.

He sighed heavily. Yes, if she ever does. And John Eekong waited in the wings. Jealousy raged inside him like a fire that refused to be put out.

Derek wanted to talk to Tammy before he left for Philadelphia, so he hurried out of the room and down the hall.

He knocked on her door before entering the room. "Tammy, it's me."

"Did it work? Can Augusta see?"

"Yes, but I want you to pretend that you don't already know. I'm sure she wants to tell you herself. Listen, I haven't got much time. I just wanted to touch base with you before I left. Call me when you and Augusta get back home. You can tell me how she's doing then."

"Derek, why can't you..."

"Seeing my face might bring back in vivid detail all that I have done to her. I know I have to give her space. But in the meantime, I want you to keep me posted."

"Of course I will. You know that. One day she'll call you. She loves you, Derek. Please just hang in there, she'll come around."

"I hope you're right, Tammy. Well, I'd better be going. Someone should be in any minute to take you to Augusta."

"Derek, I wish things could be different for you and Augusta."

"So do I. Goodbye, Tammy."

She heard Derek turn to leave and considered breaking her promise to Augusta and telling him the truth, but at the last second changed her mind.

"Bye, Derek."

"I'm so glad for you, Augusta," Tammy exclaimed minutes later.

"I can hardly believe it." She cherished seeing her foster daughter's face. Tammy was a very pretty girl. But what she longed for most was to see Derek's face. What would happen once she went back to Philadelphia?

"When are you going to tell Derek about the baby?"

"I don't know the answer to that yet, Tammy, but I will tell him."

"Does that mean that you and he might..."

"Tammy, you're beginning to sound like a remix. I don't want to talk about it. Not now."

Augusta's vision sharpened with each passing day until one day, two weeks later, she was ready to leave the clinic. She was dressed in one of the many bright-colored outfits she'd brought with her to Nigeria. She would never take colors for granted again. A knock sounded at the door.

"May I come in, dear lady?"

She smiled. "Of course, John."

"We are going to miss you around here.'

"As I am going to miss all of you."

"Our prayers and best wishes go with you, Augusta. If you should have any problems, you will call me, yes?"

"You know I will." The warm look in his eyes confirmed her earlier suspicions. John was interested in her as a woman. "John, I..."

"You do not have to say it. I know where your heart lies."

"I'm sorry, John."

"Do not be. None of us has a say in whom we fall in love with. In my case it was not meant to be. But if you should change your mind, I..."

"I won't."

He smiled slightly. "Well, if that is how it is to be, then as I have said before, I wish you all the best, Augusta."

Her eyes misted. "Thank you, John."

"Goodbye, Augusta," he said before quietly exiting the room.

Augusta and Tammy sat waiting for the driver to come for them.

Shortly she heard a knock at the door.

"Come in."

A slender, dark-skinned man entered. "I am Solango. I am here to pick up your bags and drive you to the airport."

Augusta was disappointed, for it wasn't the driver she had before.

"Do you know a driver named Oswan?"

"No, madam, I am not familiar with that name. However, I have only been working for the clinic three weeks."

"Oh, I see." She cleared her throat. "The bags are over there."

During the ride to the airport, she wondered what had happened to Oswan. Had he quit? She didn't know why it should matter to her. But there had been something about the man. Well, that was that. She had a future to think about and plan for, as well as a baby on the way.

The ache in her heart was almost unbearable. When she thought about the baby, invariably her thoughts drifted to Derek. Her feelings for him wouldn't go away. They never would, of that she was sure.

Augusta looked at the world through different eyes now as she watched the clouds and blue sky float by the plane window. Like the average person, she'd taken sight for granted, but never again. She glanced at Tammy sitting next to her and regretted that nothing could be done about getting her sight back, at least for now. But Tammy was a survivor, and she would make her way in the world with or without sight. In a few months she would be going away to Julliard, submerging herself in her music.

"Augusta, what's it like getting your sight back?" Tammy asked.

"Like a whole new beginning."

"It can be a whole new beginning for you and Derek and the baby, if you will only give him a chance."

"Tammy," Augusta sighed. "You don't understand how betrayed I feel about what he did. If he loved me as much as he said he did, he would have been honest with me instead of letting me—I don't want to talk about it."

"Not talking about it won't change anything, Augusta. Won't you even think about getting together with Derek? You're having his baby. That has to figure in your plans, doesn't it?"

"I wonder if Derek knows that he has in you a cheering section the likes of which the 76ers would envy. All right, Tammy, I'll think about it. Now can we change the subject, please?"

Tammy smiled. "All right. How soon do you think it'll be before you return to the hospital?"

"I don't know. I have to get board certified, and that can take a while."

"Do you think it'll happen before you have the baby?"

"I think so." Where did this leave her feelings for Derek? She still loved him despite everything. She did get her sight back. God, she had some heavy thinking to do.

CHAPTER XXIII

Augusta and Tammy waited at the airport arrival gate for the Hastings' to meet them. Augusta smiled when she saw them and, putting down her bag, went into Myra's welcoming arms.

"I'm so glad you're back, Augusta," Myra said, her eyes brimming with happy tears.

"I'm glad to be back. It's wonderful to be able to see your face again." Augusta took a step back away from Myra, lowering her gaze to her friend's protruding stomach. "You're blooming, girlfriend."

"Yeah, thanks to me." Ben stuck his chest out proudly.

"Ben Hastings!" Myra exclaimed.

"What, my love?" he asked, flashing her his most innocent, boyish smile.

Myra looked to Augusta. "What am I going to do with him?"

"Just keep loving him, I guess," Augusta answered softly.

"Like you love Derek, Augusta?" Ben pointedly asked.

"Ben," Augusta shot him a warning glance.

"Did I lie? You do happen to love the man, don't you?"

Augusta didn't answer him.

Tammy answered for her. "She knows it's the truth, Dr. Hastings. That's why she's not saying anything. And there's another more important reason why she should..."

"That's enough of that, young lady," Augusta said more sharply than she intended, in an effort to avert attention away from what Tammy nearly revealed.

"Augusta, you belong with Derek, especially now," Tammy continued, as if Augusta hadn't spoken.

"Myra and I both agree with you, Tammy," Ben said simply. "We'd better get you two home. Myra and I have opened up the house and had it aired and cleaned, ready and waiting for you to get back."

"Thank you, Ben and Myra. I am anxious to get home."

Augusta couldn't help wishing that Derek had come to the airport with Ben and Myra.

What did you expect? You said goodbye to the man and told him that you didn't want to see him.

After a few minutes, Myra noticed her friend's almost forlorn expression. "Augusta, you're awfully quiet. Is anything wrong?" she asked when they reached the car.

"No, I'm just tired. Kind of like you."

"What?"

Augusta decided to tell Myra and Ben about the baby. "I'm pregnant."

Ben looked sternly at Augusta. "I didn't pick up on what Tammy said earlier. But now that I know, I definitely agree with her. The baby is all the more reason why you and Derek should get back together."

Augusta didn't answer, refusing to be drawn into a discussion on the subject.

Ben put the luggage in the trunk and then got into the car. Ignoring Augusta's silent warning to desist, he started in on her again. "What did Derek say when you told him about the baby? You haven't told him, have you?" Ben asked, already having guessed the answer. "Isn't this carrying pride and stubbornness a little bit too far?"

"Of course you'd think so, you're a man and Derek's friend."

"And yours, too, I thought."

"You are, but..."

"But you don't want to hear what I have to say. Right?"

"Ben, why do you always do this to me?" Augusta sighed tiredly. "I'm not going to argue the point with you, just drive Tammy and me home, please."

He realized by the pinched lock on Augusta's face that he was really upsetting her. And he didn't want to do that. It wasn't good for her or the baby.

"All right, Augusta. I'll let it ride for now."

"Thank you, Ben."

Augusta watched the Hastings' car back out of the drive. A feeling of guilt washed over her. She hoped that she hadn't managed to alienate them with her attitude.

"Dr. Hastings is right, you know."

"Tammy, you're not going to pick up where Ben left off, are you? Because if you are, please don't. I'm just too tired to hear it."

"No, I'm not. It wouldn't do any good, so I guess I'll leave you alone."

"Tammy, I…"

"It's all right, Augusta. I'm tired too."

"I have to call the Seeing Eye Center and tell them I've gotten my sight back so they can release Bella to work with someone else.

"Oh, no! I love her so much, Augusta! Maybe you could convince them to let me have her."

"I don't know if they'll agree to that, but I'll ask the head of the Center."

The next day Augusta walked over to the desk to have a word with the head of the Seeing Eye Center.

"I'm Henry Lang. What can I help you with?"

"My name is Augusta Humphrey. I don't know if you'll remember me, but I came here about a year ago to get a seeing eye dog."

"The name's not familiar, but I never forget a face."

"You know the name Todd Winters?"

"Why yes, he's with the Philadelphia branch of the Braille Institute. I remember now. You're a doctor, aren't you? And you came here with Mr. Winters."

"Yes I am, and yes I did come here with him. I just recently got my sight back and came about my dog. My foster daughter is blind, and I thought that since she knew Bella it might be possible to assign Bella to her."

"We hardly pass our dogs among family members, Doctor."

"I know you don't, but maybe you could make an exception in this case. You see, my daughter is seventeen and will be starting college in the summer session. I thought…"

"I see. And since your daughter and the dog are already acquainted you thought it would be the ideal solution. I'll need to meet your daughter first before I make a decision."

Augusta smiled. "Thank you, Mr. Lang. I can't ask for any more than that."

Tammy lovingly wrapped her arms around Bella's neck. "I never thought I'd be kicking it with you again, girl. Thank you, Augusta."

"You don't have to thank me. You did it yourself. Mr. Lang was impressed with you, I could tell."

"Augusta..."

"I know what you want to talk about, Tammy. I have been thinking about—my situation."

"And?"

"I think it best that we leave things the way they are for the time being."

"What about your job at the Institute?"

"I don't know Since I'm no longer blind, they may not..."

"Want you? They will, believe me. It's because of the kind of person you are that they hired you. Todd—I mean Derek told me so."

"He said that?"

"Yes, when you refused to give up on me. I'm glad you didn't—give up on me, I mean."

Augusta smiled. "So am I. I would have deprived myself of a wonderful daughter if I had."

"I love hearing you say that, Augusta. You're the best."

Augusta rested for the remainder of the week before putting her comeback plan into motion. She and Tammy spent a lot of the time planning the clothes they would buy for her college wardrobe and discussing the baby and the things they would buy for it.

Tammy returned to the Institute the following week. Before that, she had contacted Derek to let him know how Augusta was adjusting to having her sight back…

"I'm glad to hear that she's doing so well. Has she said anything about us?"

"No. She won't discuss you with me. I think she's still thinking about everything, though."

"I'd say our relationship was the last thing on her mind right now. She has her career back if she wants it, and everything is going her way. Maybe there's no room in her life for me."

"Don't talk like that, Derek. Just give her a little more time, please."

"All right, I'll wait, but not forever."

Over the next few weeks, Augusta became caught up in being reinstated to the surgical board and returning to her position at the hospital. And once she got recertified, she was excited and found it hard to contain her enthusiasm.

One evening she, Ben, and Myra celebrated by going out to dinner at the Staircase. Tammy spent the evening with Melody at the Cummings' house. Matters there had generally improved. Melody and her parents and Kevin and his parents had gotten together to solve their problems. And although Augusta and Jean would never be bosom buddies, they treated each other with respect.

As soon as Augusta and the Hastings' were seated at their table, Augusta said, "I know why you decided to come here, you two, and it won't work."

"I don't know what you're talking about, Augusta," Ben replied innocently.

"Oh, give me a break, Ben. I read you like a book."

Myra laughed. "I bet it's one hell of an interesting read."

"No comments from the peanut gallery." He glared at his very pregnant wife in mock indignation. "Besides, my love, you of all people know how interesting I am," he said, smiling wickedly as he looked at her stomach and then shifted his gaze to her face.

A heated blush infused Myra's cheeks.

Augusta smiled. "Listen, guys, I know what you're both trying to do and I appreciate it, but I don't want to talk about Derek tonight."

"Have you talked to the man since you got back?" Ben probed.

"No, I haven't. And I don't intend to. It's over, Ben."

"How can you say that, knowing you're carrying his child? It doesn't have to be over. It could be a new beginning for you both."

"If you're going to preach to me—"

Ben held up a hand. "I'll step down from my soapbox. Not another word on the subject. We're here to celebrate your return to surgery. Since you and my beautiful wife are both pregnant, it will have to be ginger ale, the other bubbly."

Augusta laughed with Ben and Myra, but she felt less than ecstatic. She seemingly had everything going for her, but it didn't feel right somehow; something was very wrong with the picture. And that something was the man she loved. The fabric of her existence had a hole in it.

Do I dare to trust him?

You have some serious soul searching to do, girlfriend.

Ben watched Augusta closely. He could see the turmoil on her face and wanted so much to speak his mind. In the past he'd never had a problem with it. But in this case, he was afraid to rock the boat. Augusta had to be thinking about her and Derek's situation and whether to risk trusting him again.

Augusta loved the man, damn it! And he loved her! How could he get them back together? Then suddenly he sighed deeply, realizing it wasn't up to him. Augusta and Derek would have to work this out for themselves. Whatever conclusions Augusta came to had be from her heart. He felt so damned helpless.

Augusta tiredly shrugged out of her surgical scrubs. It had been several weeks since her return to the hospital routine. Her surgical skills, a bit rusty at first, had sharpened quickly. The chief of staff had tried her out on minor operations to accustom her to operating again. So far, everything seemed to be going all right.

Although happy to be operating again, she felt…she didn't really know how she felt. Learning to fix defective hearts had been her dream since her mother died. Ironically, fixing her own heart problems seemed beyond her capability.

Heading home from the hospital, Augusta came to the fatal intersection. She remembered vividly what it had felt like to get into a car and slide behind the driver's seat for the first time after her accident…

Tammy had offered to go with her to get another car, but she had refused, and later wished she had taken her up on the offer. Beads of sweat had broken out on her forehead, and she had trembled with apprehension. She chose a car similar to the one totaled in the accident.

She had forced herself to turn the key in the ignition. Her hands shook for a moment, then steadied. Maneuvering the car out onto the streets of Philadelphia in the rushing flow of traffic had been the acid test.

She had driven around several blocks before venturing out into the traffic on the freeway. Her first brush with a reckless driver nearly unnerved her, but she got past that and returned safely to the car lot…

Switching her thoughts back to the intersection where she now waited to turn, it dawned on her that since her accident, the city had installed four-way streetlights. Had they done it when they had promised they would, she wouldn't have lost nearly two years of her career and her life.

You would never have had Tammy and fallen in love with Derek, either. And you wouldn't be carrying his child.

She banished those thoughts to the back of her mind.

Augusta pulled into her driveway minutes later. Looking at her watch when she got to the hospital earlier that morning, she realized she had automatically fastened on her Braille watch when dressing.

That watch brought back so many memories of the man she loved that it drew tears from her eyes.

She would have to stop this. Augusta quickly channeled her thoughts to her foster daughter and her home. Still at the Institute, Tammy wouldn't be home for at least another hour.

Augusta gazed at her home. She never failed to appreciate it. On this spring day her garden promised an abundance of bouquets. In the one year almost to the day since Derek had come into her life, so much had happened.

She checked her mailbox. Finding a letter from Elaine, Augusta went into the house to sit down and read it. A smile came to her lips when she discovered an invitation to Elaine's June graduation from Tulane, along with a note. She wouldn't be able to go, but she would send her a nice gift.

Minutes later Augusta walked into her kitchen and foraged in the refrigerator for something to eat. She felt a strange craving for crab leg stew. Until now, she had never believed in cravings, thinking them the stuff of old wives' tales. She had to admit that she also craved the sight of the man she associated with crab leg stew.

Augusta slipped into a roomy pair of jeans and a big white sweater. The jeans fit snugly around the waist. Very soon she would have to abandon them for maternity jeans. Grabbing up her keys, she headed for the only place in Philadelphia that made a decent crab leg stew: Mama's-on-the-River, which also happened to be Derek's favorite place and his favorite food.

Augusta felt odd going to Mama's without Derek. As she got out of her car, she breathed in the scent of river water, fresh spring grass, and wet sand.

"I heard you got your sight back, honey," Mama said when Augusta walked in.

"You've seen…"

Mama guided Augusta to an empty booth. "Derek? No."

"Then how did you know?"

"I have a cousin who works at Philadelphia General. I haven't seen Derek in a long time."

"You knew his name wasn't Todd Winters all those times we were in here."

Mama sat down across the table from Augusta. "Yes, I did. But it wasn't my place to question why. I figured that he had his own reasons for using the other name. What would you like, honey?" Mama smiled. "You don't have to answer that. I already know what you want and why."

"You do? How?"

"You have that special glow a lot of pregnant women get. When's the baby due?"

"The middle of October."

"You and Derek going to—"

Augusta cut across her. "No, I'm afraid not."

She shook her head and frowned. "Why not, for God's sake? I know you love him, honey."

Augusta lowered her eyes. "It's a long story, Mama."

"Isn't it always? Well, it's none of my business, but I think it's a shame if you two don't get back together." Mama rose from the seat. "I'll get you that order of crab leg stew."

As she sat at her kitchen table eating the stew, Augusta thought about Derek. She couldn't go on like this. Either she wanted him back or…

Or what, girlfriend?

I miss him so much.

Call him.

I can't do that.

Why not? You love the man, don't you?

But can I trust him with my heart?

You trusted him with your body and your heart when you were blind.

Yeah, and see what it got me.

A baby you already love and your sight back.

Augusta got up and washed the dishes, then went into the living room and switched on the stereo. The song "There's a Right and a Wrong Way to Love Somebody" by Keith Sweat came on the radio.

Tears came to her eyes. Maybe Derek hadn't gone about love the right way. What was the right way? No matter what it was, God, how she loved him!

Wasn't the way you treated him the wrong way?

I never wanted to hurt him.

Didn't you, Augusta? Be honest. Didn't a part of you want to hurt him the way he hurt you?

He was everything I despised in a man.

That was in the past. You know he's changed. He's no longer the reckless fool who blinded you, but a caring, selfless human being. Admit it, Augusta, you no longer think of him as that other kind of man.

But he lied to me.

It was the only way he could get close to you. He's learned a valuable lesson about life since coming to know you.

He did help me at a time when all I wanted to do was wallow in self pity and do nothing for myself.

You're damn right he did!

He tried to make amends the only way he knew how. Ben said he donated more than just his fair share of time at the Institute. And he's donated a huge amount of money to the Eye Research Foundation.

Doesn't that tell you something?

That night after Tammy had gone to her room, Augusta turned off the lights and locked up the house. In her own room she eased down on the bed and lay thinking.

What good was having her sight back when she couldn't see the one person who made her life worth living?

But will he still want me after all the awful things I've said?

Could you blame him if he didn't?

No, I couldn't.

There's only one thing left to do.

Augusta reached for the phone and dialed Derek's number. A recorded, computerized message announced that the line was no longer in service and there was no new number. There had to be a mistake, she thought, and tried it again with the same results.

She frowned. Where was Derek? If he had moved, then why didn't he...It didn't make any sense.

She remembered the oddly sad expression on Tammy's face when she had gotten home a little over an hour ago. Augusta slid off the bed, shed her clothes, and padded into the bathroom. There were no towels.

Tears welled in her eyes as a memory of Derek filled her mind. There were never any towels in his bathroom. She recalled telling him that she would take care of him. She closed her eyes and put her head down. "Oh, Derek, I miss you so much. I love you and want to be with you."

She'd find out in the morning what Tammy knew about this. And surely Barry Hawkins, Derek's business manager, would know how to get in touch with him. And of course, Diane and John.

Augusta waited for Tammy to come into the kitchen for breakfast.

"What do you want for breakfast?" Augusta asked.

"I'm not really hungry. Juice is all I want."

"Okay, Tammy, out with it."

"I don't know—"

"Tammy, when was the last time you spoke to Derek?"

"A couple of weeks ago."

"Come again?"

"All right. His last day at the Institute."

"What?"

"He couldn't wait any longer for you to contact him and he quit."

"I don't believe that. His job at the Institute was too important to him."

"You just don't get it, do you, Augusta?"

"Get what?"

"It was too painful for him without you. He loves you. You mean more to him than anything."

"I'm taking you to the Institute this morning. I have to talk to Diane."

Augusta saw the bud of hope blossom on Tammy's face, and she wondered why it had taken her stubborn mind so long to acknowledge that her heart knew the best thing for her.

"When did you know that Todd Winters wasn't Derek's real name, Diane?" Augusta asked.

"From the beginning. He wouldn't tell me why, but when Ben explained later, I decided to go along with it."

"Where is he?"

"I can't answer that."

"But I don't understand, Diane."

"He had been sad for a long time, Augusta. Oh, he still cared for his students, but he was different after he came back."

"Came back? From where?"

"From Africa."

"What?"

"He took a leave of absence from the Institute several months ago."

"And he told you he was going to Africa?"

"Yes. Surely you knew that. He went there to be with you."

"I'm afraid I didn't. And he wasn't with me." When Augusta thought about it, she knew that he had been. She realized why the driver Oswan had sounded so familiar; he was Derek. And all those times when she had felt that someone was watching over her—it was Derek's presence she'd drawn comfort from.

"I have to find him, Diane."

"I wish I could be of more help to you."

"Thanks, you've helped me more than you realize."

Diane smiled. She could have volunteered information that could help Augusta, but she decided to stay out of it. If it was meant to be, Derek and Augusta would get together.

"This is Barry Hawkins."

"Mr. Hawkins, this is Augusta Humphrey. Can you give me Derek Morgan's new phone number?"

"I'm sorry, Ms. Humphrey, but I'm not at liberty to—"

"I've got to talk with him," she said impatiently. "It's extremely urgent."

"I can't help you."

"Can't or won't? You don't understand, I—"

"I'm sorry."

"Thanks for nothing." She hung up.

Augusta paced back and forth in her living room.

Ben!

She reached for the phone.

"Is Ben in, Rebba? This is Augusta Humphrey."

"I'm sorry, Doctor. He's away at a conference in Montreal and won't be back for another two days."

"Isn't there a number where I can reach him? It's a matter of life or death."

"Hold on, I'll get it for you." The line was silent for a few moments and then she came back on the phone and gave Augusta the number.

She wrote it down, then hung up and dialed.

"Montreal Hotel."

"Dr. Ben Hastings' room, please."

"He's in a meeting at the moment. Can I have him call you back when he gets out?"

"Yes." Augusta left her number. She was about to go crazy. Where was Derek, and why hadn't he left a number where he could be reached?

Augusta had to operate that afternoon. Because of complications, the surgery ran longer than expected. It was well after six o'clock when she got home, but there were no messages on the answering machine.

Tammy came home.

"Augusta, what's wrong? I sense that you're really freaked out about something. Didn't you get in touch with Derek?"

"No. You knew that Derek was in Africa, didn't you?"

"How did you find out?"

"It doesn't matter how I found out. You knew and didn't tell me. I want to know why."

"Derek asked me not to. He'd been in touch with Dr. Eekong all along. He even watched when they took your bandages off."

"He told you the result before I did, didn't he? You don't have to answer. I thought at the time that you didn't sound very surprised to hear my news."

"Have you found out where Derek is?"

"No. And I'm getting damned frustrated."

CHAPTER XXIV

Later Augusta wondered why Ben hadn't gotten back to her. She dialed the number of the hotel.

"I'm sorry, but Dr. Hastings checked out an hour ago."

"Thank you." She cradled the phone.

"Damn you, Ben!"

First thing the next morning, Augusta was back on the phone.

"Hello," came the sleepy voice of Myra Hastings.

"Myra, this is Augusta. Is Ben there?"

"Yeah, but he's asleep. He didn't get home until two o'clock in the morning. Why? What's up?"

"I really need to talk to him."

"Can't you tell me?"

"No offense, but I have to talk to Ben."

"He'll be into the office at eleven-thirty. Can't it wait until then? He's really done in from his late-night flight."

Augusta considered. "I guess so. Tell him I'll be waiting there. No excuses."

Myra yawned. "I'll tell him."

"I'm sorry I woke you up. Go back to sleep."

After the longest five hours on record, the moment of truth finally arrived. Augusta walked into Ben's reception room at eleven-thirty on the dot.

"He'll be with you in a moment, Doctor," Rebba assured her.

Ben came out to meet her.

"Come on in, Augusta."

She preceded him inside.

"No calls for the next twenty minutes, Rebba."

"Yes, Doctor."

Ben took a deep breath and entered his office, closed the door, then headed for his seat behind his desk.

"All right, Augusta."

"Where is Derek, Ben?"

"Why do you want to know?"

"Ben don't play twenty questions with me. I'm definitely not in the mood."

"Augusta, I—"

"Tell me, damn you!"

"Hasn't the guy suffered enough? You've made it plain he has no part in your life. You haven't tried to get in touch with him once since you got your sight back, have you? Of all the ungrateful—Now, all of a sudden you want to talk to him? Why, Augusta?"

"Ben, I want to—"

"What? Hurt him some more?"

"No, I don't," she said, affronted. "If you know where he is, you've got to tell me. I tried his phone number and got a computerized message saying his number was no longer in service. I grilled Tammy and came up empty. I talked to Diane, but she doesn't know anything. His manager refuses to give me any information. There's been no answer at any door I've knocked on. Finally, out of desperation, I went by his apartment building. He'd moved out and left no forwarding address. All of his mail is forwarded to his business manager."

Ben leaned back in his chair. "Why do you want to see him?"

"I have something to tell him. Ben, please, I..." She twisted her hands in her lap and tears trickled down her cheeks. "I love him, Ben. I have to tell him how much."

Ben got up from his chair and came around his desk to hand her a tissue.

"He's left Philadelphia, Augusta."

She looked up from the tissue. "He's left town! Where has he gone? Is he coming back? Please, Ben, you've got to tell me."

Ben sat on the edge of his desk. "He waited and waited for you to contact him when you got back from Africa. After a while he gave up. He said he couldn't take being in the same city with you any longer. Said it would tear him apart if he saw you or ran into you. I couldn't get him to tell me where he was going."

Augusta's heart lurched painfully. Had she lost him? Was he gone from her life for good? "What am I..." She made a choking sound. "Ben, what can I do?"

"Derek loves you. Maybe he'll come back on his own, in time."

"Do you really believe that?"

Ben shifted uncomfortably. How could he be sure of what Derek might do? The man was in love and hurting. Ben had to wonder what his own reaction would be if it were he and Myra.

Ben's silence was answer enough for Augusta.

Hurt, pride, and her inability to forgive had caused her present misery. She had no one to blame but herself. She stood and walked over to the window and looked out.

She eased her fingers over the slight swell of her abdomen. What about their baby? Not only had she deprived Derek of knowing he would have a child, but she was also going to deprive their child of a wonderful father. And Augusta knew instinctively that he would be that and more. He would also be a fantastic, loving husband. If she'd only given him a chance. Now it was too late. He was gone. Her body began to shake, and the tears came.

Ben came up behind her and put his hands on her shoulders. "I'll do everything I can to help you find him, you know that, but if a man doesn't want to be found..." His voiced trailed away.

Ben didn't have to finish the sentence. Augusta knew better than he that a person didn't have to physically remove himself to not want to be found. There were so many ways to escape from unendurable pain. Had she inflicted more pain on the man she proclaimed to love than he could bear?

That night Augusta sat in front of the fireplace remembering the wonderful times when she and Derek had made love in a room illuminated and warmed by a fire, how gentle he could be and at other times savagely tender. Her heart ached for him. Her body craved his touch.

Oh, God, what am I going to do if he doesn't come back?

Just then the baby moved. She rubbed her stomach. "You want him too, don't you?"

Over the next few weeks, Augusta tried, with very little success, to get on with her life. But no matter how long her work day, it was never long enough to relieve the pain, or sense of loss, she felt at its end.

Tammy had entered a talent competition scheduled to take place in a few days. Augusta loved her adopted daughter as her own. And so did Derek. Her heart began to beat a little faster, filling with hope. Was there a chance that…? Surely he wouldn't miss her performance. Augusta had to wonder if she were just clutching at straws. Her heart sank the next moment. *If* he knew about it.

Derek left the city because of you.

If he didn't come back it would be her fault.

Derek did know about Tammy's performance. He'd made it his business to know everything that was going on with both Tammy and Augusta through his business manager." before he'd left for San Francisco.

He debated whether he should go to the talent competition, but he knew deep down that nothing, not even Augusta's soul-destroying presence, would stop him. And Augusta would definitely be there. He groaned and then closed his eyes. His heart lurched, and his lower body hardened achingly at the thought of how good it had been between him and Augusta.

He wasn't sure he wouldn't go off the deep end when he saw her. His days he could handle, but his nights were pure hell. He had no one to blame but himself. He would eventually have to accept that it was over between him and Augusta. But, God, he didn't know how he was going to do it. And he had the night of the competition to get through.

"I'm so nervous, Augusta," Tammy said as she sat down in the easy chair in Augusta's living room, Bella parked at her feet.

"You'll do fine, Tammy. With a talent like yours, you're sure to win."

"In a few hours I'll be in front of all those people. Jeffrey said I was ready for this and that he thought I had it made. I just wish I had as much confidence as both of you." She was quiet for a minute. "Do you think Derek will come?"

"I don't know He loves you very much. If he knows—"

"Oh, he knows about it, all right."

Augusta's face molded into a confused frown.

Tammy hurried on to explain. "I received a message from him by way of his business manager

"What did the message say?"

"If there was anything I needed to let Mr. Hawkins know."

"When did this happen?"

"Two or three weeks ago. Now don't get mad! I didn't mention it because I knew you would get upset. You know your doctor is concerned about you since you've been through so much in the last few months."

Augusta sighed. "Nothing hurts me more than knowing it's my fault Derek and I aren't together. You know what you've told me means, don't you? It means that he *will* be there. This may be my last chance to win him back."

"You could tell him about the baby."

"No, I couldn't. I won't use our baby like that. Derek has to come back to me because he loves me and doesn't want to live his life without me."

"You'll get the answer you want. I know you will. If you can't get him to see reason, I'll lock him in the dressing room, if I have to."

Augusta laughed. "I'm sure you won't have to resort to anything that drastic, but if it comes to that..."

"I hear you. You know Ben and Myra will help." Tammy rubbed Bella's furry head. "And you'll help too, won't you, girl?"

The dog barked in agreement.

"You see, Augusta, everyone wants to help you two get back together."

"With friends like mine there's no way I can lose, right?"

As she changed into a flowing, yet concealing, dress of mint-green silk, Augusta remembered that Derek loved seeing her wear that color. She wished she could have seen the look on his face that day she'd first worn it. The tingling sensation she'd felt when he had touched her bare skin…

Augusta smoothed her hand up and down the front of the dress. She'd purposely chosen this particular style because she knew it would camouflage her pregnancy. She had to find out if he still loved and wanted her for herself. If she failed, she didn't know what she was going to do.

But she wouldn't fail.

"How do I look?"

Augusta came out of her reverie and turned to study her daughter. "Like a million dollars." She walked over to Tammy and hugged her. "I feel sorry for the kids competing against you. They haven't got a chance."

"You sound like a typical stage mother. I wish you had been my real mother from the jump."

Augusta's eyes misted. "Me too."

"Do I really look all right?"

"Yes, you do. Red is very definitely your color. Don't worry, Tammy, you look good, good enough to win. And you will."

She hugged Augusta. "I love you."

"I love you too. Now, we had better get a move on. We don't want you to be late."

Derek waited until everyone was seated before sliding into the back of the theater. Finally Tammy's turn to sing arrived. He spotted Jeffrey Osborne and his family sitting in the front row seats. Derek's heart skipped a beat when his gaze settled on Augusta seated beside the Osbornes. His throat went dry as he stood glued to the spot. An attendant walked over to him and asked him to find his seat.

God, Augusta was beautiful, and she was wearing the color he liked best on her. There seemed to be a glow about her, or maybe his imagination was conjuring up that image. His body stiffened with desire, and he felt an overwhelming urge to run to her, take her in his arms, and make her see that they belonged together.

She doesn't want you, man. You may as well forget about her and get on with your life.

What life? He had no life without Augusta.

Well, what are you going to do about it?

The fire of determination ignited within him. He relaxed and enjoyed the rest of the show.

Tammy sang, "There's Nothing Better Than Love." She sang it with so much heart that emotion flooded Augusta. If she'd only let love lead the way as the song said, she'd have Derek by her side right now.

She was sure he was somewhere in the audience. She could feel his presence.

The cheers from the audience died down, and the emcee gained everyone's attention.

"While our judges are making their decision, there will be a short musical program."

The moment everyone was waiting for finally arrived. Tammy sat between Augusta and the Hastings', listening to the names of the runnersup. As the drum roll preceded the announcement of the finalists, Augusta squeezed Tammy's hand. "Ready to receive your award?"

The emcee announced the third place winner. "Allen Filmore."

Crunch time. Only two people were left, and only one would come away the winner. Tammy and the second place winner tensed.

"This year's winner is..." Complete silence. "Tammy Gibson."

Happy tears streamed down Tammy's cheeks. Augusta hugged and kissed her. Jeffrey Osborne escorted her to the stage.

Derek watched, overflowing with pride.

When she reached the platform, Tammy received a standing ovation led by the Hastings'.

"I think the judges weren't the only ones to agree on who our winner is," the emcee commented.

"I don't know what to say. I had hoped—I want to thank my mother, Augusta, and my father, Derek. Without their help, encouragement, and love I wouldn't be standing here accepting this award. I want to give special thanks to Mr. Jeffrey Osborne. He is a fantastic person who took time away from his busy schedule to help me. And I want to thank the judges who voted for me. And you, the audience, for so warmly receiving me. Thank you."

Jeffrey Osborne and Ben and Myra stood, leading the applause.

"I told you she would win," Ben whispered to Myra.

She whispered back, "Who told who?"

Derek eased from his seat just as the show wound down and headed backstage to wait for Tammy—and Augusta.

After the crowd thinned, Augusta made her way backstage with Tammy. She had a feeling they would find Derek waiting for them. Her heart lurched violently when she saw the object of her thoughts standing just outside the dressing room door. She had to stop to gather her composure.

"What's wrong, Augusta?" Tammy asked.

A memory of the day of the accident flashed before her mind's eye when she saw Derek's face up close—intense brown eyes, stunned and guilty, staring back at her for just a moment before impact. He was as good looking as she remembered, only more so with her new awareness of him. "Derek is here," she said to Tammy.

A smile lit up Tammy's face. "Now it's time for you to do your thing. Go, Momma, get Daddy back."

"I'm going to try my best," Augusta laughed.

"By the way, I'll be spending the night with Ben and Myra, to give you and Derek some privacy."

"Whose idea was this? Yours or Ben's? You don't have to do that, I—"

"Nothing negative, promise me, Momma?"

Augusta smiled, "All right, daughter. But don't you think you're jumping the gun? Derek may not even want—"

"Nothing negative, remember?"

Derek tensed when he saw Tammy and Augusta walking toward him. He steeled himself for the meeting. For so long he had yearned to see that light of awareness in her eyes when she looked at him. His stomach turned over when it happened. He wanted his woman back, and he was going to give this encounter his best shot.

"You were fantastic as always, Tammy." Derek pulled her into his embrace. "I knew you could do it."

"Derek, I'm so happy you're here. I've missed you so much. And so has Augusta."

"Talking about dropping out of sight…" Ben added, bringing up the rear.

"Oh, be quiet. Are you ready, Tammy?" Myra asked.

"Yes, I'm ready. All I need to do is get Bella. She's waiting for me in the dressing mom."

Augusta stood staring at the man she loved, drinking in his handsome features. She agreed with Elaine; Derek Morgan had incredible brown eyes, a cross between sherry brown and cinnamon. She recalled trying to get Derek to describe the color of his eyes. He'd labeled them as "just an ordinary shade of brown."

There was nothing ordinary about this man that she loved. His build was magnificent, but *then* she didn't need her sight back to know that. She'd had a more intimate knowledge of his body when she was blind. And how she missed making love with him. She missed him. Period.

"Augusta," Derek took her hand. That same electricity was there, currenting between them.

Augusta felt it, too, and closed her eyes. Opening them again, she looked into his. "Derek.'

Entranced with each other, neither noticed that Ben, Myra, Tammy, and Bella had left them alone.

"Derek…"

"Augusta…"

They spoke at the same time.

"You go first," Derek proffered anxiously.

"I think that we should go to my house so we can talk," Augusta suggested, looking at the stage people milling around.

"I think you're right," he said quietly.

Augusta couldn't stand the awkwardness between them. "We can go in my car."

"It's ironic that cars should play such a major role in our lives."

"Yes, I met you because…"

"I was an irresponsible…"

Augusta put her finger across his lips. "That part of our lives is over, Derek. As I once told you, yesterday is gone, and we can't do anything to change it. We only have today; tomorrow is not promised."

"I'll leave my rental car here and pick it up later." He didn't want to miss out on any time he had with her. Every moment was too precious.

Augusta wondered what Derek was thinking. Was there any hope that they might get back together?

Derek wanted to believe that imploring look in her eyes meant what he hoped it did.

During the ride to her house, Augusta prayed that she would say the right words, do the right thing to convince him that she loved him and badly wanted a life with him.

Even in the darkness, everything was so familiar to Derek. How many times had he walked through this gate? How many times had they made love in Augusta's bed? He smiled, thinking of other places, remembering how they had brought in the new year making wild, savage love in the shower. They had gotten so carried away that any thought of protection had gone down the drain. He had been worried that Augusta might become pregnant. But in actuality, he would have happily welcomed any child they created. He would have had another tie to bind her to him.

Augusta pushed the key in the lock and turned the knob. She'd left the air conditioning on to combat Philadelphia's summer humidity, and the living room felt comfortably cool when they walked inside.

"Sit down, Derek. Can I get you anything?"

Yes, you, Augusta. "No, thank you," he replied, seating himself on the couch.

He's being so polite. Had that special wild intimacy they'd once shared died? Augusta wondered. Had she killed it with her stubborn determination to deny what they had? What should she do now? How was she going to get into this?

"What do we have to talk about, Augusta? I thought you said it all when you never called me after you got back from Africa."

"Back then I did all of the talking and none of the listening."

"Are you telling me you're ready to listen?"

"That's exactly what I'm telling you."

"How do we begin?" he asked warily. "Where do we begin?"

Augusta noticed as she studied his guarded expression that Derek seemed thinner than when she had last been with him. He'd never acted so distant before. She'd done that to him. What was he feeling? She offered up a little prayer. *God, please help me to do this right. Guide my thoughts and direct my words so they reach deeper than his heart, to his very soul.*

The nerves in Augusta's stomach were behaving like hyper butterflies. Was he glad to see her? Would he let her back into his life after the way she had treated him, the things she'd said? The thought that he might not tortured her relentlessly.

"The afternoon of the accident is as good a place as any, I guess." He sighed

Augusta's heart went out to him. His pained expression made her want to draw him into her arms and comfort him. "Anywhere you want to start, Derek."

"I want to make something clear before we start. Up until that day I *was* a wild, irresponsible fool. I told you once that I'd had it easy all my life. My father's electronic business was a good, solid company, and he lavishly spent the proceeds on my mother and me."

"I was their only child. I became the spoiled brat to top all spoiled brats. I breezed through school and later college. Anything I wanted, my father and mother moved heaven and earth to get for me. If I got into trouble, they automatically bailed me out."

"When they died, I was alone for the first time in my spoiled existence. I went through women and gambled and drank like there was no tomorrow. I'd developed an intense interest in drag racing. The day of the accident I had decided to take a short cut."

Derek got up and walked over to the window and looked out.

"I'd just bought a new, bright yellow Porsche and was itching to try it out. I realized too late the tree limb was obstructing the view of the stop sign. I know it's no excuse for my actions, and believe me, I'm not trying to justify them, but..."

Augusta remembered about that tree near the stop sign. She and several other people in the neighborhood had complained to the city council about the long splaying branches that obstructed the sign.

Taking action was another thing the council pushed to the back of the agenda.

Derek continued. "When I saw Kelsey, I put on the brakes, but I was going too fast and couldn't stop." His eyes reflected pain and regret. "You were so brave, zooming your car between mine and that little girl. Following the impact, when I saw your face covered with blood from the shattered glass, my heart stopped. I died a thousand deaths when I watched the paramedics take you away."

"I tried to talk to you after you came out of surgery, but you refused to see me. I felt so damned guilty. If it hadn't been for me, you would have been practicing surgery instead of going through it yourself. When I learned that you would probably be permanently blind, I made up my mind to trade in my useless existence for something worthwhile, make myself useful to someone."

"I visited the Braille Institute. I wanted to learn all I could about working with the blind. I worked hard, something I'd never done in my adult life because I'd never had a reason before. During those long months following the accident, I kept up with your condition while at the same time mastering Braille and learning techniques for helping the blind cope with their handicap."

"I made sure you saw only the top specialists. I wanted you to get your sight back so badly. I became even more determined to help you adjust when I learned that you'd had no success with the specialists and clinics you'd gone to. I contacted Ben after that. The rest you know."

"As each day passed after meeting you, I grew to love you more and more. It wasn't just the guilt, Augusta. My feelings for you transcended that. I knew in my heart and soul the love I felt for you was genuine."

"How do you feel about me now?"

When he didn't answer right away, Augusta's heart started to pound very fast.

Oh, God, let him still love me…

"Why did you leave town, Derek?" Augusta asked, her voice so weak that it threatened to desert her entirely.

"We'll get to that in a minute. First, I have a confession to make. I went to Nigeria ahead of you and talked to Dr. Eekong. In fact, I picked you and Tammy up at the airport and drove you to the clinic."

Augusta smiled. "I knew there was something familiar about Oswan's voice, and so did Tammy." She was quiet for a moment. "You were there watching over me during the course of my treatment, weren't you?"

"I plead guilty as charged. I kept in touch with Tammy. I also convinced Dr. Eekong to let me watch when your bandages came off."

"I also have a confession to make. I knew you'd gone to Africa. Not at first, but when I went to see Diane after I got back to the States, she told me."

"Still it didn't move you to call me? Why, Augusta?"

"My stubborn pride, I guess. I had to find out the hard way what I needed, what was more important to me."

"And did you?"

"What I want to know is how you feel about me now, Derek."

He turned away from the window to face her. "Baby, I love you more than mere words can convey," he said in an emotion-charged voice.

Augusta crossed the room, slipped her arms around his neck, and kissed him.

"My darling, I love you too. I've been a selfish fool. Even after I found out the truth, I knew deep in my heart it didn't matter what you had done in the past because I had already fallen in love with you. But I was hurt, disillusioned, and disappointed." She stroked his cheek. "You've gone through hell, haven't you?"

"I lived through it. You lent me some of your amazing strength. You changed my life, Augusta, made me a better man—and I'll always be grateful to you."

"Gratitude? I hope you feel more than gratitude for me. I want you to..." She stopped talking and rubbed her body against his, touched her lips to his, sensuously moving them from side to side, neglecting no part of his. Augusta darted her tongue into Derek's mouth with tiny, hot, quicksilver movements and felt him shudder violently at the intimacy.

He groaned. "If you keep that up..."

"I intend to do more than that, sweet man."

"More?"

"Hmmm." Augusta stroked his tongue with her own, tasting, devouring. She'd missed this.

Desire rippled through Derek's body, flowing hotly, breaking down the guarded control he'd built up against these feelings.

"Make love to me, Derek," Augusta murmured. "I'm your woman and you're my man."

He pulled a little away. "Augusta," he breathed heavily, reaching for his quickly disappearing control.

He watched her eyelids lower sexily, almost closing, to open moments later glowing radiantly with passion.

"I love you," she whispered, letting her breath flow warmly across his lips.

"Have mercy," groaned Derek as he let himself be drawn irresistibly back into intimate contact with her body.

"Not now, not while I have you where I want you."

"You definitely have me, baby."

Augusta licked her tongue over his lips again and again, driving him crazy with a desire to possess her. He let out a groan and took her mouth even as she took his.

He savored the heated feel of her soft, hot lips. Suddenly he couldn't hold her close enough, taste enough of her sweetness. Before the kiss ended he was aroused beyond anything he'd ever experienced, urgently needing her as he'd never needed her before.

"I want you so bad, Derek."

To hear her say that she wanted him this much was like an aphrodisiac to his senses.

He lifted her in his arms and carried her in the direction of the bedroom.

"Hurry, Derek, I want you inside me."

He st opped without warning and looked into her eyes, the eyes he had been responsible for blinding and then restoring to sight. He took her mouth with the hard thrust of his tongue and triumphantly laughed as the force of her own passion made her tremble.

"I love you, Augusta, and God how I want to be inside you." When they reached her bedroom, he pushed the door open with his shoulder then lowered her feet to the floor.

Augusta began to undress him. When he stood completely naked, she drank her fill of his fine body, something she'd not been able to do until now. He was wonderfully made.

Derek kissed her again, searching out the hot-sweet texture of her mouth, slowly stroking her with the rough wetness of his tongue. He heard the sounds of pleasure welling up from deep in her throat and wondered if he would ever get enough of this woman, even when he was buried inside her.

"You're driving me crazy, woman. I don't know if I'll be able to let you go long enough to undress you."

With shaky hands, he unzipped her dress and let it fall to the floor. Derek gasped at the telling swell of her stomach. His mouth hung open in shock.

Augusta was pregnant!

But they had used protection every time they'd made love—except that one time in the shower on New Year's Eve.

"You've got to be at least five months pregnant! That means you knew you were carrying my baby before the treatments started. And so did Dr. Eekong, yet he didn't tell me—and neither did you."

Augusta sat down on the bed. "I planned to tell you, but wasn't sure how you'd react. I'd rejected you and refused to talk, or even hear you out before I left for Africa. I wasn't sure you'd want me back, and if you did, whether it would be because of the baby. I didn't want you to come back to me for that reason."

"What you're saying is that you didn't know if you could trust my love for you after what I had done?"

"When I found out you'd left town, all my fears seemed trivial in comparison to losing you. But I had to know how you felt about me before I told you about the baby. If you'd said that you no longer loved me, then I wouldn't have told you until later. I always meant to tell you, though."

Derek wanted to say something in answer to that, but decided that it was water under the bridge. He had his woman back in his arms, in his life where she belonged—and that was all that mattered to him. He eased her back against the pillows. "Now that we've straightened that out, I want to tell you, you're one hell of mom, Gusto."

"How—Who—Ben, right?"

"You got it. The name fits. You go all out in whatever you undertake. I hope that will extend into your personal life."

"Oh, it definitely does, especially when I'm aroused."

"And are you—aroused, I mean?"

"Why don't you find out?"

With slow, easy movements, Derek brushed his lips across one nipple and then the other. He felt the passionate quiver of her response. As she cried out his name, imploring him to give her more, he drew the taut peaks into his mouth, caressing her as though he could seduce the breath and the very life itself from her body.

Not for long moments did he release her, long enough for her to shudder, long enough for her skin to grow as sensuously hot as his.

Augusta tried to pull him over her, but he moved to the side.

"Not so fast, my hot little darling, I want to see you. I've never seen anything to compare to your beauty."

She blushed as his eyes roved over the swell of her stomach.

"You're carrying the from of our love beneath your heart. You've never looked more beautiful."

"Remember when I wanted to get my hands around your neck in a less-than-lover-like manner?"

"Yes, I remember. As I recall, you wanted to do more than caress that part of my anatomy."

"I'm definitely not talking about your neck this time." She reached out and grasped the hard male part of him that had given her so much pleasure in the past and had planted the precious child stirring inside her.

"You're one hell of a man, Derek Morgan. And I love you with all my heart. Why won't you hurry up and make us one?"

"Ssh." He traced a finger across her bottom lip. "Be quiet and let me love you the way I want to."

"By all means, go ahead, mister, get on with it."

He kissed her deeply, druggingly, until a sigh of pleasure eased from between her lips. He tangled his fingers in the jet curls concealing her femininity. When he delved his fingers into her liquid, satiny heat to the softness awaiting him beyond, he knew how ready she was for his lovemaking.

Trickles of ecstasy stole through her stomach, stopping just above the cradle of her femininity.

With his thumb, Derek coaxed the giving folds between her legs to velvety wetness. Her thighs trembled, and she arched herself against his questing fingers.

"Oh, my God, Augusta! You're so wet and ready." With an eagerness that surprised him, Derek continued to stroke her until Augusta writhed wildly, crying out his name.

"Derek, oh, Derek, now!" she gasped. "I can't wait."

His breathing was heavy, the blood in his veins thick with passion, but he somehow managed to utter, "Not yet, my love. Let me please you."

"Oh, you are, you are!"

He reversed their positions and slid her over him. "I don't want to hurt the baby."

She opened her body, slowly sheathing him inside her, and began to move her hips, beckoning him to start the rhythm of the loving process he was so good at.

"Baby, now, now!" she leaned forward and murmured breathlessly into his ear.

The warmth of her breath and the softness of her lips as they touched his throat made him lose control. With a low growl, he raised his hips, marrying his flesh with hers deep in her moist heat. He cried out when he felt her inner muscles tightening around him.

She gazed into his eyes as pleasure throbbed through her.

Lowering her hips, he thrust upward again and again. The friction of flesh against flesh built the tension higher and higher.

He caressed that most sensitive part of her and Augusta began to shudder. The convulsing movements of her inner body swept him into a quaking epicenter of rapture, and they exploded together.

Long moments later, his voice ragged, Derek muttered, "I love you."

Augusta's breathing, just as ragged, whispered, "Not as much as I love you."

"That, woman, is a matter of opinion."

"All right, I'll take your word for it. I don't want to argue, I want to make love."

"My sentiments exactly. I have something of yours." He reached for his jacket and brought out a small black box. He flipped the top open, taking the ring out and placing it on her finger. "Now it's back where it belongs."

Augusta gasped in awe. It was her engagement ring. "It's every bit as beautiful as I had imagined. You kept it."

"I couldn't do anything else. I had it especially made for you. Now when are you going to marry me?"

She kissed his chest and laved his male nipple with her tongue and answered, "Whenever you say."

Without uttering another word, Derek slid over her and into her, loving her again.

EPILOGUE

"Are you happy living here, Augusta?" Derek asked.

She sighed contently. "Yes."

"You don't miss Philadelphia?"

"No. Oh, I miss Ben and Myra and little Olivia. And most of all Tammy. But Ben and Myra can come out here to visit, and Tammy will be here during semester break."

He smiled. "I miss Tammy, too. And that Liv is going to be a real heartbreaker one day. Ben had better get his shotgun ready."

"Do you think D.J. will notice?"

"I'll have to clue him in. If he's anything like Derek Senior, he won't be able to resist beautiful women."

Augusta pinched him.

"Ouch!"

"Beautiful women, huh?"

"You're all the woman I'll ever need or ever want, baby. Does that sound better?"

He kissed her neck and next went on to her mouth.

"A little," she answered. "We'd better turn in soon. I have early surgery tomorrow."

"San Francisco Memorial isn't Philadelphia General. Are you sure you don't mind the change?"

"No, I'm happy here with you and our son."

"Are you ready to try for a girl this time?"

"I'm out of practice. Mind if I take a refresher course first?"

"As long as I'm your teacher."

"I'm looking forward to being teacher's pet."

2008 Reprint Mass Market Titles

January

Cautious Heart
Cheris F. Hodges
ISBN-13: 978-1-58571-301-1
ISBN-10: 1-58571-301-5
$6.99

Suddenly You
Crystal Hubbard
ISBN-13: 978-1-58571-302-8
ISBN-10: 1-58571-302-3
$6.99

February

Passion
T. T. Henderson
ISBN-13: 978-1-58571-303-5
ISBN-10: 1-58571-303-1
$6.99

Whispers in the Sand
LaFlorya Gauthier
ISBN-13: 978-1-58571-304-2
ISBN-10: 1-58571-304-x
$6.99

March

Life Is Never As It Seems
J. J. Michael
ISBN-13: 978-1-58571-305-9
ISBN-10: 1-58571-305-8
$6.99

Beyond the Rapture
Beverly Clark
ISBN-13: 978-1-58571-306-6
ISBN-10: 1-58571-306-6
$6.99

April

A Heart's Awakening
Veronica Parker
ISBN-13: 978-1-58571-307-3
ISBN-10: 1-58571-307-4
$6.99

Breeze
Robin Lynette Hampton
ISBN-13: 978-1-58571-308-0
ISBN-10: 1-58571-308-2
$6.99

May

I'll Be Your Shelter
Giselle Carmichael
ISBN-13: 978-1-58571-309-7
ISBN-10: 1-58571-309-0
$6.99

Careless Whispers
Rochelle Alers
ISBN-13: 978-1-58571-310-3
ISBN-10: 1-58571-310-4
$6.99

June

Sin
Crystal Rhodes
ISBN-13: 978-1-58571-311-0
ISBN-10: 1-58571-311-2
$6.99

Dark Storm Rising
Chinelu Moore
ISBN-13: 978-1-58571-312-7
ISBN-10: 1-58571-312-0
$6.99

2008 Reprint Mass Market Titles (continued)

July

Object of His Desire
A.C. Arthur
ISBN-13: 978-1-58571-313-4
ISBN-10: 1-58571-313-9
$6.99

Angel's Paradise
Janice Angelique
ISBN-13: 978-1-58571-314-1
ISBN-10: 1-58571-314-7
$6.99

August

Unbreak My Heart
Dar Tomlinson
ISBN-13: 978-1-58571-315-8
ISBN-10: 1-58571-315-5
$6.99

All I Ask
Barbara Keaton
ISBN-13: 978-1-58571-316-5
ISBN-10: 1-58571-316-3
$6.99

September

Icie
Pamela Leigh Starr
ISBN-13: 978-1-58571-275-5
ISBN-10: 1-58571-275-2
$6.99

At Last
Lisa Riley
ISBN-13: 978-1-58571-276-2
ISBN-10: 1-58571-276-0
$6.99

October

Everlastin' Love
Gay G. Gunn
ISBN-13: 978-1-58571-277-9
ISBN-10: 1-58571-277-9
$6.99

Three Wishes
Seressia Glass
ISBN-13: 978-1-58571-278-6
ISBN-10: 1-58571-278-7
$6.99

November

Yesterday Is Gone
Beverly Clark
ISBN-13: 978-1-58571-279-3
ISBN-10: 1-58571-279-5
$6.99

Again My Love
Kayla Perrin
ISBN-13: 978-1-58571-280-9
ISBN-10: 1-58571-280-9
$6.99

December

Office Policy
A.C. Arthur
ISBN-13: 978-1-58571-281-6
ISBN-10: 1-58571-281-7
$6.99

Rendezvous With Fate
Jeanne Sumerix
ISBN-13: 978-1-58571-283-3
ISBN-10: 1-58571-283-3
$6.99

2008 New Mass Market Titles

January

Where I Want To Be
Maryam Diaab
ISBN-13: 978-1-58571-268-7
ISBN-10: 1-58571-268-X
$6.99

Never Say Never
Michele Cameron
ISBN-13: 978-1-58571-269-4
ISBN-10: 1-58571-269-8
$6.99

February

Stolen Memories
Michele Sudler
ISBN-13: 978-1-58571-270-0
ISBN-10: 1-58571-270-1
$6.99

Dawn's Harbor
Kymberly Hunt
ISBN-13: 978-1-58571-271-7
ISBN-10: 1-58571-271-X
$6.99

March

Undying Love
Renee Alexis
ISBN-13: 978-1-58571-272-4
ISBN-10: 1-58571-272-8
$6.99

Blame It On Paradise
Crystal Hubbard
ISBN-13: 978-1-58571-273-1
ISBN-10: 1-58571-273-6
$6.99

April

When A Man Loves A Woman
La Connie Taylor-Jones
ISBN-13: 978-1-58571-274-8
ISBN-10: 1-58571-274-4
$6.99

Choices
Tammy Williams
ISBN-13: 978-1-58571-300-4
ISBN-10: 1-58571-300-7
$6.99

May

Dream Runner
Gail McFarland
ISBN-13: 978-1-58571-317-2
ISBN-10: 1-58571-317-1
$6.99

Southern Fried Standards
S.R. Maddox
ISBN-13: 978-1-58571-318-9
ISBN-10: 1-58571-318-X
$6.99

June

Looking for Lily
Africa Fine
ISBN-13: 978-1-58571-319-6
ISBN-10: 1-58571-319-8
$6.99

Bliss, Inc.
Chamein Canton
ISBN-13: 978-1-58571-325-7
ISBN-10: 1-58571-325-2
$6.99

2008 New Mass Market Titles (continued)

July

Love's Secrets
Yolanda McVey
ISBN-13: 978-1-58571-321-9
ISBN-10: 1-58571-321-X
$6.99

Things Forbidden
Maryam Diaab
ISBN-13: 978-1-58571-327-1
ISBN-10: 1-58571-327-9
$6.99

August

Storm
Pamela Leigh Starr
ISBN-13: 978-1-58571-323-3
ISBN-10: 1-58571-323-6
$6.99

Passion's Furies
AlTonya Washington
ISBN-13: 978-1-58571-324-0
ISBN-10: 1-58571-324-4
$6.99

September

Three Doors Down
Michele Sudler
ISBN-13: 978-1-58571-332-5
ISBN-10: 1-58571-332-5
$6.99

Mr Fix-It
Crystal Hubbard
ISBN-13: 978-1-58571-326-4
ISBN-10: 1-58571-326-0
$6.99

October

Moments of Clarity
Michele Cameron
ISBN-13: 978-1-58571-330-1
ISBN-10: 1-58571-330-9
$6.99

Lady Preacher
K.T. Richey
ISBN-13: 978-1-58571-333-2
ISBN-10: 1-58571-333-3
$6.99

November

This Life Isn't Perfect Holla
Sandra Foy
ISBN: 978-1-58571-331-8
ISBN-10: 1-58571-331-7
$6.99

Promises Made
Bernice Layton
ISBN-13: 978-1-58571-334-9
ISBN-10: 1-58571-334-1
$6.99

December

A Voice Behind Thunder
Carrie Elizabeth Greene
ISBN-13: 978-1-58571-329-5
ISBN-10: 1-58571-329-5
$6.99

The More Things Change
Chamein Canton
ISBN-13: 978-1-58571-328-8
ISBN-10: 1-58571-328-7
$6.99

Other Genesis Press, Inc. Titles

A Dangerous Deception	J.M. Jeffries	$8.95
A Dangerous Love	J.M. Jeffries	$8.95
A Dangerous Obsession	J.M. Jeffries	$8.95
A Drummer's Beat to Mend	Kei Swanson	$9.95
A Happy Life	Charlotte Harris	$9.95
A Heart's Awakening	Veronica Parker	$9.95
A Lark on the Wing	Phyliss Hamilton	$9.95
A Love of Her Own	Cheris F. Hodges	$9.95
A Love to Cherish	Beverly Clark	$8.95
A Risk of Rain	Dar Tomlinson	$8.95
A Taste of Temptation	Reneé Alexis	$9.95
A Twist of Fate	Beverly Clark	$8.95
A Will to Love	Angie Daniels	$9.95
Acquisitions	Kimberley White	$8.95
Across	Carol Payne	$12.95
After the Vows (Summer Anthology)	Leslie Esdaile T.T. Henderson Jacqueline Thomas	$10.95
Again My Love	Kayla Perrin	$10.95
Against the Wind	Gwynne Forster	$8.95
All I Ask	Barbara Keaton	$8.95
Always You	Crystal Hubbard	$6.99
Ambrosia	T.T. Henderson	$8.95
An Unfinished Love Affair	Barbara Keaton	$8.95
And Then Came You	Dorothy Elizabeth Love	$8.95
Angel's Paradise	Janice Angelique	$9.95
At Last	Lisa G. Riley	$8.95
Best of Friends	Natalie Dunbar	$8.95
Beyond the Rapture	Beverly Clark	$9.95
Blaze	Barbara Keaton	$9.95
Blood Lust	J. M. Jeffries	$9.95
Blood Seduction	J.M. Jeffries	$9.95

Other Genesis Press, Inc. Titles (continued)

Bodyguard	Andrea Jackson	$9.95
Boss of Me	Diana Nyad	$8.95
Bound by Love	Beverly Clark	$8.95
Breeze	Robin Hampton Allen	$10.95
Broken	Dar Tomlinson	$24.95
By Design	Barbara Keaton	$8.95
Cajun Heat	Charlene Berry	$8.95
Careless Whispers	Rochelle Alers	$8.95
Cats & Other Tales	Marilyn Wagner	$8.95
Caught in a Trap	Andre Michelle	$8.95
Caught Up In the Rapture	Lisa G. Riley	$9.95
Cautious Heart	Cheris F Hodges	$8.95
Chances	Pamela Leigh Starr	$8.95
Cherish the Flame	Beverly Clark	$8.95
Class Reunion	Irma Jenkins/ John Brown	$12.95
Code Name: Diva	J.M. Jeffries	$9.95
Conquering Dr. Wexler's Heart	Kimberley White	$9.95
Corporate Seduction	A.C. Arthur	$9.95
Crossing Paths, Tempting Memories	Dorothy Elizabeth Love	$9.95
Crush	Crystal Hubbard	$9.95
Cypress Whisperings	Phyllis Hamilton	$8.95
Dark Embrace	Crystal Wilson Harris	$8.95
Dark Storm Rising	Chinelu Moore	$10.95
Daughter of the Wind	Joan Xian	$8.95
Deadly Sacrifice	Jack Kean	$22.95
Designer Passion	Dar Tomlinson Diana Richeaux	$8.95
Do Over	Celya Bowers	$9.95
Dreamtective	Liz Swados	$5.95

Other Genesis Press, Inc. Titles (continued)

Ebony Angel	Deatri King-Bey	$9.95
Ebony Butterfly II	Delilah Dawson	$14.95
Echoes of Yesterday	Beverly Clark	$9.95
Eden's Garden	Elizabeth Rose	$8.95
Eve's Prescription	Edwina Martin Arnold	$8.95
Everlastin' Love	Gay G. Gunn	$8.95
Everlasting Moments	Dorothy Elizabeth Love	$8.95
Everything and More	Sinclair Lebeau	$8.95
Everything but Love	Natalie Dunbar	$8.95
Falling	Natalie Dunbar	$9.95
Fate	Pamela Leigh Starr	$8.95
Finding Isabella	A.J. Garrotto	$8.95
Forbidden Quest	Dar Tomlinson	$10.95
Forever Love	Wanda Y. Thomas	$8.95
From the Ashes	Kathleen Suzanne Jeanne Sumerix	$8.95
Gentle Yearning	Rochelle Alers	$10.95
Glory of Love	Sinclair LeBeau	$10.95
Go Gentle into that Good Night	Malcom Boyd	$12.95
Goldengroove	Mary Beth Craft	$16.95
Groove, Bang, and Jive	Steve Cannon	$8.99
Hand in Glove	Andrea Jackson	$9.95
Hard to Love	Kimberley White	$9.95
Hart & Soul	Angie Daniels	$8.95
Heart of the Phoenix	A.C. Arthur	$9.95
Heartbeat	Stephanie Bedwell-Grime	$8.95
Hearts Remember	M. Loui Quezada	$8.95
Hidden Memories	Robin Allen	$10.95
Higher Ground	Leah Latimer	$19.95
Hitler, the War, and the Pope	Ronald Rychiak	$26.95
How to Write a Romance	Kathryn Falk	$18.95

Other Genesis Press, Inc. Titles (continued)

I Married a Reclining Chair	Lisa M. Fuhs	$8.95
I'll Be Your Shelter	Giselle Carmichael	$8.95
I'll Paint a Sun	A.J. Garrotto	$9.95
Icie	Pamela Leigh Starr	$8.95
Illusions	Pamela Leigh Starr	$8.95
Indigo After Dark Vol. I	Nia Dixon/Angelique	$10.95
Indigo After Dark Vol. II	Dolores Bundy/ Cole Riley	$10.95
Indigo After Dark Vol. III	Montana Blue/ Coco Morena	$10.95
Indigo After Dark Vol. IV	Cassandra Colt/	$14.95
Indigo After Dark Vol. V	Delilah Dawson	$14.95
Indiscretions	Donna Hill	$8.95
Intentional Mistakes	Michele Sudler	$9.95
Interlude	Donna Hill	$8.95
Intimate Intentions	Angie Daniels	$8.95
It's Not Over Yet	J.J. Michael	$9.95
Jolie's Surrender	Edwina Martin-Arnold	$8.95
Kiss or Keep	Debra Phillips	$8.95
Lace	Giselle Carmichael	$9.95
Last Train to Memphis	Elsa Cook	$12.95
Lasting Valor	Ken Olsen	$24.95
Let Us Prey	Hunter Lundy	$25.95
Lies Too Long	Pamela Ridley	$13.95
Life Is Never As It Seems	J.J. Michael	$12.95
Lighter Shade of Brown	Vicki Andrews	$8.95
Love Always	Mildred E. Riley	$10.95
Love Doesn't Come Easy	Charlyne Dickerson	$8.95
Love Unveiled	Gloria Greene	$10.95
Love's Deception	Charlene Berry	$10.95
Love's Destiny	M. Loui Quezada	$8.95
Mae's Promise	Melody Walcott	$8.95

Other Genesis Press, Inc. Titles (continued)

Magnolia Sunset	Giselle Carmichael	$8.95
Many Shades of Gray	Dyanne Davis	$6.99
Matters of Life and Death	Lesego Malepe, Ph.D.	$15.95
Meant to Be	Jeanne Sumerix	$8.95
Midnight Clear	Leslie Esdaile	$10.95
(Anthology)	Gwynne Forster	
	Carmen Green	
	Monica Jackson	
Midnight Magic	Gwynne Forster	$8.95
Midnight Peril	Vicki Andrews	$10.95
Misconceptions	Pamela Leigh Starr	$9.95
Montgomery's Children	Richard Perry	$14.95
My Buffalo Soldier	Barbara B. K. Reeves	$8.95
Naked Soul	Gwynne Forster	$8.95
Next to Last Chance	Louisa Dixon	$24.95
No Apologies	Seressia Glass	$8.95
No Commitment Required	Seressia Glass	$8.95
No Regrets	Mildred E. Riley	$8.95
Not His Type	Chamein Canton	$6.99
Nowhere to Run	Gay G. Gunn	$10.95
O Bed! O Breakfast!	Rob Kuehnle	$14.95
Object of His Desire	A. C. Arthur	$8.95
Office Policy	A. C. Arthur	$9.95
Once in a Blue Moon	Dorianne Cole	$9.95
One Day at a Time	Bella McFarland	$8.95
One in A Million	Barbara Keaton	$6.99
One of These Days	Michele Sudler	$9.95
Outside Chance	Louisa Dixon	$24.95
Passion	T.T. Henderson	$10.95
Passion's Blood	Cherif Fortin	$22.95
Passion's Journey	Wanda Y. Thomas	$8.95
Past Promises	Jahmel West	$8.95

Other Genesis Press, Inc. Titles (continued)

Title	Author	Price
Path of Fire	T.T. Henderson	$8.95
Path of Thorns	Annetta P. Lee	$9.95
Peace Be Still	Colette Haywood	$12.95
Picture Perfect	Reon Carter	$8.95
Playing for Keeps	Stephanie Salinas	$8.95
Pride & Joi	Gay G. Gunn	$8.95
Promises to Keep	Alicia Wiggins	$8.95
Quiet Storm	Donna Hill	$10.95
Reckless Surrender	Rochelle Alers	$6.95
Red Polka Dot in a World of Plaid	Varian Johnson	$12.95
Reluctant Captive	Joyce Jackson	$8.95
Rendezvous with Fate	Jeanne Sumerix	$8.95
Revelations	Cheris F. Hodges	$8.95
Rivers of the Soul	Leslie Esdaile	$8.95
Rocky Mountain Romance	Kathleen Suzanne	$8.95
Rooms of the Heart	Donna Hill	$8.95
Rough on Rats and Tough on Cats	Chris Parker	$12.95
Secret Library Vol. 1	Nina Sheridan	$18.95
Secret Library Vol. 2	Cassandra Colt	$8.95
Secret Thunder	Annetta P. Lee	$9.95
Shades of Brown	Denise Becker	$8.95
Shades of Desire	Monica White	$8.95
Shadows in the Moonlight	Jeanne Sumerix	$8.95
Sin	Crystal Rhodes	$8.95
Small Whispers	Annetta P. Lee	$6.99
So Amazing	Sinclair LeBeau	$8.95
Somebody's Someone	Sinclair LeBeau	$8.95
Someone to Love	Alicia Wiggins	$8.95
Song in the Park	Martin Brant	$15.95
Soul Eyes	Wayne L. Wilson	$12.95

Other Genesis Press, Inc. Titles (continued)

Soul to Soul	Donna Hill	$8.95
Southern Comfort	J.M. Jeffries	$8.95
Still the Storm	Sharon Robinson	$8.95
Still Waters Run Deep	Leslie Esdaile	$8.95
Stolen Kisses	Dominiqua Douglas	$9.95
Stories to Excite You	Anna Forrest/Divine	$14.95
Subtle Secrets	Wanda Y. Thomas	$8.95
Suddenly You	Crystal Hubbard	$9.95
Sweet Repercussions	Kimberley White	$9.95
Sweet Sensations	Gwendolyn Bolton	$9.95
Sweet Tomorrows	Kimberly White	$8.95
Taken by You	Dorothy Elizabeth Love	$9.95
Tattooed Tears	T. T. Henderson	$8.95
The Color Line	Lizzette Grayson Carter	$9.95
The Color of Trouble	Dyanne Davis	$8.95
The Disappearance of Allison Jones	Kayla Perrin	$5.95
The Fires Within	Beverly Clark	$9.95
The Foursome	Celya Bowers	$6.99
The Honey Dipper's Legacy	Pannell-Allen	$14.95
The Joker's Love Tune	Sidney Rickman	$15.95
The Little Pretender	Barbara Cartland	$10.95
The Love We Had	Natalie Dunbar	$8.95
The Man Who Could Fly	Bob & Milana Beamon	$18.95
The Missing Link	Charlyne Dickerson	$8.95
The Mission	Pamela Leigh Starr	$6.99
The Perfect Frame	Beverly Clark	$9.95
The Price of Love	Sinclair LeBeau	$8.95
The Smoking Life	Ilene Barth	$29.95
The Words of the Pitcher	Kei Swanson	$8.95
Three Wishes	Seressia Glass	$8.95
Ties That Bind	Kathleen Suzanne	$8.95

Other Genesis Press, Inc. Titles (continued)

Tiger Woods	Libby Hughes	$5.95
Time is of the Essence	Angie Daniels	$9.95
Timeless Devotion	Bella McFarland	$9.95
Tomorrow's Promise	Leslie Esdaile	$8.95
Truly Inseparable	Wanda Y. Thomas	$8.95
Two Sides to Every Story	Dyanne Davis	$9.95
Unbreak My Heart	Dar Tomlinson	$8.95
Uncommon Prayer	Kenneth Swanson	$9.95
Unconditional Love	Alicia Wiggins	$8.95
Unconditional	A.C. Arthur	$9.95
Until Death Do Us Part	Susan Paul	$8.95
Vows of Passion	Bella McFarland	$9.95
Wedding Gown	Dyanne Davis	$8.95
What's Under Benjamin's Bed	Sandra Schaffer	$8.95
When Dreams Float	Dorothy Elizabeth Love	$8.95
When I'm With You	LaConnie Taylor-Jones	$6.99
Whispers in the Night	Dorothy Elizabeth Love	$8.95
Whispers in the Sand	LaFlorya Gauthier	$10.95
Who's That Lady?	Andrea Jackson	$9.95
Wild Ravens	Altonya Washington	$9.95
Yesterday Is Gone	Beverly Clark	$10.95
Yesterday's Dreams, Tomorrow's Promises	Reon Laudat	$8.95
Your Precious Love	Sinclair LeBeau	$8.95

Ignite
The Flame!

Order Form

Mail to: Genesis Press, Inc.
P.O. Box 101
Columbus, MS 39703

Name _______________
Address _______________
City/State _______________ Zip _______________
Telephone _______________

Ship to (if different from above)
Name _______________
Address _______________
City/State _______________ Zip _______________
Telephone _______________

Credit Card Information
Credit Card # _______________ ☐ Visa ☐ Mastercard
Expiration Date (mm/yy) _______________ ☐ AmEx ☐ Discover

Qty.	Author	Title	Price	Total

Use this order form, or call 1-888-INDIGO-1

Total for books _______________
Shipping and handling:
$5 first two books,
$1 each additional book _______________
Total S & H _______________
Total amount enclosed _______________

Mississippi residents add 7% sales tax

Visit www.genesis-press.com for latest releases and excerpts.